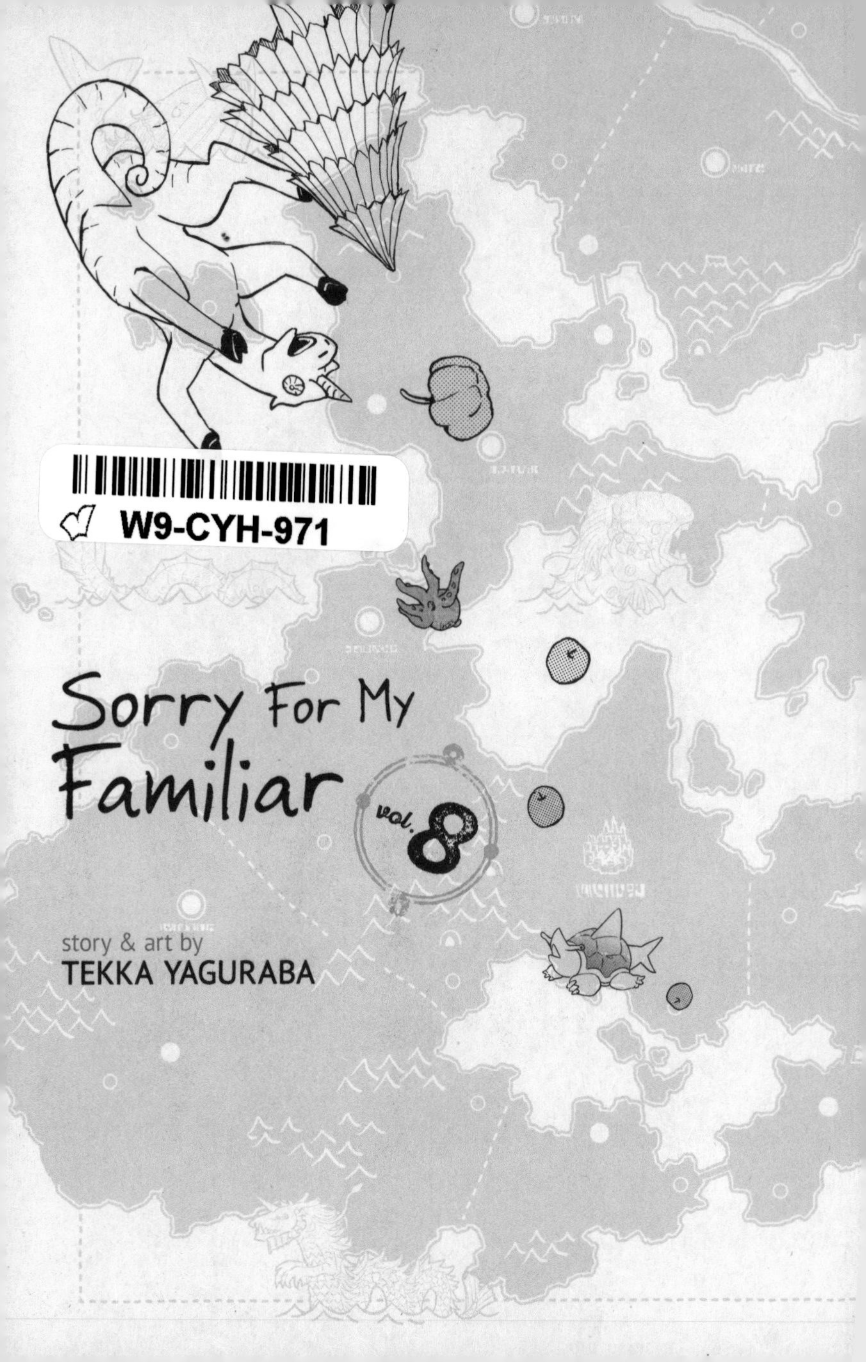

Sorry For My Familiar

vol. 8

story & art by
TEKKA YAGURABA

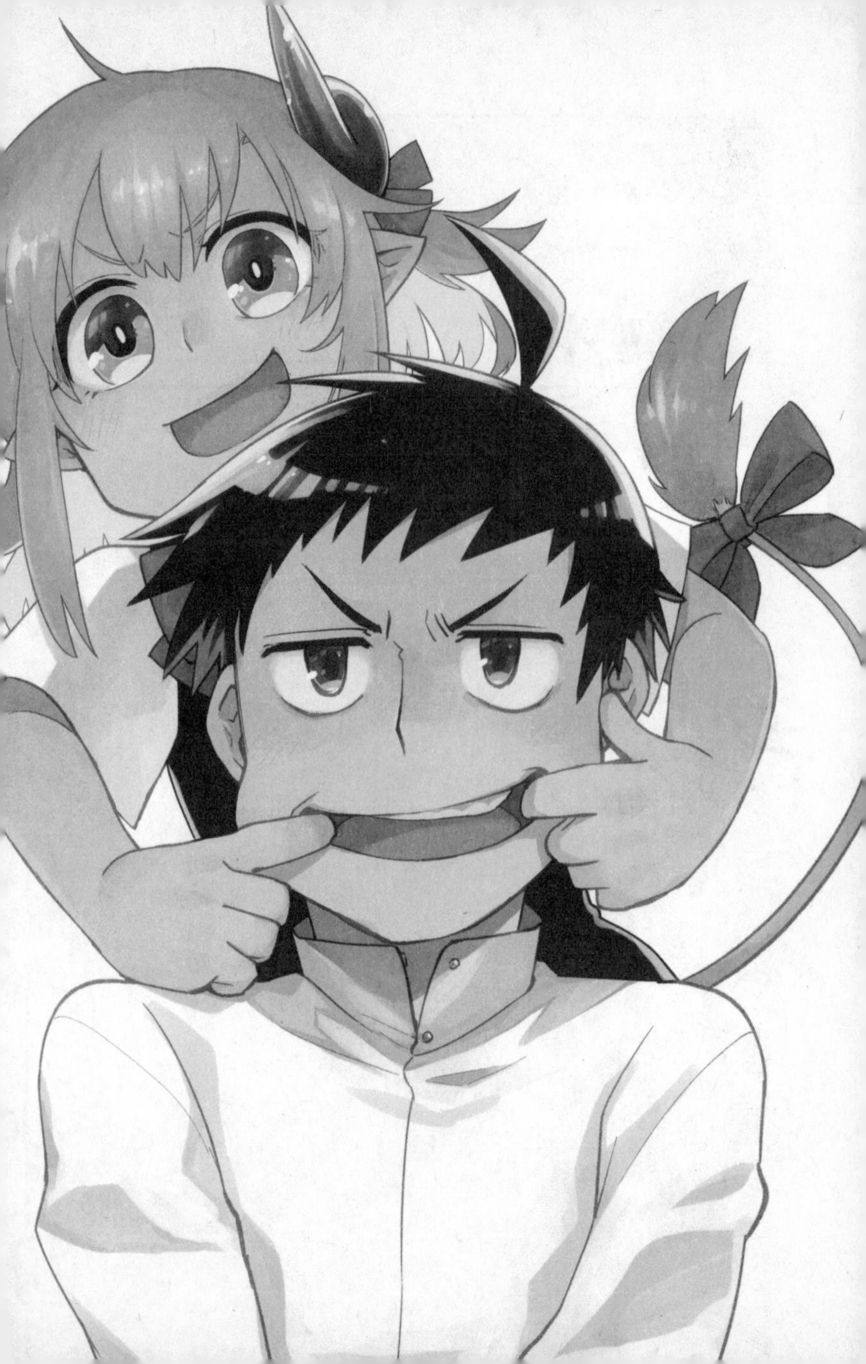

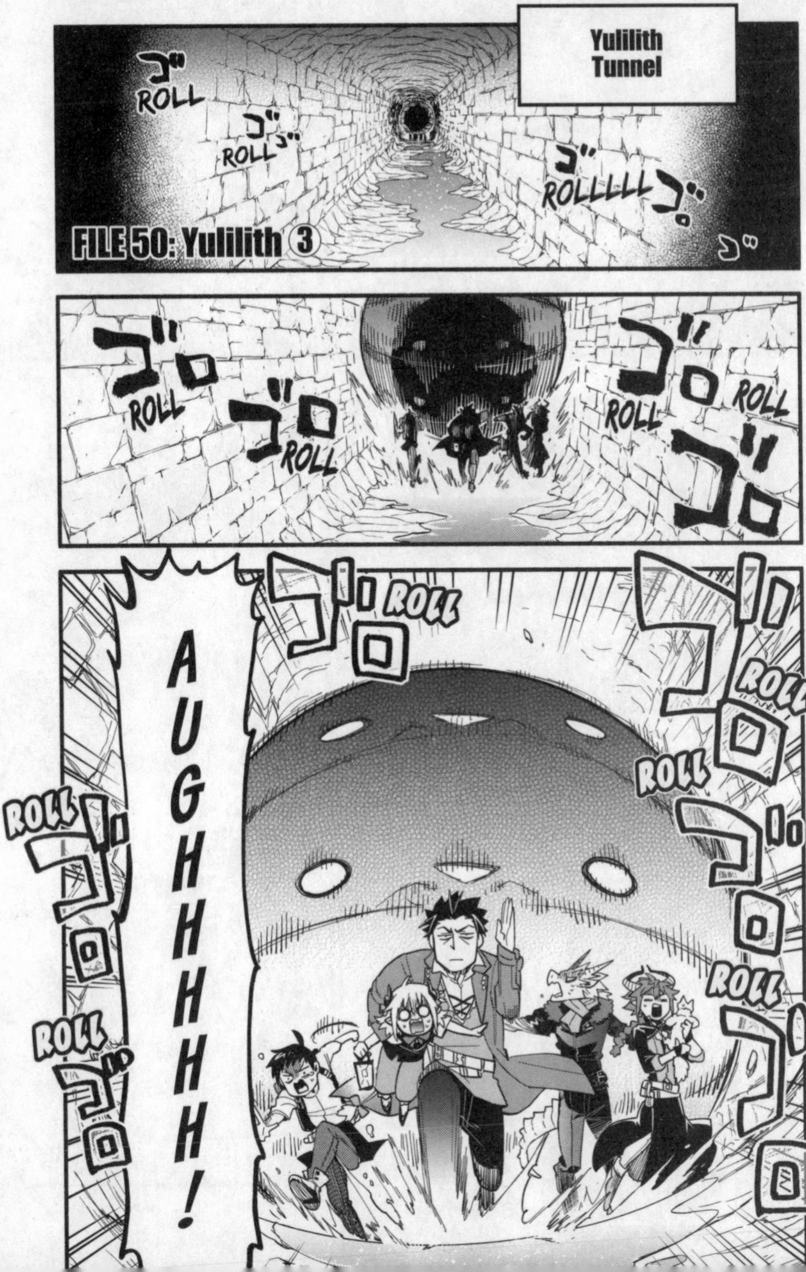

Yulilith Tunnel
FILE 50: Yulilith ③
ゴ ROLL
ゴゴ ROLL
ゴ ROLLLLLL ゴ
ゴ
ゴロ ROLL
ゴロ ROLL
ゴロ ROLL
ROLL ゴロ
ゴロ ROLL
AUGHHHHHH!
ゴロ ROLL
ゴロ ROLL
ゴロ ROLL
ゴロ ROLL
ゴロ ROLL
ゴロ

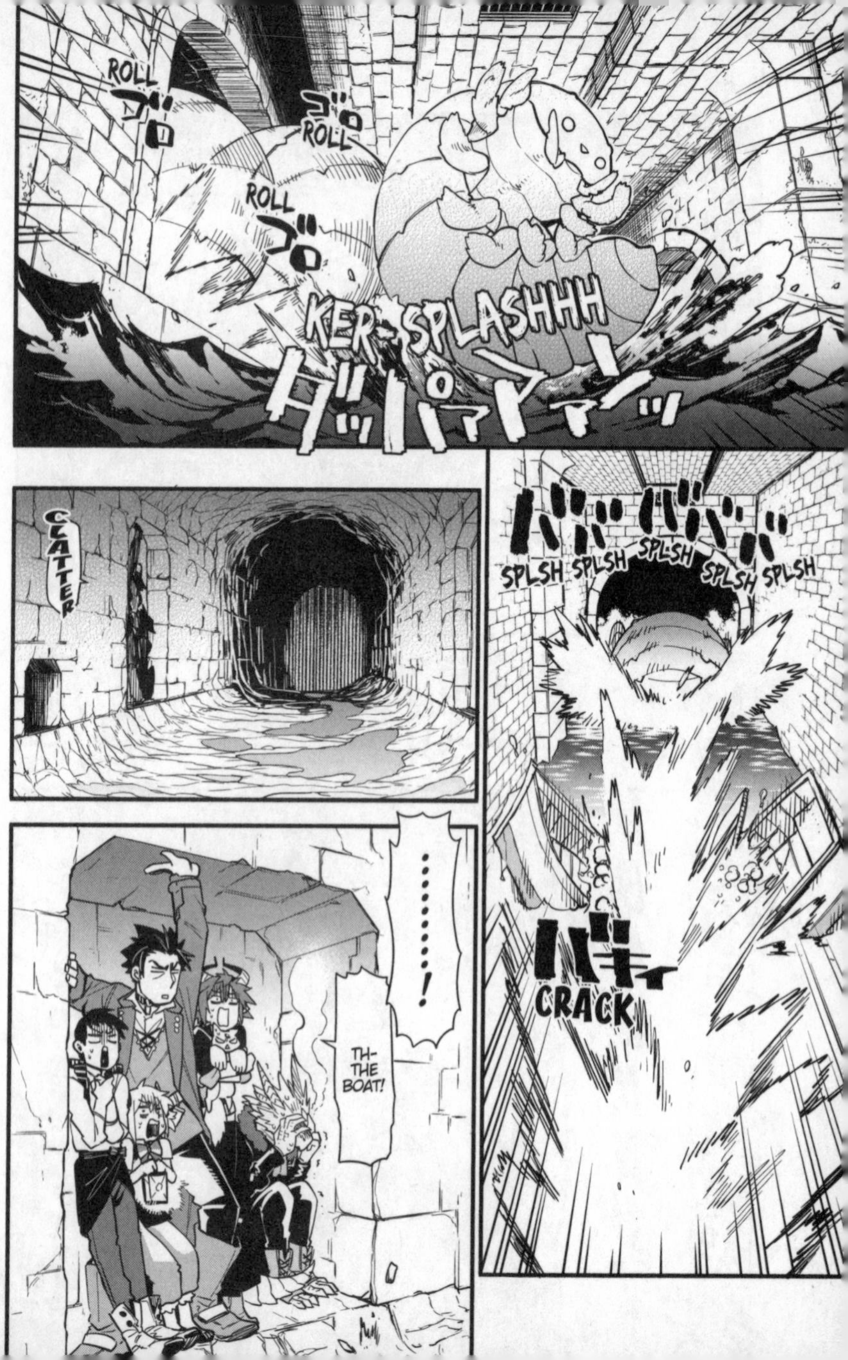

ゴロ
ROLL
ROLL
ゴロ
ROLL
ゴロ
KER-SPLASHHH
SPLSH SPLSH SPLSH SPLSH SPLSH
バキ
CRACK
CLATTER
......!
TH-THE BOAT!

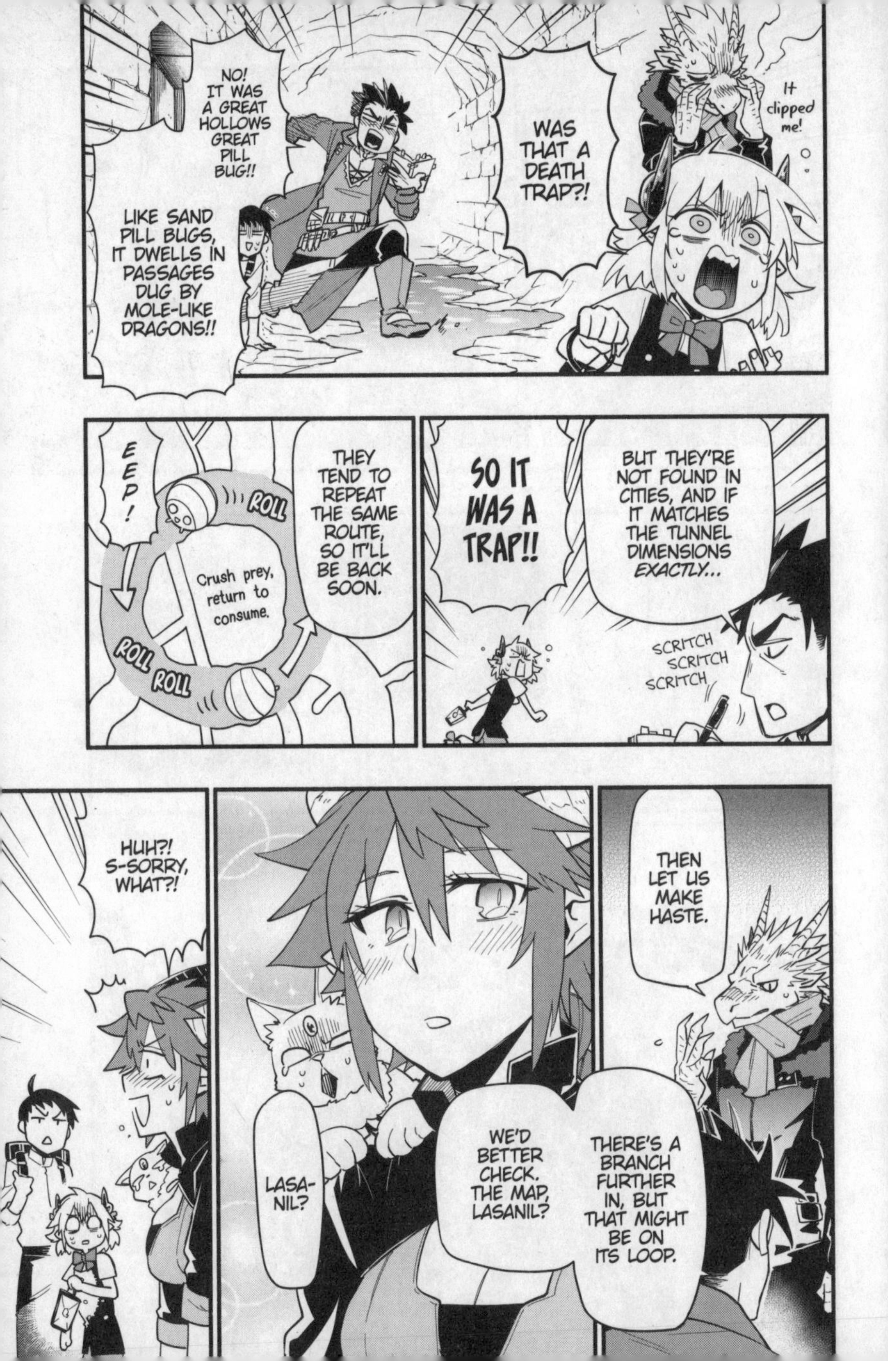
WAS THAT A DEATH TRAP?!
It clipped me!
NO! IT WAS A GREAT HOLLOWS GREAT PILL BUG!!
LIKE SAND PILL BUGS, IT DWELLS IN PASSAGES DUG BY MOLE-LIKE DRAGONS!!
BUT THEY'RE NOT FOUND IN CITIES, AND IF IT MATCHES THE TUNNEL DIMENSIONS *EXACTLY*...
SO IT WAS A TRAP!!
SCRITCH SCRITCH SCRITCH
THEY TEND TO REPEAT THE SAME ROUTE, SO IT'LL BE BACK SOON.
ROLL
Crush prey, return to consume.
ROLL ROLL
EEP!
THEN LET US MAKE HASTE.
THERE'S A BRANCH FURTHER IN, BUT THAT MIGHT BE ON ITS LOOP.
WE'D BETTER CHECK. THE MAP, LASANIL?
LASA-NIL?
HUH?! S-SORRY, WHAT?!

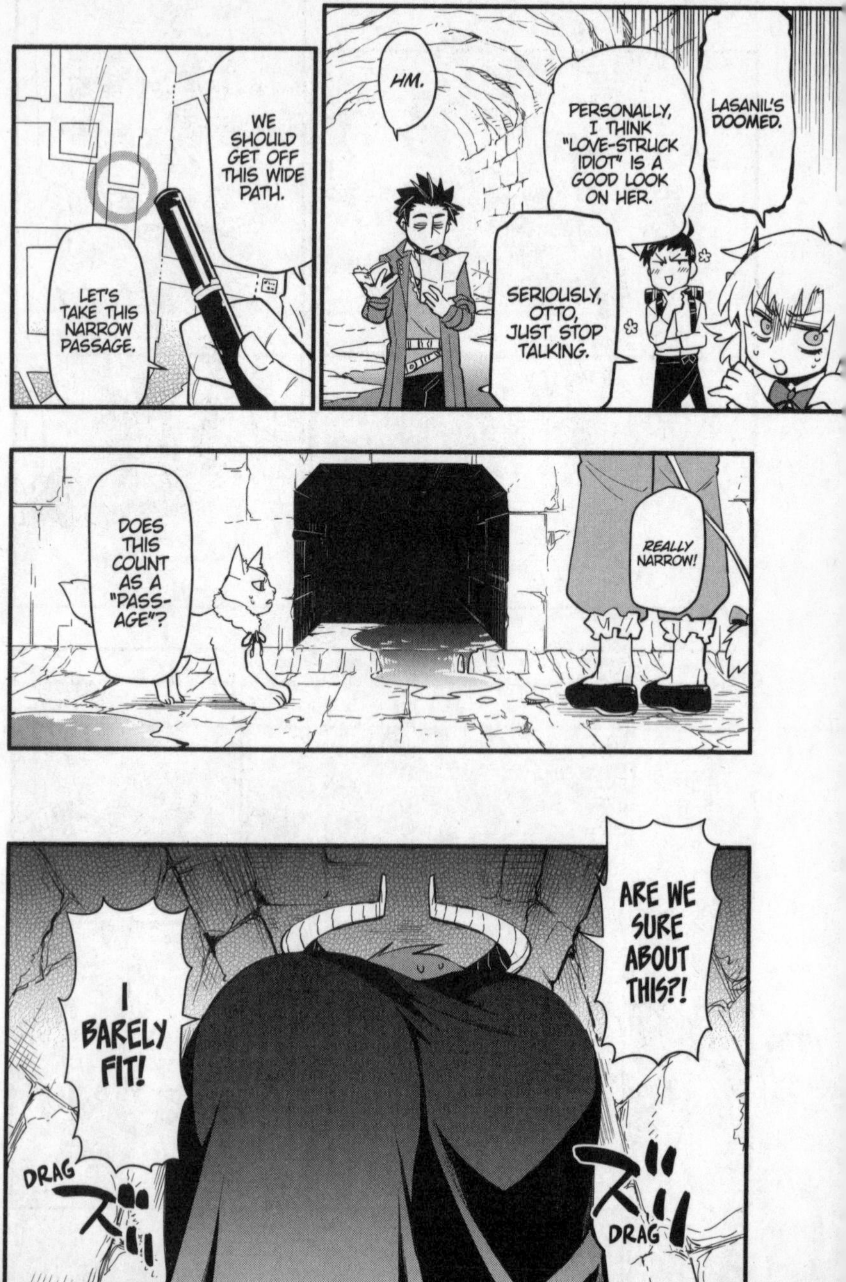
LASANIL'S DOOMED.
PERSONALLY, I THINK "LOVE-STRUCK IDIOT" IS A GOOD LOOK ON HER.
HM.
SERIOUSLY, OTTO, JUST STOP TALKING.
WE SHOULD GET OFF THIS WIDE PATH.
LET'S TAKE THIS NARROW PASSAGE.
REALLY NARROW!
DOES THIS COUNT AS A "PASS-AGE"?
ARE WE SURE ABOUT THIS?!
I BARELY FIT!
DRAG
DRAG

THERE SHOULD BE AN EXIT NEARBY!
JUST... HAVE TO... ENDURE!
JAZER, YOU OKAY BACK THERE?
WHAP
WHAP
I-I CAN HANDLE IT!
Just hair in my eyes!
TUMP
PATTY!
I CAN'T FIT!
UGH! I WAS AFRAID OF THAT!

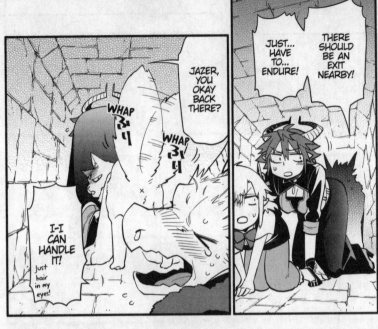

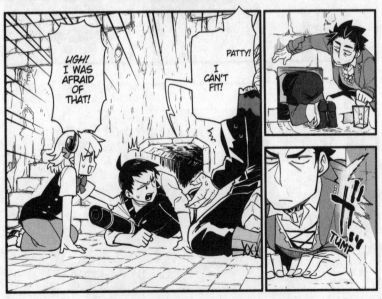

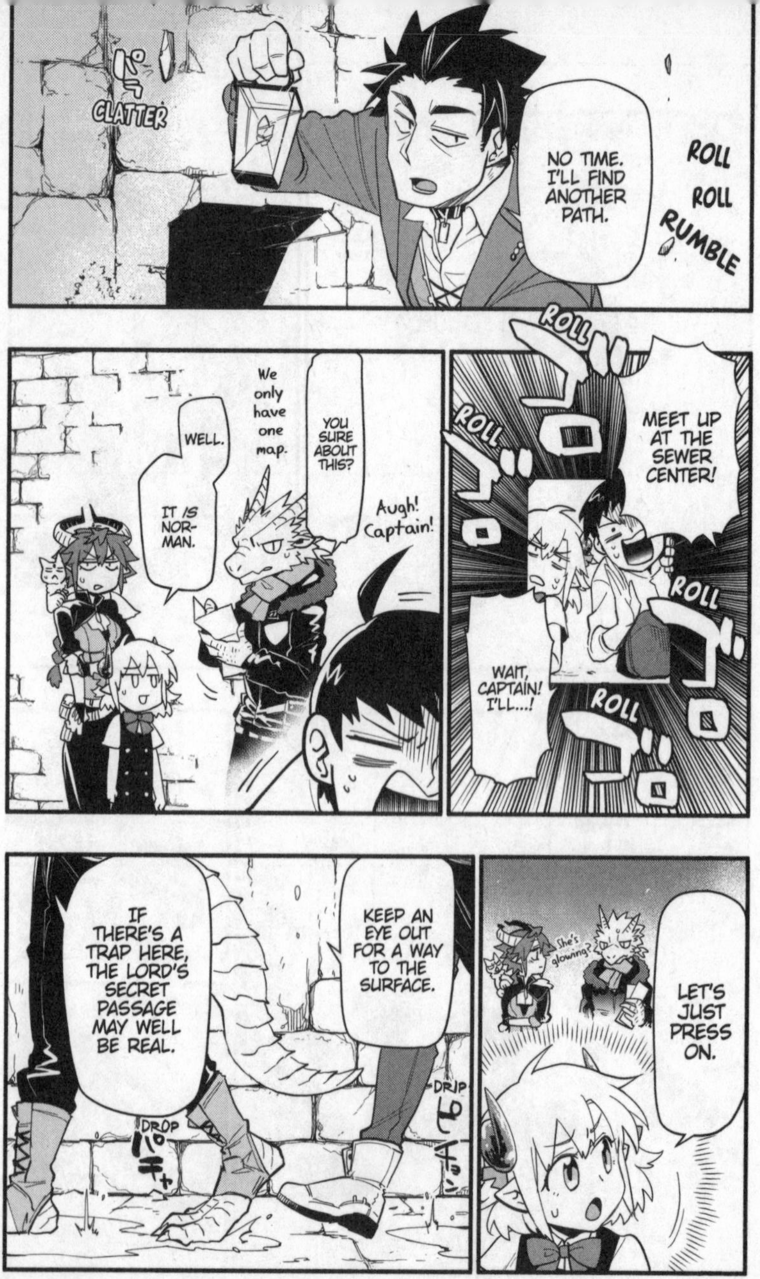
CLATTER
NO TIME. I'LL FIND ANOTHER PATH.
ROLL
ROLL
RUMBLE
ROLL
MEET UP AT THE SEWER CENTER!
ROLL
ROLL
WAIT, CAPTAIN! I'LL...!
ROLL
Augh! Captain!
YOU SURE ABOUT THIS?
We only have one map.
WELL.
IT IS NORMAN.
She's glowing?
LET'S JUST PRESS ON.
KEEP AN EYE OUT FOR A WAY TO THE SURFACE.
IF THERE'S A TRAP HERE, THE LORD'S SECRET PASSAGE MAY WELL BE REAL.
DRIP
DROP

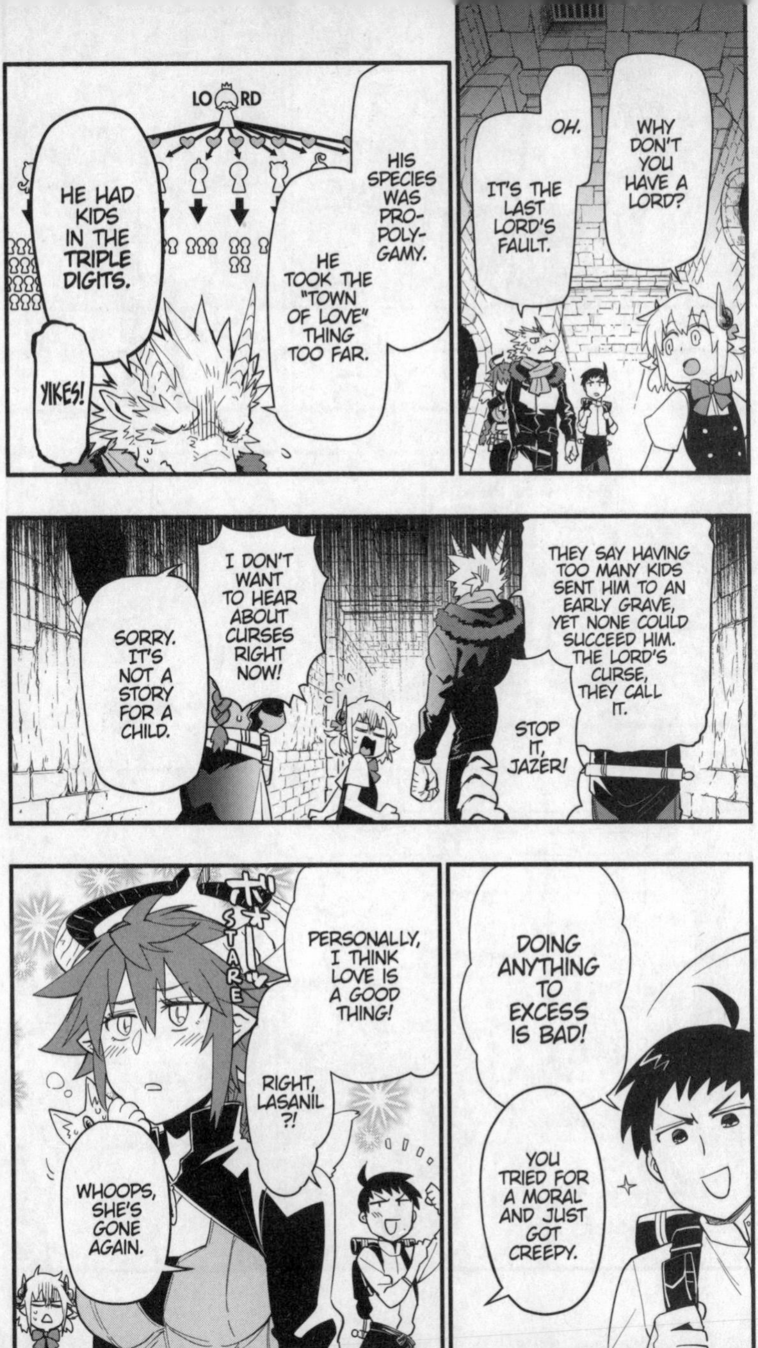
WHY DON'T YOU HAVE A LORD?
OH.
IT'S THE LAST LORD'S FAULT.
HIS SPECIES WAS PRO-POLYGAMY.
HE TOOK THE "TOWN OF LOVE" THING TOO FAR.
LORD
HE HAD KIDS IN THE TRIPLE DIGITS.
YIKES!
THEY SAY HAVING TOO MANY KIDS SENT HIM TO AN EARLY GRAVE, YET NONE COULD SUCCEED HIM. THE LORD'S CURSE, THEY CALL IT.
STOP IT, JAZER!
I DON'T WANT TO HEAR ABOUT CURSES RIGHT NOW!
SORRY. IT'S NOT A STORY FOR A CHILD.
DOING ANYTHING TO EXCESS IS BAD!
YOU TRIED FOR A MORAL AND JUST GOT CREEPY.
PERSONALLY, I THINK LOVE IS A GOOD THING!
RIGHT, LASANIL?!
STARE
WHOOPS, SHE'S GONE AGAIN.

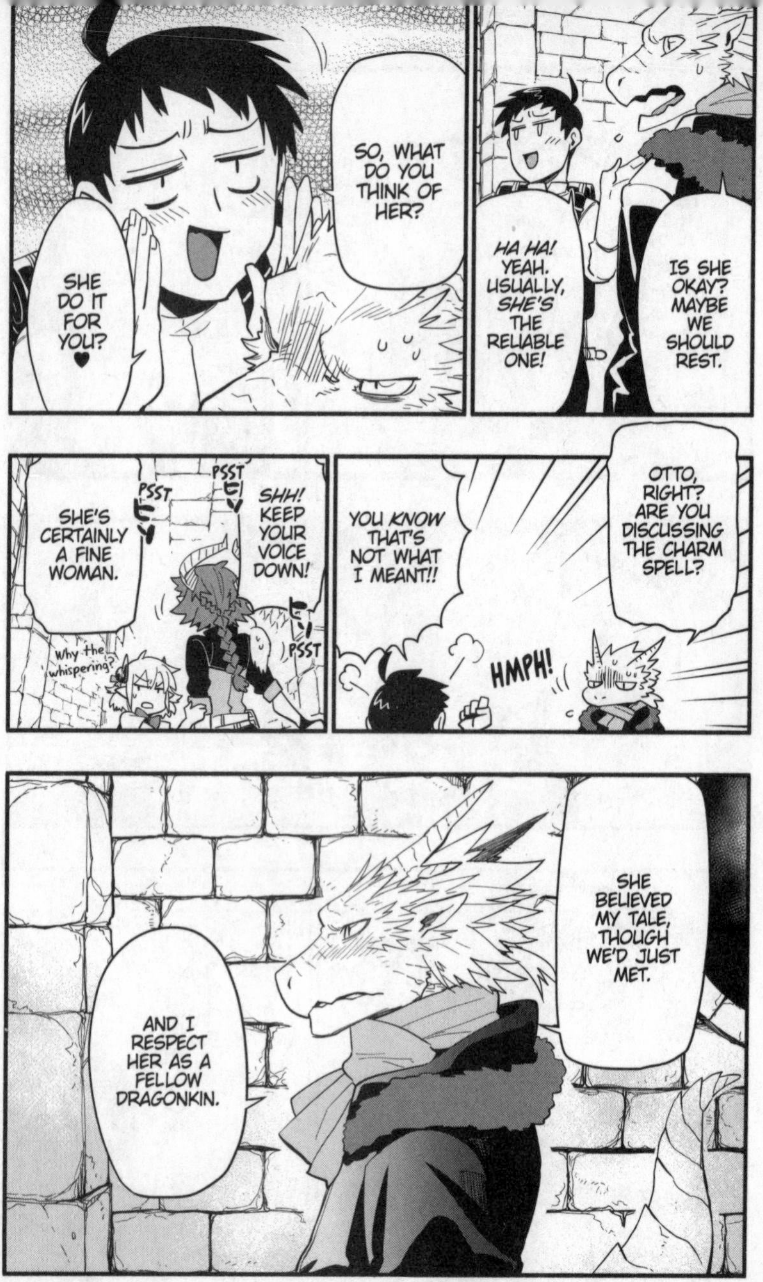
IS SHE OKAY? MAYBE WE SHOULD REST.
HA HA! YEAH. USUALLY, SHE'S THE RELIABLE ONE!
SO, WHAT DO YOU THINK OF HER?
SHE DO IT FOR YOU? ♥
OTTO, RIGHT? ARE YOU DISCUSSING THE CHARM SPELL?
HMPH!
YOU KNOW THAT'S NOT WHAT I MEANT!!
SHH! KEEP YOUR VOICE DOWN!
PSST
PSST
PSST
SHE'S CERTAINLY A FINE WOMAN.
Why the whispering?
SHE BELIEVED MY TALE, THOUGH WE'D JUST MET.
AND I RESPECT HER AS A FELLOW DRAGONKIN.

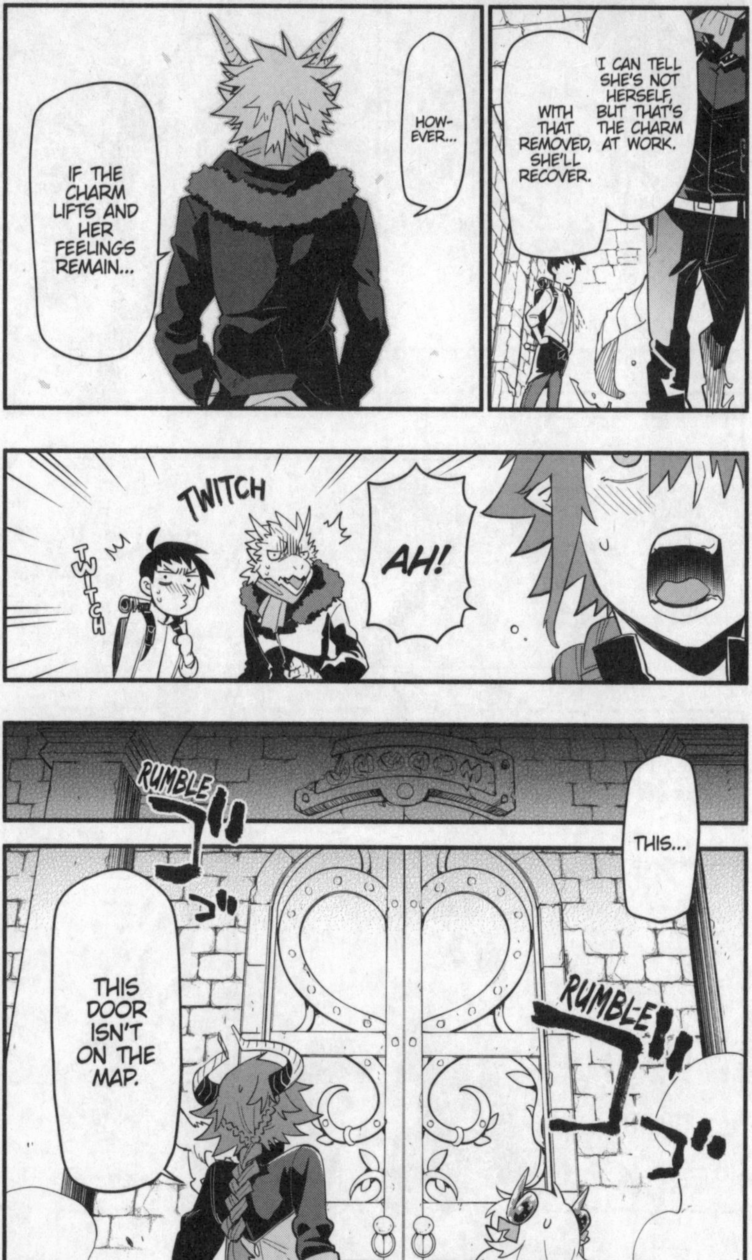
I CAN TELL SHE'S NOT HERSELF, BUT THAT'S THE CHARM AT WORK.
WITH THAT REMOVED, SHE'LL RECOVER.
HOW-EVER...
IF THE CHARM LIFTS AND HER FEELINGS REMAIN...
AH!
TWITCH
TWITCH
RUMBLE
THIS...
RUMBLE
THIS DOOR ISN'T ON THE MAP.

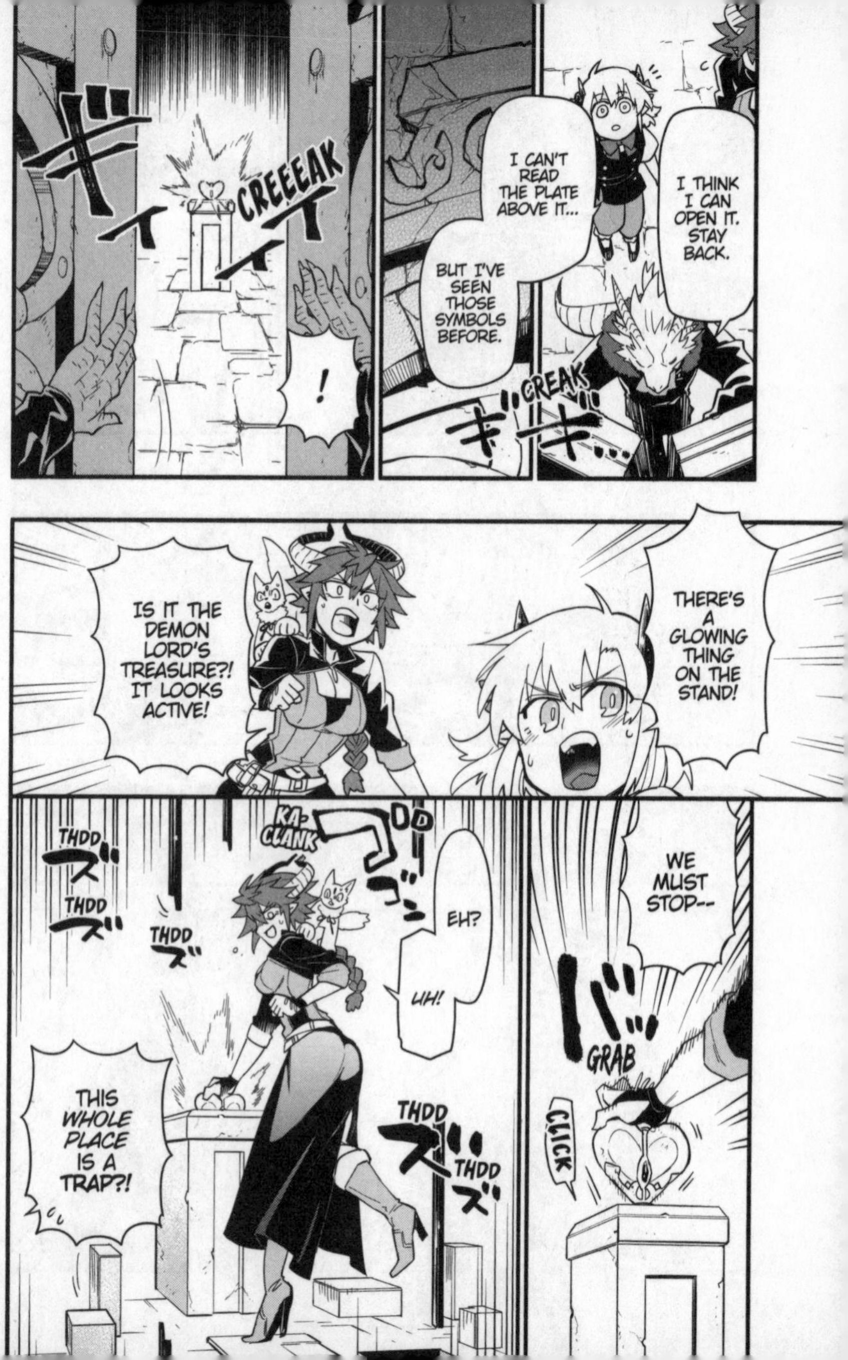
I THINK I CAN OPEN IT. STAY BACK.
I CAN'T READ THE PLATE ABOVE IT...
BUT I'VE SEEN THOSE SYMBOLS BEFORE.
CREAK
CREEEAK
!
THERE'S A GLOWING THING ON THE STAND!
IS IT THE DEMON LORD'S TREASURE?! IT LOOKS ACTIVE!
WE MUST STOP--
GRAB
CLICK
KA-CLANK
EH?
UH!
THDD
THDD
THDD
THDD
THDD
THIS WHOLE PLACE IS A TRAP?!

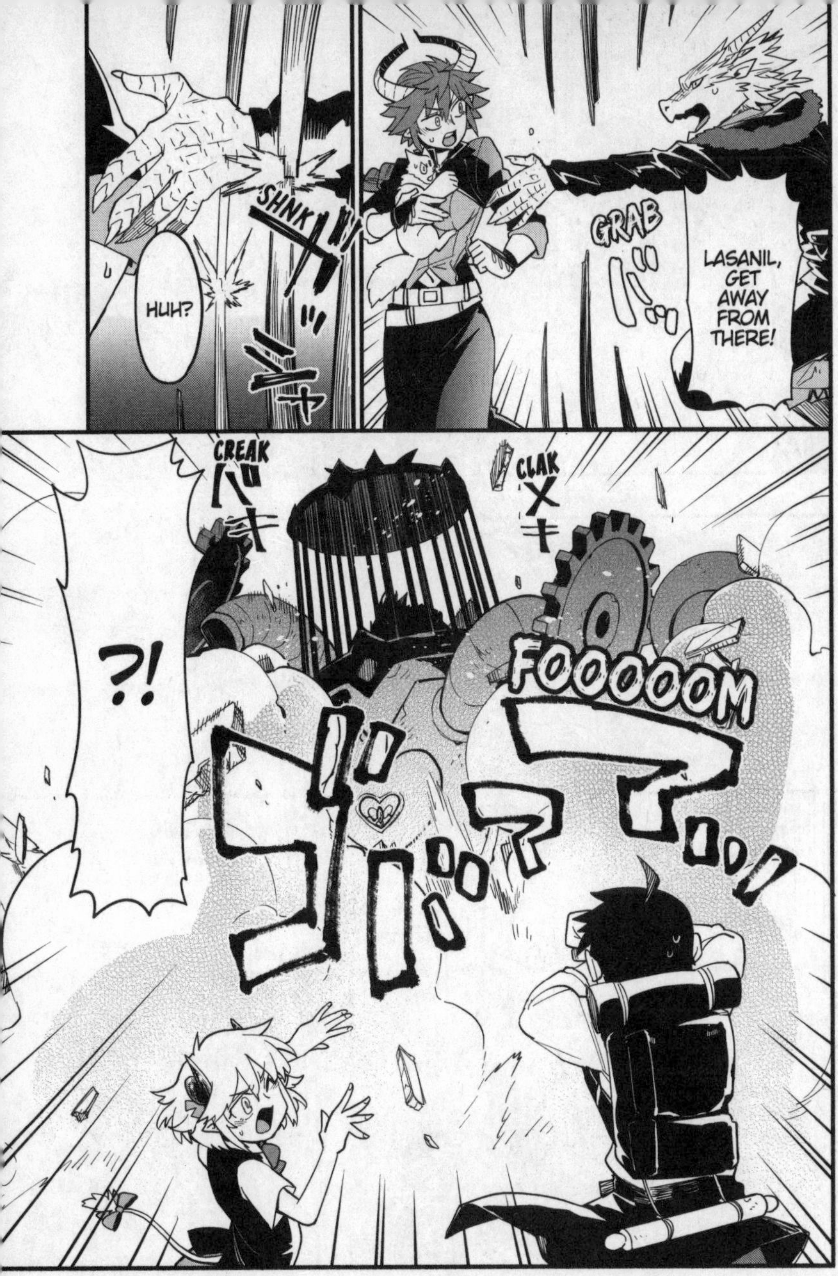
LASANIL, GET AWAY FROM THERE!
GRAB
SHNK
HUH?
CLAK
CREAK
FOOOOOOM
?!

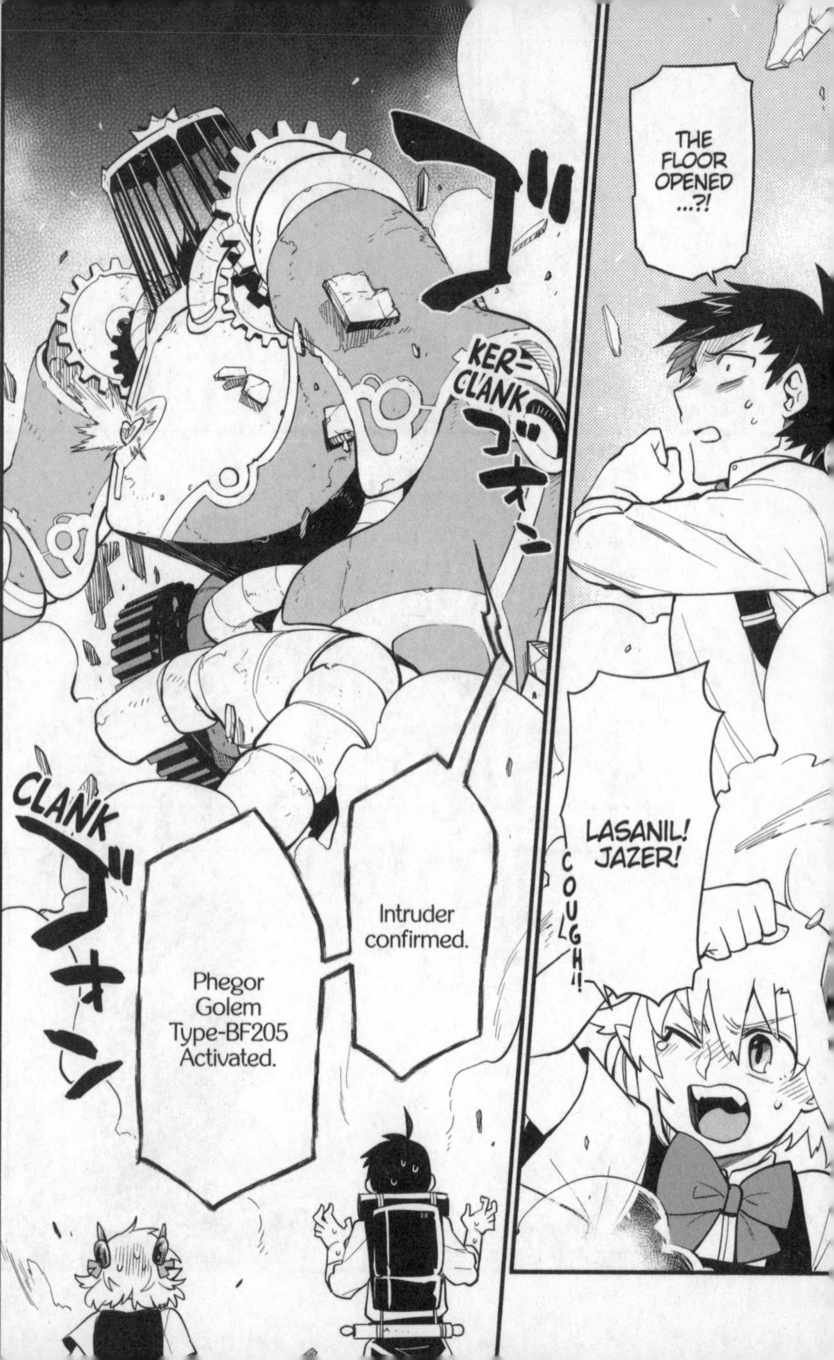
THE FLOOR OPENED ...?!
LASANIL! JAZER!
COUGH!
KER-CLANK
CLANK
Intruder confirmed.
Phegor Golem Type-BF205 Activated.

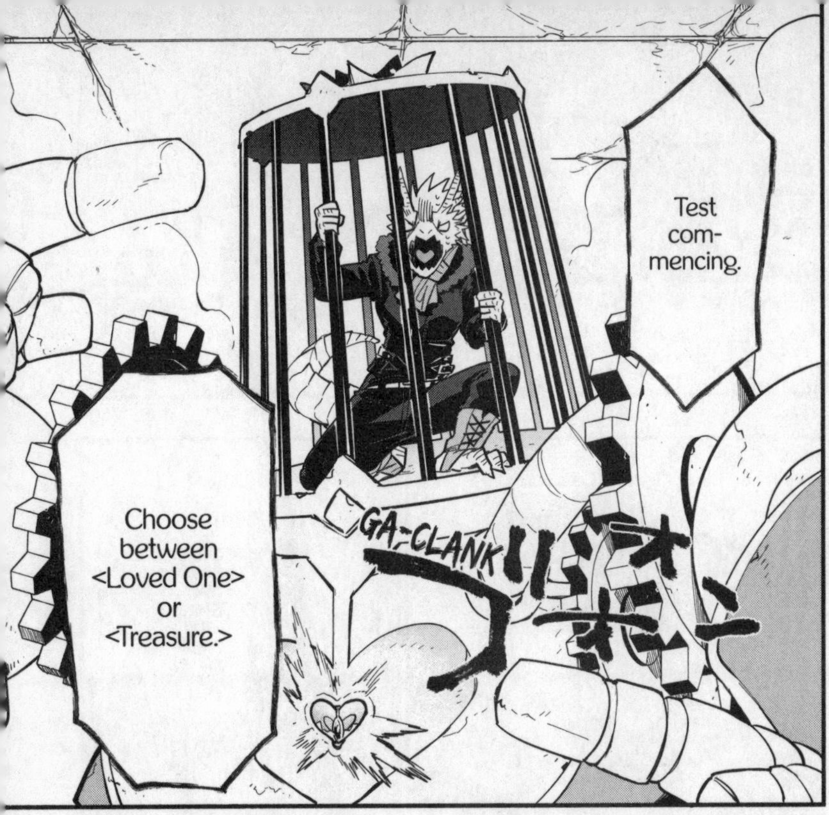
Test commencing.
Choose between <Loved One> or <Treasure.>
GA-CLANK

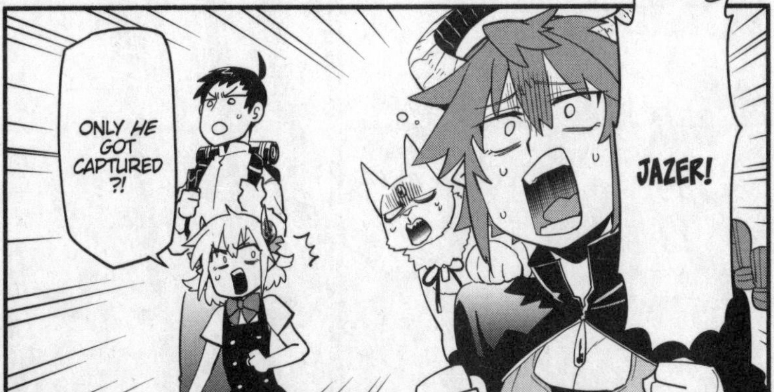
JAZER!
ONLY HE GOT CAPTURED?!

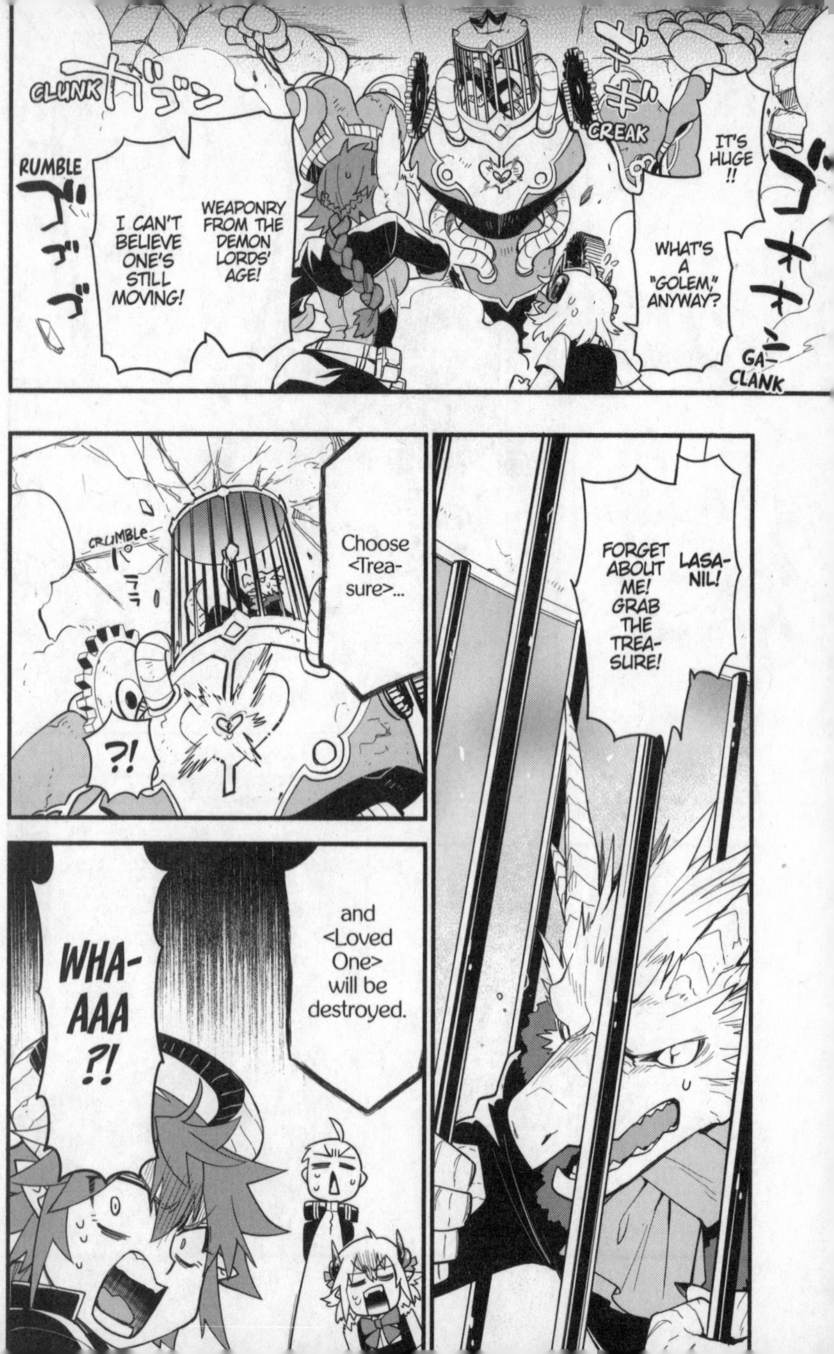
GA-CLANK
IT'S HUGE!!
WHAT'S A "GOLEM," ANYWAY?
CREAK
ギギ
WEAPONRY FROM THE DEMON LORDS' AGE!
I CAN'T BELIEVE ONE'S STILL MOVING!
CLUNK
ガゴン
RUMBLE
ゴゴゴ
LASA-NIL!
FORGET ABOUT ME! GRAB THE TREA-SURE!
CRUMBLE
Choose <Trea-sure>...
?!
and <Loved One> will be destroyed.
WHA-AAA?!

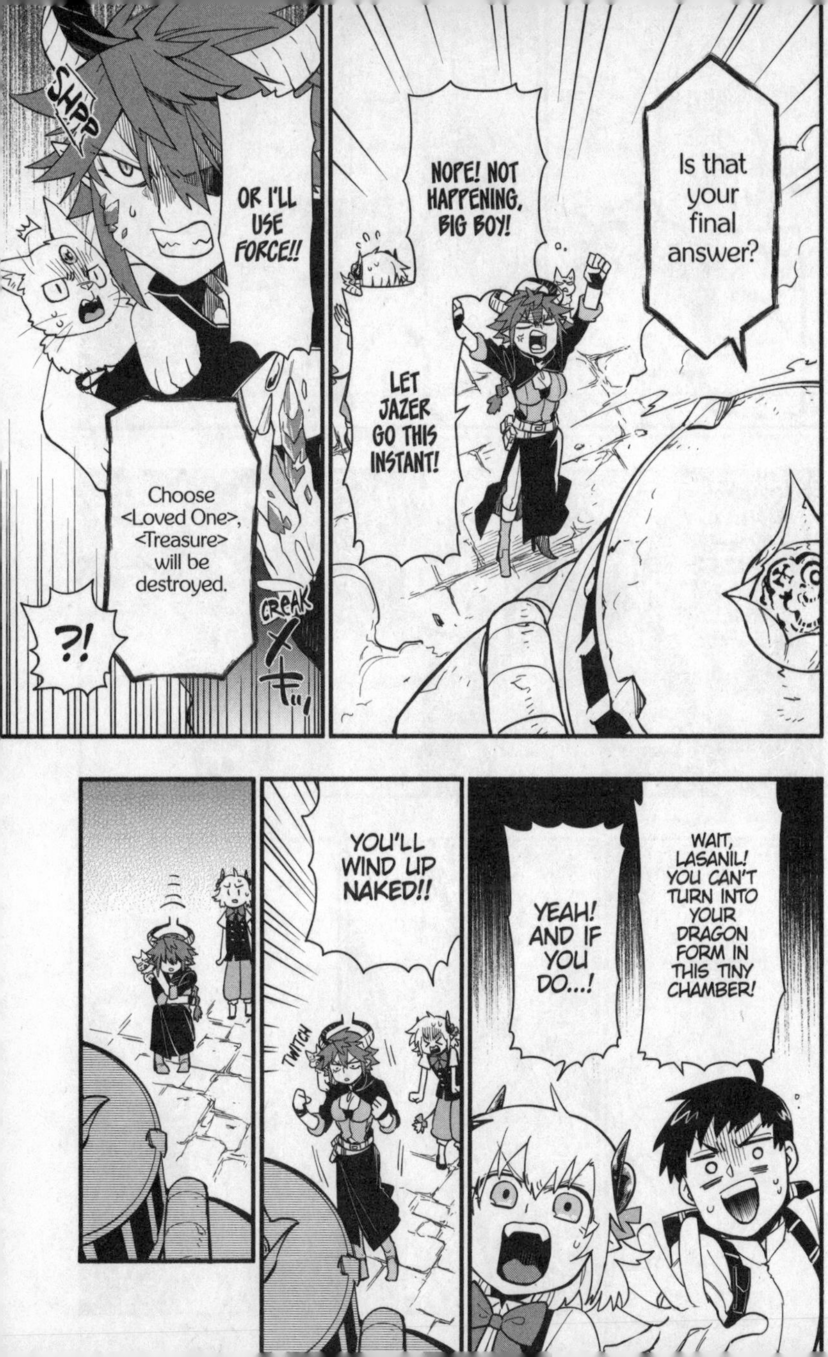
Is that your final answer?
NOPE! NOT HAPPENING, BIG BOY!
LET JAZER GO THIS INSTANT!
SHPP
OR I'LL USE FORCE!!
Choose <Loved One>, <Treasure> will be destroyed.
?!
CREAK
WAIT, LASANIL! YOU CAN'T TURN INTO YOUR DRAGON FORM IN THIS TINY CHAMBER!
YEAH! AND IF YOU DO...!
YOU'LL WIND UP NAKED!!
TWITCH

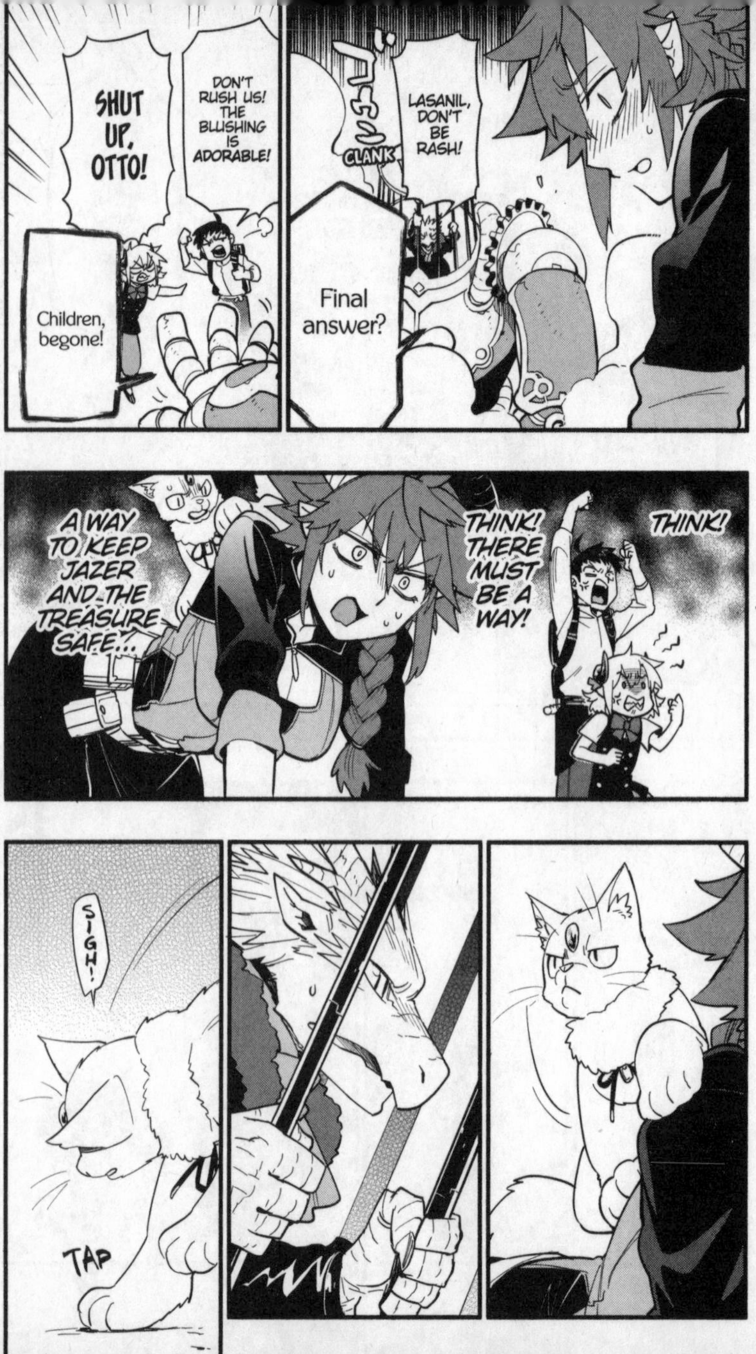
LASANIL, DON'T BE RASH!
CLANK
Final answer?
DON'T RUSH US! THE BLUSHING IS ADORABLE!
SHUT UP, OTTO!
Children, begone!
THINK!
THINK! THERE MUST BE A WAY!
A WAY TO KEEP JAZER AND THE TREASURE SAFE...
SIGH!
TAP

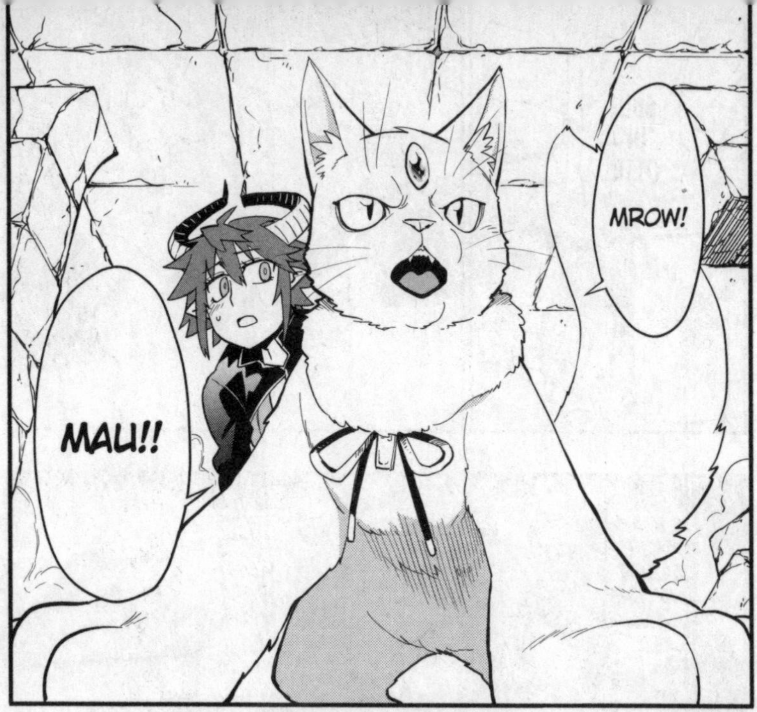
MROW!
MAU!!

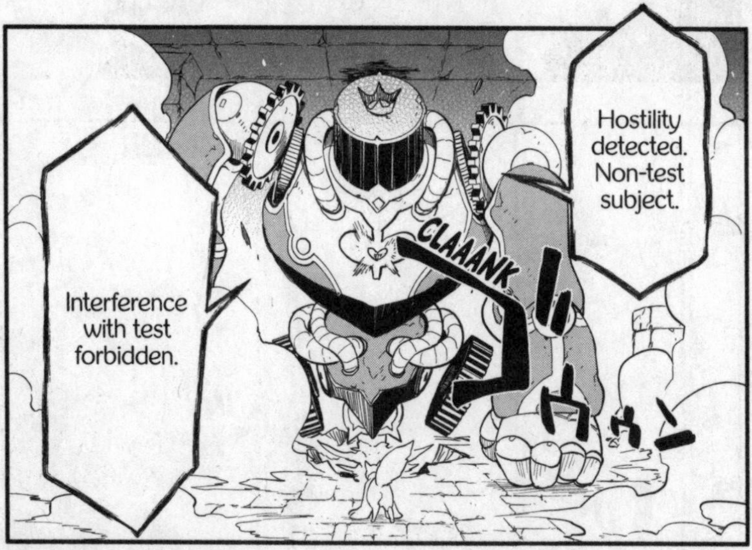
Hostility detected. Non-test subject.
CLAAANK
Interference with test forbidden.

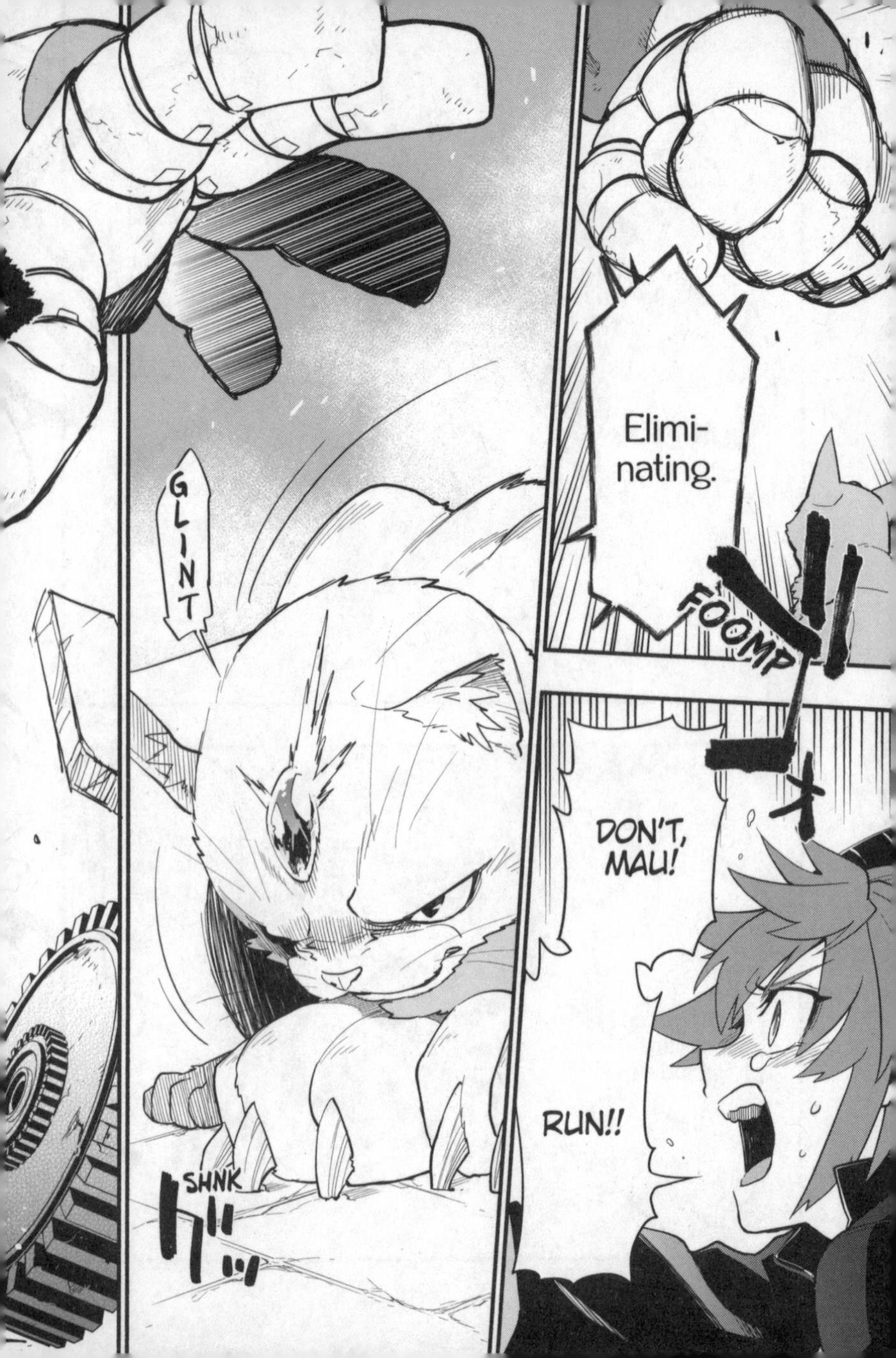
Elimi-
nating.
FOOMP
DON'T,
MAU!
RUN!!
GLINT
SHNK

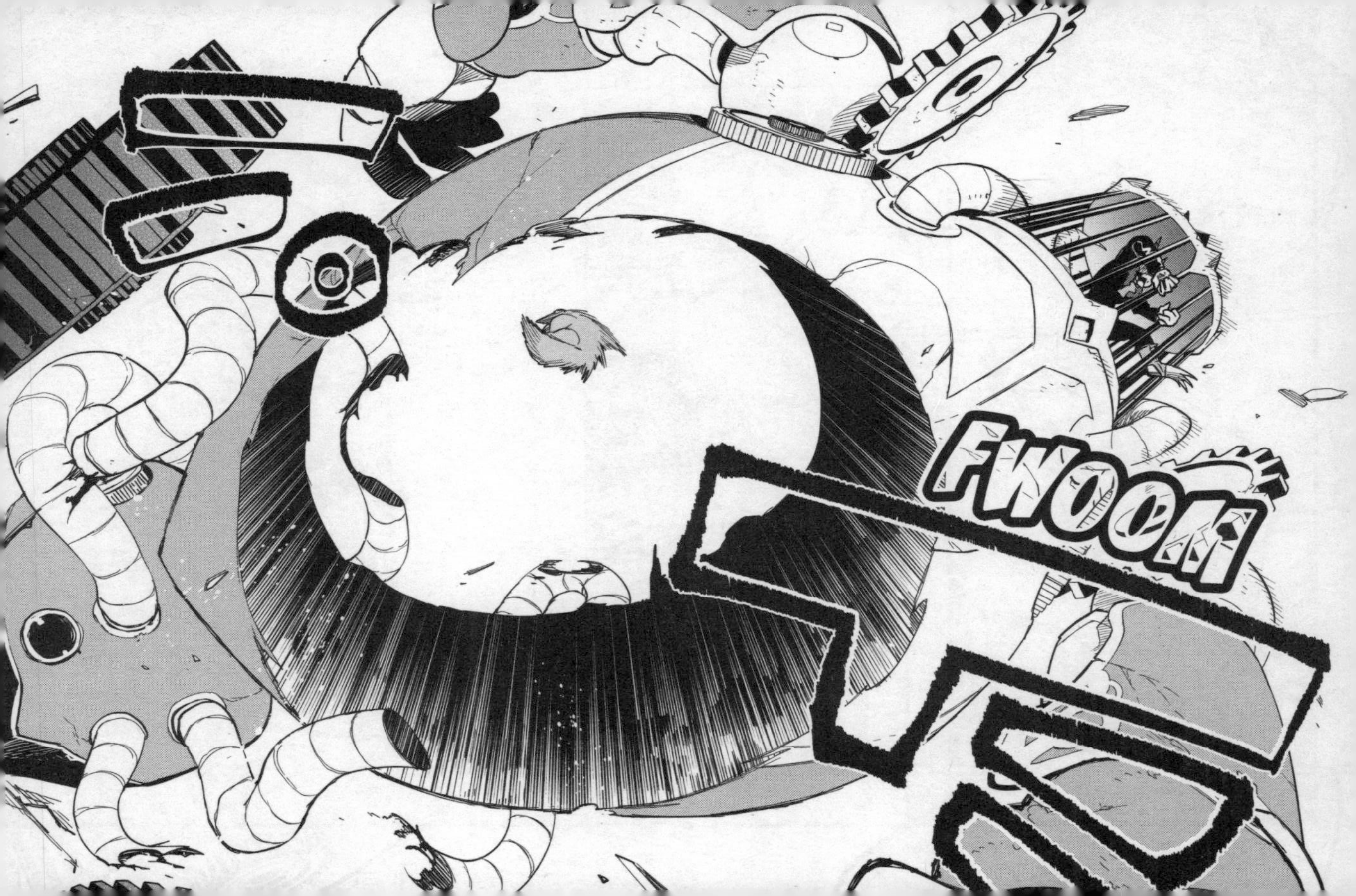
FWOOM

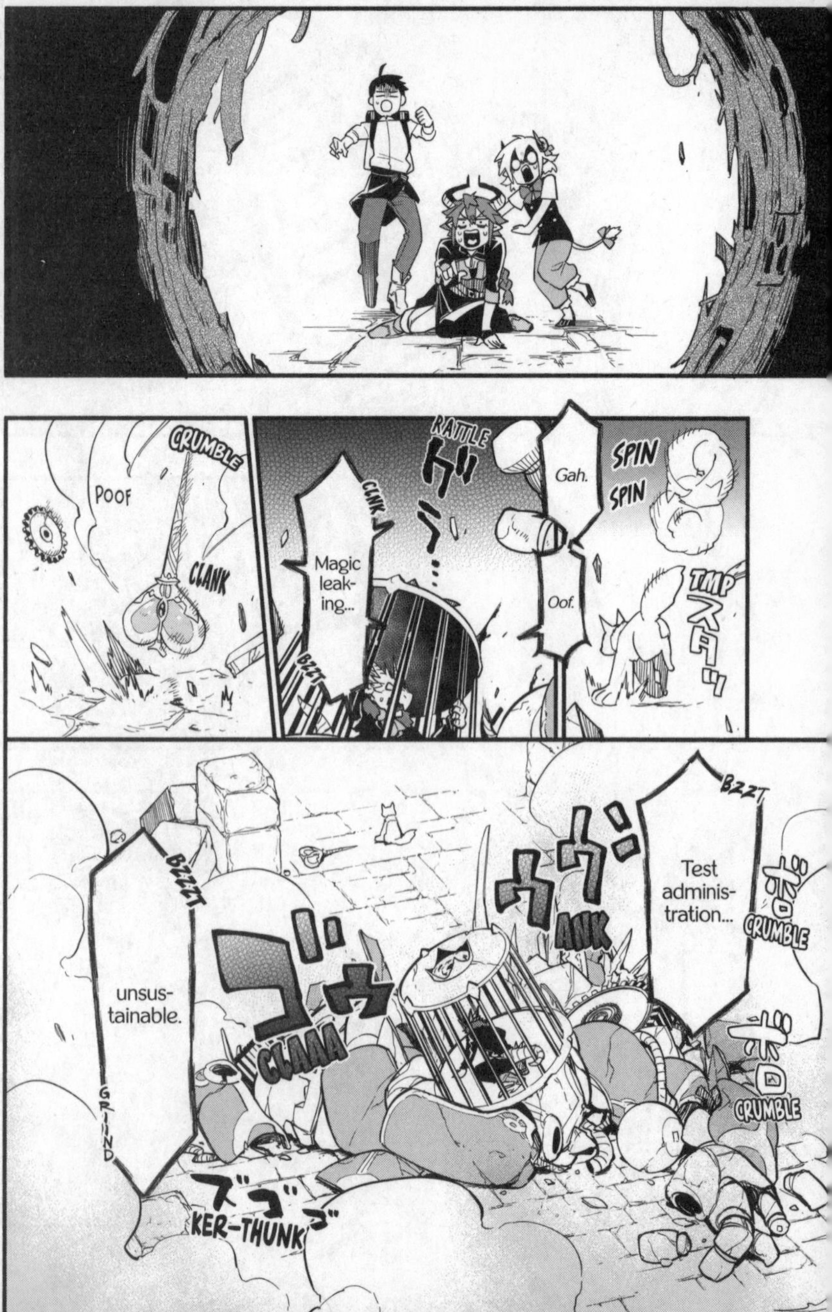
Gah.
SPIN SPIN
Oof.
TMP スタッ
RATTLE グラ…
CLNK
Magic leaking...
BZZT
CRUMBLE
POOF
CLANK
BZZT
Test administration...
ボロ CRUMBLE
ウウ ANK
ゴウ CLAAA
BZZZT
unsustainable.
GRIND
ズゴゴ KER-THUNK
ボロ CRUMBLE

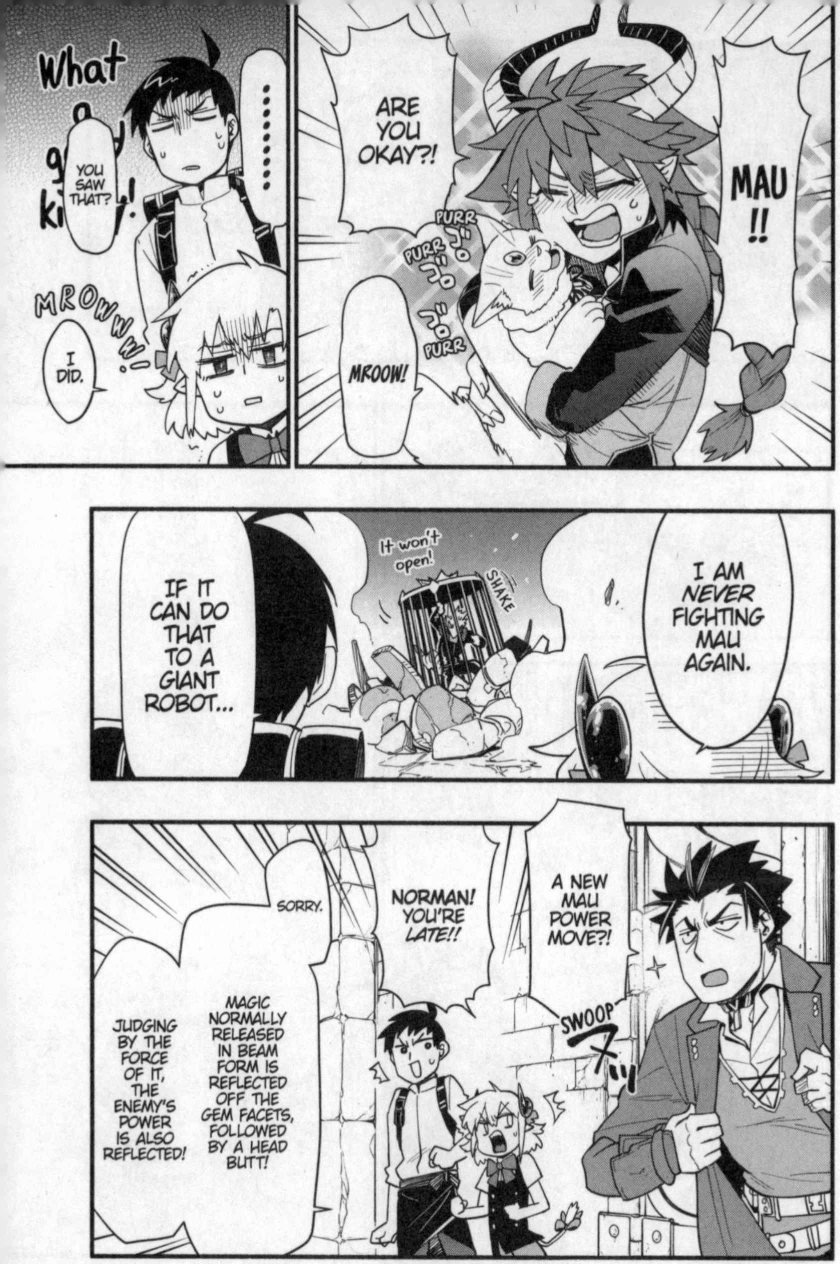

MAU!!
ARE YOU OKAY?!
PURR
PURR
PURR
MROOW!
......
YOU SAW THAT?
I DID.
MROWWW!
What
I AM NEVER FIGHTING MAU AGAIN.
It won't open!
SHAKE
IF IT CAN DO THAT TO A GIANT ROBOT...
A NEW MAU POWER MOVE?!
SWOOP
NORMAN! YOU'RE LATE!!
SORRY.
MAGIC NORMALLY RELEASED IN BEAM FORM IS REFLECTED OFF THE GEM FACETS, FOLLOWED BY A HEAD BUTT!
JUDGING BY THE FORCE OF IT, THE ENEMY'S POWER IS ALSO REFLECTED!

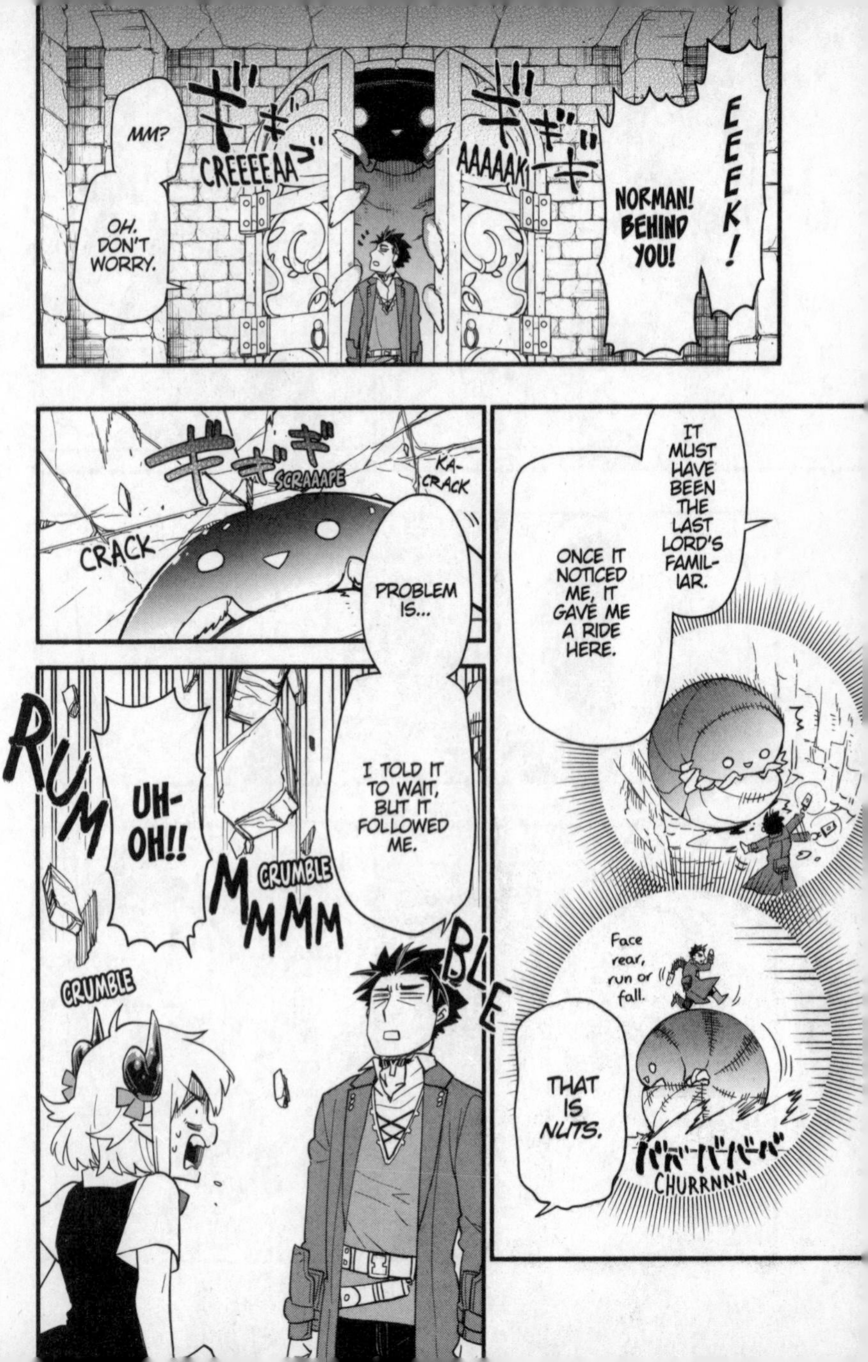
EEEK!
NORMAN! BEHIND YOU!
ギギギ
AAAAAK
ギギ
CREEEEAA
MM?
OH. DON'T WORRY.
IT MUST HAVE BEEN THE LAST LORD'S FAMIL-IAR.
ONCE IT NOTICED ME, IT GAVE ME A RIDE HERE.
Face rear, run or fall.
THAT IS NUTS.
ババババ
CHURRNNN
KA-CRACK
ギギギ
SCRAAAPE
CRACK
PROBLEM IS...
I TOLD IT TO WAIT, BUT IT FOLLOWED ME.
BLE
MMMM
CRUMBLE
UH-OH!!
RUM
CRUMBLE

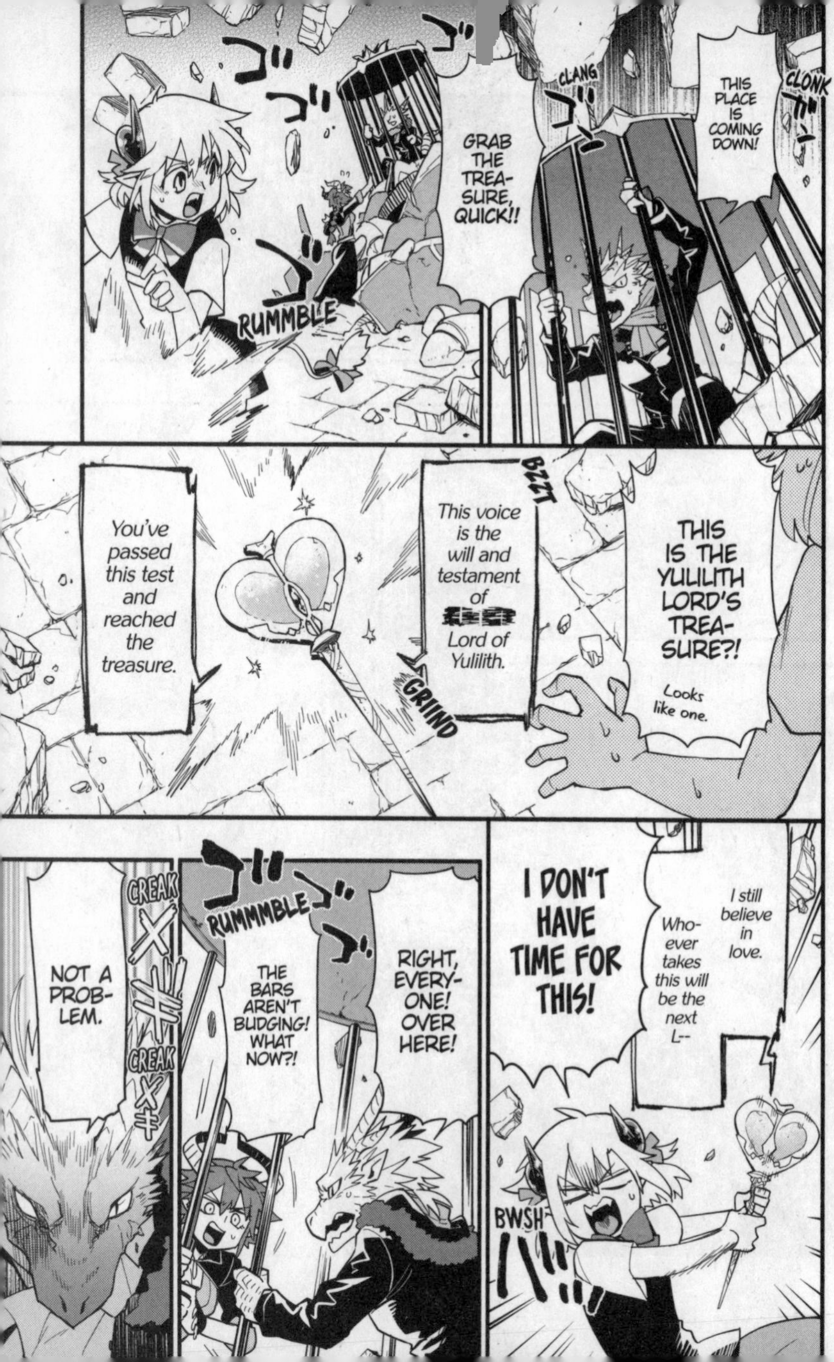
THIS PLACE IS COMING DOWN!
CLONK
CLANG
GRAB THE TREASURE, QUICK!!
RUMMBLE
THIS IS THE YULILITH LORD'S TREASURE?!
Looks like one.
BZZT
This voice is the will and testament of [redacted] Lord of Yulilith.
GRIIND
You've passed this test and reached the treasure.
I still believe in love.
Whoever takes this will be the next L--
I DON'T HAVE TIME FOR THIS!
BWSH
RIGHT, EVERYONE! OVER HERE!
THE BARS AREN'T BUDGING! WHAT NOW?!
RUMMMBLE
CREAK
CREAK
NOT A PROBLEM.

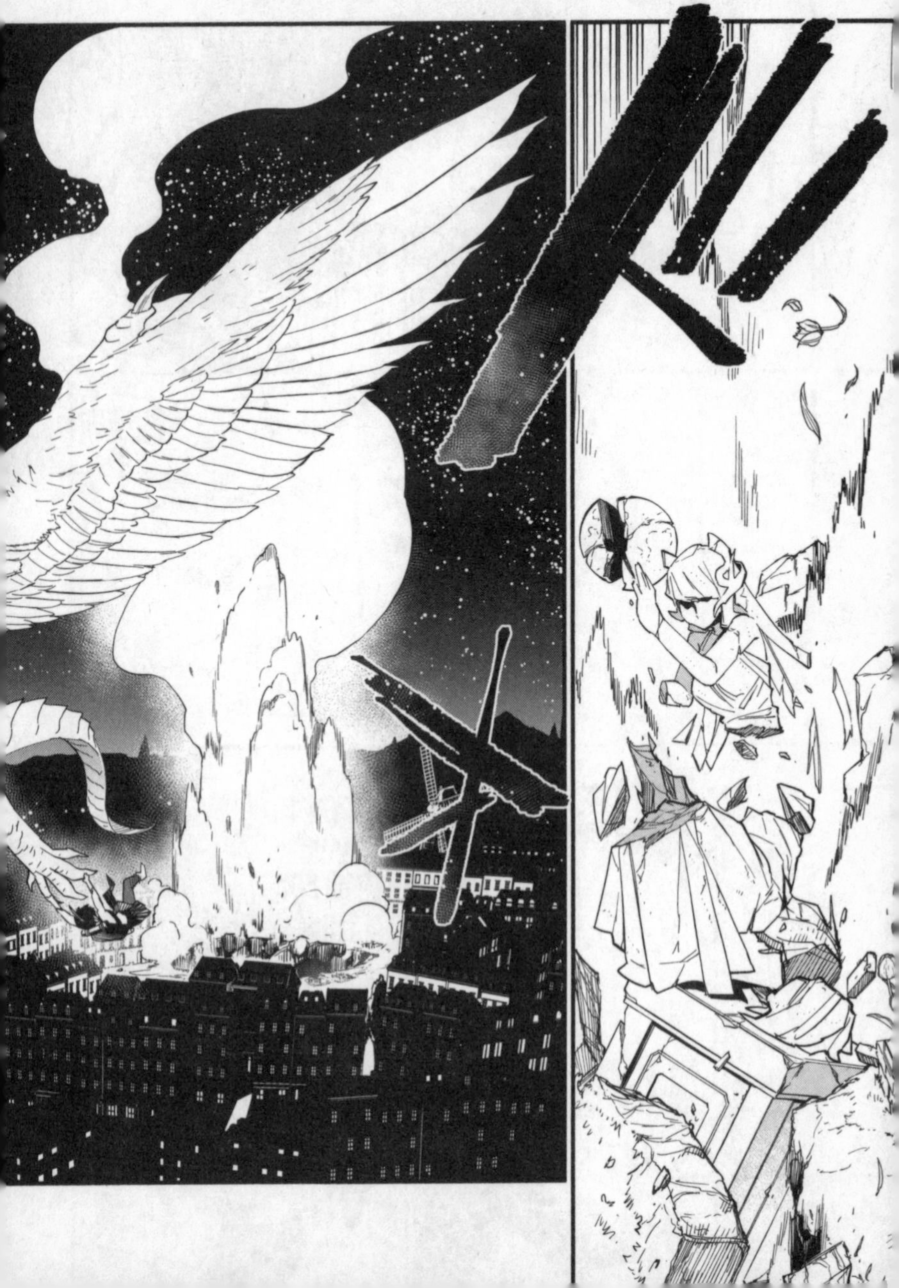

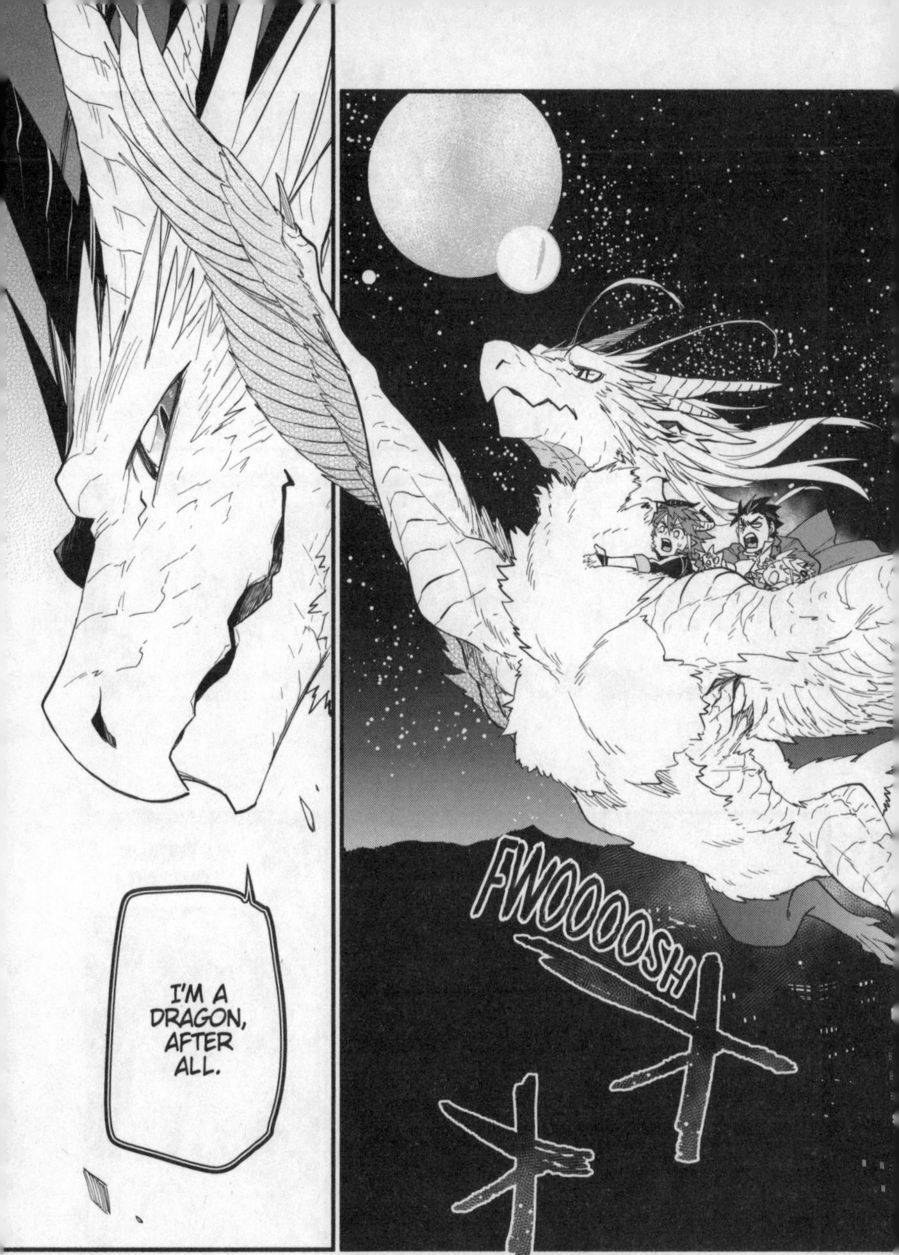
FWOOOOSH
I'M A DRAGON, AFTER ALL.

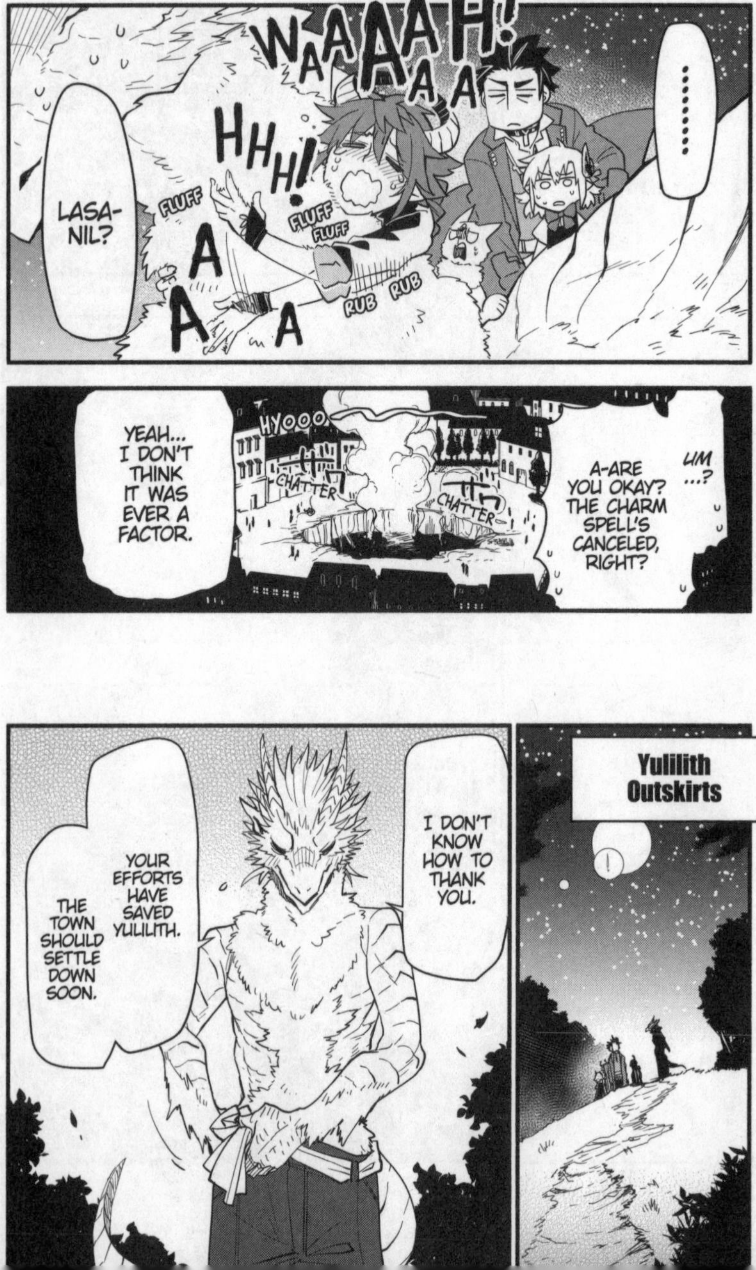

......
WAAAAAH! AAA HHH! AAAA
FLUFF
FLUFF FLUFF
RUB RUB
LASA-NIL?
UM ...?
A-ARE YOU OKAY? THE CHARM SPELL'S CANCELED, RIGHT?
HYOOO
CHATTER
CHATTER
YEAH... I DON'T THINK IT WAS EVER A FACTOR.
Yulilith Outskirts
!
I DON'T KNOW HOW TO THANK YOU.
YOUR EFFORTS HAVE SAVED YULILITH.
THE TOWN SHOULD SETTLE DOWN SOON.

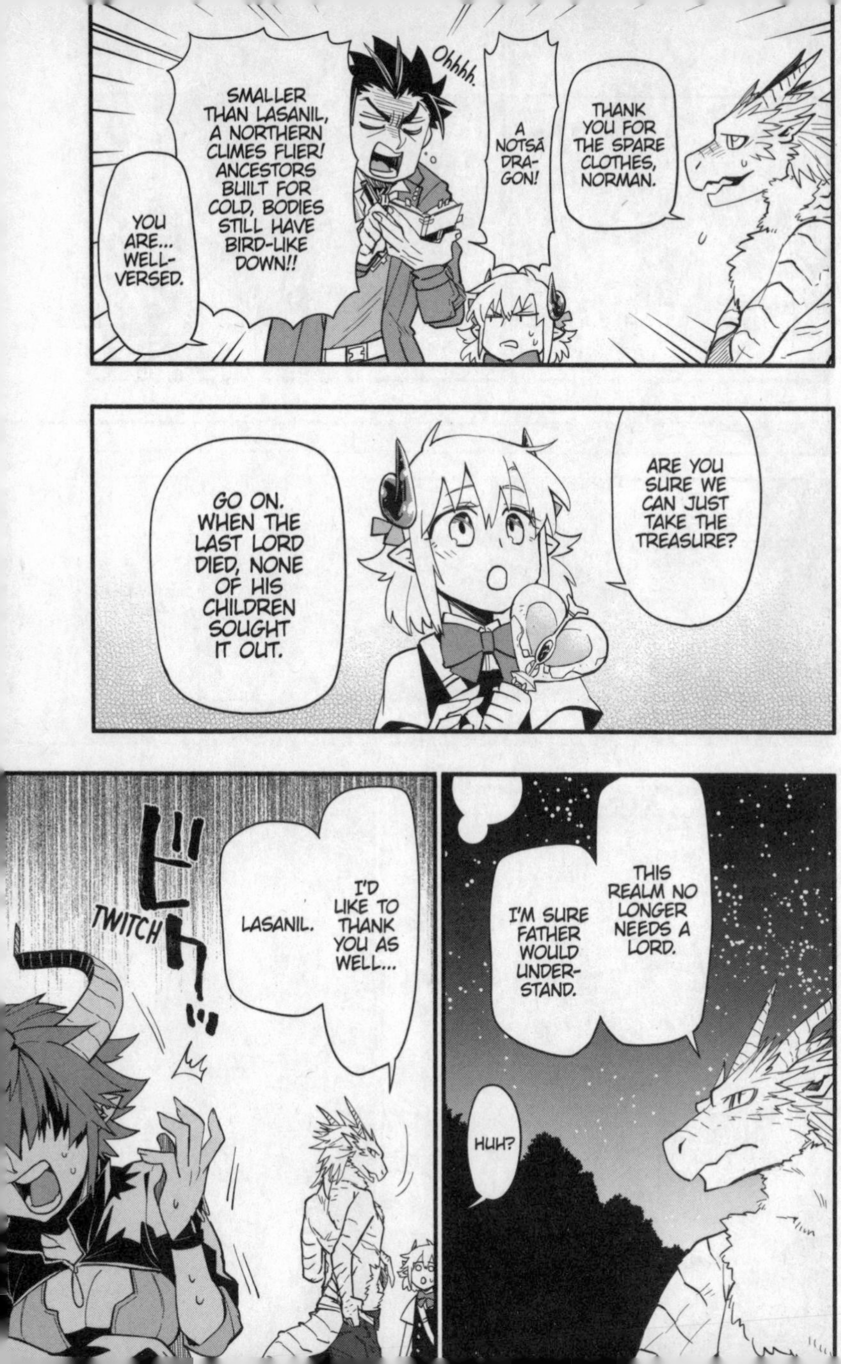
THANK YOU FOR THE SPARE CLOTHES, NORMAN.
A NOTSĀ DRAGON!
Ohhhh.
SMALLER THAN LASANIL, A NORTHERN CLIMES FLIER! ANCESTORS BUILT FOR COLD, BODIES STILL HAVE BIRD-LIKE DOWN!!
YOU ARE... WELL-VERSED.
ARE YOU SURE WE CAN JUST TAKE THE TREASURE?
GO ON. WHEN THE LAST LORD DIED, NONE OF HIS CHILDREN SOUGHT IT OUT.
THIS REALM NO LONGER NEEDS A LORD.
I'M SURE FATHER WOULD UNDERSTAND.
HUH?
I'D LIKE TO THANK YOU AS WELL...
LASANIL.
ビクッ
TWITCH

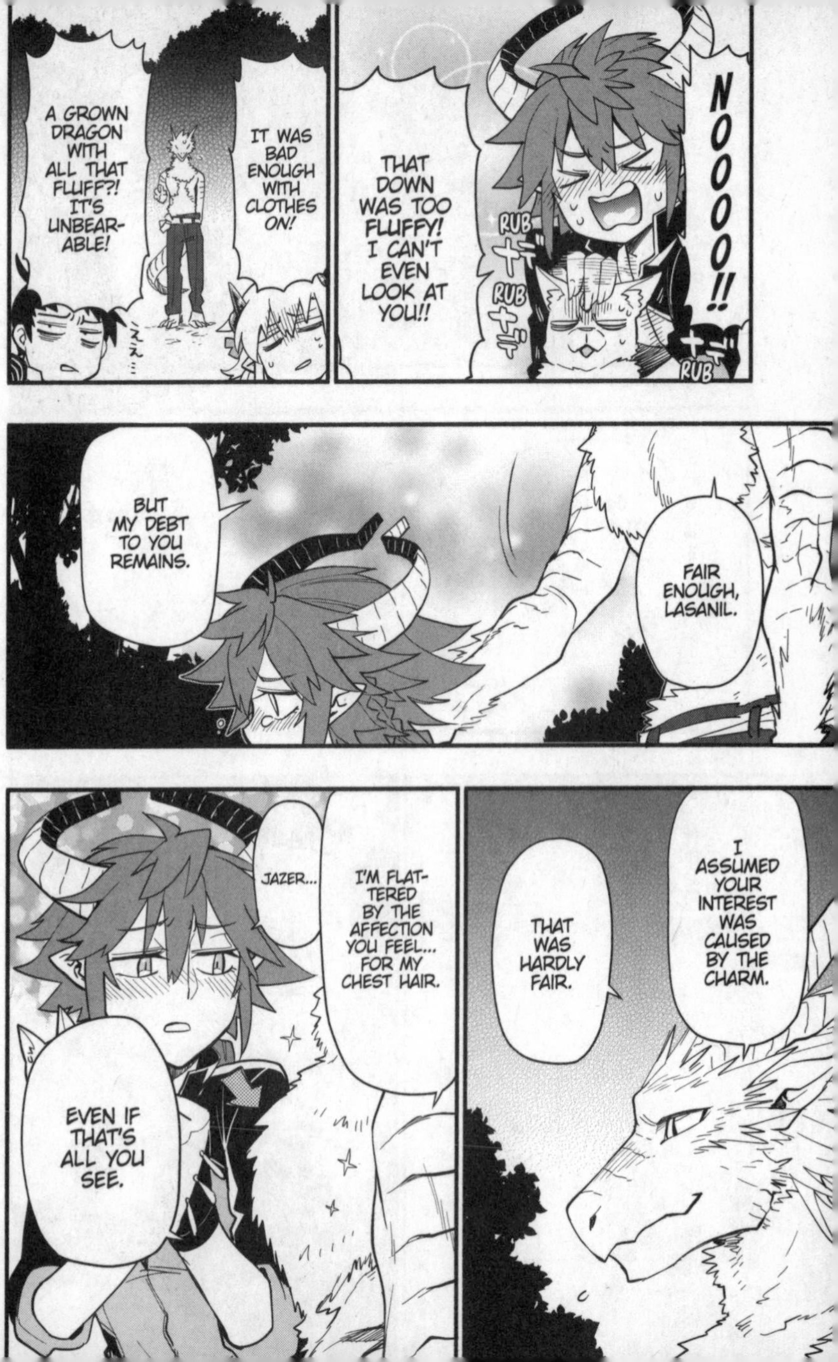
NOOOOO!!
THAT DOWN WAS TOO FLUFFY! I CAN'T EVEN LOOK AT YOU!!
RUB
RUB
RUB
IT WAS BAD ENOUGH WITH CLOTHES ON!
A GROWN DRAGON WITH ALL THAT FLUFF?! IT'S UNBEAR-ABLE!
FAIR ENOUGH, LASANIL.
BUT MY DEBT TO YOU REMAINS.
I ASSUMED YOUR INTEREST WAS CAUSED BY THE CHARM.
THAT WAS HARDLY FAIR.
JAZER...
I'M FLAT-TERED BY THE AFFECTION YOU FEEL... FOR MY CHEST HAIR.
EVEN IF THAT'S ALL YOU SEE.

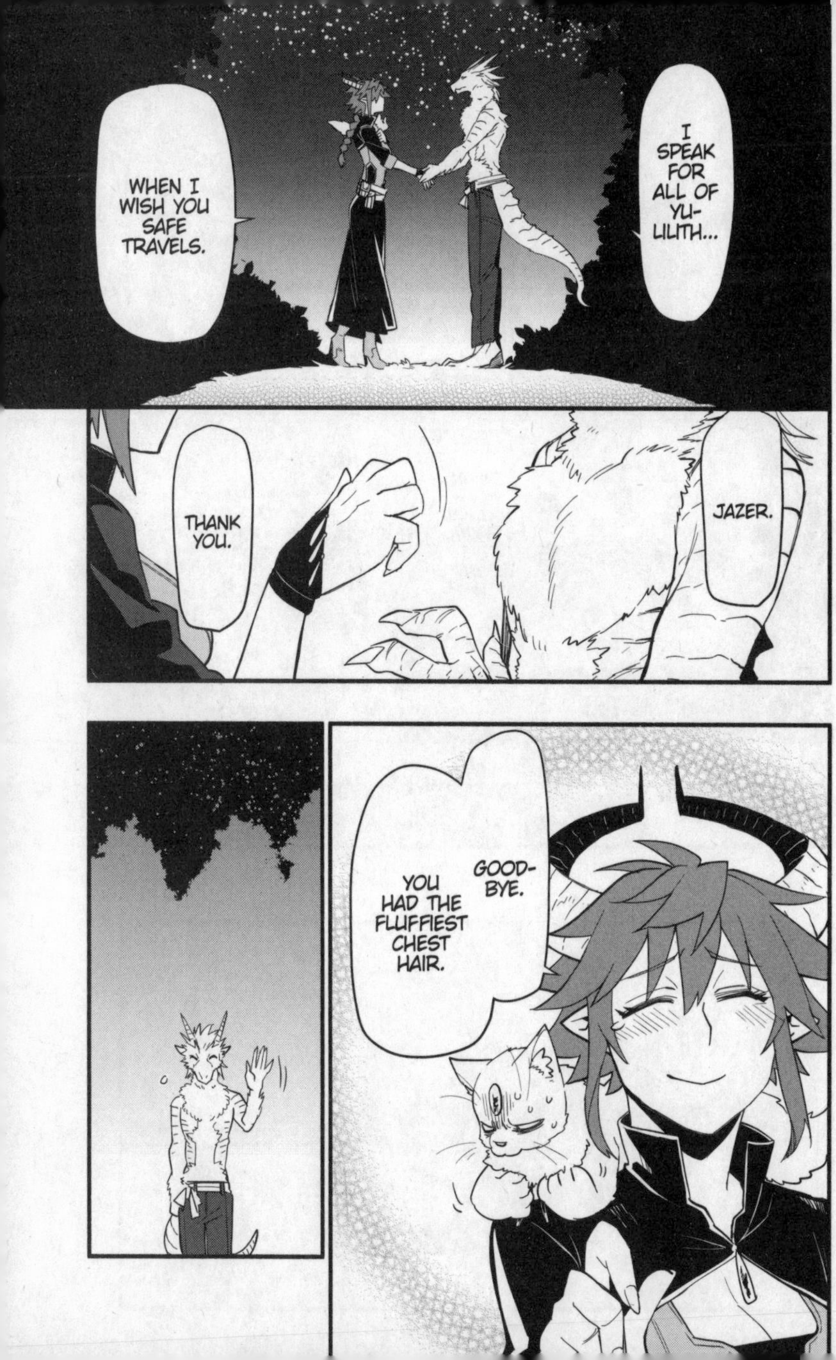
I SPEAK FOR ALL OF YU-LILITH...
WHEN I WISH YOU SAFE TRAVELS.
JAZER.
THANK YOU.
GOOD-BYE. YOU HAD THE FLUFFIEST CHEST HAIR.

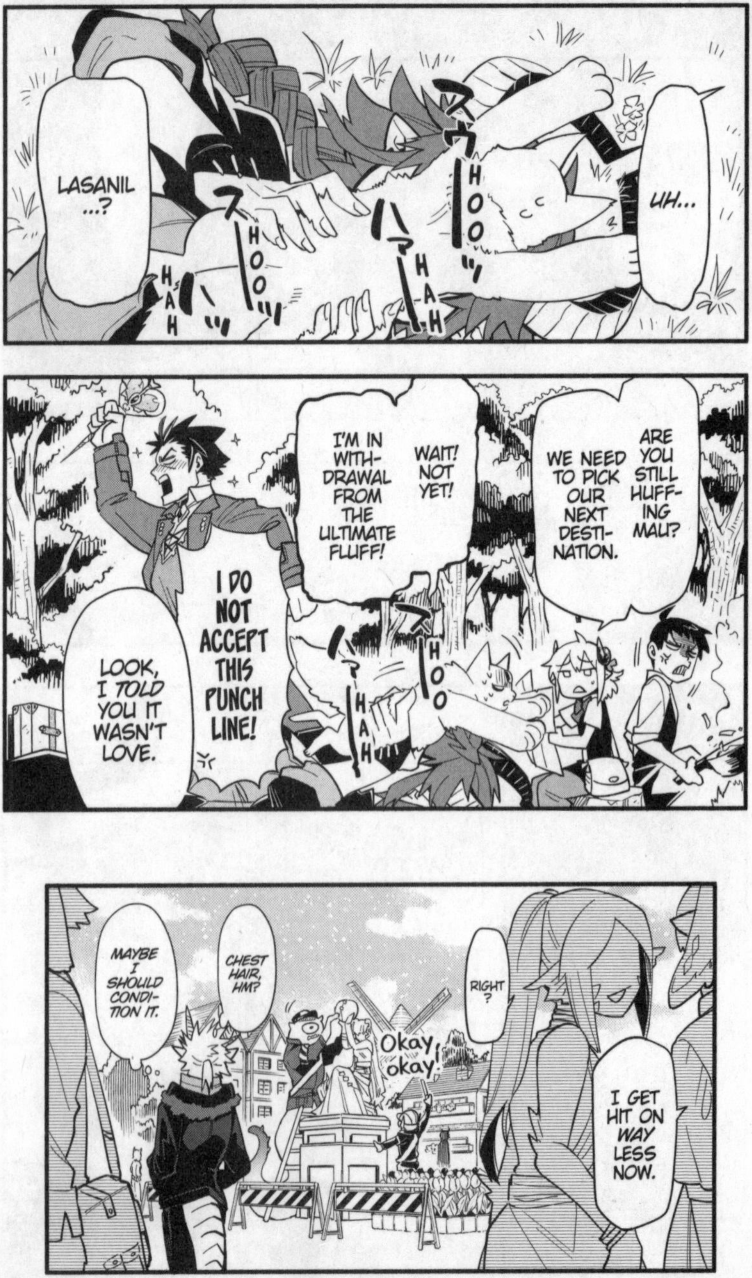
UH...
HOO
HAH
HOO
HAH
LASANIL ...?
ARE YOU STILL HUFF-ING MAU?
WE NEED TO PICK OUR NEXT DESTI-NATION.
WAIT! NOT YET!
I'M IN WITH-DRAWAL FROM THE ULTIMATE FLUFF!
HOO
HAH
I DO NOT ACCEPT THIS PUNCH LINE!
LOOK, I *TOLD* YOU IT WASN'T LOVE.
I GET HIT ON *WAY* LESS NOW.
RIGHT?
Okay, okay!
CHEST HAIR, HM?
MAYBE I SHOULD CONDI-TION IT.

File 51

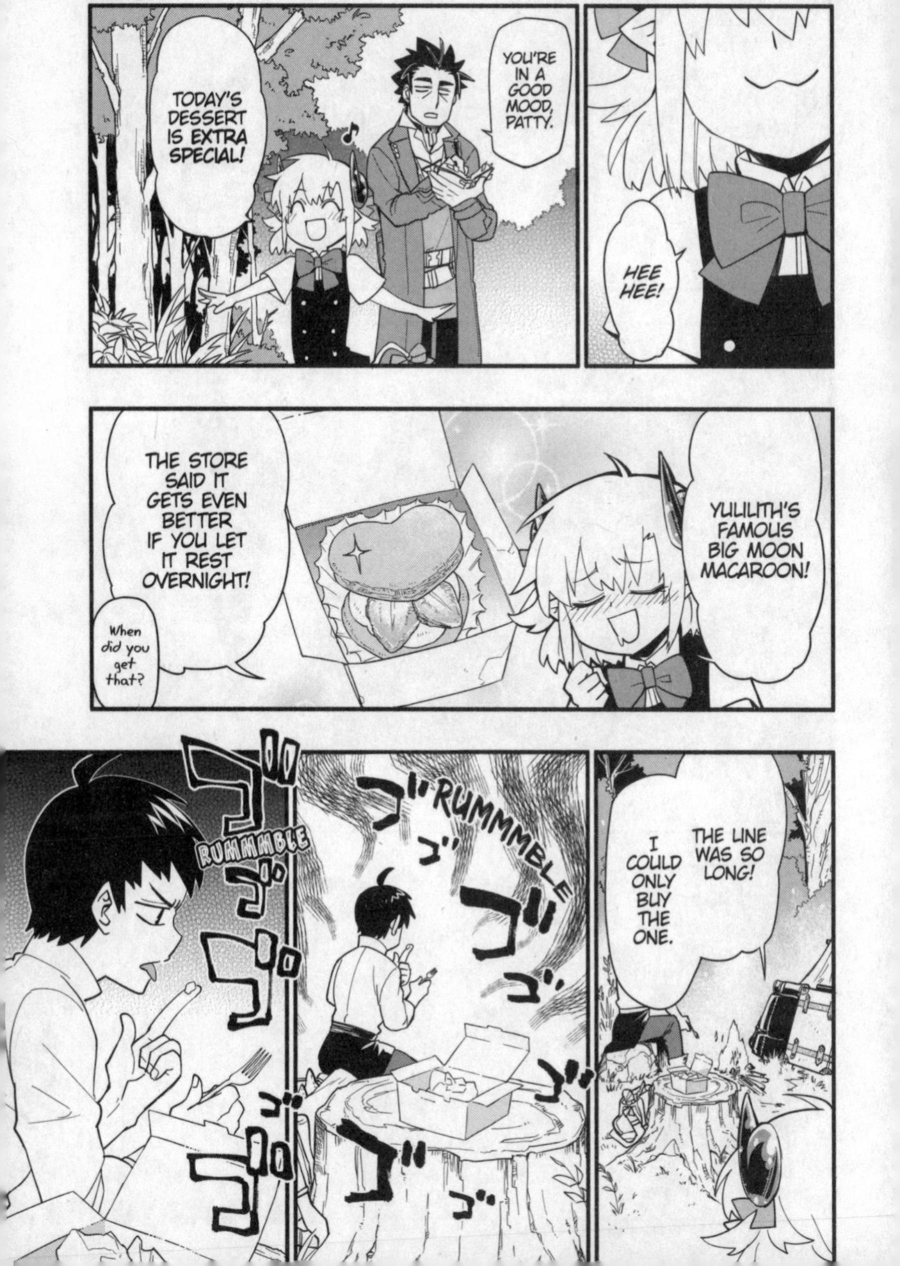
TODAY'S DESSERT IS EXTRA SPECIAL!
YOU'RE IN A GOOD MOOD, PATTY.
HEE HEE!
YUULITH'S FAMOUS BIG MOON MACAROON!
THE STORE SAID IT GETS EVEN BETTER IF YOU LET IT REST OVERNIGHT!
When did you get that?
RUMMMBLE
RUMMMBLE
THE LINE WAS SO LONG!
I COULD ONLY BUY THE ONE.

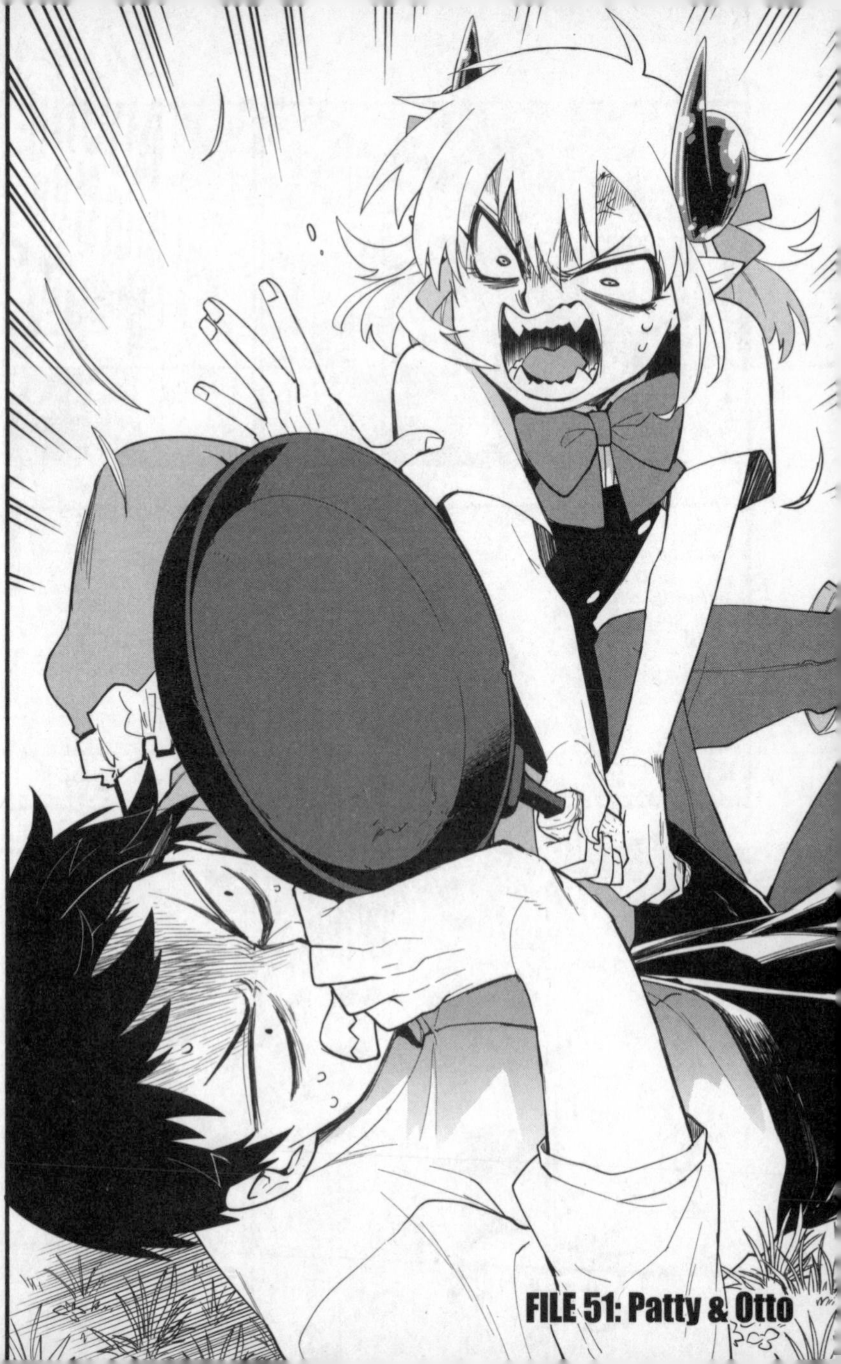
FILE 51: Patty & Otto

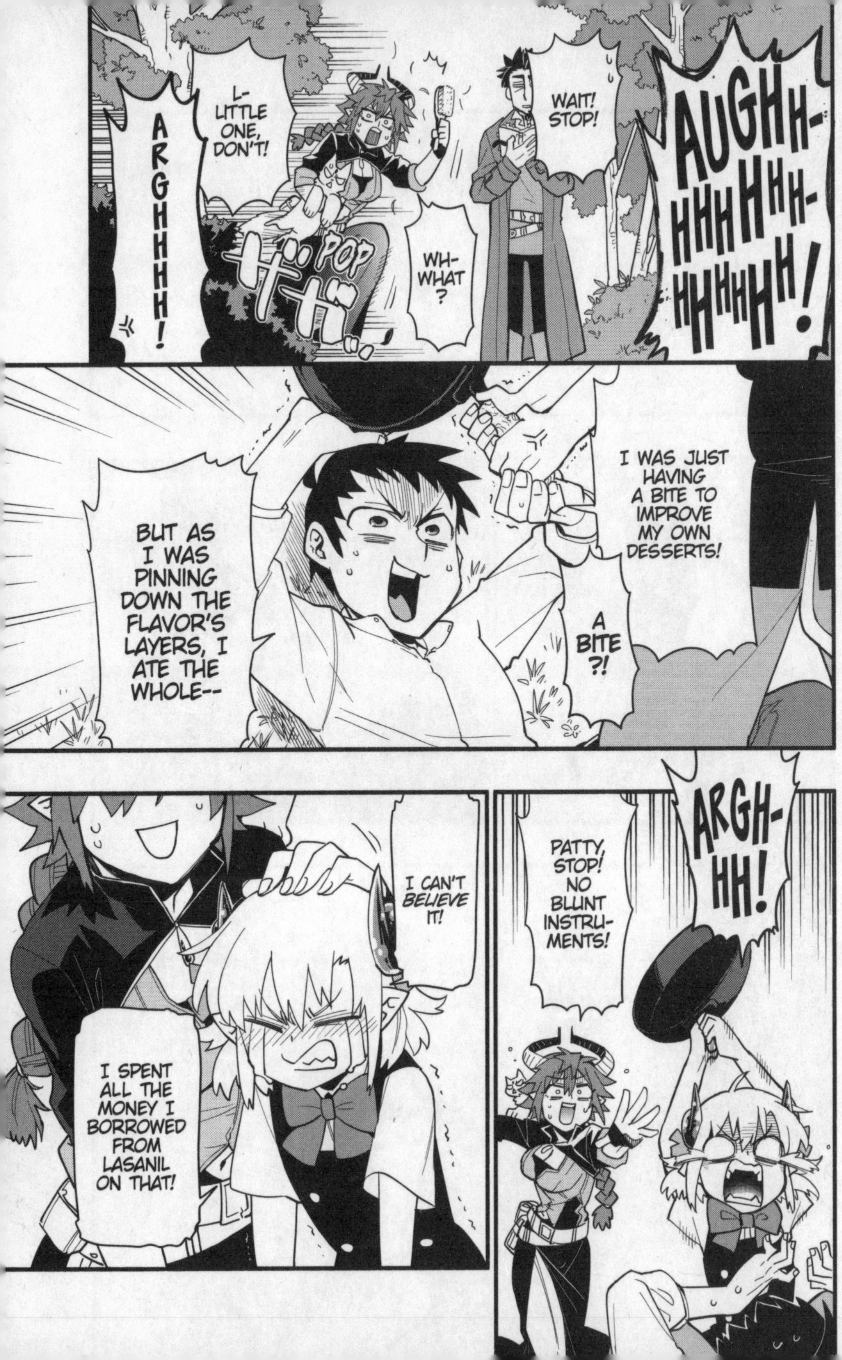
AUGHH-HHHHHH-HHHHHH!
WAIT! STOP!
WH-WHAT?
L-LITTLE ONE, DON'T!
POP
ARGHHHHH!
I WAS JUST HAVING A BITE TO IMPROVE MY OWN DESSERTS!
A BITE?!
BUT AS I WAS PINNING DOWN THE FLAVOR'S LAYERS, I ATE THE WHOLE--
ARGH-HH!
PATTY, STOP! NO BLUNT INSTRU-MENTS!
I CAN'T BELIEVE IT!
I SPENT ALL THE MONEY I BORROWED FROM LASANIL ON THAT!

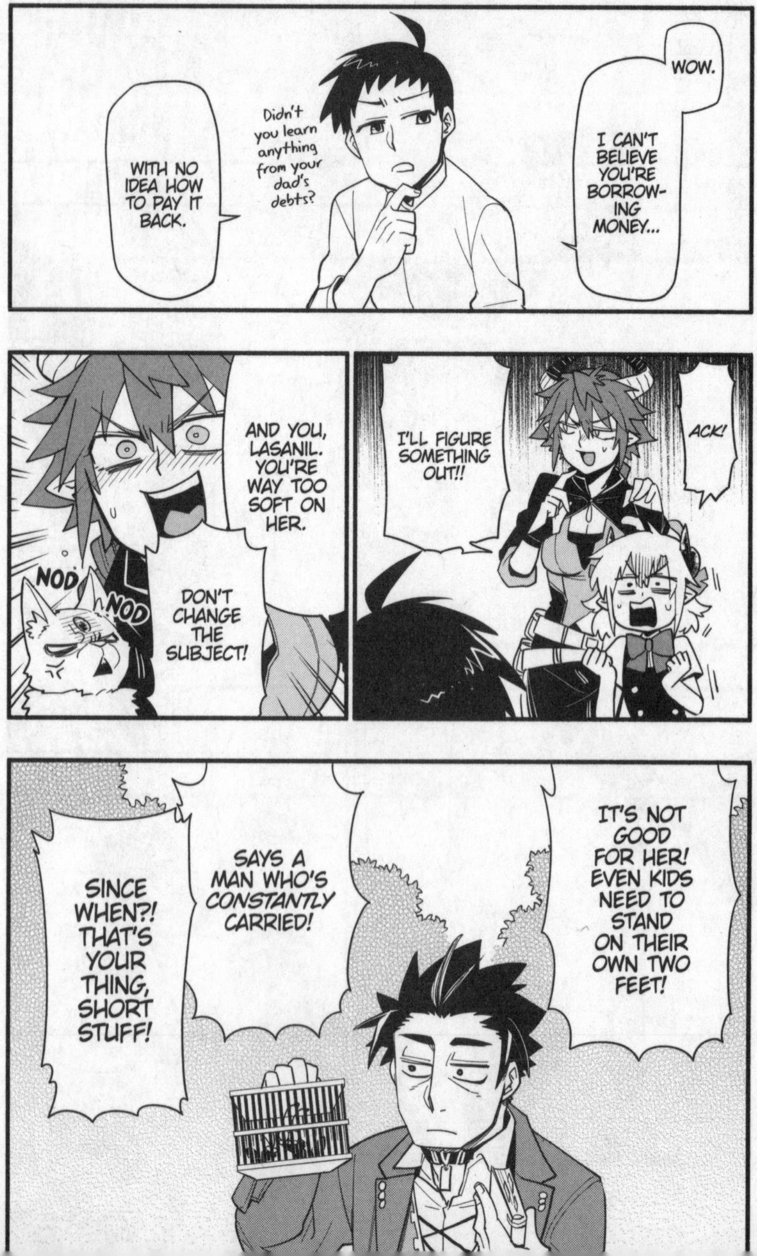
WOW.
I CAN'T BELIEVE YOU'RE BORROWING MONEY...
WITH NO IDEA HOW TO PAY IT BACK.
Didn't you learn anything from your dad's debts?
ACK!
I'LL FIGURE SOMETHING OUT!!
AND YOU, LASANIL. YOU'RE WAY TOO SOFT ON HER.
DON'T CHANGE THE SUBJECT!
NOD
NOD
IT'S NOT GOOD FOR HER! EVEN KIDS NEED TO STAND ON THEIR OWN TWO FEET!
SAYS A MAN WHO'S CONSTANTLY CARRIED!
SINCE WHEN?! THAT'S YOUR THING, SHORT STUFF!

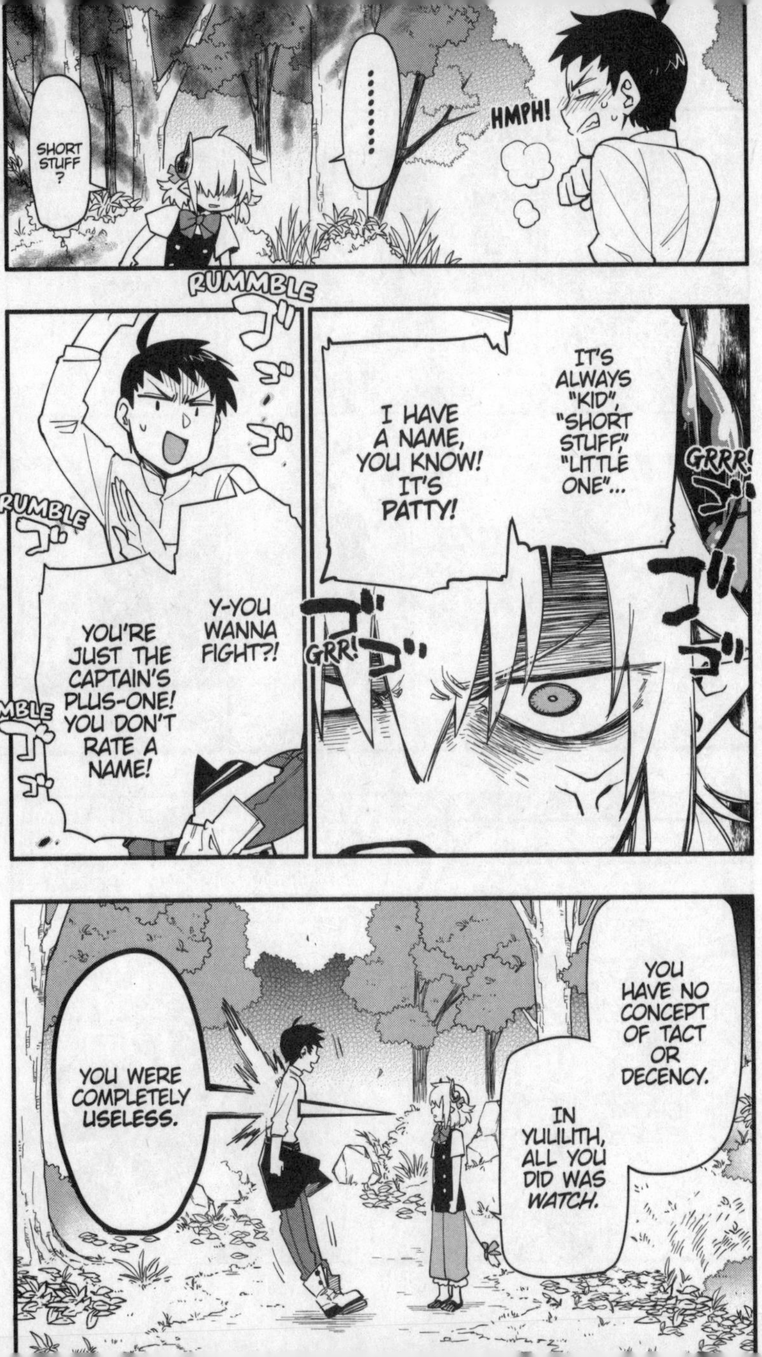
HMPH!
......
SHORT STUFF?
RUMMBLE
IT'S ALWAYS "KID", "SHORT STUFF," "LITTLE ONE"...
I HAVE A NAME, YOU KNOW! IT'S PATTY!
GRRR!
GRR!
Y-YOU WANNA FIGHT?!
YOU'RE JUST THE CAPTAIN'S PLUS-ONE! YOU DON'T RATE A NAME!
RUMBLE
RUMBLE
YOU HAVE NO CONCEPT OF TACT OR DECENCY.
IN YULILITH, ALL YOU DID WAS *WATCH*.
YOU WERE COMPLETELY USELESS.

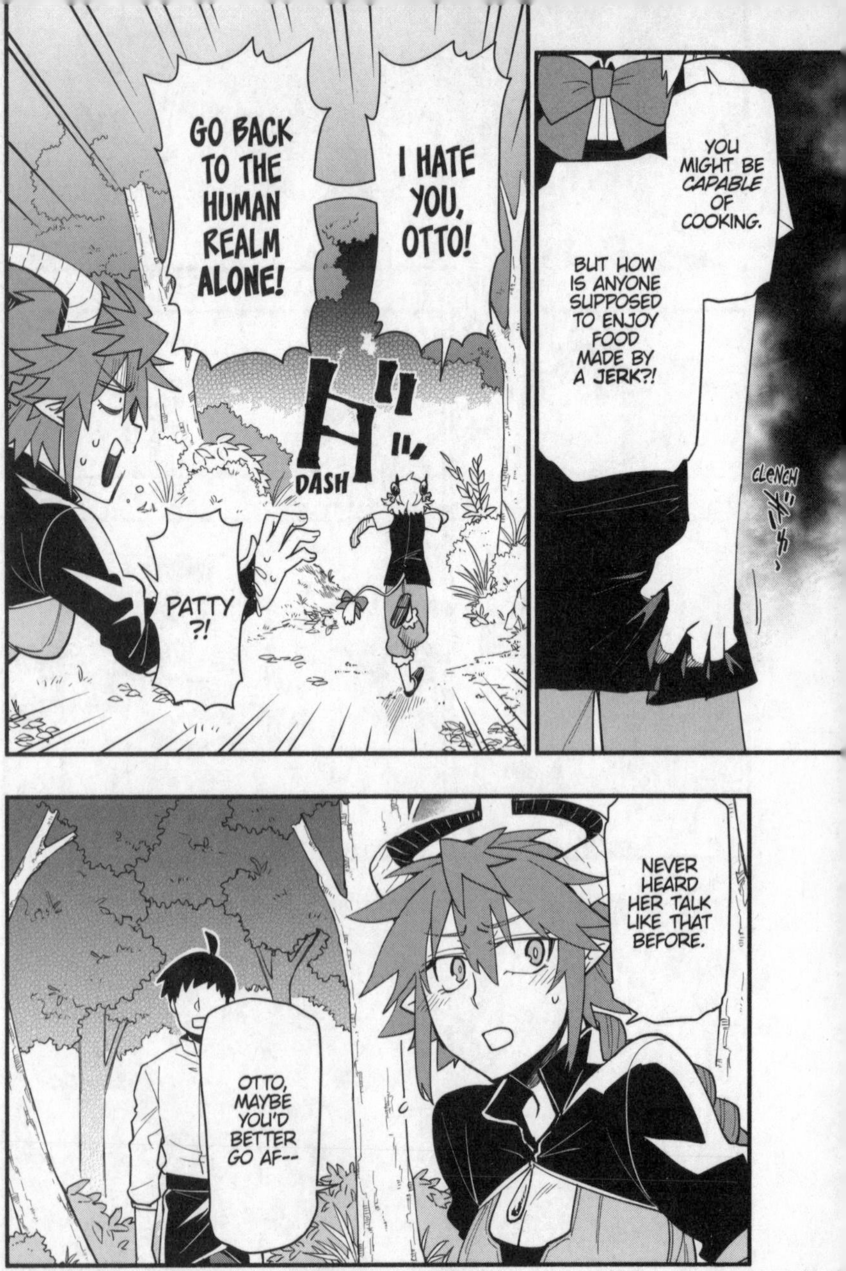
YOU MIGHT BE CAPABLE OF COOKING.
BUT HOW IS ANYONE SUPPOSED TO ENJOY FOOD MADE BY A JERK?!
CLENCH
I HATE YOU, OTTO!
GO BACK TO THE HUMAN REALM ALONE!
DASH
PATTY?!
NEVER HEARD HER TALK LIKE THAT BEFORE.
OTTO, MAYBE YOU'D BETTER GO AF--

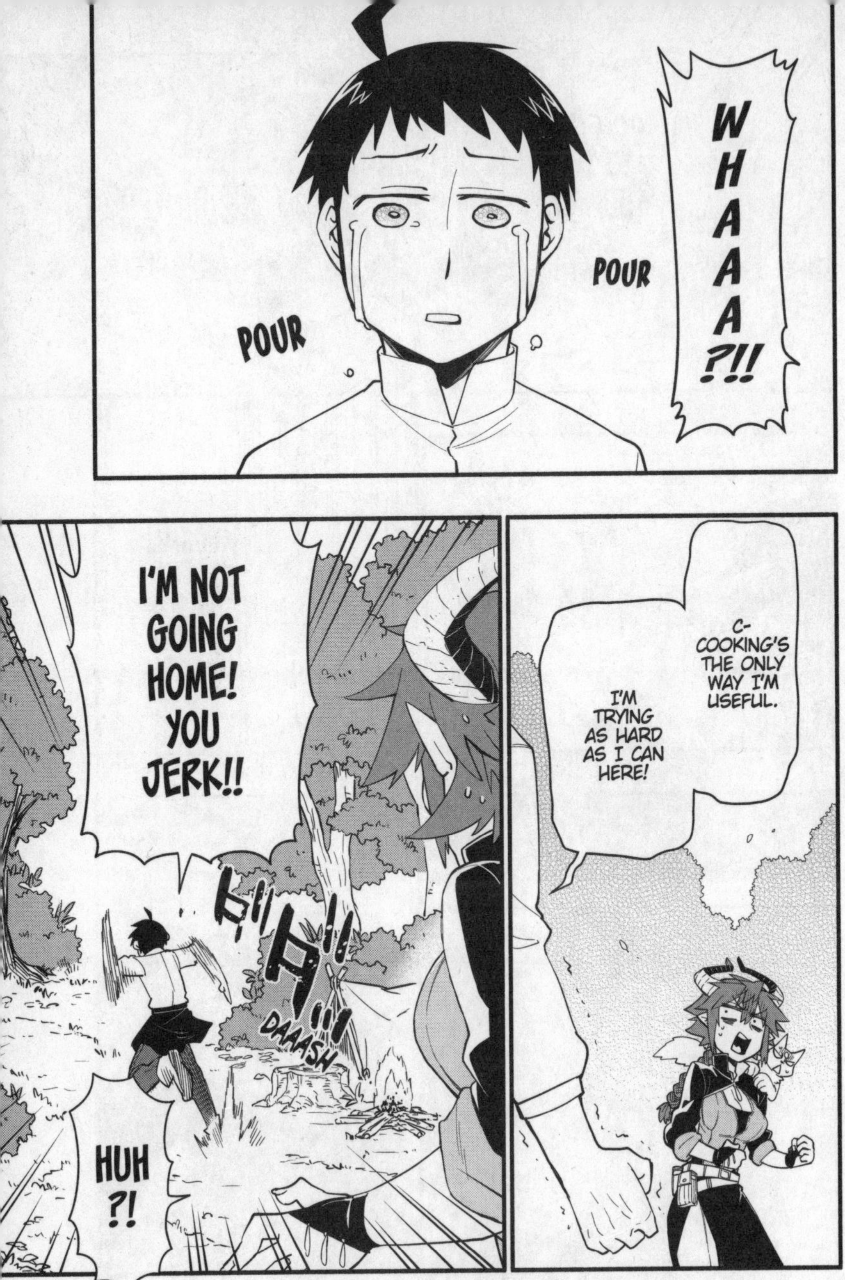
WHAAAA?!!
POUR
POUR
C-COOKING'S THE ONLY WAY I'M USEFUL.
I'M TRYING AS HARD AS I CAN HERE!
I'M NOT GOING HOME! YOU JERK!!
DAAASH
HUH?!

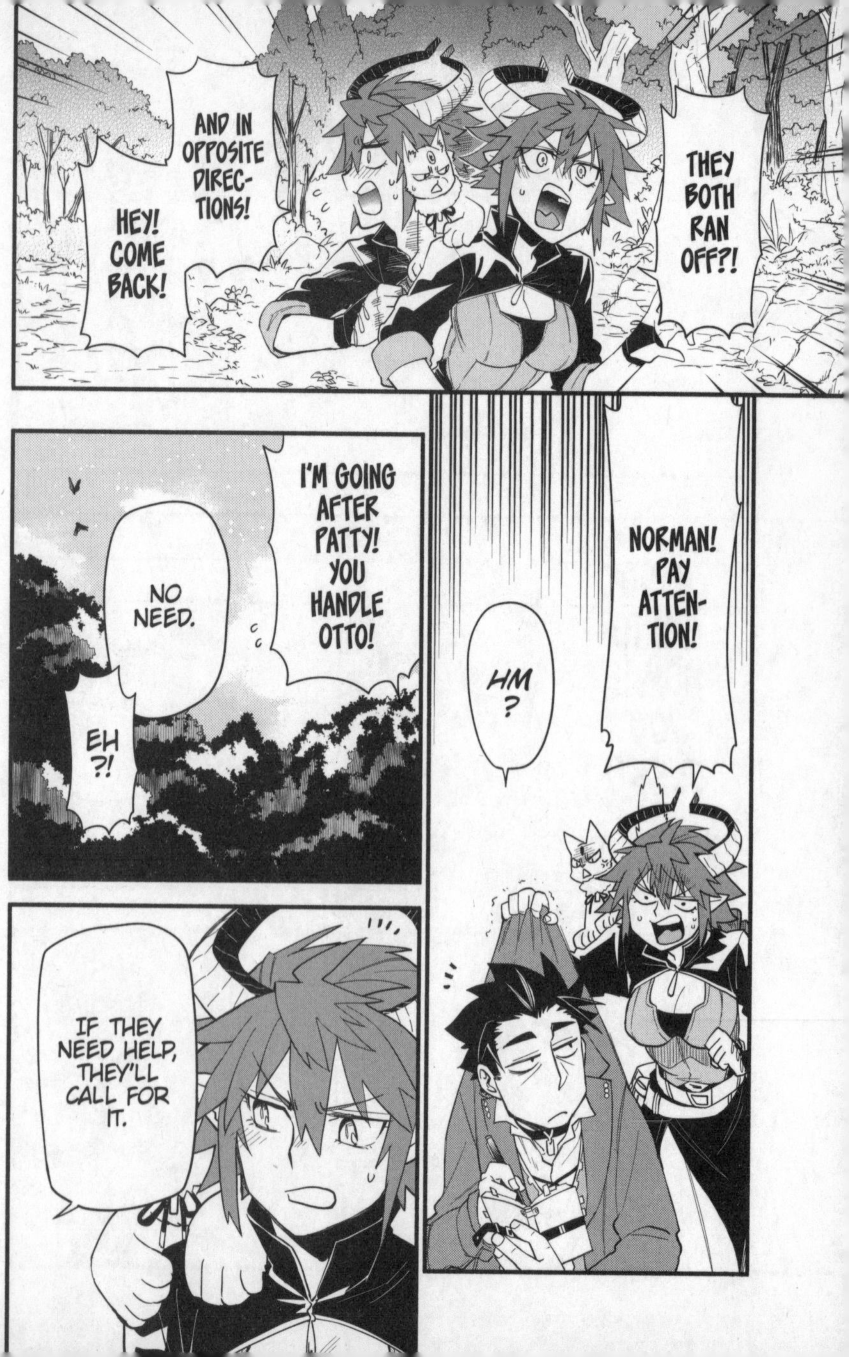
THEY BOTH RAN OFF?!
AND IN OPPOSITE DIREC-TIONS!
HEY! COME BACK!
NORMAN! PAY ATTEN-TION!
HM?
I'M GOING AFTER PATTY! YOU HANDLE OTTO!
NO NEED.
EH?!
IF THEY NEED HELP, THEY'LL CALL FOR IT.

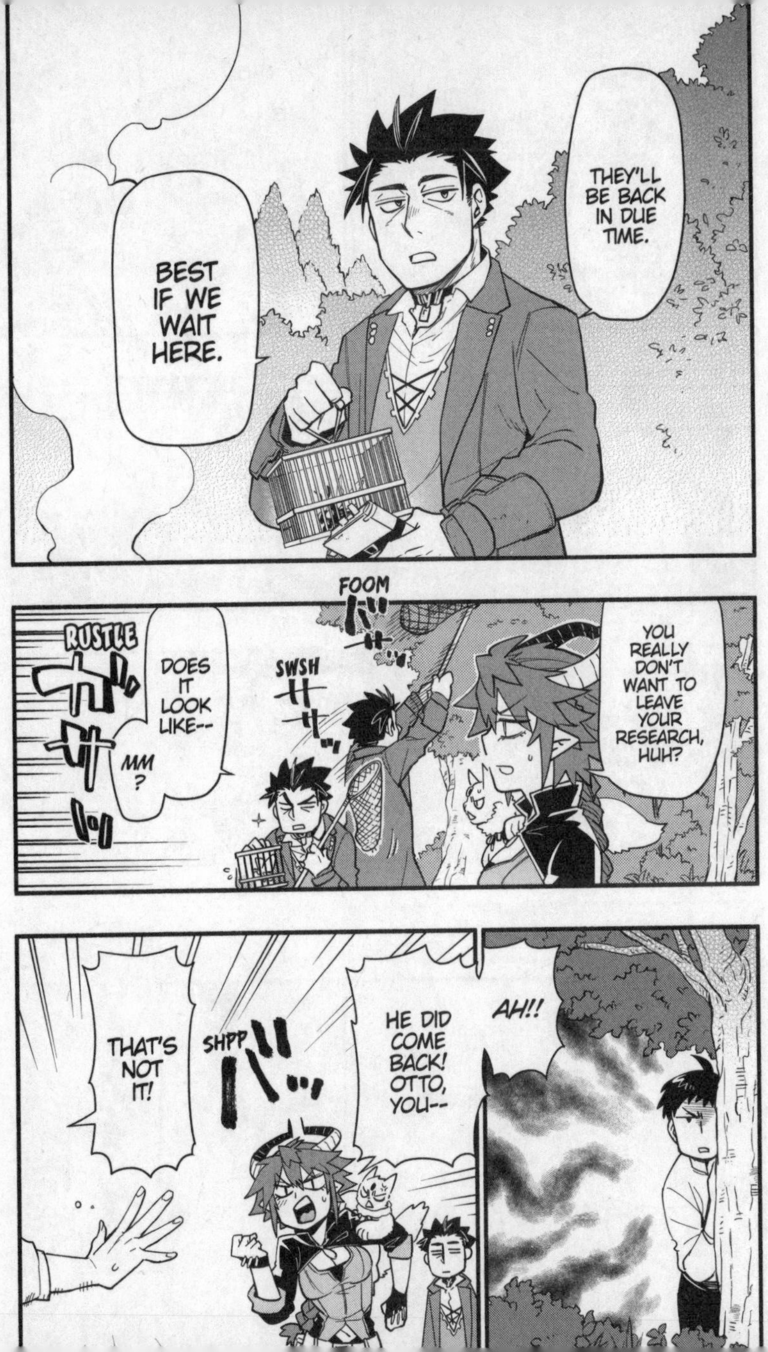
THEY'LL BE BACK IN DUE TIME.
BEST IF WE WAIT HERE.
FOOM
YOU REALLY DON'T WANT TO LEAVE YOUR RESEARCH, HUH?
SWSH
DOES IT LOOK LIKE--
RUSTLE
MM?
AH!!
HE DID COME BACK! OTTO, YOU--
SHPP
THAT'S NOT IT!

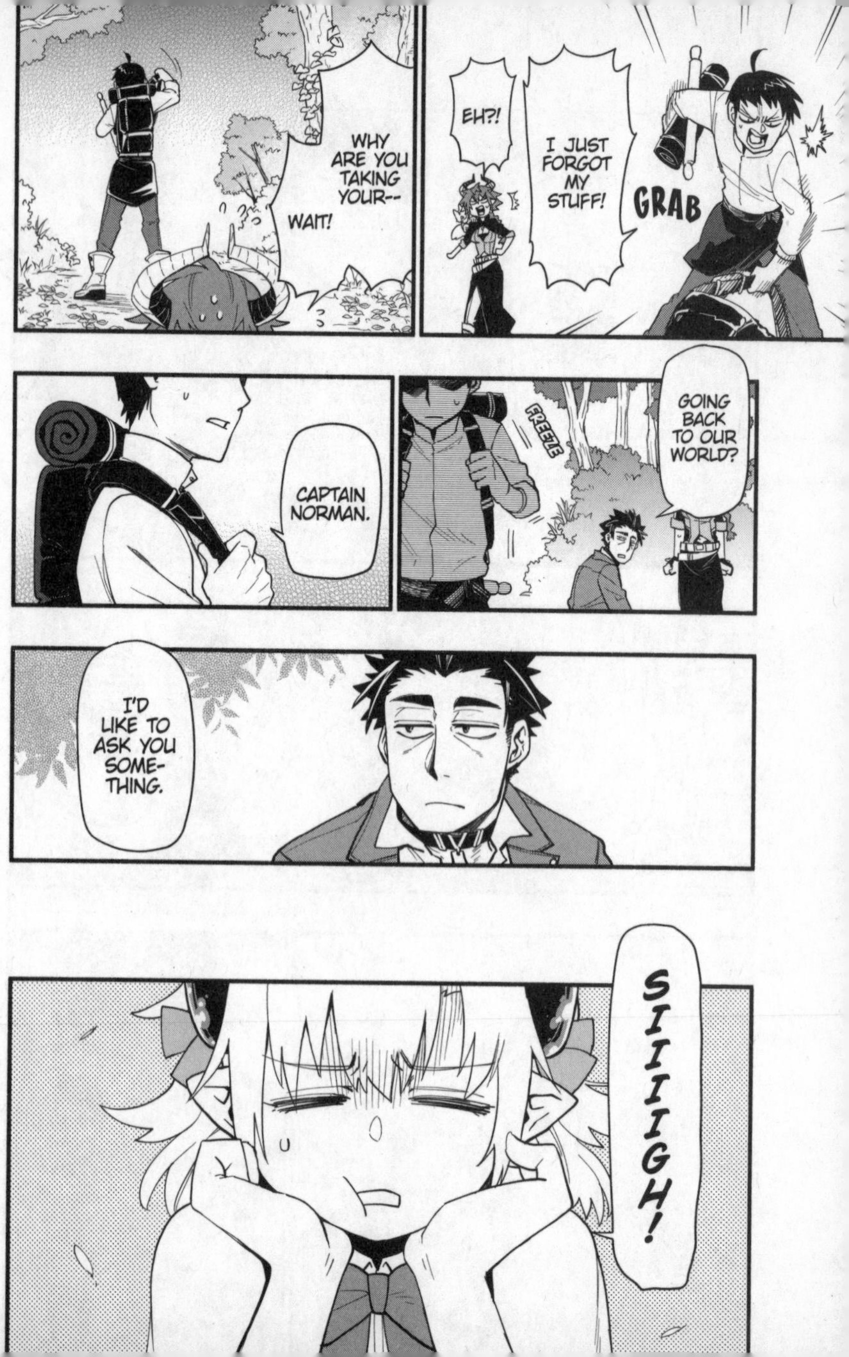
GRAB
I JUST FORGOT MY STUFF!
EH?!
WHY ARE YOU TAKING YOUR--
WAIT!
GOING BACK TO OUR WORLD?
FREEZE
CAPTAIN NORMAN.
I'D LIKE TO ASK YOU SOME-THING.
SIIIIGH!

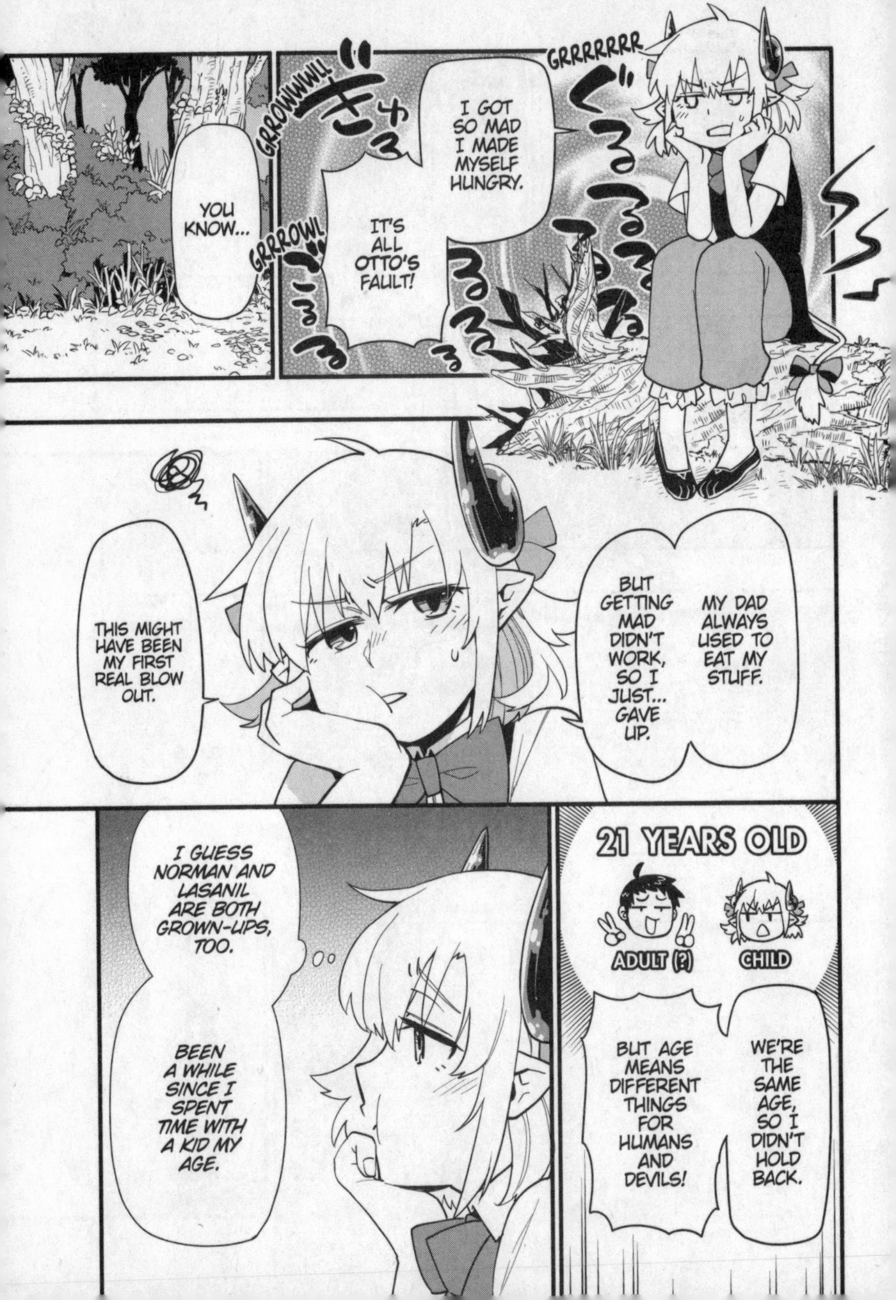
GRRRRRRR
I GOT SO MAD I MADE MYSELF HUNGRY.
IT'S ALL OTTO'S FAULT!
GRROWWWLL
GRRROWL
YOU KNOW...
MY DAD ALWAYS USED TO EAT MY STUFF.
BUT GETTING MAD DIDN'T WORK, SO I JUST... GAVE UP.
THIS MIGHT HAVE BEEN MY FIRST REAL BLOW OUT.
21 YEARS OLD
ADULT (?)
CHILD
WE'RE THE SAME AGE, SO I DIDN'T HOLD BACK.
BUT AGE MEANS DIFFERENT THINGS FOR HUMANS AND DEVILS!
I GUESS NORMAN AND LASANIL ARE BOTH GROWN-UPS, TOO.
BEEN A WHILE SINCE I SPENT TIME WITH A KID MY AGE.

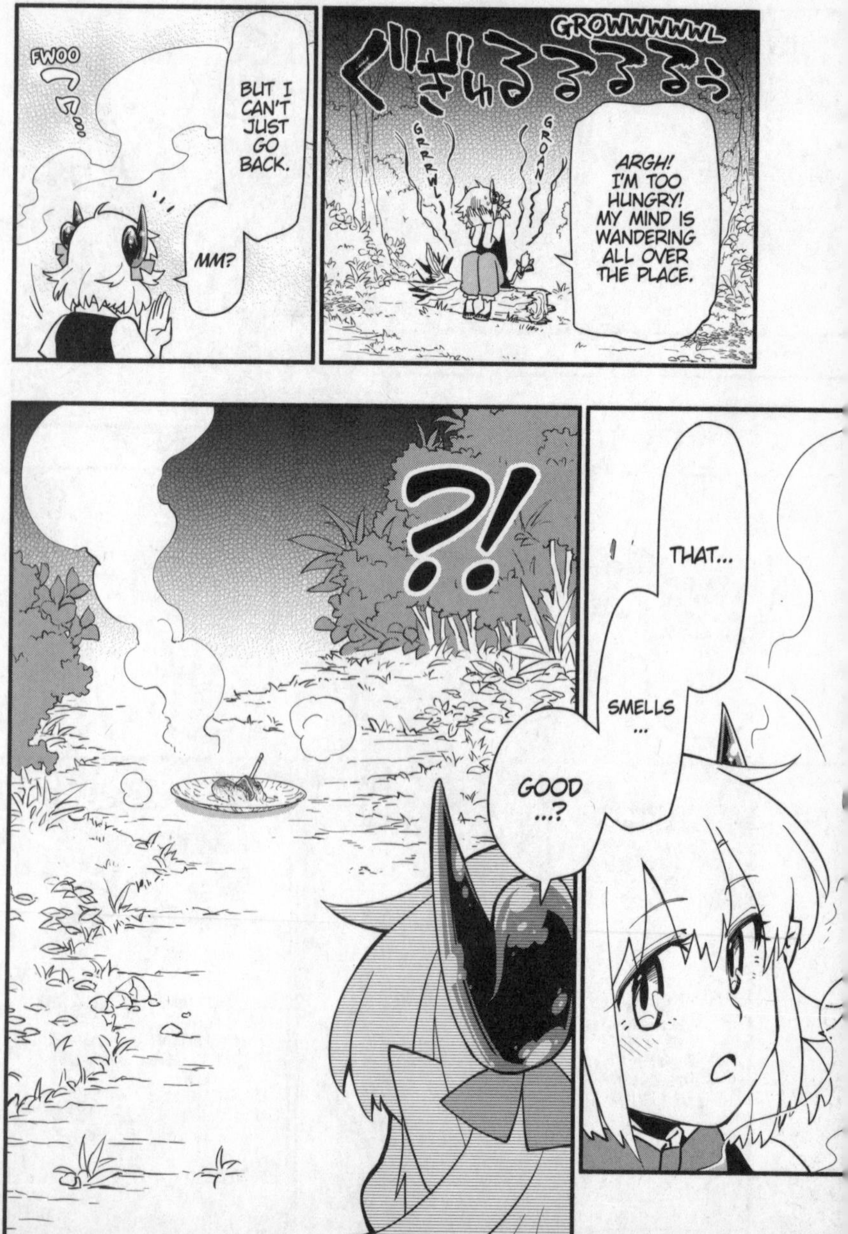
GROWWWWWL
くぎゅるるるるぅ
GRRRWL
GROAN
ARGH! I'M TOO HUNGRY! MY MIND IS WANDERING ALL OVER THE PLACE.
BUT I CAN'T JUST GO BACK.
FWOO
MM?
THAT...
SMELLS...
GOOD...?
?!

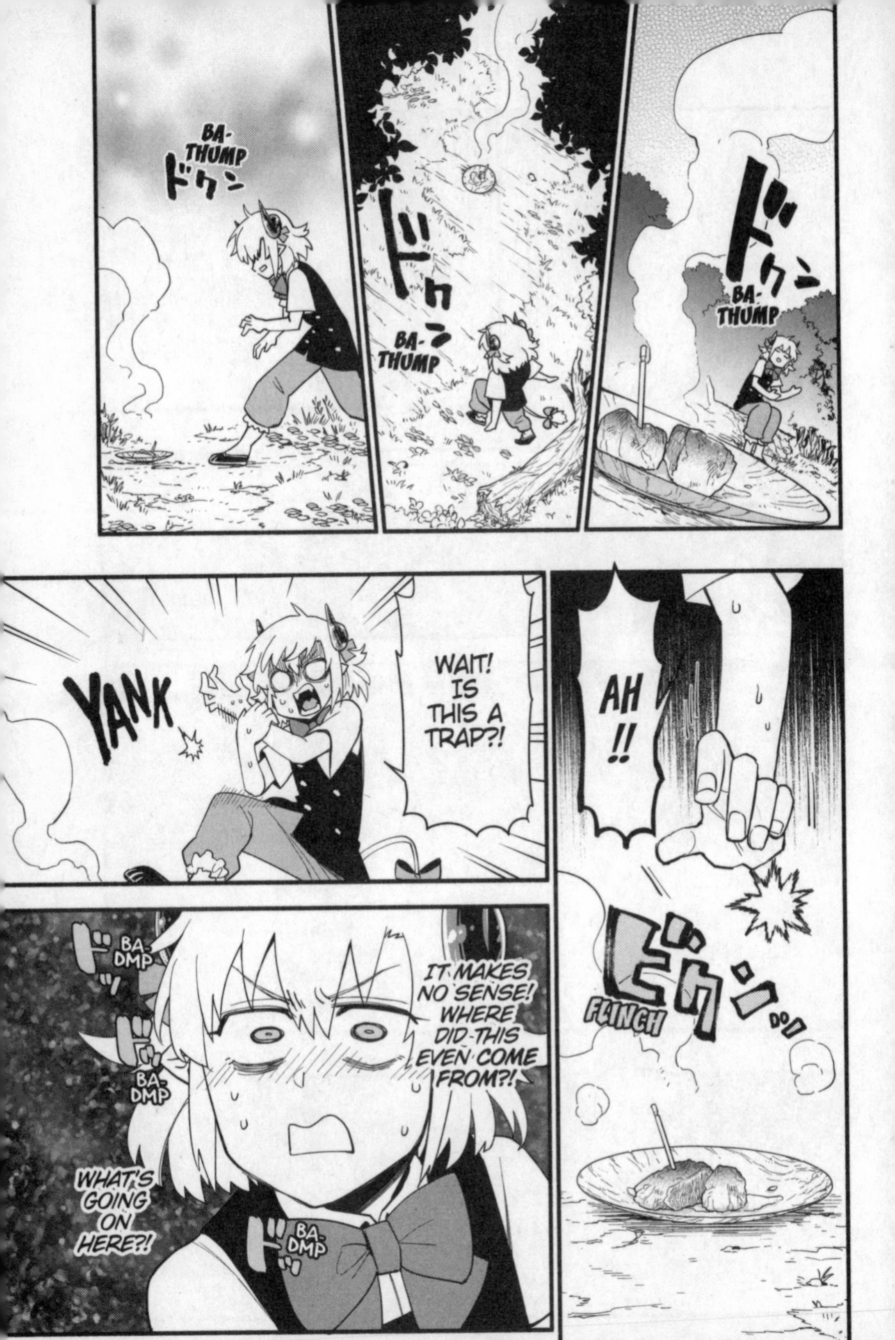
ドクン
BA-THUMP
BA-THUMP
BA-THUMP
ドクン
AH !!
ビクンッ
FLINCH
WAIT! IS THIS A TRAP?!
YANK
BA-DMP
BA-DMP
BA-DMP
IT MAKES NO SENSE! WHERE DID THIS EVEN COME FROM?!
WHAT'S GOING ON HERE?!

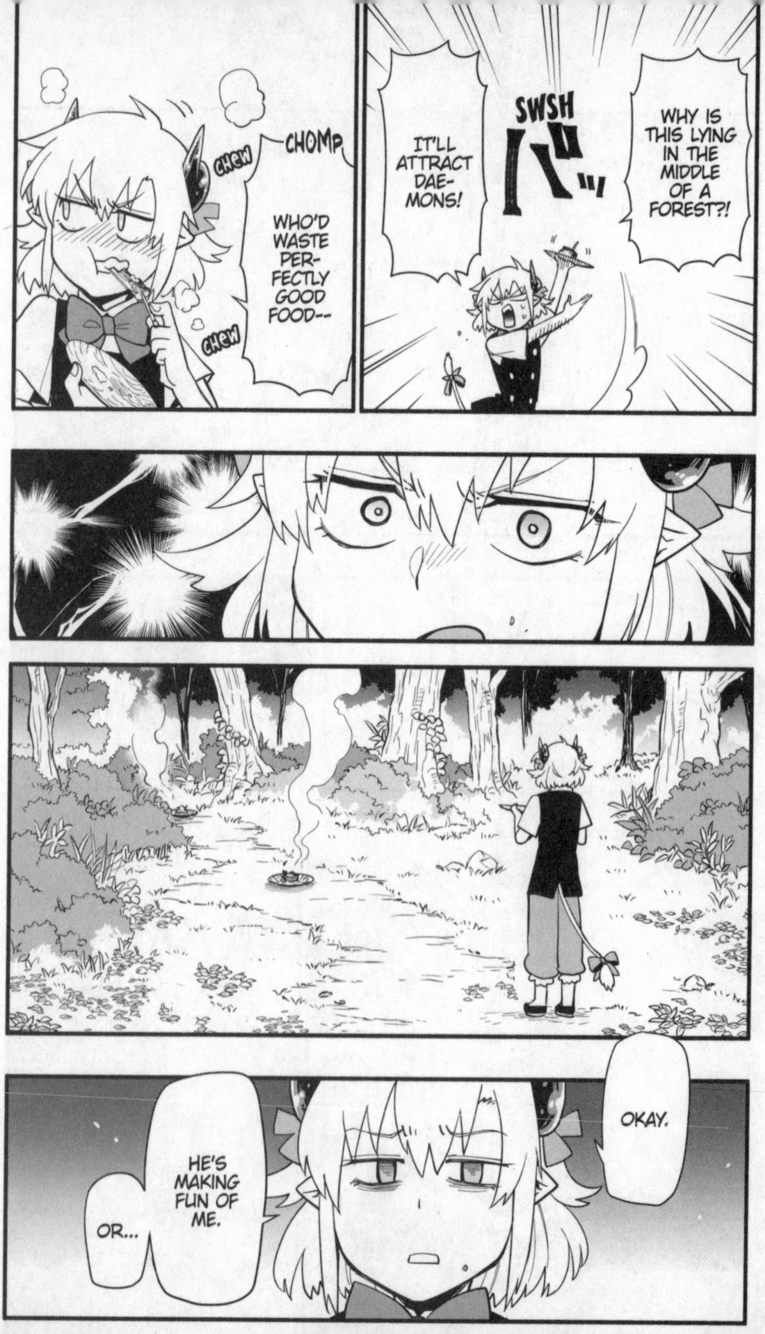
WHY IS THIS LYING IN THE MIDDLE OF A FOREST?!
SWSH
バッ
IT'LL ATTRACT DAE-MONS!
CHOMP
CHEW
WHO'D WASTE PER-FECTLY GOOD FOOD--
CHEW
OKAY.
HE'S MAKING FUN OF ME.
OR...

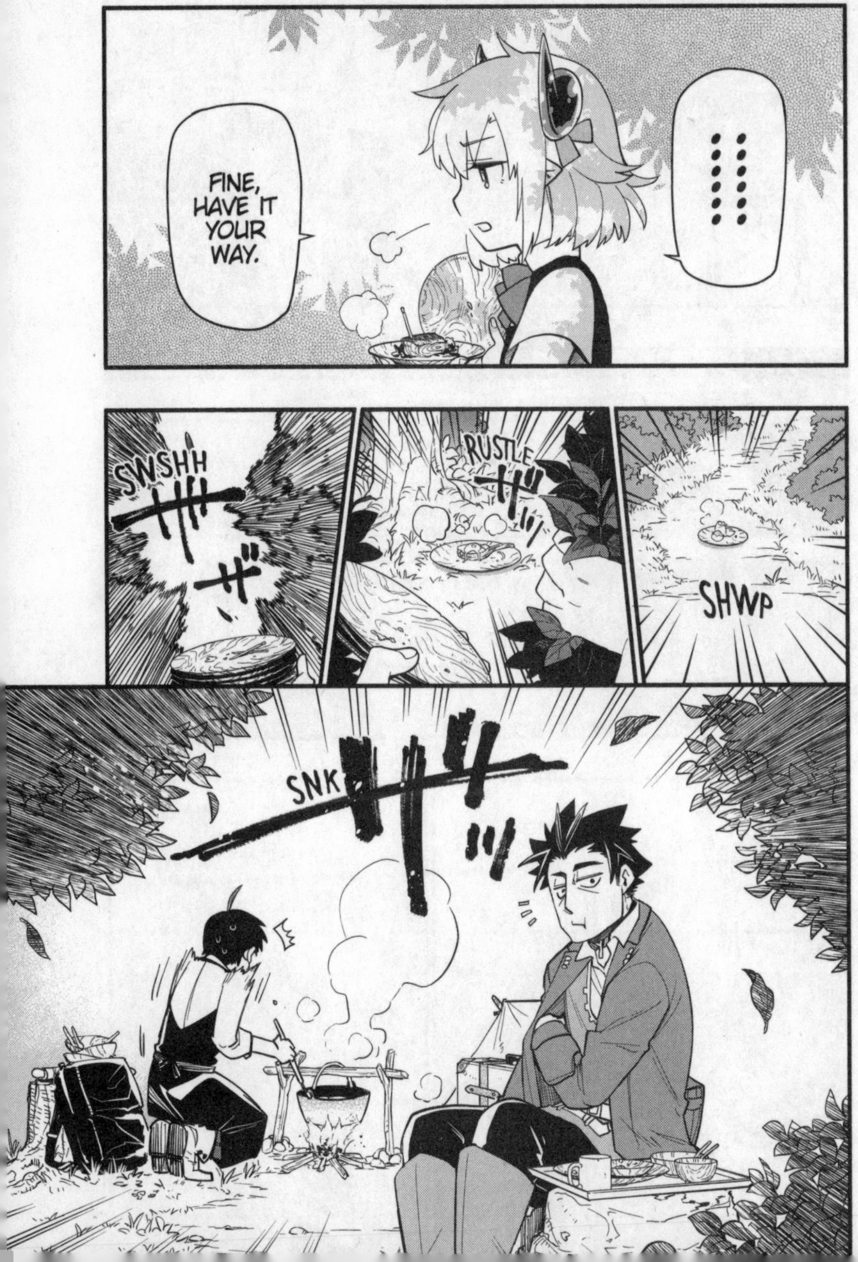
......
FINE, HAVE IT YOUR WAY.
SHWP
RUSTLE
SWSHH
SNK

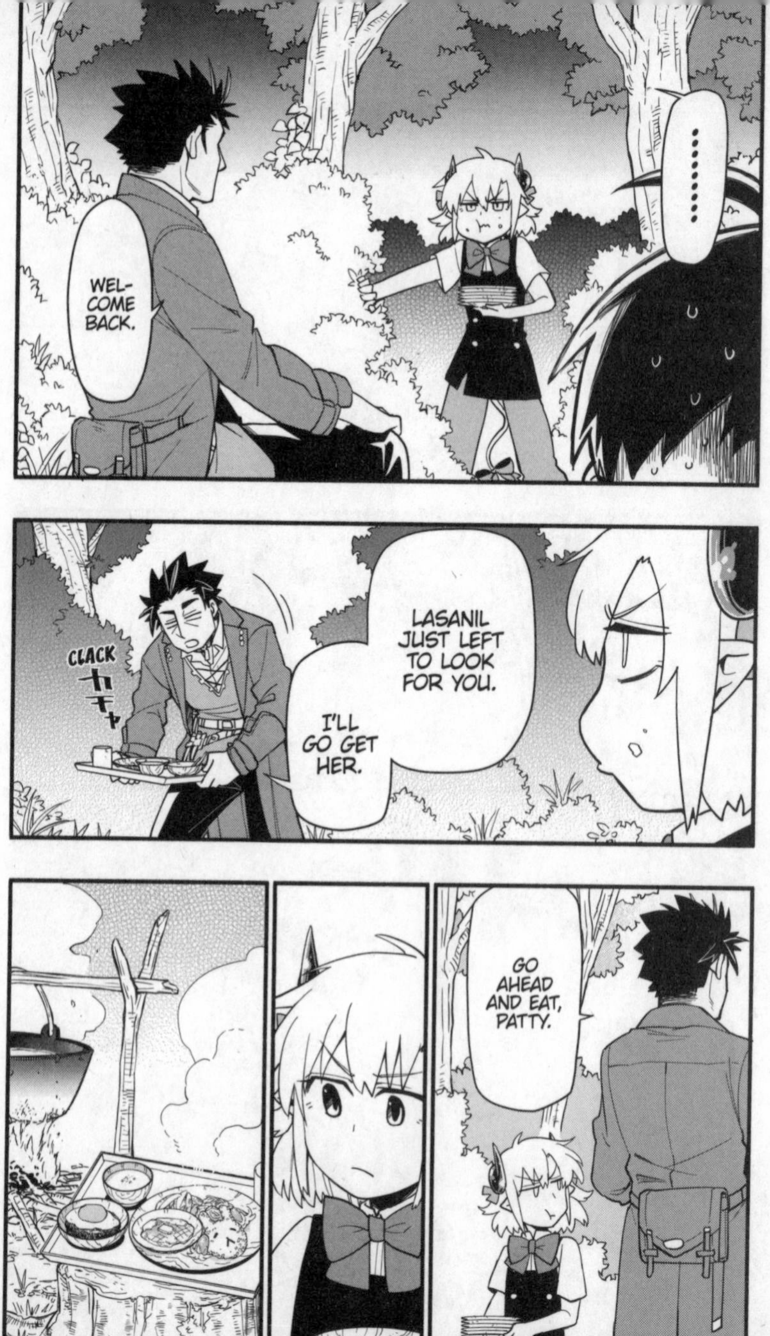
WEL-COME BACK.
......
LASANIL JUST LEFT TO LOOK FOR YOU.
I'LL GO GET HER.
CLACK
カチャ
GO AHEAD AND EAT, PATTY.

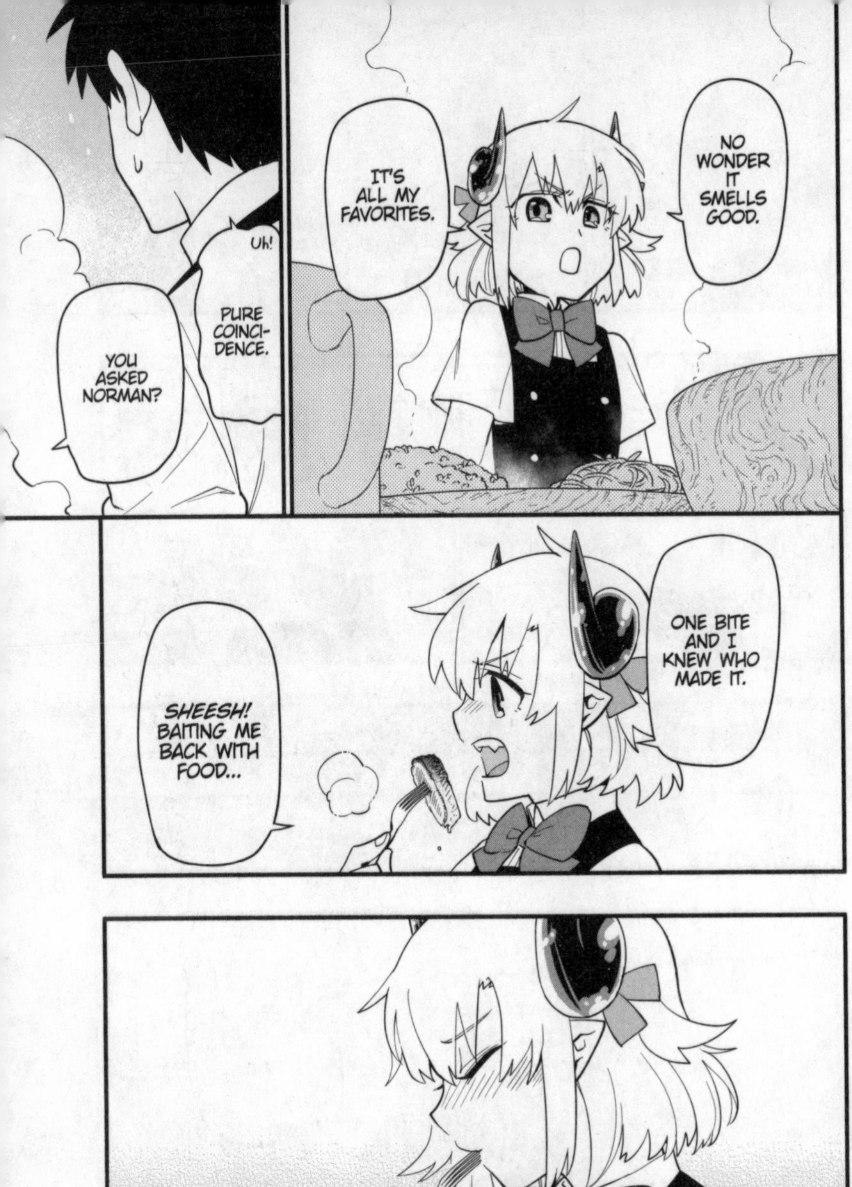
NO WONDER IT SMELLS GOOD.
IT'S ALL MY FAVORITES.
Uh!
PURE COINCI-DENCE.
YOU ASKED NORMAN?
ONE BITE AND I KNEW WHO MADE IT.
SHEESH! BAITING ME BACK WITH FOOD...

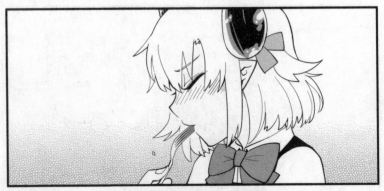

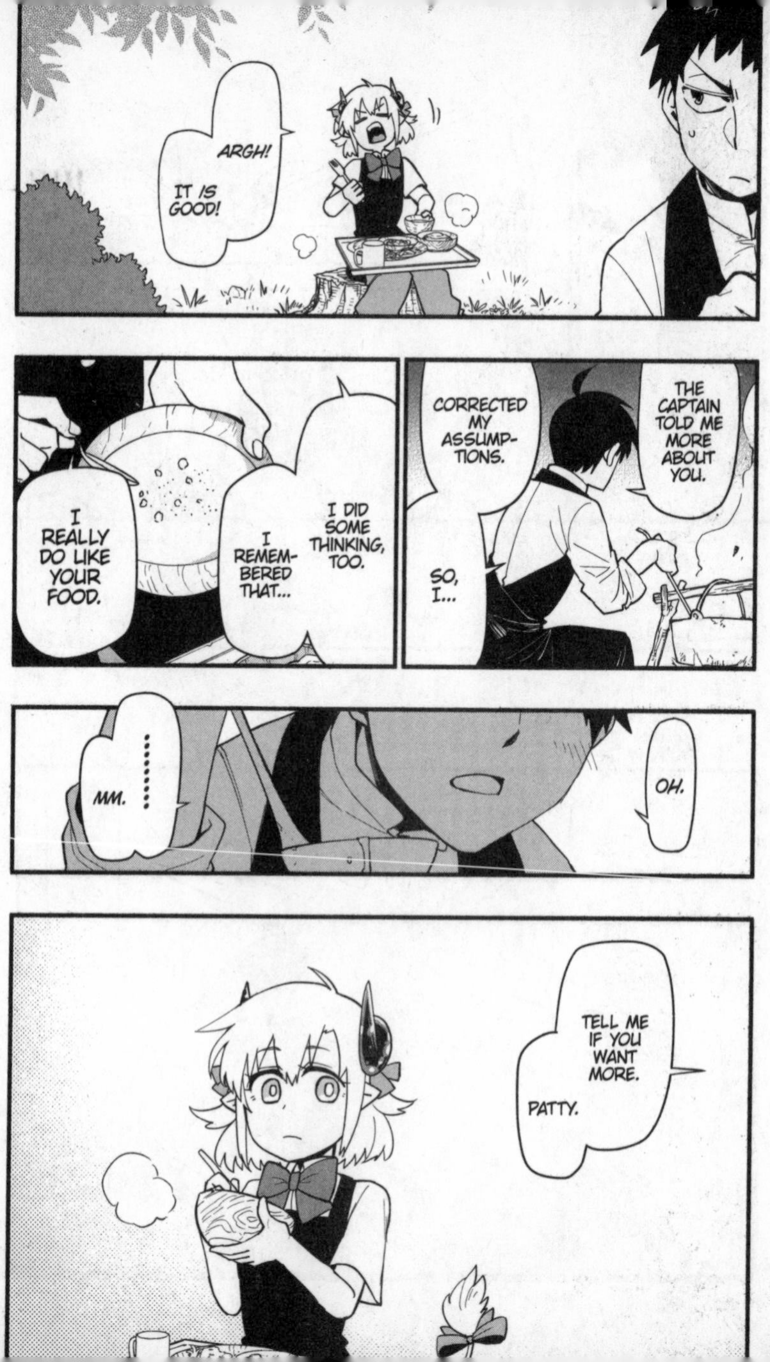
ARGH! IT IS GOOD!
THE CAPTAIN TOLD ME MORE ABOUT YOU.
CORRECTED MY ASSUMP-TIONS.
SO, I...
I DID SOME THINKING, TOO.
I REMEM-BERED THAT...
I REALLY DO LIKE YOUR FOOD.
OH.
......
MM.
TELL ME IF YOU WANT MORE.
PATTY.

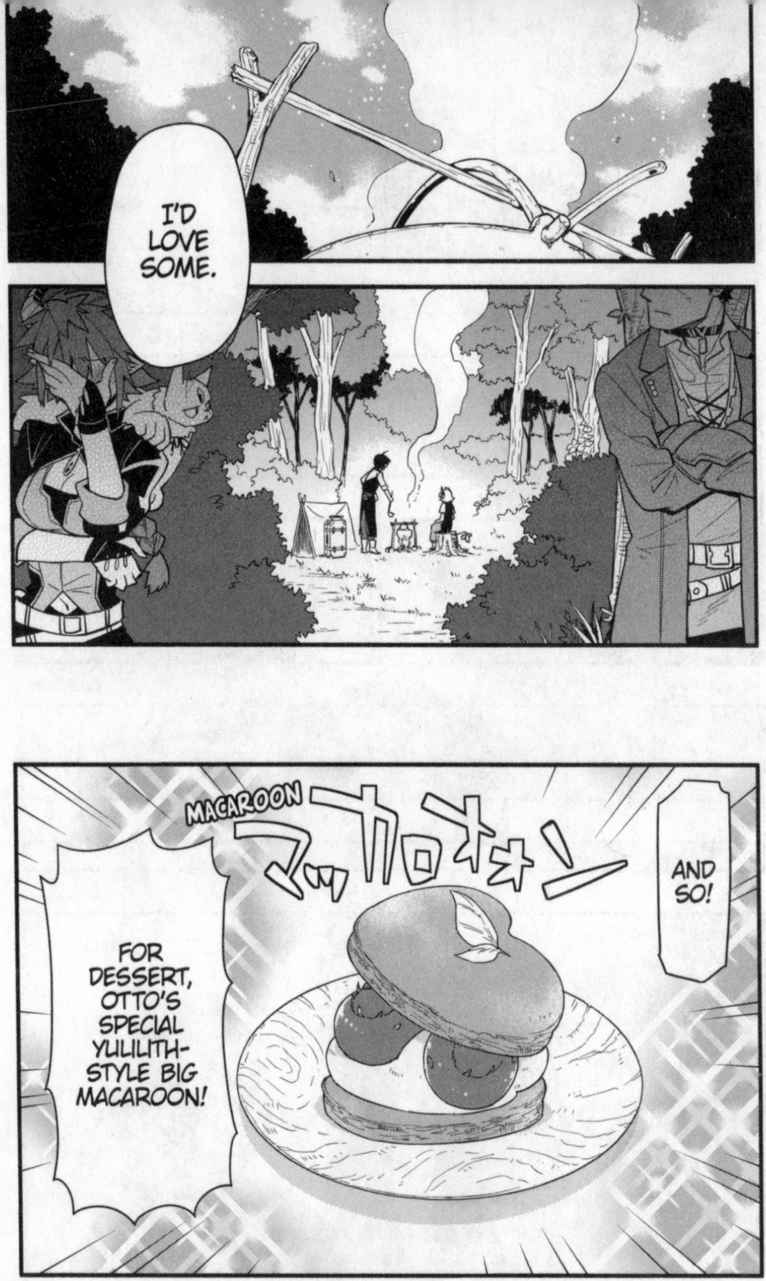
I'D LOVE SOME.
AND SO!
MACAROON
FOR DESSERT, OTTO'S SPECIAL YULILITH-STYLE BIG MACAROON!

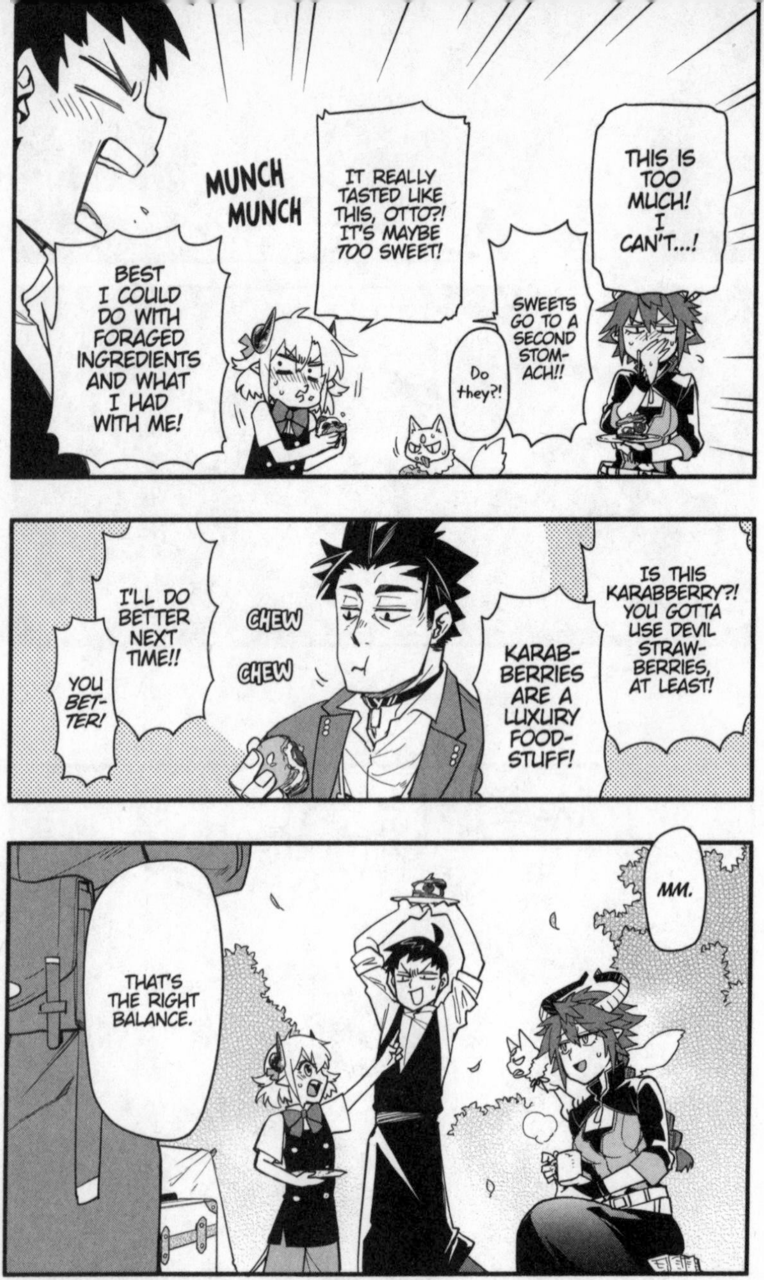
THIS IS TOO MUCH! I CAN'T...!
SWEETS GO TO A SECOND STOM-ACH!!
Do they?!
IT REALLY TASTED LIKE THIS, OTTO?! IT'S MAYBE TOO SWEET!
MUNCH MUNCH
BEST I COULD DO WITH FORAGED INGREDIENTS AND WHAT I HAD WITH ME!
IS THIS KARABBERRY?! YOU GOTTA USE DEVIL STRAW-BERRIES, AT LEAST!
KARAB-BERRIES ARE A LUXURY FOOD-STUFF!
CHEW
CHEW
I'LL DO BETTER NEXT TIME!!
YOU BET-TER!
MM.
THAT'S THE RIGHT BALANCE.

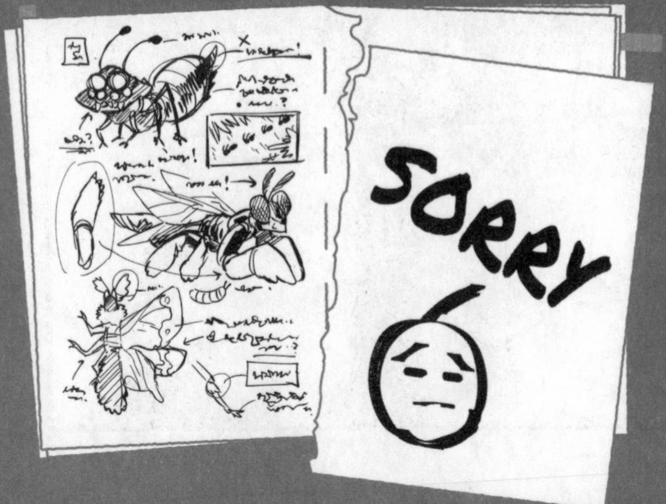
SORRY

Sorry For My Familiar

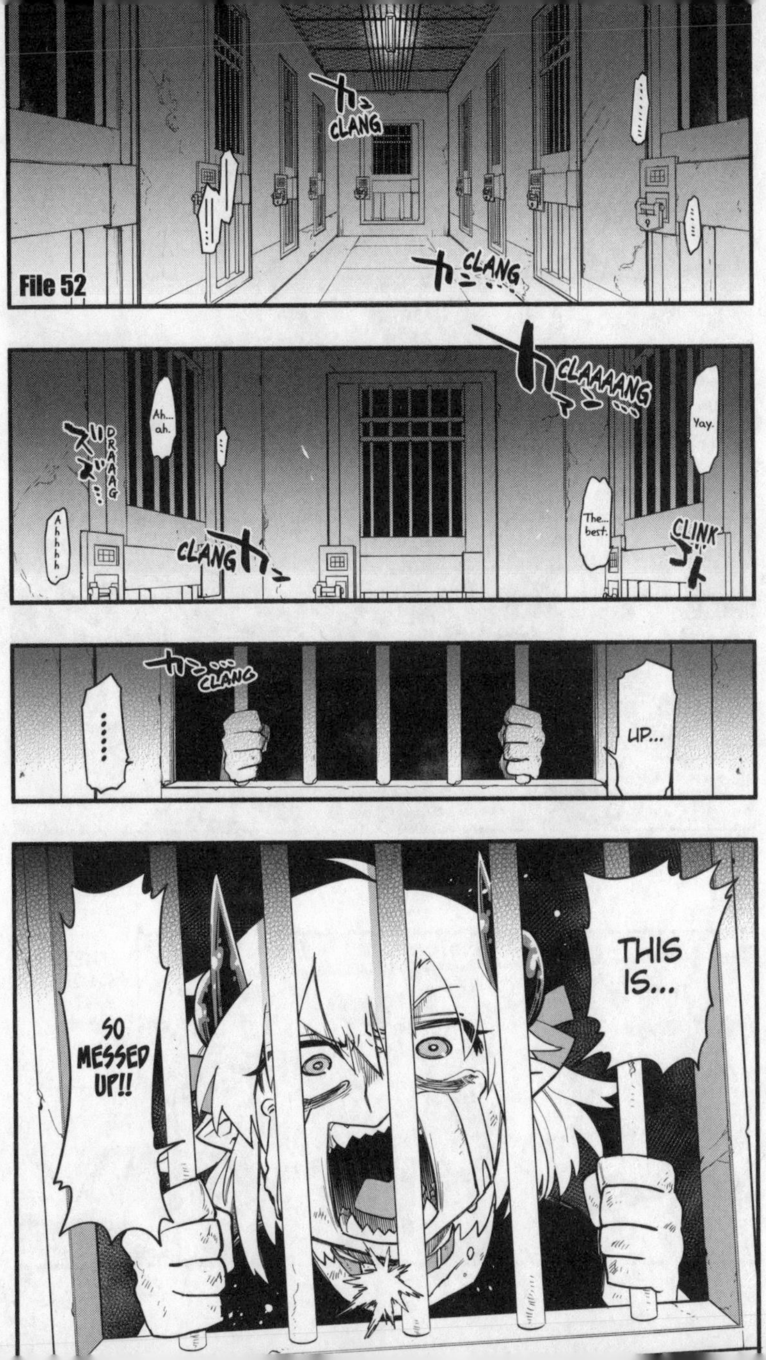
File 52
......
...
CLANG
...
CLANG
CLAAAANG
Yay.
The... best.
CLINK
CLANG
...
Ah... ah.
DRAAAG
Ahhhh.
UP...
CLANG
......
THIS IS...
SO MESSED UP!!

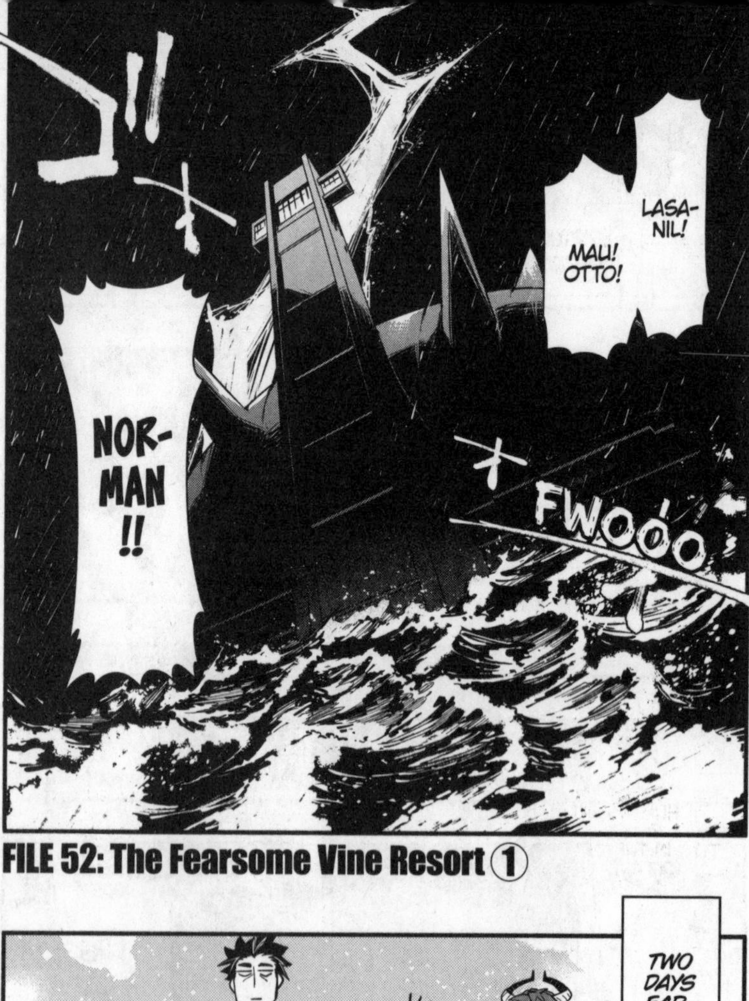
LASA-NIL!
MAU! OTTO!
NOR-MAN!!
FWOOO

FILE 52: The Fearsome Vine Resort ①

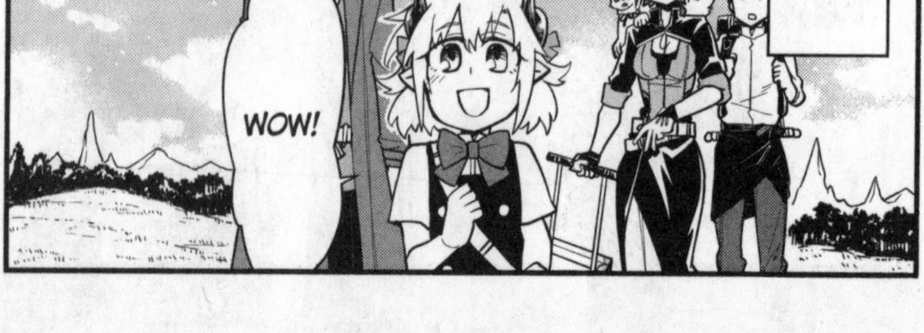
TWO DAYS EAR-LIER.
WOW!

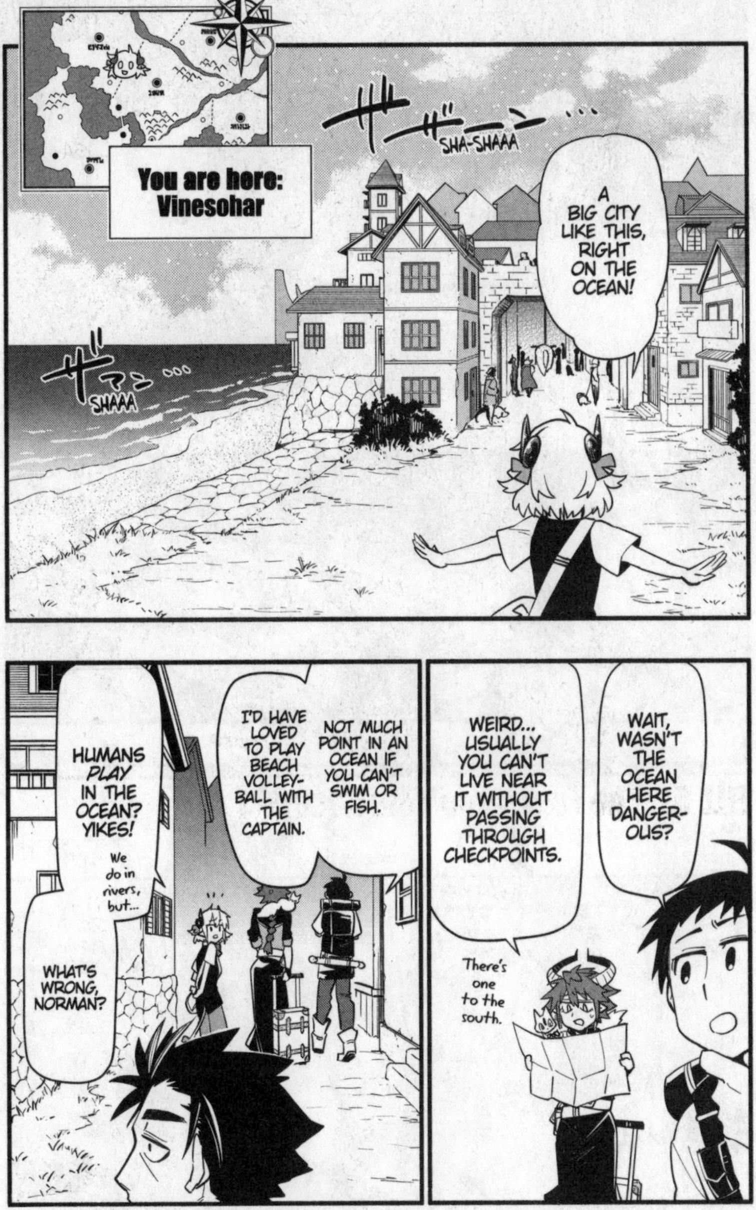
You are here: Vinesohar
SHA-SHAAA
A BIG CITY LIKE THIS, RIGHT ON THE OCEAN!
SHAAA
WAIT, WASN'T THE OCEAN HERE DANGER-OUS?
WEIRD... USUALLY YOU CAN'T LIVE NEAR IT WITHOUT PASSING THROUGH CHECKPOINTS.
There's one to the south.
NOT MUCH POINT IN AN OCEAN IF YOU CAN'T SWIM OR FISH.
I'D HAVE LOVED TO PLAY BEACH VOLLEY-BALL WITH THE CAPTAIN.
HUMANS PLAY IN THE OCEAN? YIKES!
We do in rivers, but...
WHAT'S WRONG, NORMAN?

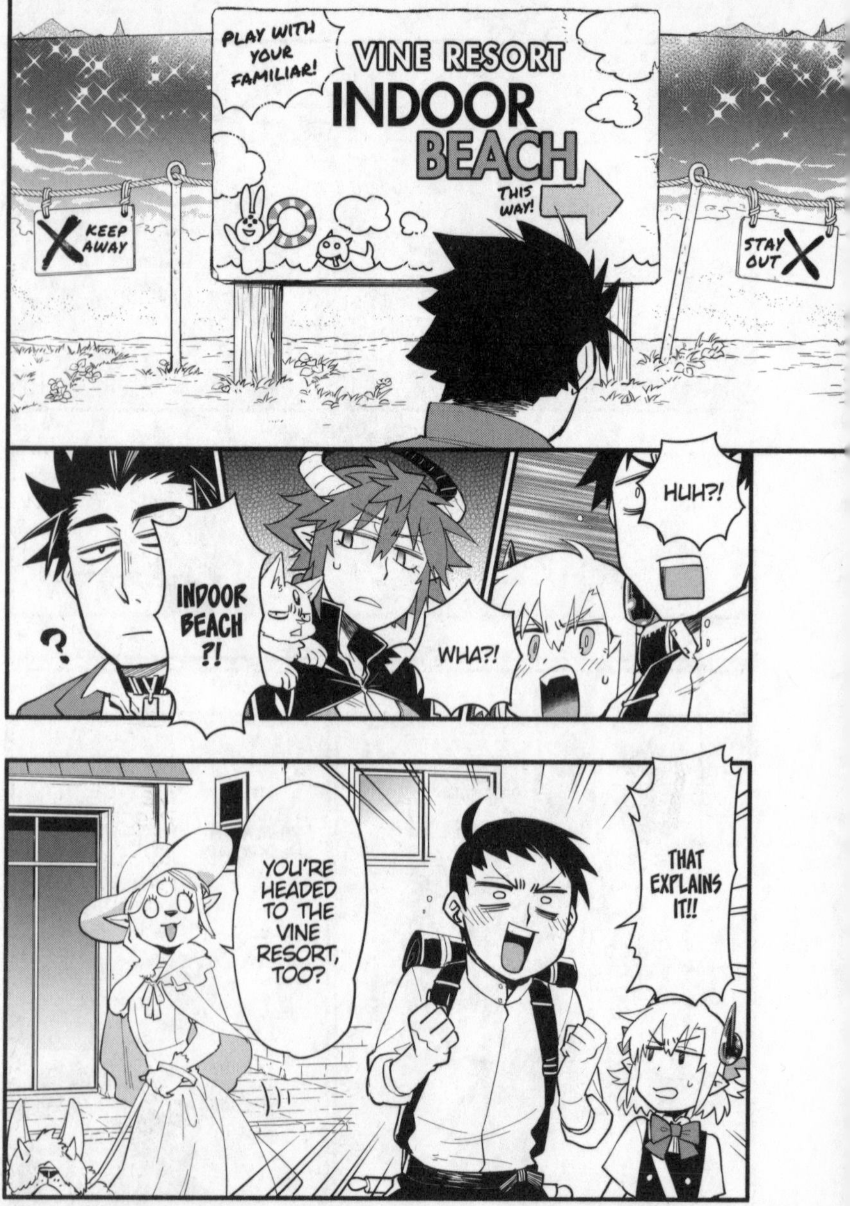
VINE RESORT
INDOOR BEACH
PLAY WITH YOUR FAMILIAR!
THIS WAY!
STAY OUT
KEEP AWAY
HUH?!
WHA?!
INDOOR BEACH?!
THAT EXPLAINS IT!!
YOU'RE HEADED TO THE VINE RESORT, TOO?

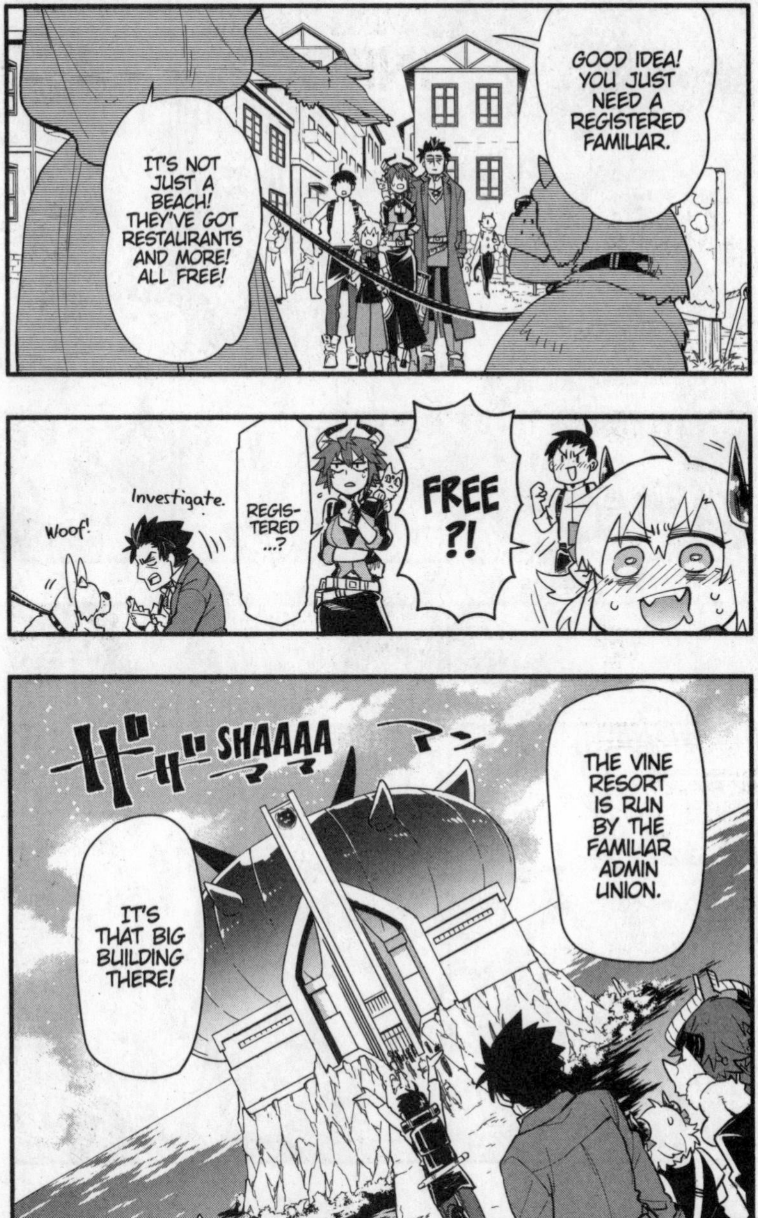
GOOD IDEA! YOU JUST NEED A REGISTERED FAMILIAR.
IT'S NOT JUST A BEACH! THEY'VE GOT RESTAURANTS AND MORE! ALL FREE!
FREE?!
REGIS-TERED ...?
Investigate.
Woof!
SHAAAA
THE VINE RESORT IS RUN BY THE FAMILIAR ADMIN UNION.
IT'S THAT BIG BUILDING THERE!

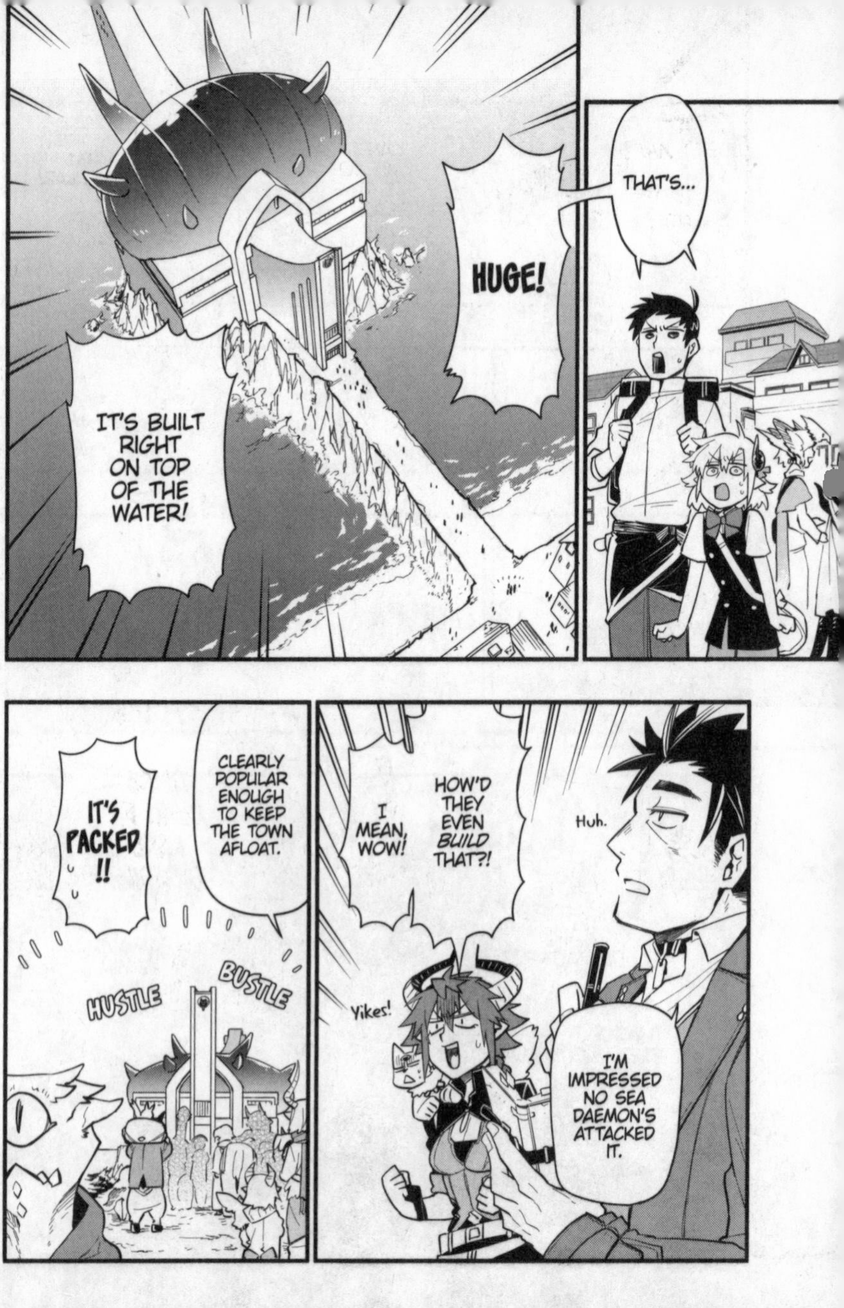
THAT'S...
HUGE!
IT'S BUILT RIGHT ON TOP OF THE WATER!
Huh.
HOW'D THEY EVEN *BUILD* THAT?!
I MEAN, WOW!
Yikes!
I'M IMPRESSED NO SEA DAEMON'S ATTACKED IT.
CLEARLY POPULAR ENOUGH TO KEEP THE TOWN AFLOAT.
IT'S PACKED!!
BUSTLE
HUSTLE

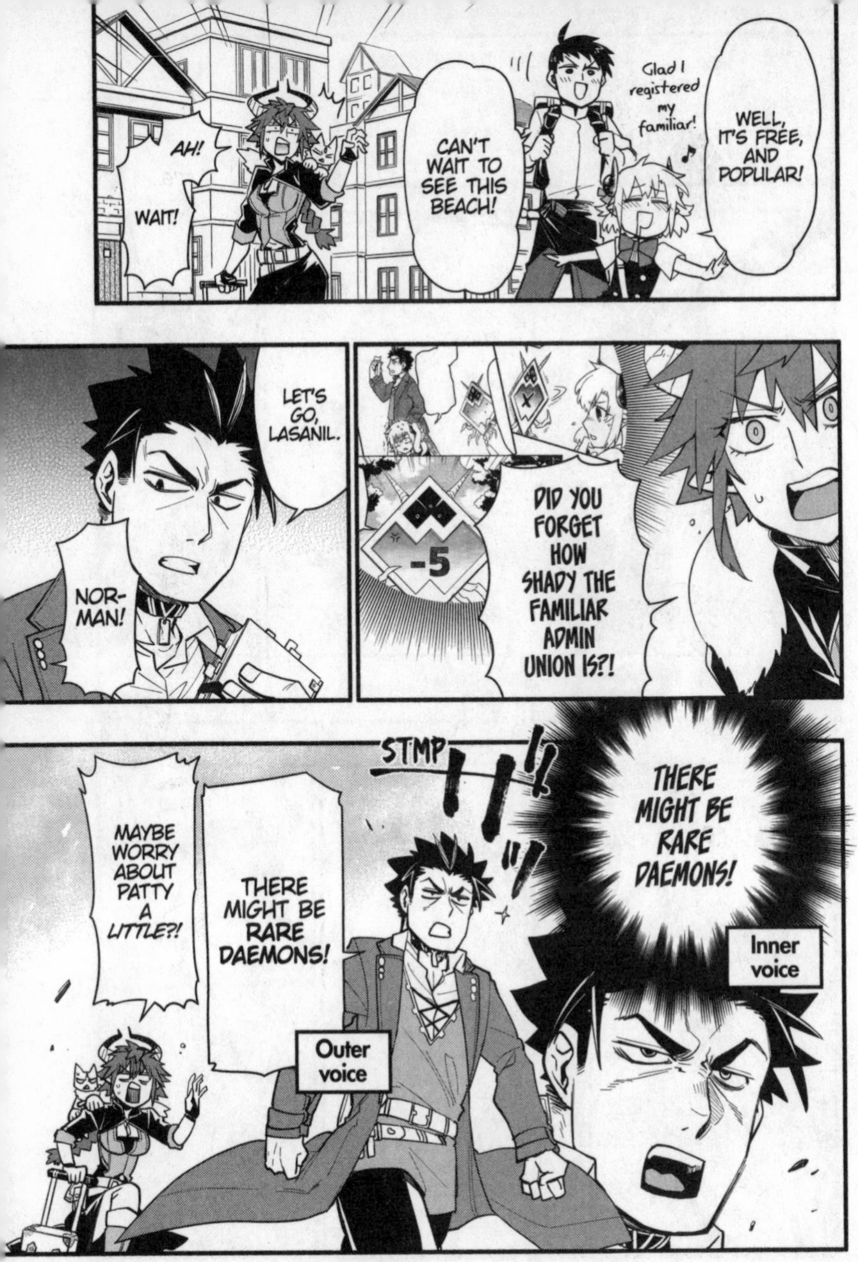
WELL, IT'S FREE, AND POPULAR!
Glad I registered my familiar!
CAN'T WAIT TO SEE THIS BEACH!
AH!
WAIT!
DID YOU FORGET HOW SHADY THE FAMILIAR ADMIN UNION IS?!
-5
LET'S GO, LASANIL.
NOR-MAN!
THERE MIGHT BE RARE DAEMONS!
Inner voice
STMP
THERE MIGHT BE RARE DAEMONS!
Outer voice
MAYBE WORRY ABOUT PATTY A LITTLE?!

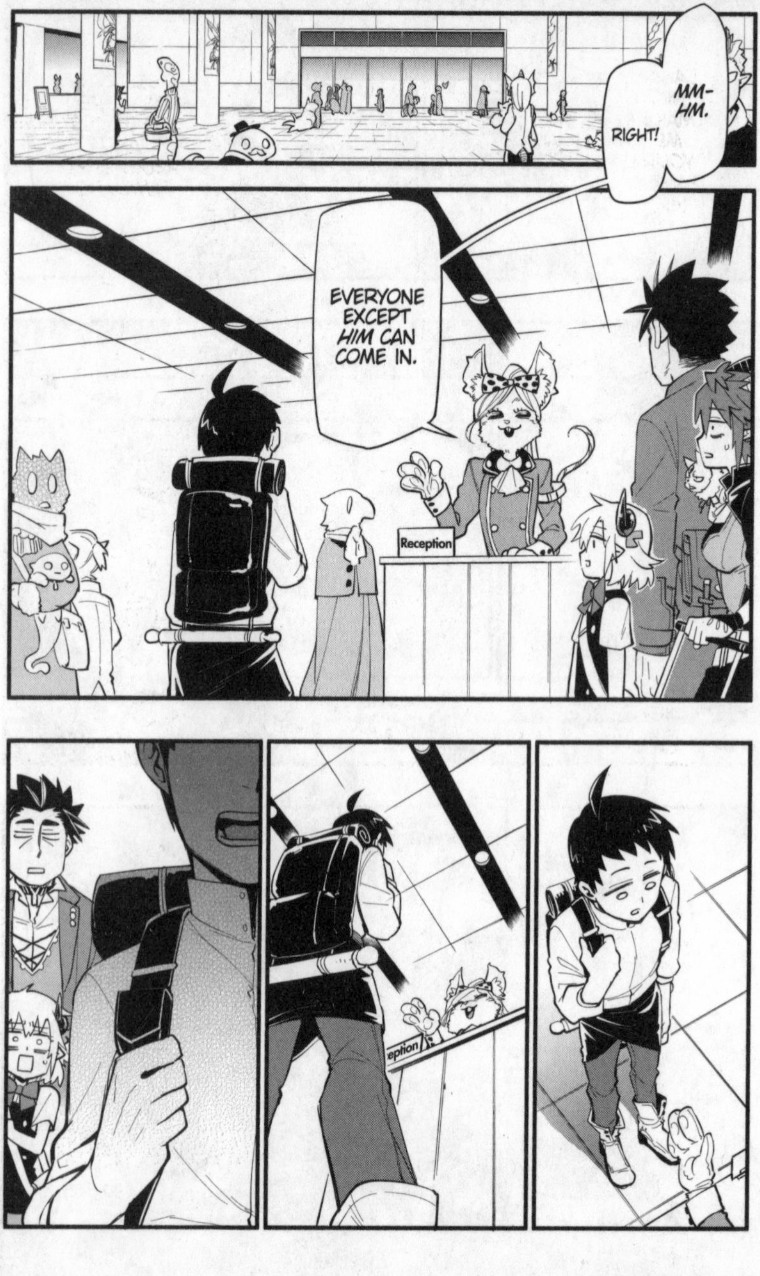
MM-HM.
RIGHT!
EVERYONE EXCEPT HIM CAN COME IN.
Reception
eption

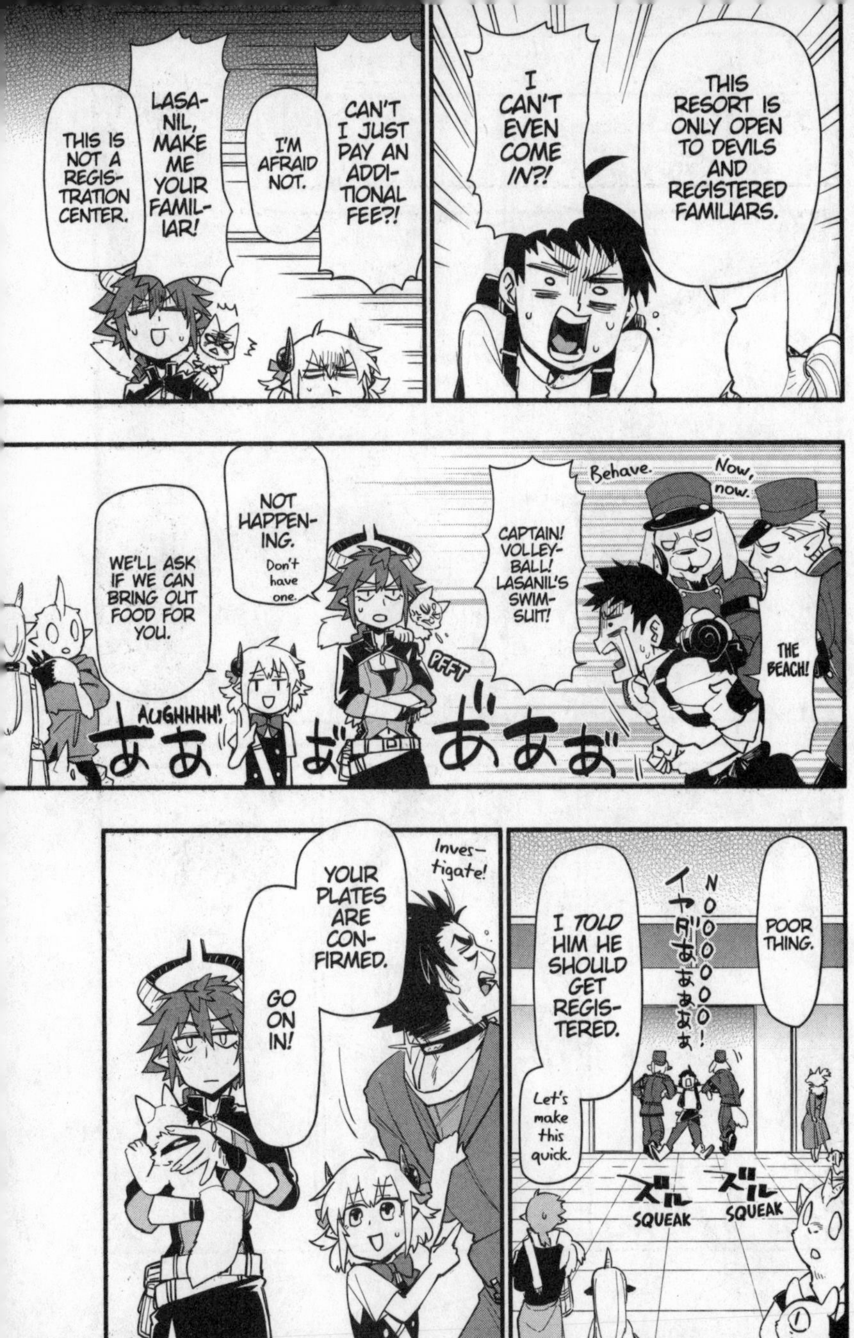
THIS RESORT IS ONLY OPEN TO DEVILS AND REGISTERED FAMILIARS.
I CAN'T EVEN COME IN?!
CAN'T I JUST PAY AN ADDITIONAL FEE?!
I'M AFRAID NOT.
LASANIL, MAKE ME YOUR FAMILIAR!
THIS IS NOT A REGISTRATION CENTER.
Now, now.
Behave.
THE BEACH!
CAPTAIN! VOLLEYBALL! LASANIL'S SWIMSUIT!
PFFT
NOT HAPPENING.
Don't have one.
WE'LL ASK IF WE CAN BRING OUT FOOD FOR YOU.
AUGHHHH!
POOR THING.
NOOOOOOO!
I TOLD HIM HE SHOULD GET REGISTERED.
Let's make this quick.
SQUEAK
SQUEAK
Investigate!
YOUR PLATES ARE CONFIRMED.
GO ON IN!

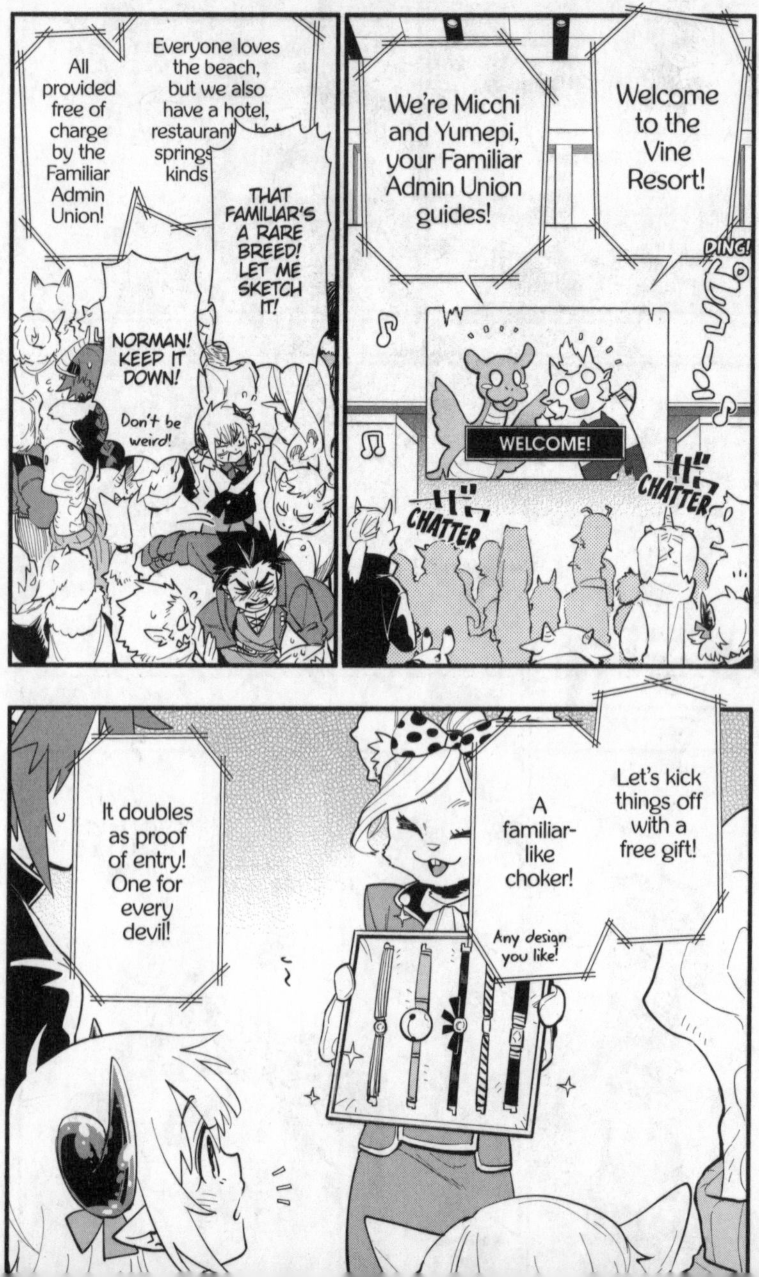

Welcome to the Vine Resort!
DING!
We're Micchi and Yumepi, your Familiar Admin Union guides!
WELCOME!
CHATTER
CHATTER
Everyone loves the beach, but we also have a hotel, restaurant springs kinds
All provided free of charge by the Familiar Admin Union!
THAT FAMILIAR'S A RARE BREED! LET ME SKETCH IT!
NORMAN! KEEP IT DOWN!
Don't be weird!
Let's kick things off with a free gift!
A familiar-like choker!
Any design you like!
It doubles as proof of entry! One for every devil!

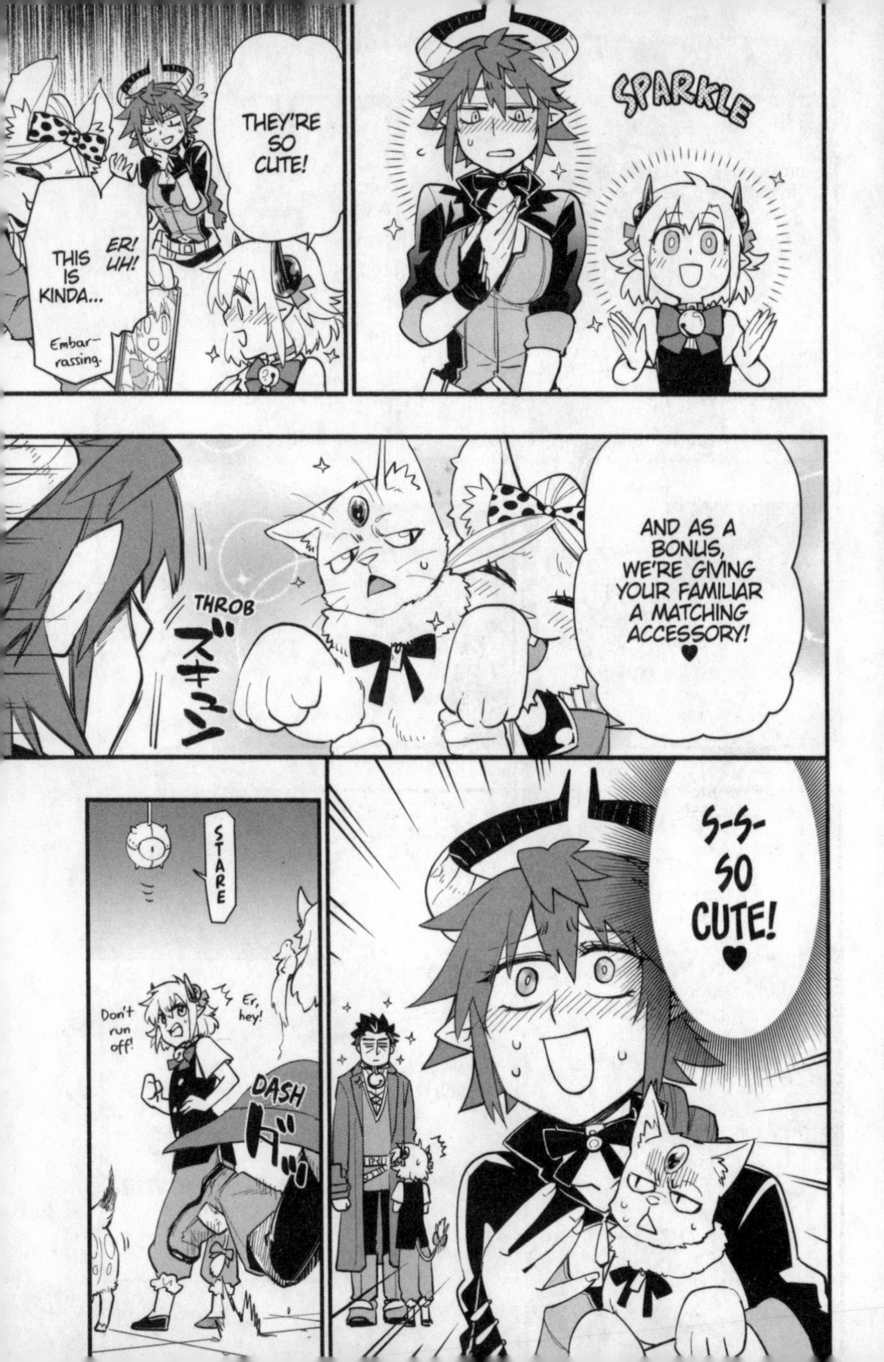
SPARKLE
THEY'RE SO CUTE!
ER! UH!
THIS IS KINDA...
Embar-rassing.
AND AS A BONUS, WE'RE GIVING YOUR FAMILIAR A MATCHING ACCESSORY! ♥
THROB
ズキュン
S-S-SO CUTE! ♥
STARE
Er, hey!
Don't run off!
DASH
ダッ

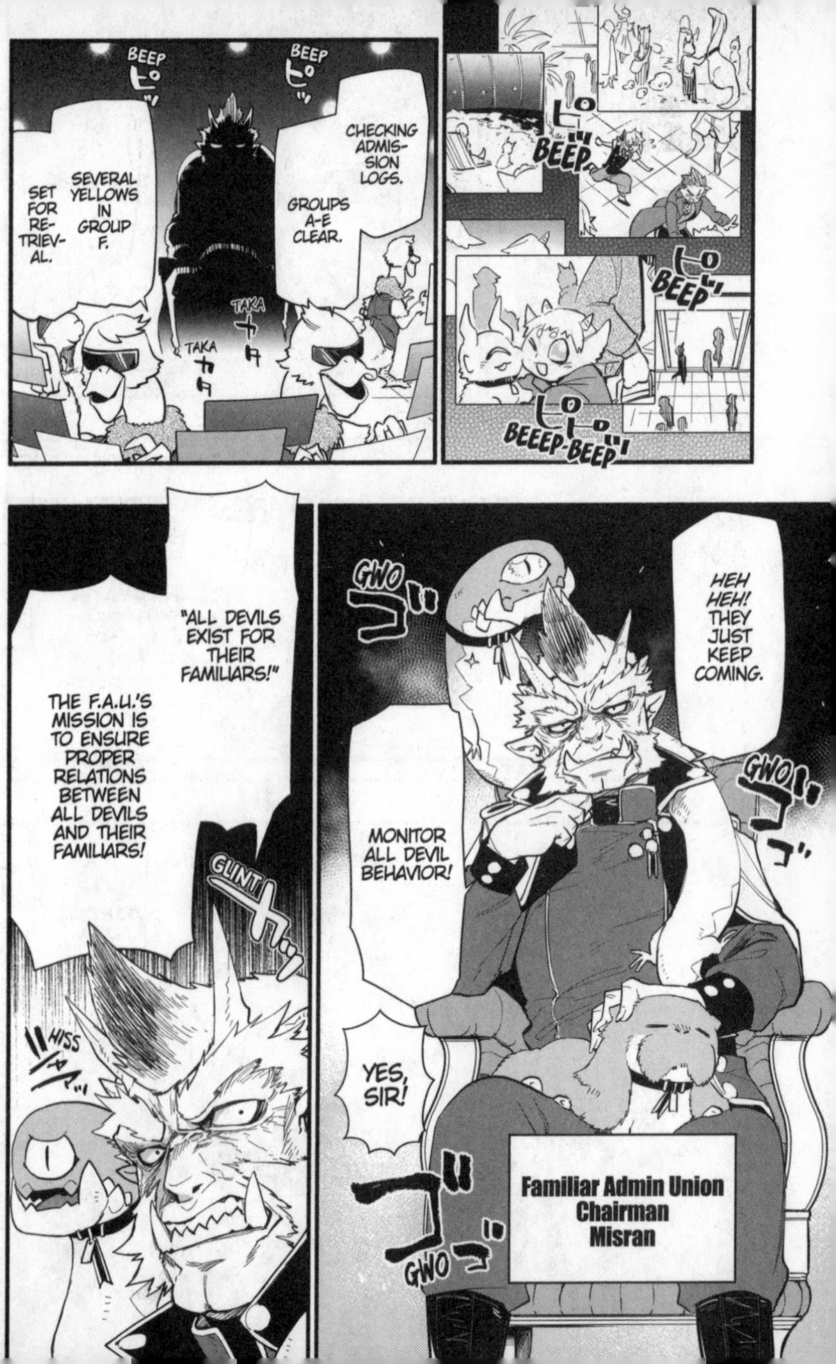
BEEP
BEEP
BEEP
BEEEP-BEEEP
BEEP
BEEP
CHECKING ADMISSION LOGS.
GROUPS A-E CLEAR.
SEVERAL YELLOWS IN GROUP F.
SET FOR RETRIEVAL.
TAKA
TAKA
GWO
HEH HEH! THEY JUST KEEP COMING.
GWO
MONITOR ALL DEVIL BEHAVIOR!
YES, SIR!
GWO
Familiar Admin Union
Chairman
Misran
"ALL DEVILS EXIST FOR THEIR FAMILIARS!"
THE F.A.U.'S MISSION IS TO ENSURE PROPER RELATIONS BETWEEN ALL DEVILS AND THEIR FAMILIARS!
GLINT
HISS

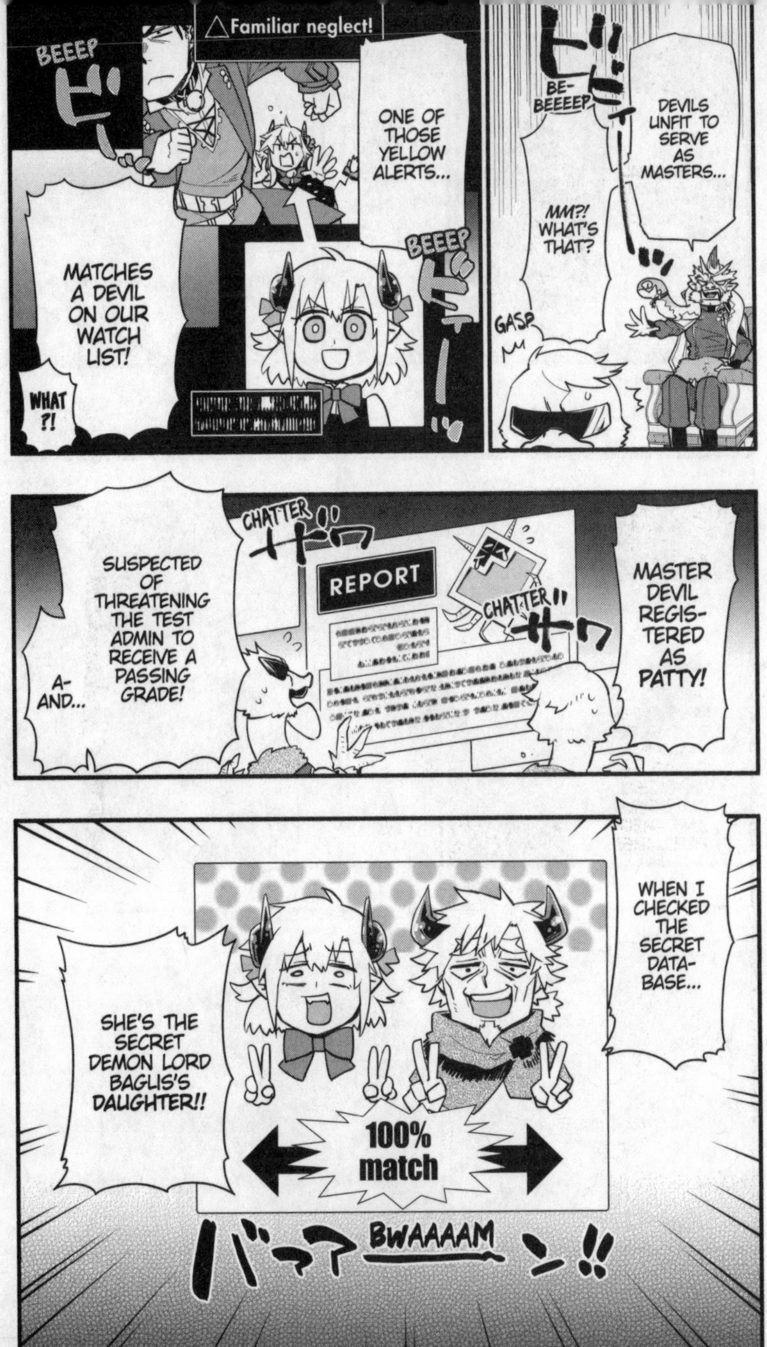
BE-BEEEEP
DEVILS UNFIT TO SERVE AS MASTERS...
MM?! WHAT'S THAT?
GASP
△Familiar neglect!
BEEEP
ONE OF THOSE YELLOW ALERTS...
BEEEP
MATCHES A DEVIL ON OUR WATCH LIST!
WHAT?!
MASTER DEVIL REGISTERED AS PATTY!
CHATTER
REPORT
CHATTER
SUSPECTED OF THREATENING THE TEST ADMIN TO RECEIVE A PASSING GRADE!
A- AND...
WHEN I CHECKED THE SECRET DATABASE...
SHE'S THE SECRET DEMON LORD BAGLIS'S DAUGHTER!!
100% match
BWAAAAM

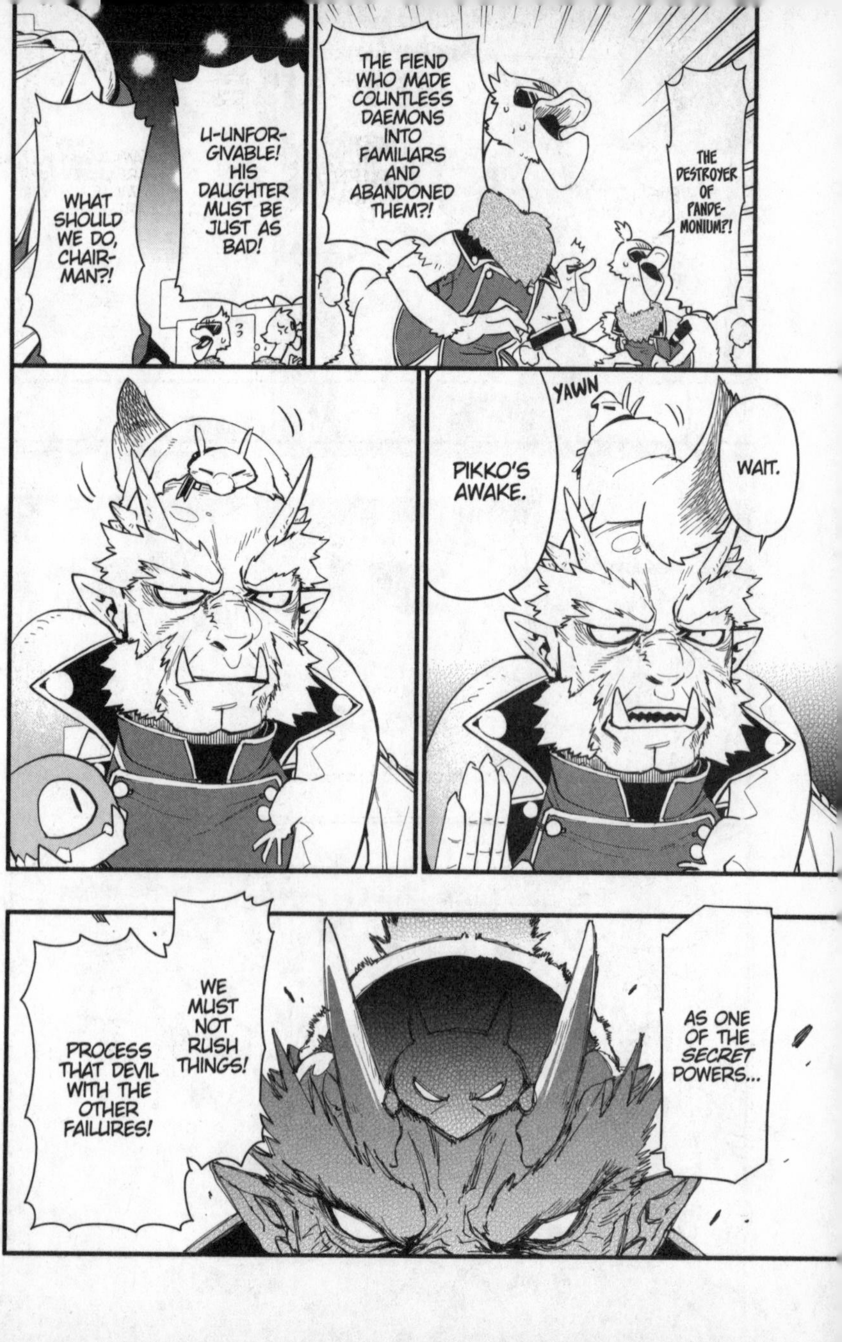
THE DESTROYER OF PANDE-MONIUM?!
THE FIEND WHO MADE COUNTLESS DAEMONS INTO FAMILIARS AND ABANDONED THEM?!
U-UNFORGIVABLE! HIS DAUGHTER MUST BE JUST AS BAD!
WHAT SHOULD WE DO, CHAIRMAN?!
WAIT.
YAWN
PIKKO'S AWAKE.
AS ONE OF THE SECRET POWERS...
WE MUST NOT RUSH THINGS!
PROCESS THAT DEVIL WITH THE OTHER FAILURES!

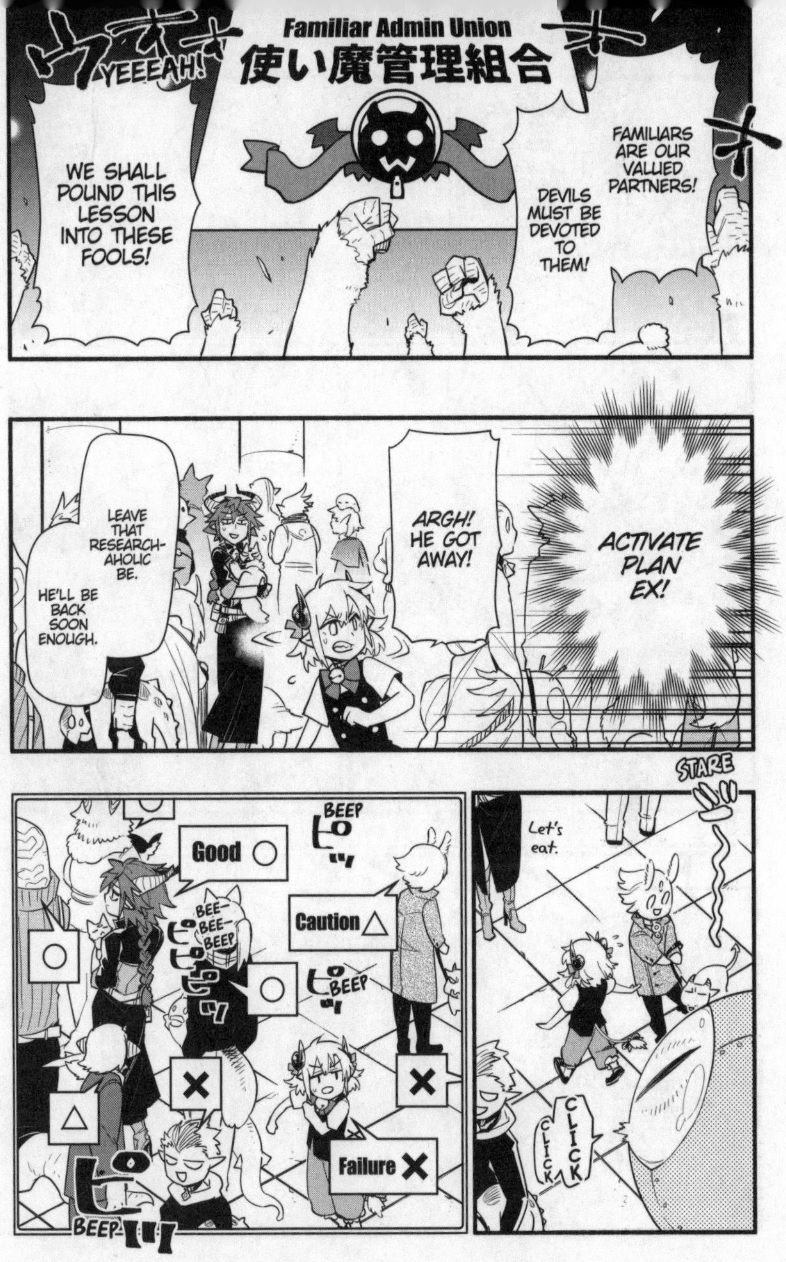

YEEEAH!
Familiar Admin Union
使い魔管理組合
FAMILIARS ARE OUR VALUED PARTNERS!
DEVILS MUST BE DEVOTED TO THEM!
WE SHALL POUND THIS LESSON INTO THESE FOOLS!
ACTIVATE PLAN EX!
ARGH! HE GOT AWAY!
LEAVE THAT RESEARCH-AHOLIC BE.
HE'LL BE BACK SOON ENOUGH.
STARE
Let's eat.
CLICK
CLICK
BEEP
Good ○
Caution △
BEE-BEE-BEEP
○
○
BEEP
×
×
△
Failure ×
BEEP

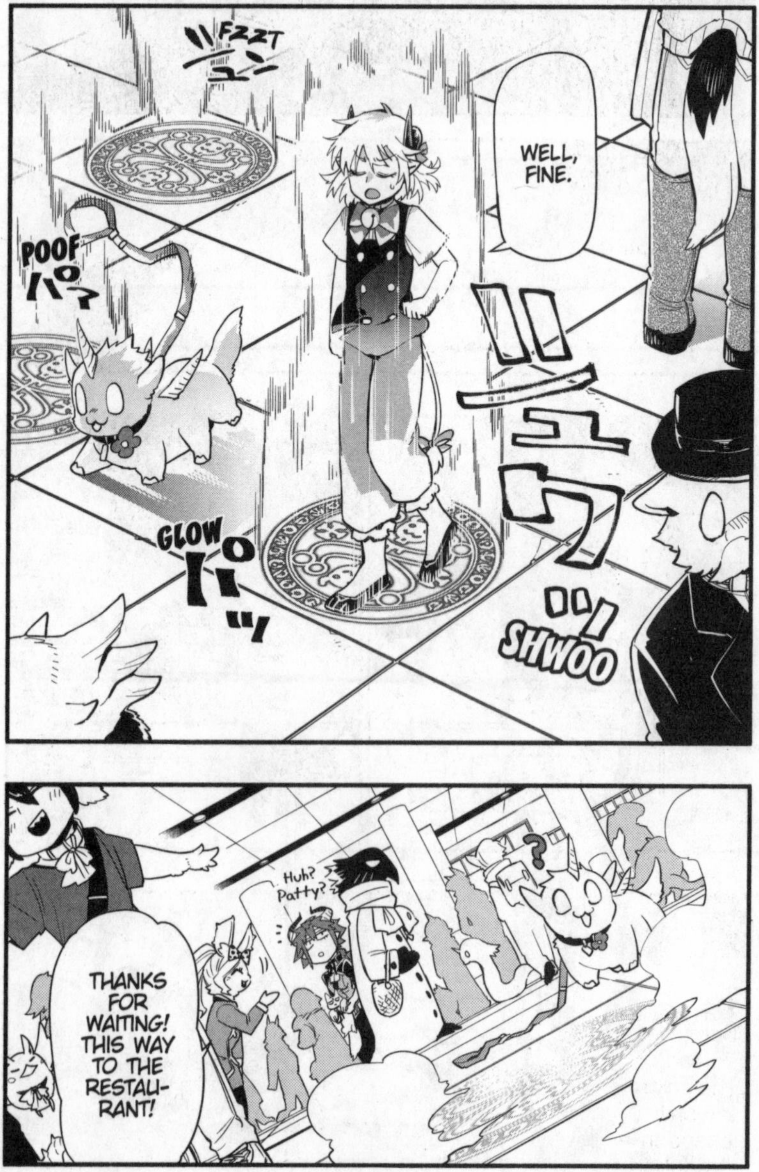
FZZT
WELL, FINE.
POOF
SHWOO
GLOW
Huh? Patty?
THANKS FOR WAITING! THIS WAY TO THE RESTAU-RANT!

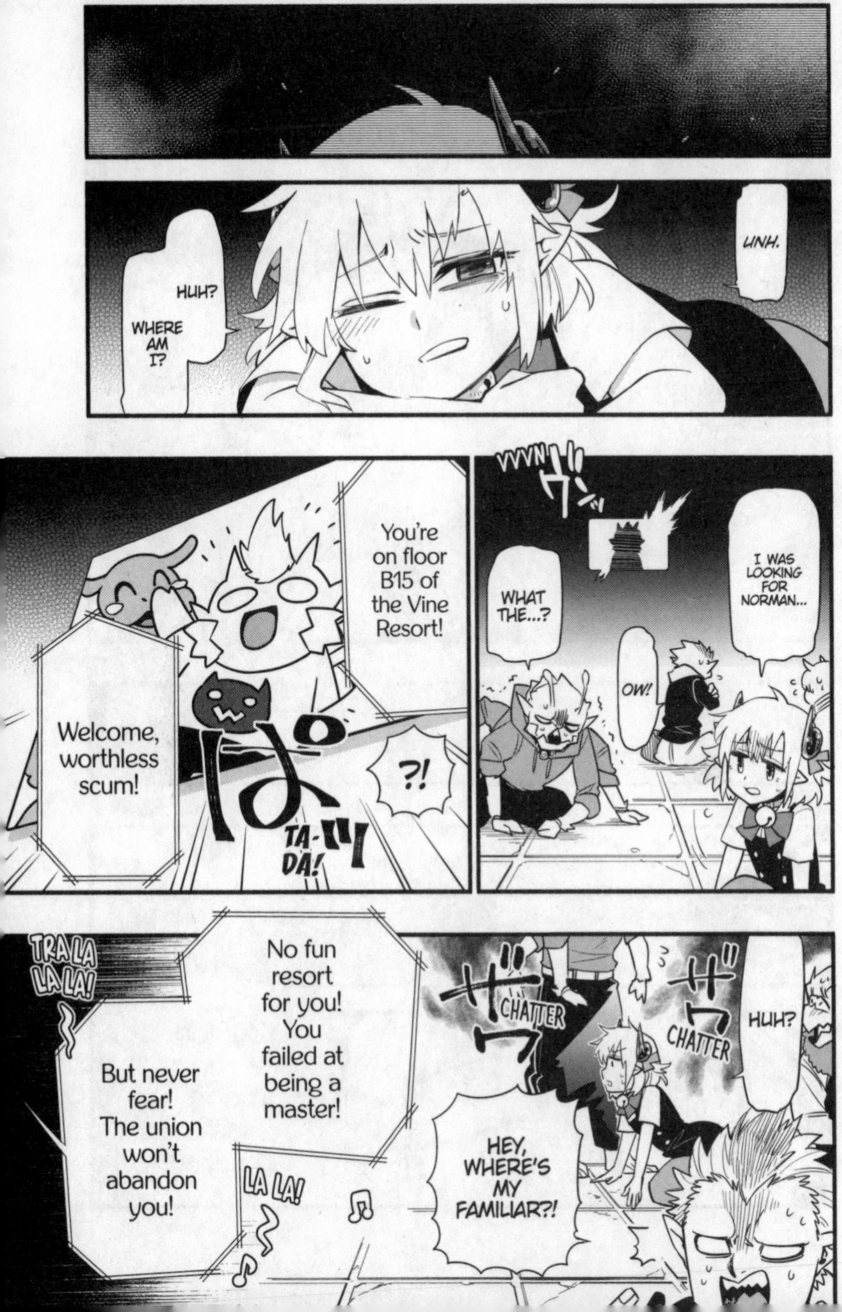
UNH.
HUH?
WHERE AM I?
VVVN
I WAS LOOKING FOR NORMAN...
OW!
WHAT THE...?
You're on floor B15 of the Vine Resort!
?!
Welcome, worthless scum!
TA-DA!
HUH?
CHATTER
CHATTER
HEY, WHERE'S MY FAMILIAR?!
No fun resort for you! You failed at being a master!
But never fear! The union won't abandon you!
TRA LA LA LA!
LA LA!

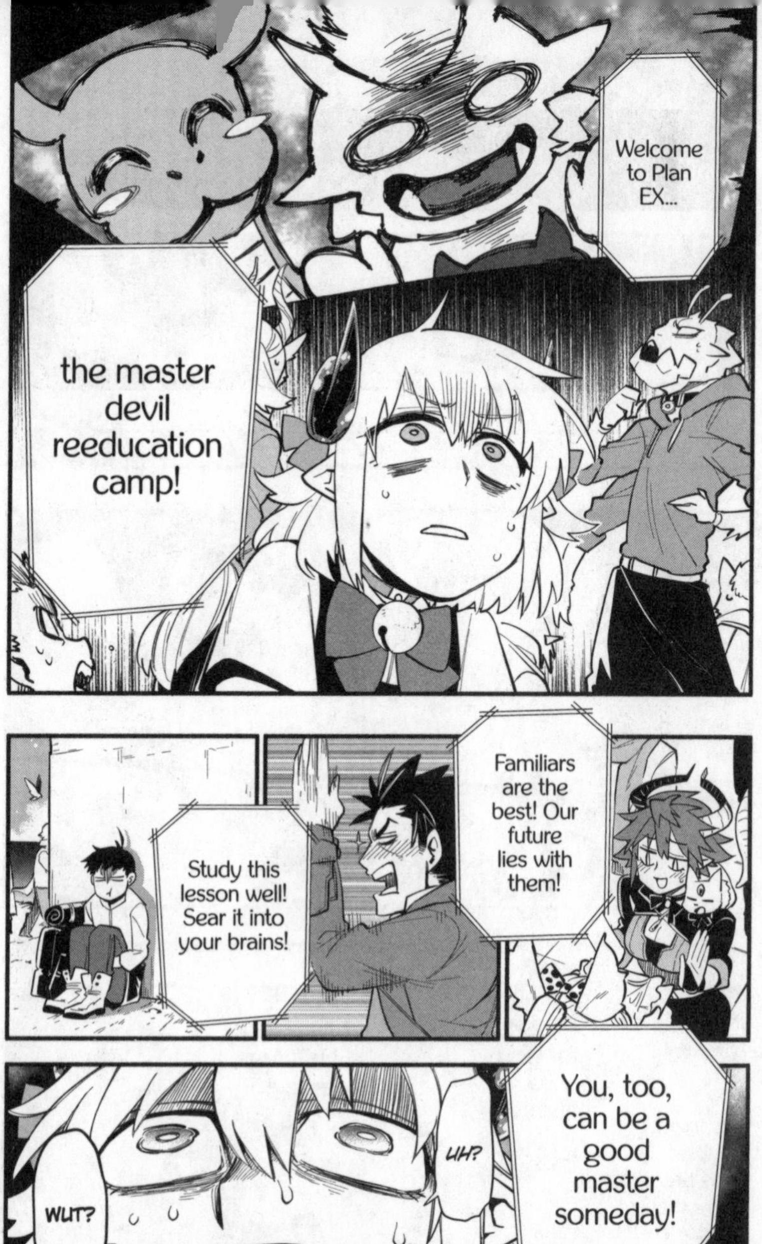
Welcome to Plan EX...
the master devil reeducation camp!
Familiars are the best! Our future lies with them!
Study this lesson well! Sear it into your brains!
You, too, can be a good master someday!
UH?
WUT?

File 53

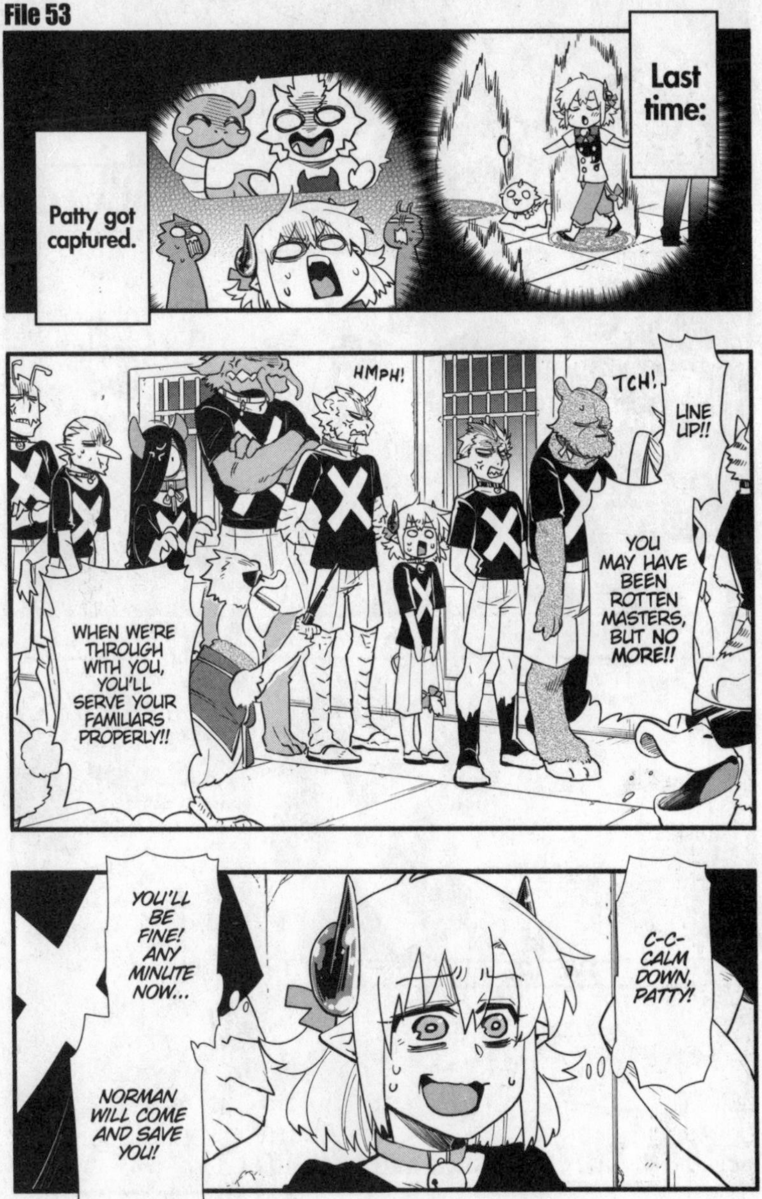
Last time:
Patty got captured.
LINE UP!!
TCH!
YOU MAY HAVE BEEN ROTTEN MASTERS, BUT NO MORE!!
HMPH!
WHEN WE'RE THROUGH WITH YOU, YOU'LL SERVE YOUR FAMILIARS PROPERLY!!
C-C-CALM DOWN, PATTY!
YOU'LL BE FINE! ANY MINUTE NOW...
NORMAN WILL COME AND SAVE YOU!

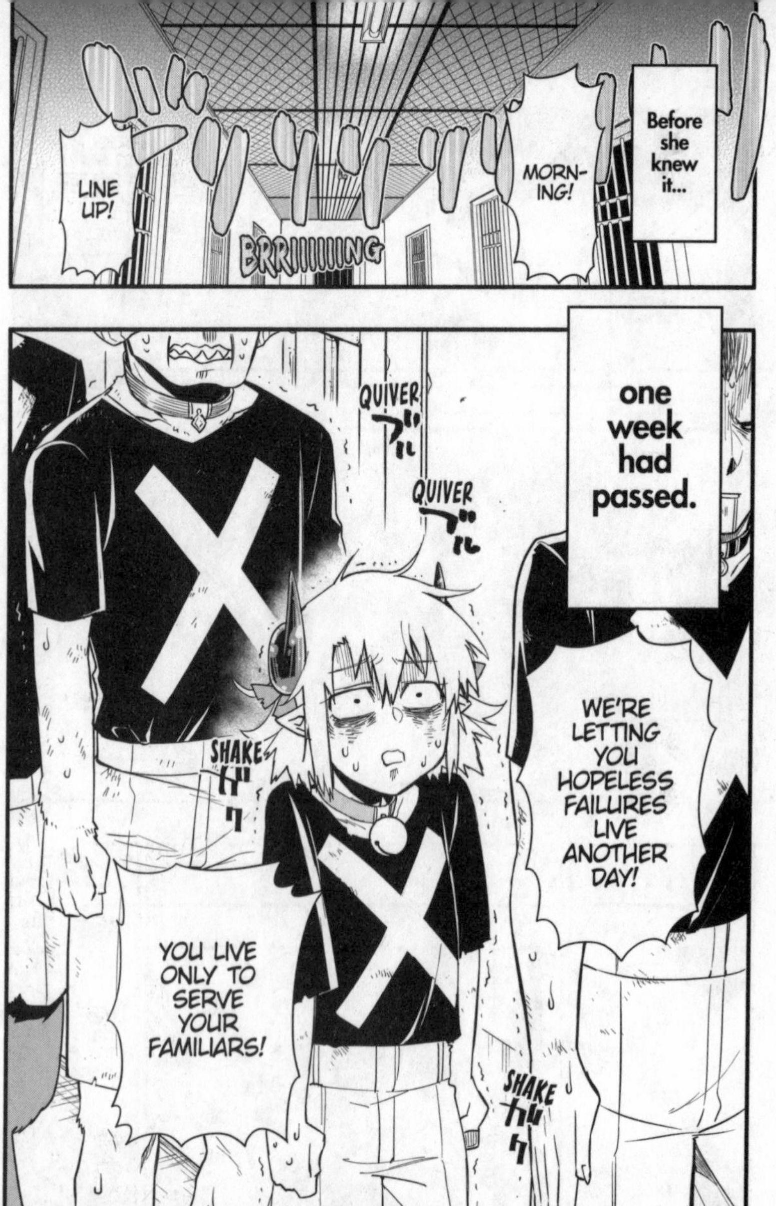
Before she knew it...
MORNING!
BRRIIIIIIING
LINE UP!
one week had passed.
QUIVER
QUIVER
WE'RE LETTING YOU HOPELESS FAILURES LIVE ANOTHER DAY!
SHAKE
YOU LIVE ONLY TO SERVE YOUR FAMILIARS!
SHAKE

FILE 53: The Fearsome Vine Resort ②

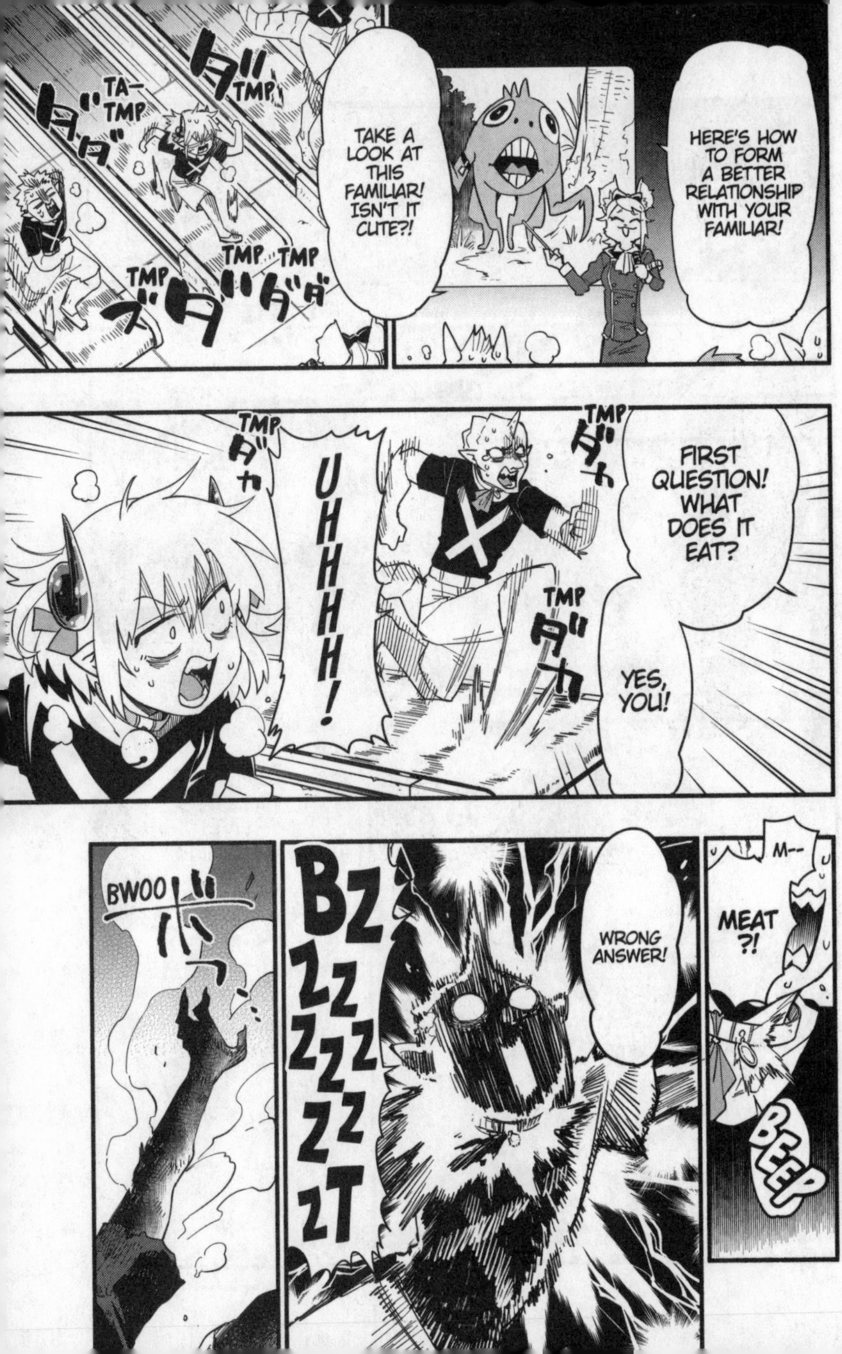

HERE'S HOW TO FORM A BETTER RELATIONSHIP WITH YOUR FAMILIAR!
TAKE A LOOK AT THIS FAMILIAR! ISN'T IT CUTE?!
TMP
TA-TMP
TMP
TMP
TMP
FIRST QUESTION! WHAT DOES IT EAT?
YES, YOU!
TMP
TMP
UHHHHH!
TMP
M--
MEAT?!
BEEP
WRONG ANSWER!
BZZZZZZZZZZZT
BWOO

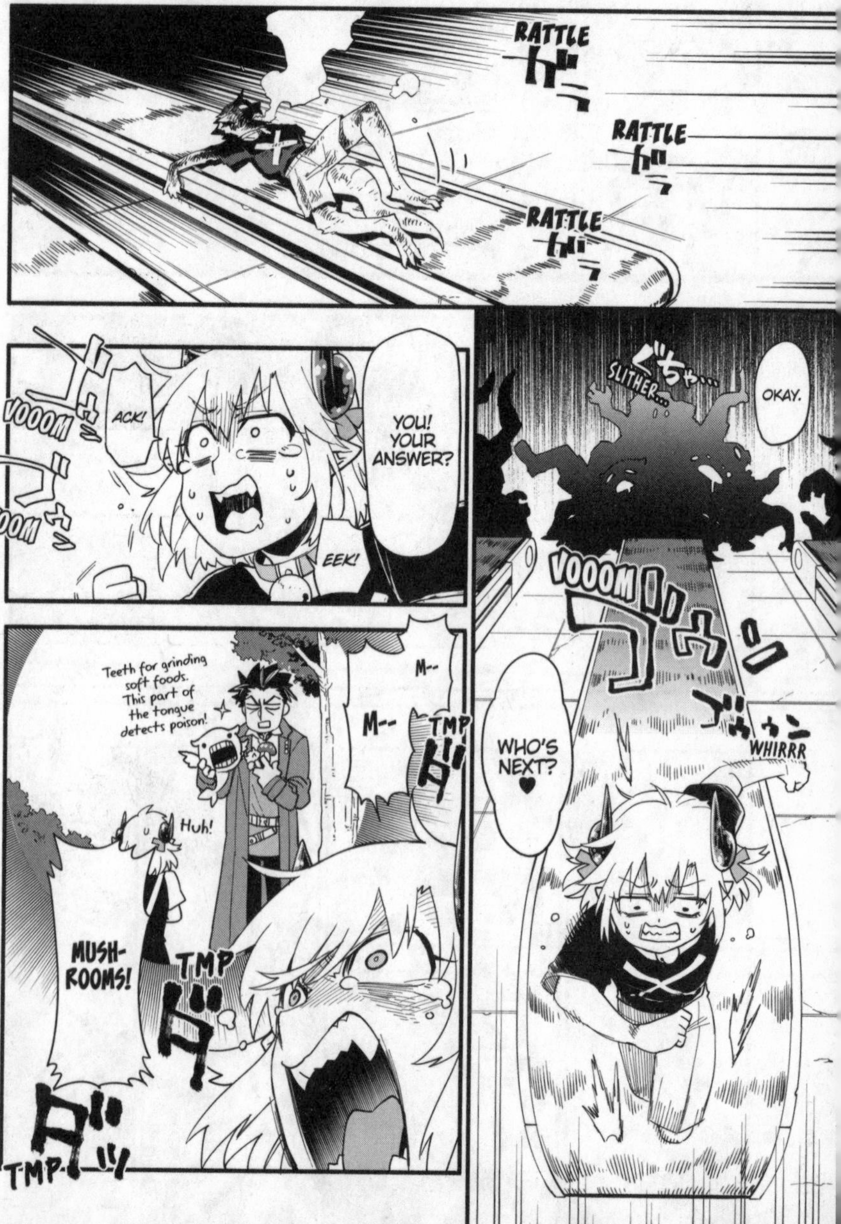
RATTLE
RATTLE
RATTLE
ぐちゃ…
SLITHER...
OKAY.
VOOOM
WHO'S NEXT? ♥
WHIRRR
YOU! YOUR ANSWER?
ACK!
EEK!
VOOOM
VOOM
M--
M--
TMP
Teeth for grinding soft foods. This part of the tongue detects poison!
Huh!
MUSH-ROOMS!
TMP
TMP

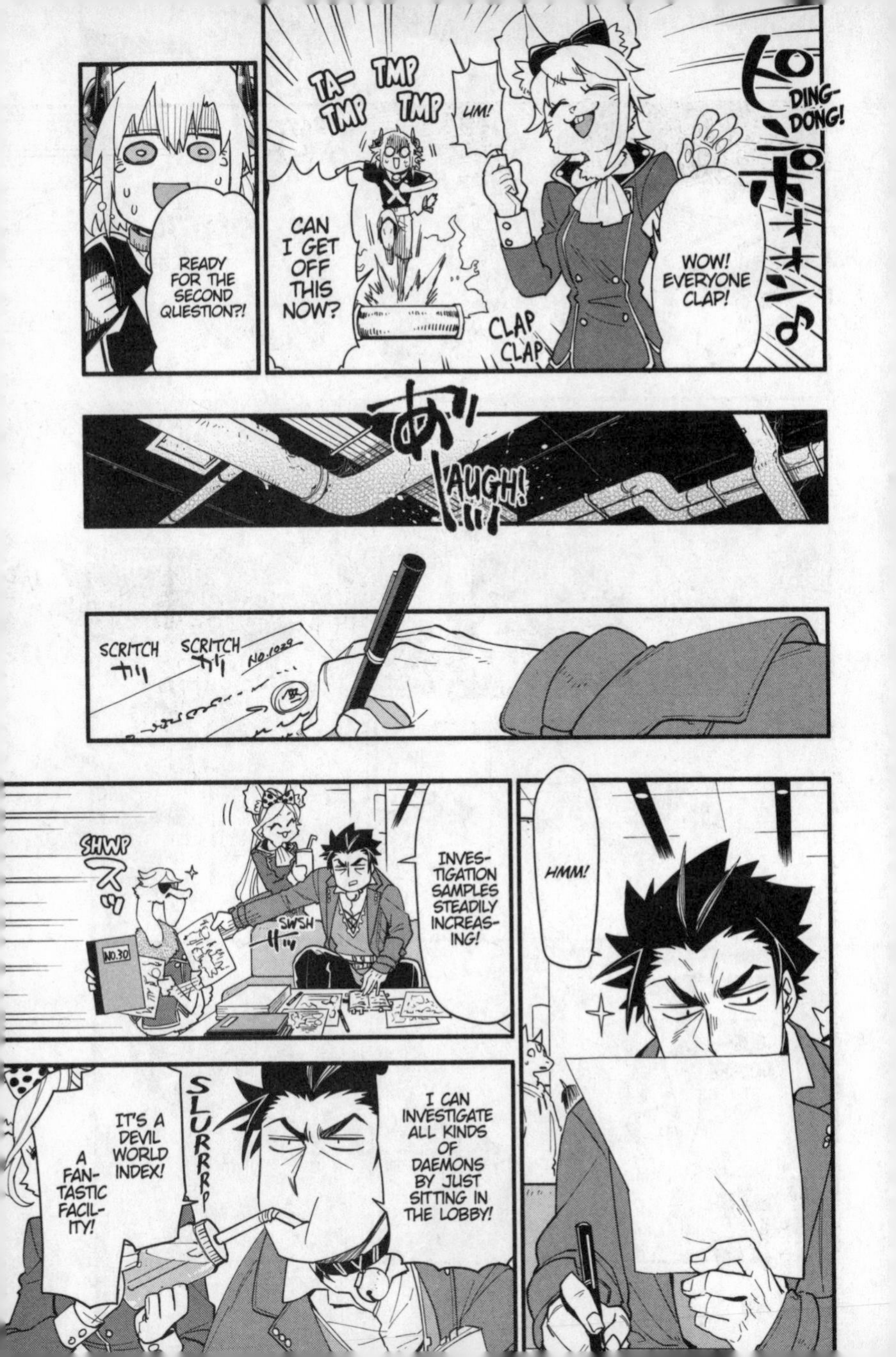
DING-DONG!
WOW! EVERYONE CLAP!
CLAP CLAP
UM!
TA-TMP TMP TMP
CAN I GET OFF THIS NOW?
READY FOR THE SECOND QUESTION?!
AUGH!
SCRITCH
SCRITCH
NO.1029
HMM!
INVESTIGATION SAMPLES STEADILY INCREASING!
SWSH
SHWP
NO.30
I CAN INVESTIGATE ALL KINDS OF DAEMONS BY JUST SITTING IN THE LOBBY!
SLURRRP
IT'S A DEVIL WORLD INDEX!
A FANTASTIC FACILITY!

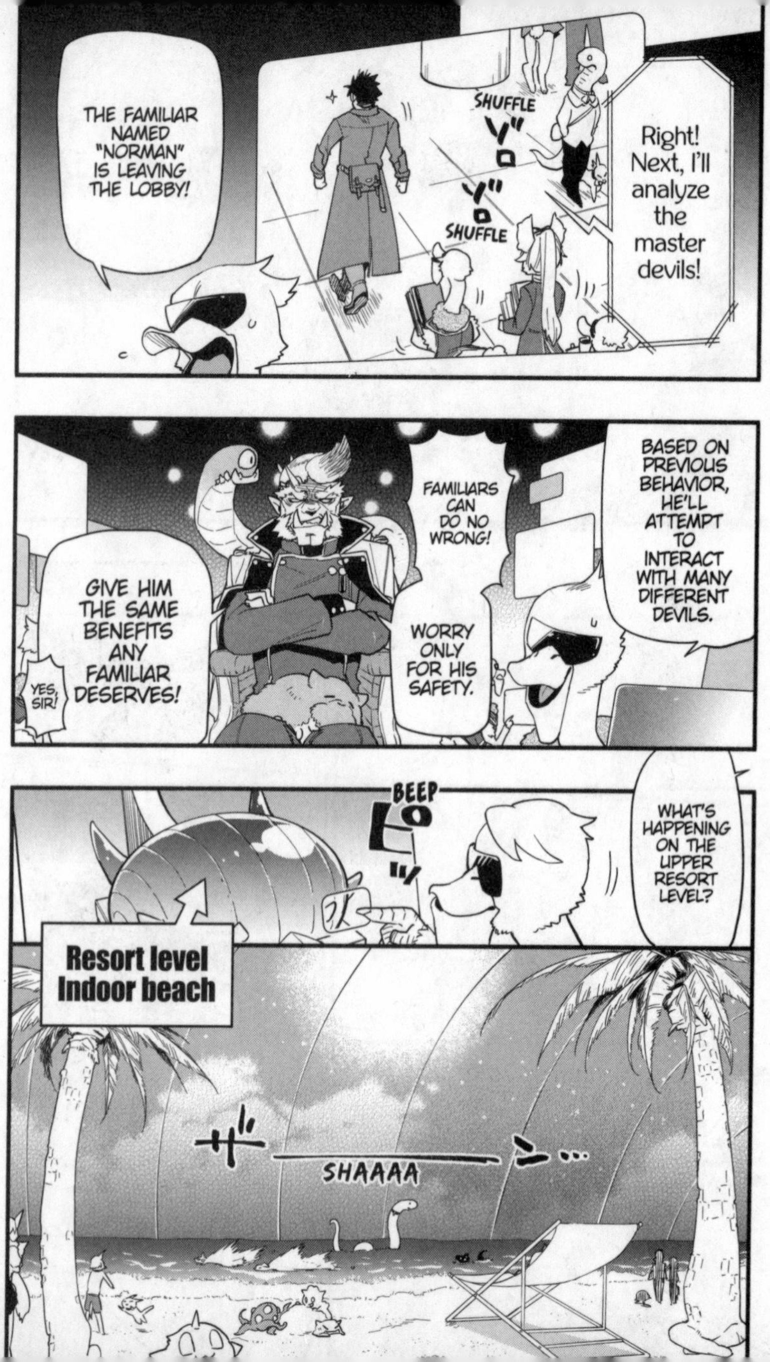
Right! Next, I'll analyze the master devils!
SHUFFLE
SHUFFLE
THE FAMILIAR NAMED "NORMAN" IS LEAVING THE LOBBY!
BASED ON PREVIOUS BEHAVIOR, HE'LL ATTEMPT TO INTERACT WITH MANY DIFFERENT DEVILS.
FAMILIARS CAN DO NO WRONG!
WORRY ONLY FOR HIS SAFETY.
GIVE HIM THE SAME BENEFITS ANY FAMILIAR DESERVES!
YES, SIR!
WHAT'S HAPPENING ON THE UPPER RESORT LEVEL?
BEEP
Resort level
Indoor beach
SHAAAA

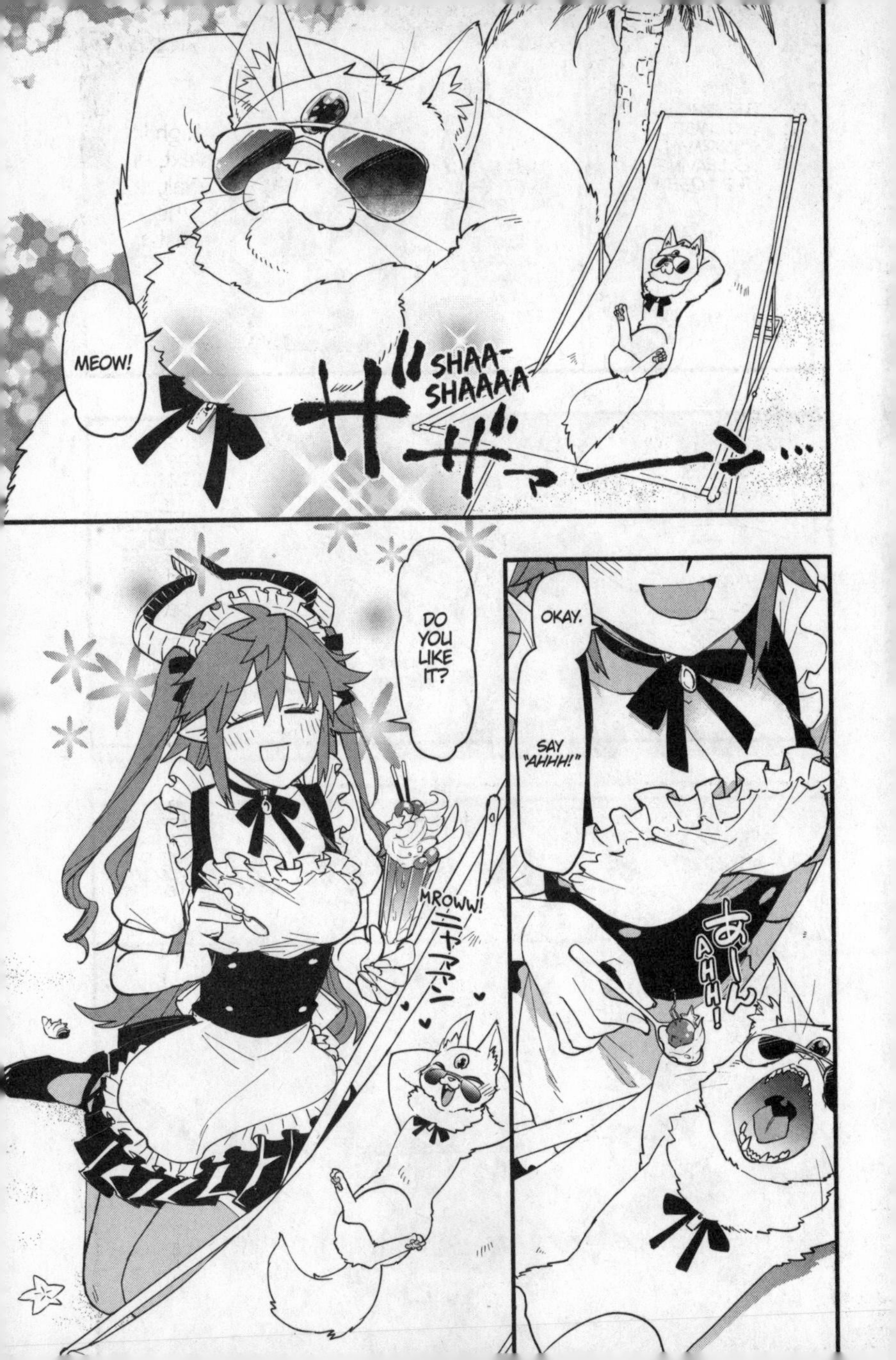
MEOW!
ザザァーーン…
SHAA-SHAAAA
DO YOU LIKE IT?
ニャアァン
MROWW!
OKAY.
SAY "AHHH!"
あーん
AHHH!

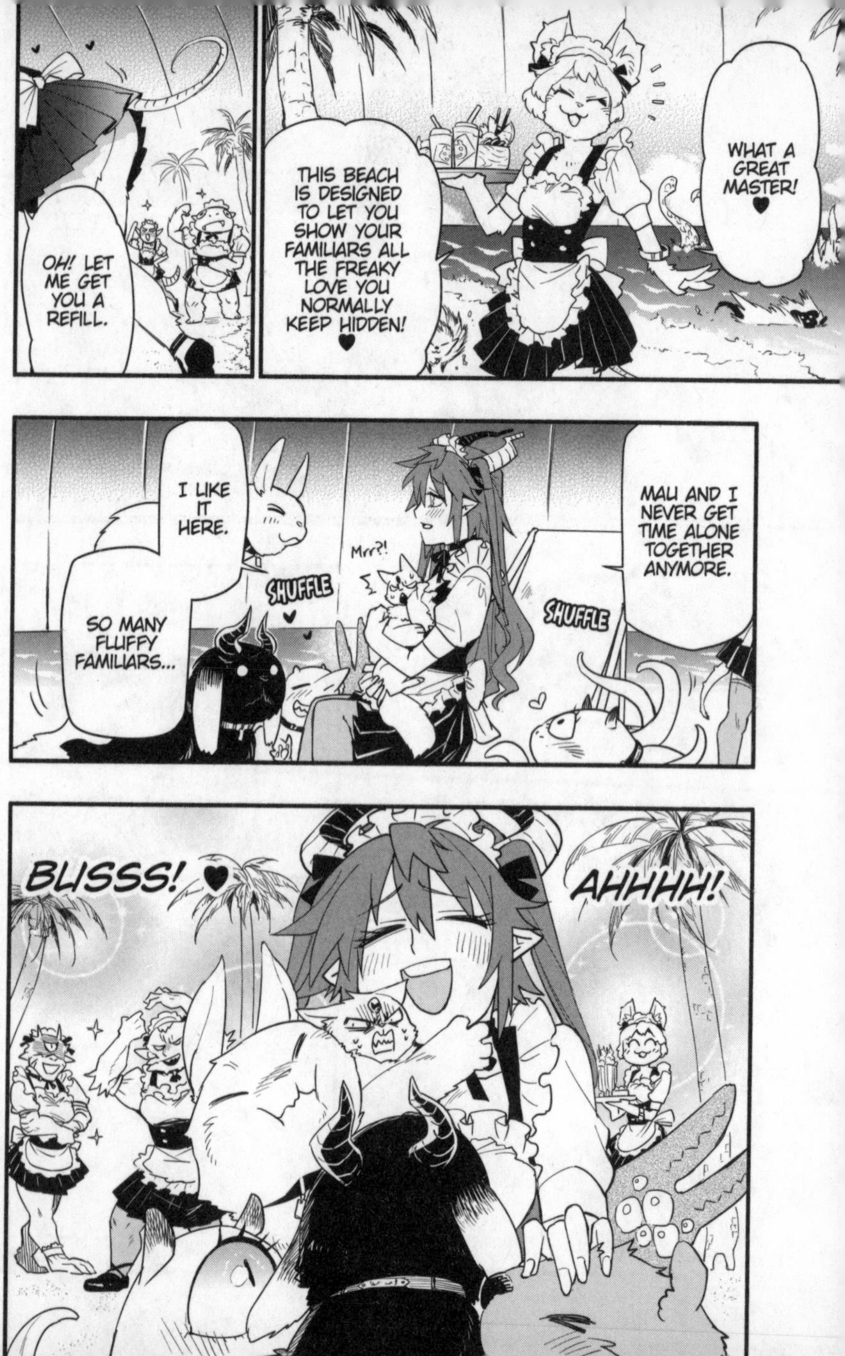
WHAT A GREAT MASTER! ♥
THIS BEACH IS DESIGNED TO LET YOU SHOW YOUR FAMILIARS ALL THE FREAKY LOVE YOU NORMALLY KEEP HIDDEN! ♥
OH! LET ME GET YOU A REFILL.
MAU AND I NEVER GET TIME ALONE TOGETHER ANYMORE.
SHUFFLE
Mrr?!
SHUFFLE
I LIKE IT HERE.
SO MANY FLUFFY FAMILIARS...
AHHHH!
BLISSS! ♥

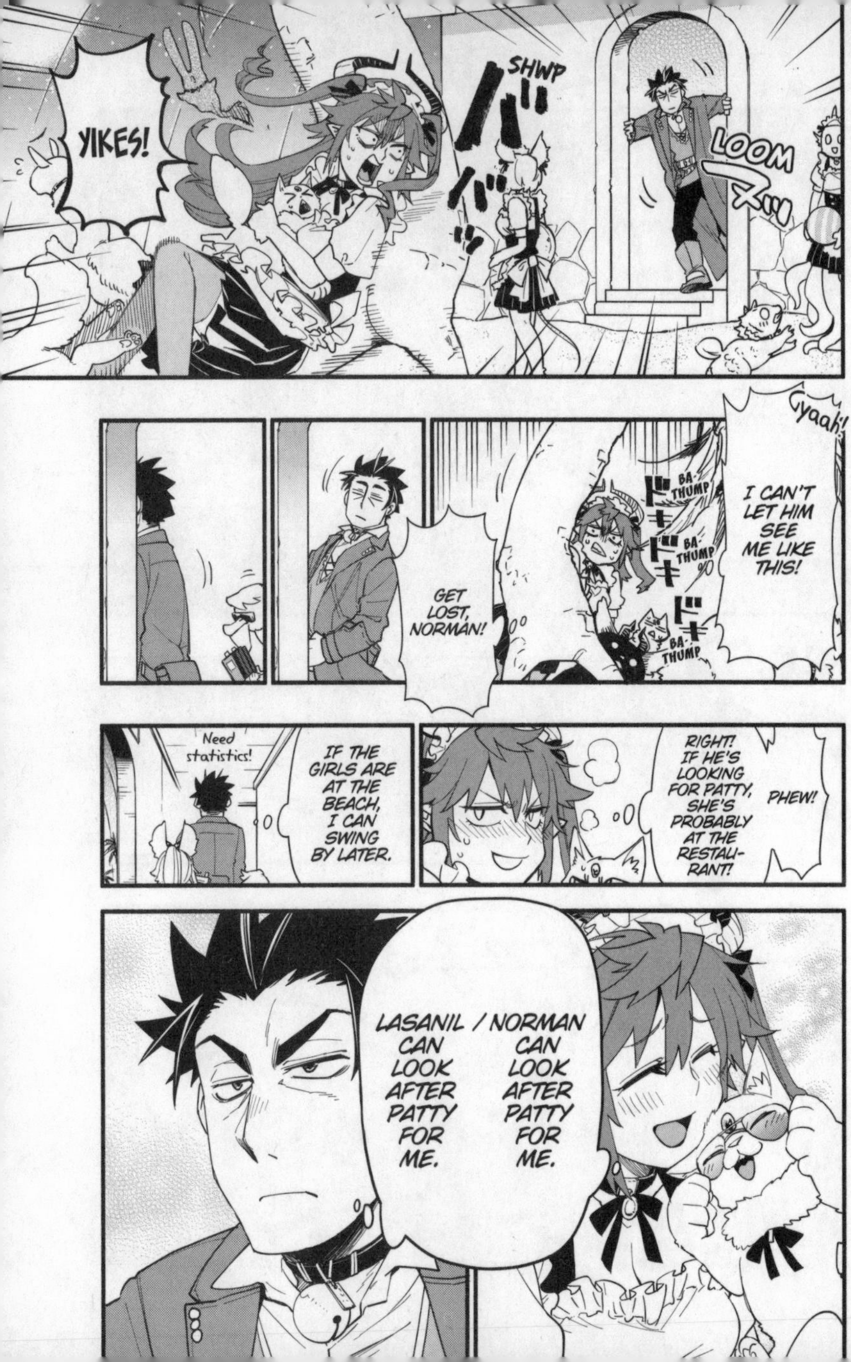
LOOM
SHWP
YIKES!
Gyaah!
I CAN'T LET HIM SEE ME LIKE THIS!
BA-THUMP
BA-THUMP
BA-THUMP
GET LOST, NORMAN!
PHEW!
RIGHT! IF HE'S LOOKING FOR PATTY, SHE'S PROBABLY AT THE RESTAURANT!
IF THE GIRLS ARE AT THE BEACH, I CAN SWING BY LATER.
Need statistics!
LASANIL / NORMAN CAN LOOK AFTER PATTY FOR ME. CAN LOOK AFTER PATTY FOR ME.

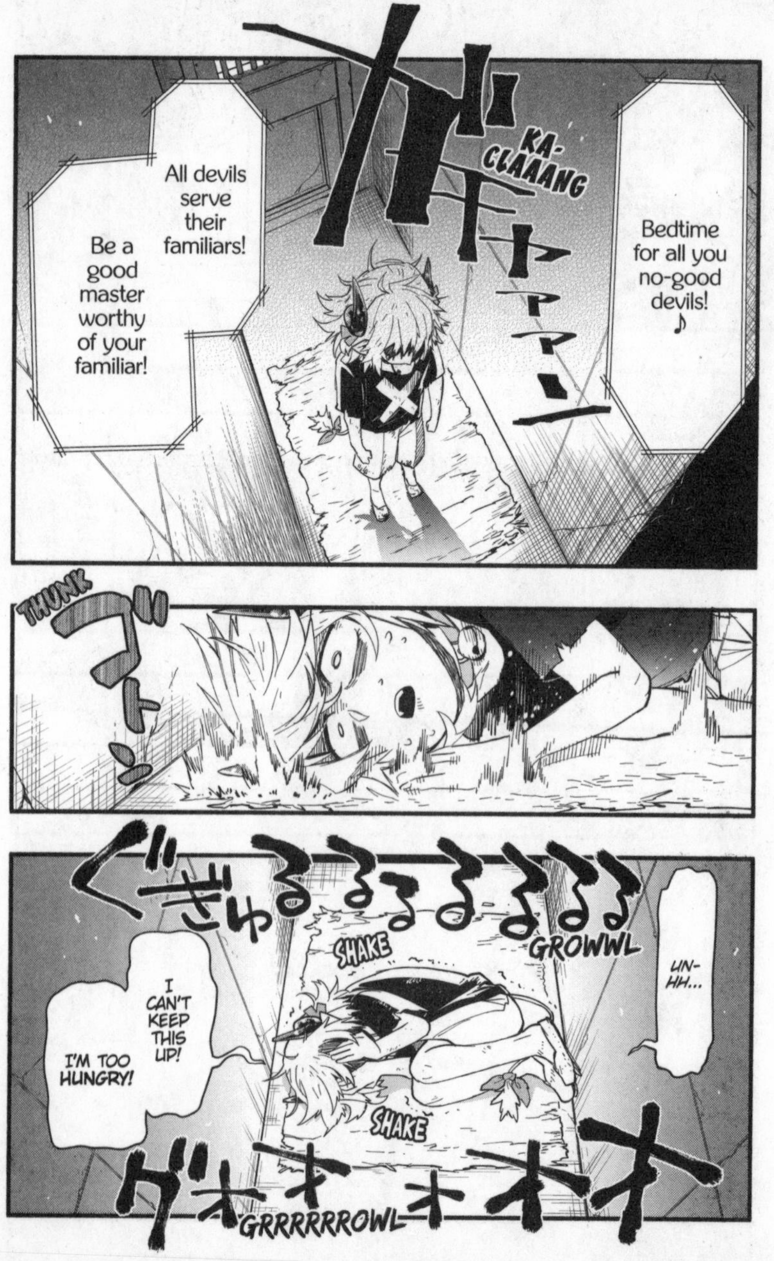
KA-CLAAANG
Bedtime for all you no-good devils! ♪
All devils serve their familiars!
Be a good master worthy of your familiar!
THUNK
GROWWL
SHAKE
UN-HH...
I CAN'T KEEP THIS UP!
I'M TOO HUNGRY!
SHAKE
GRRRRRROWL

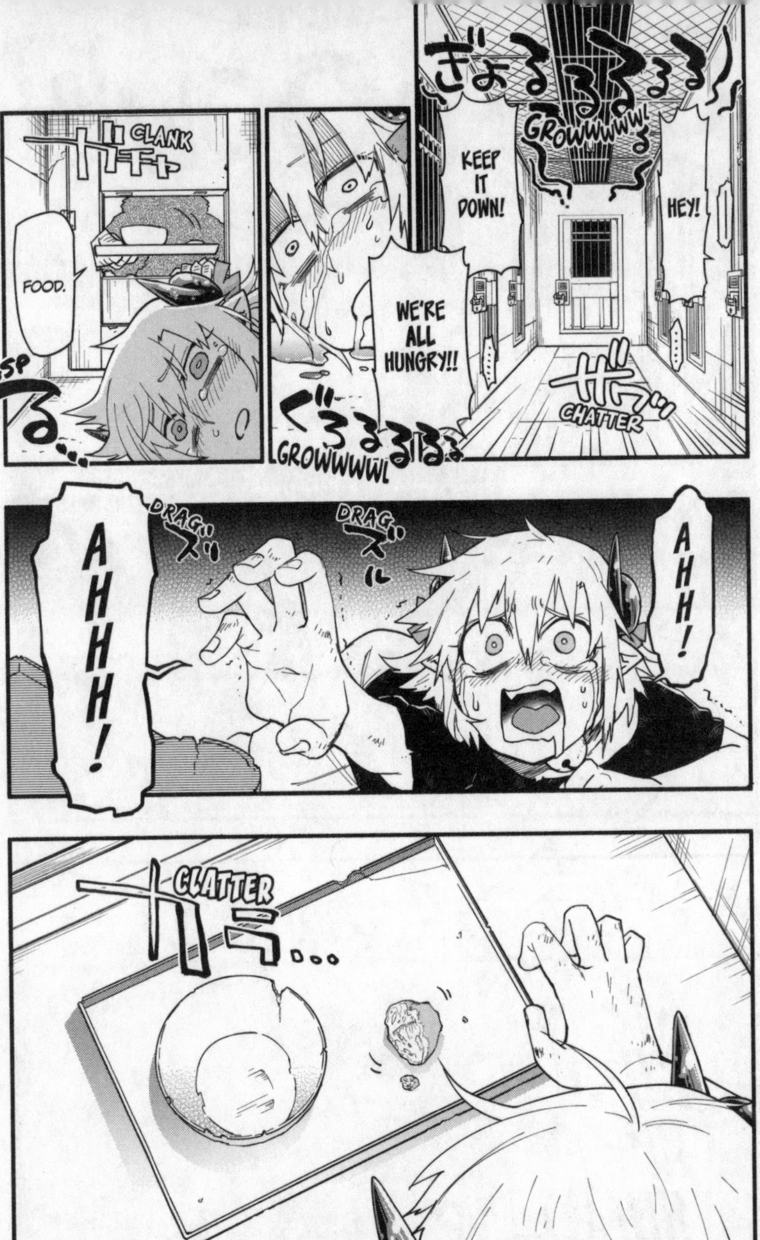
GROWWWWL
KEEP IT DOWN!
HEY!
ザワッ
CHATTER
WE'RE ALL HUNGRY!!
GROWWWWL
CLANK
FOOD.
GASP
AHH!
DRAG
ズル
DRAG
ズリ
AHHHH!
CLATTER
カラ...

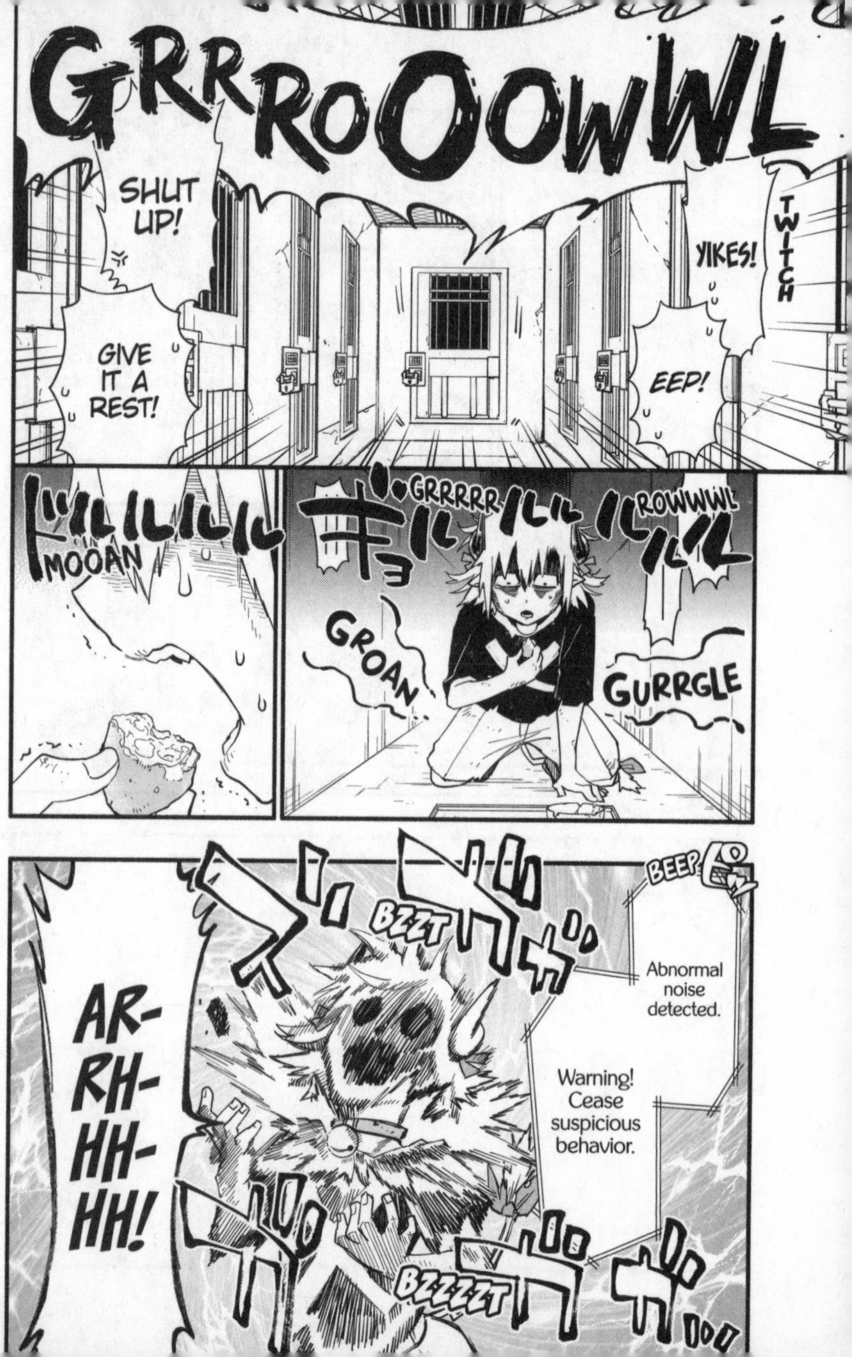
GRRROOOWWL
YIKES!
TWITCH
EEP!
SHUT UP!
GIVE IT A REST!
GRRRRR
ROWWWL
GROAN
GURRGLE
MOOAN
BEEP
BZZT
Abnormal noise detected.
Warning! Cease suspicious behavior.
AR-RH-HH-HH!
BZZZZT

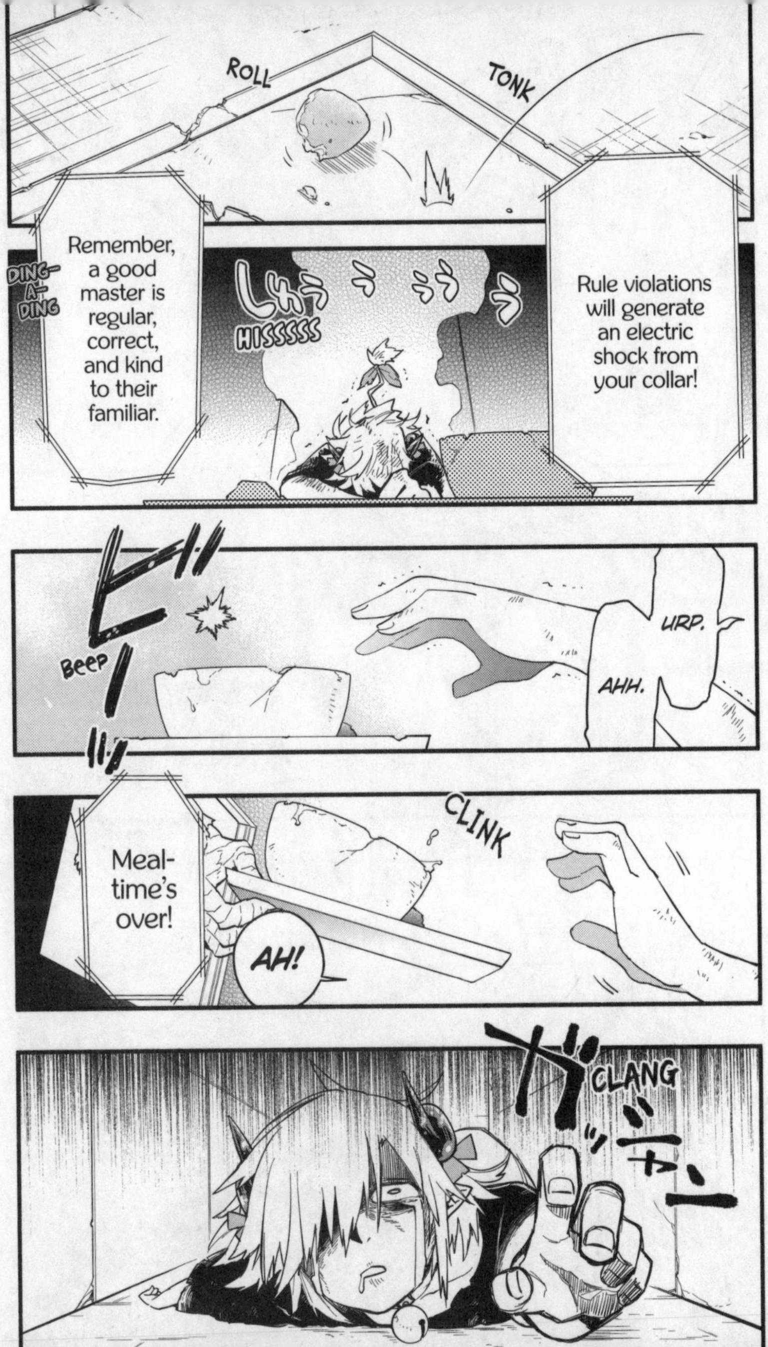
TONK
ROLL
Rule violations will generate an electric shock from your collar!
DING-A-DING
Remember, a good master is regular, correct, and kind to their familiar.
HISSSSS
URP.
AHH.
BEEP
CLINK
Meal-time's over!
AH!
CLANG

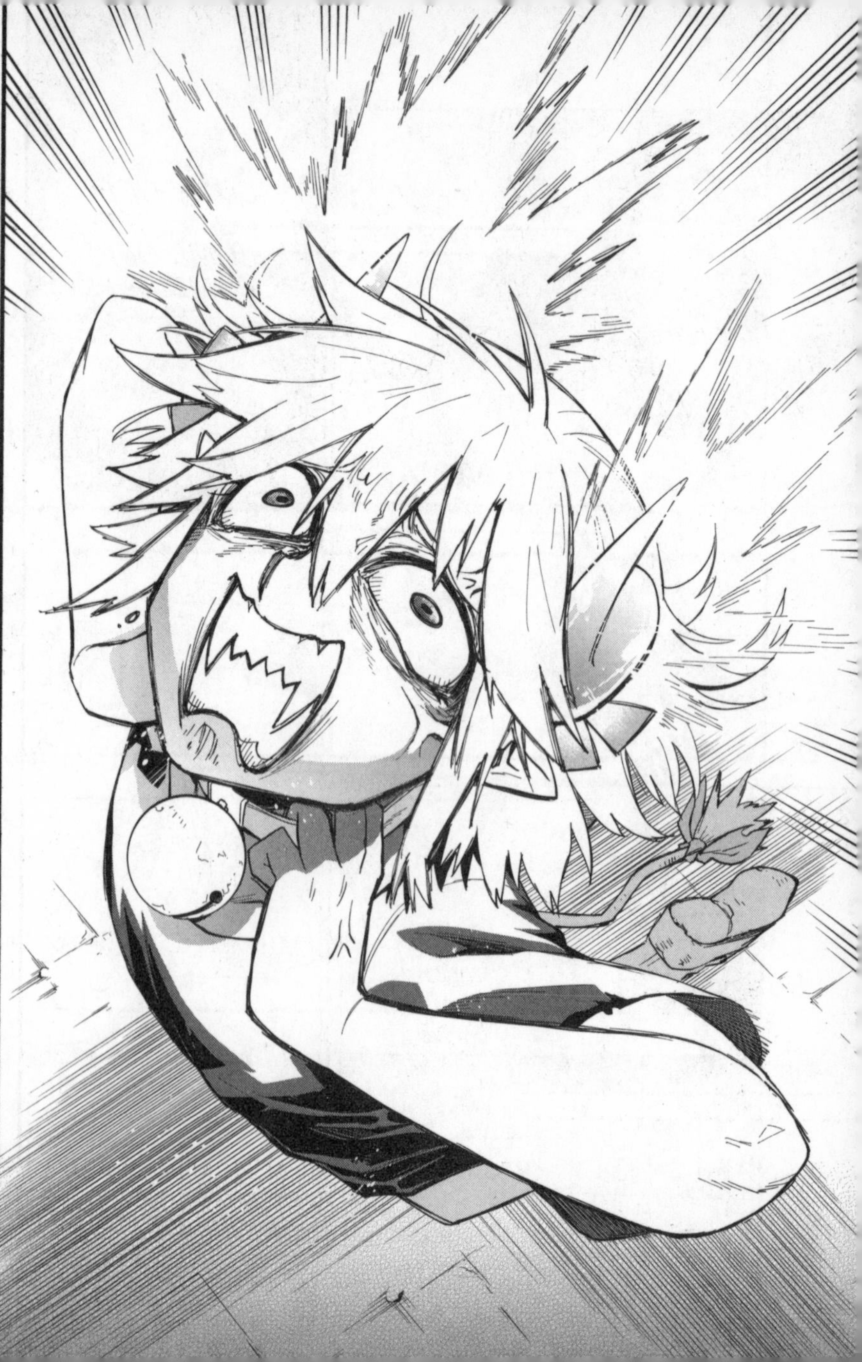

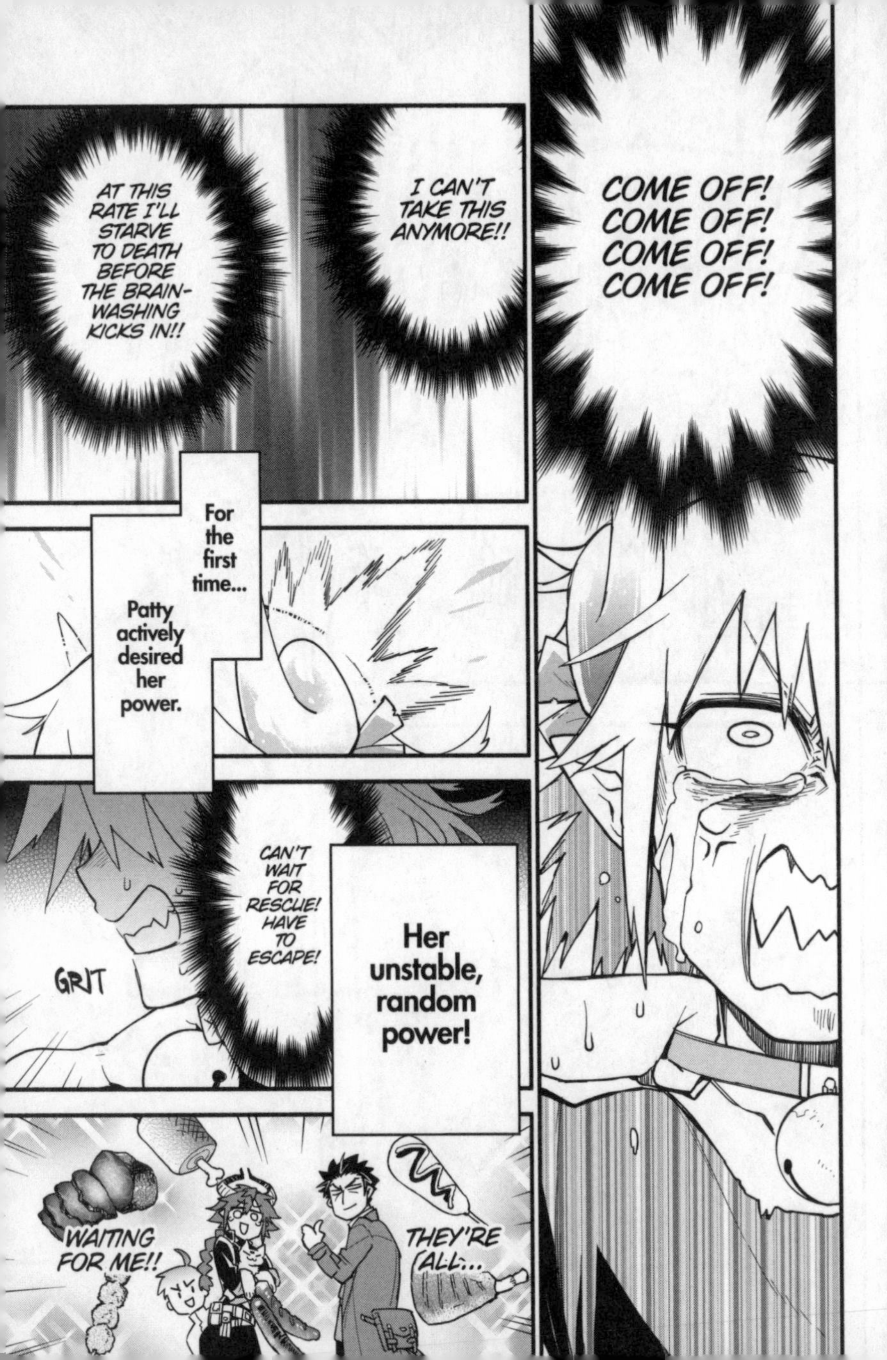

I CAN'T TAKE THIS ANYMORE!!
AT THIS RATE I'LL STARVE TO DEATH BEFORE THE BRAIN-WASHING KICKS IN!!
For the first time...
Patty actively desired her power.
CAN'T WAIT FOR RESCUE! HAVE TO ESCAPE!
GRIT
Her unstable, random power!
THEY'RE ALL...
WAITING FOR ME!!
COME OFF! COME OFF! COME OFF! COME OFF!

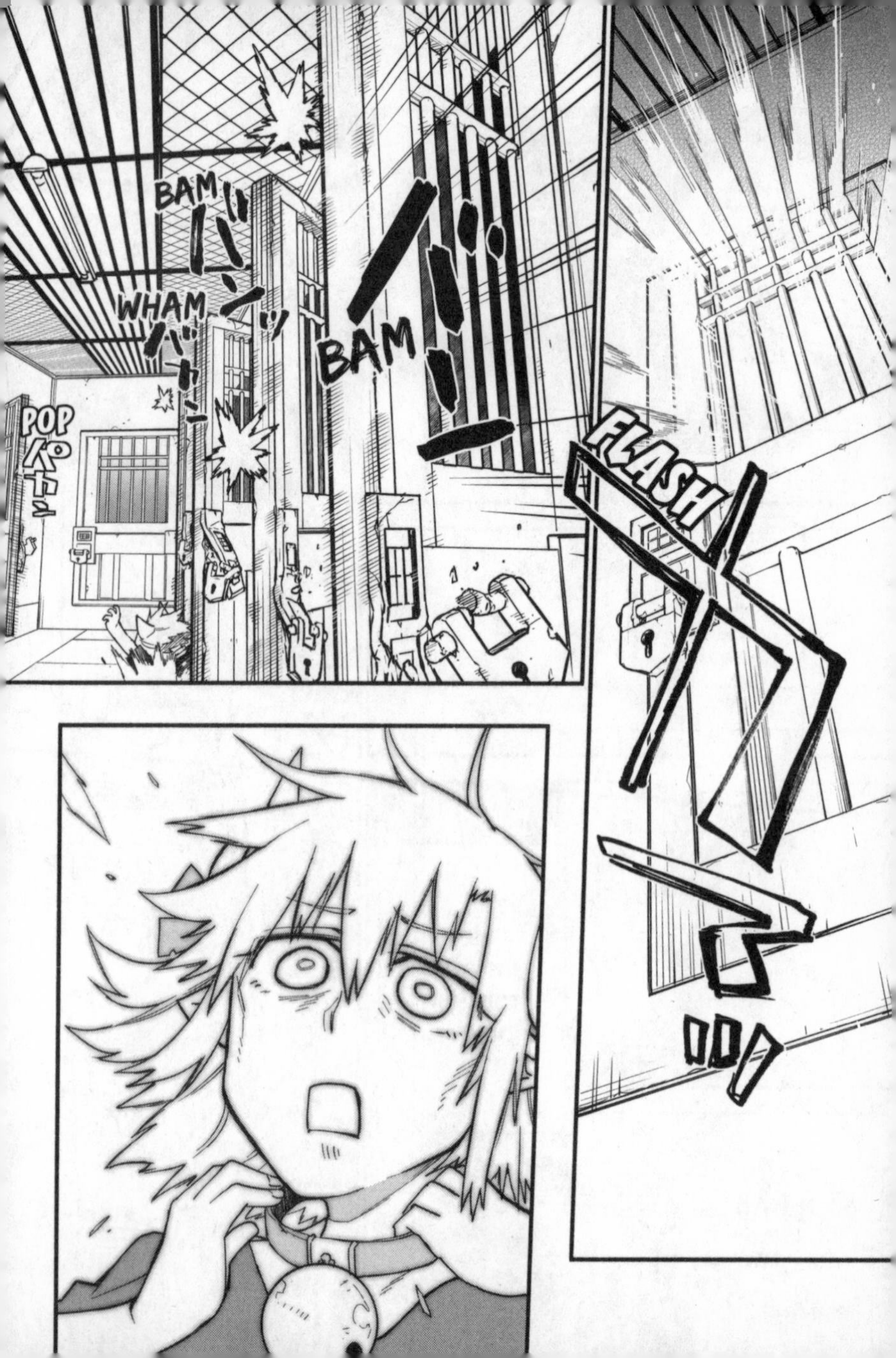
FLASH
BAM
BAM
WHAM
POP

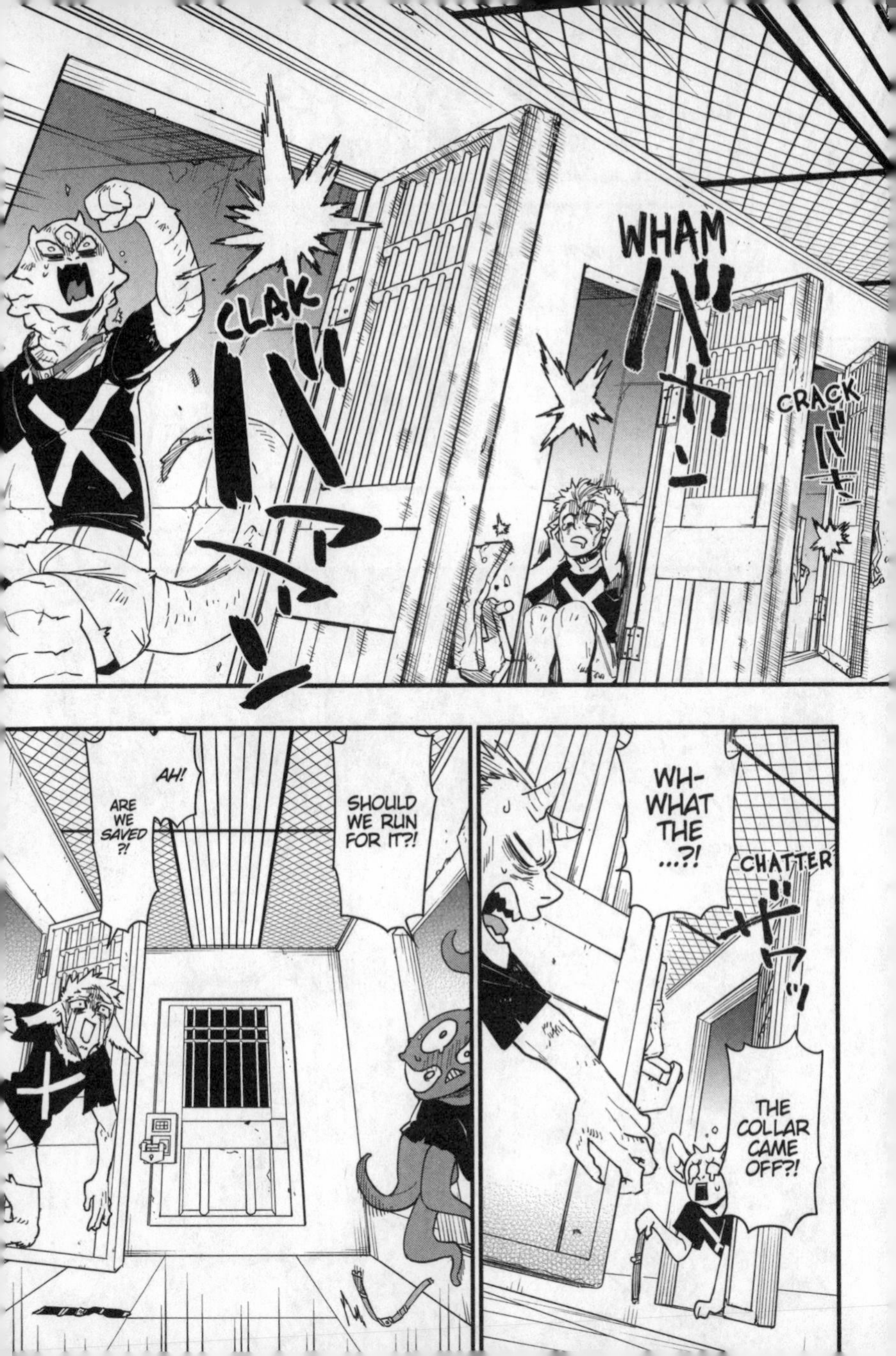
WHAM
CRACK
CLAK
WH- WHAT THE ...?!
CHATTER
THE COLLAR CAME OFF?!
SHOULD WE RUN FOR IT?!
AH!
ARE WE SAVED ?!

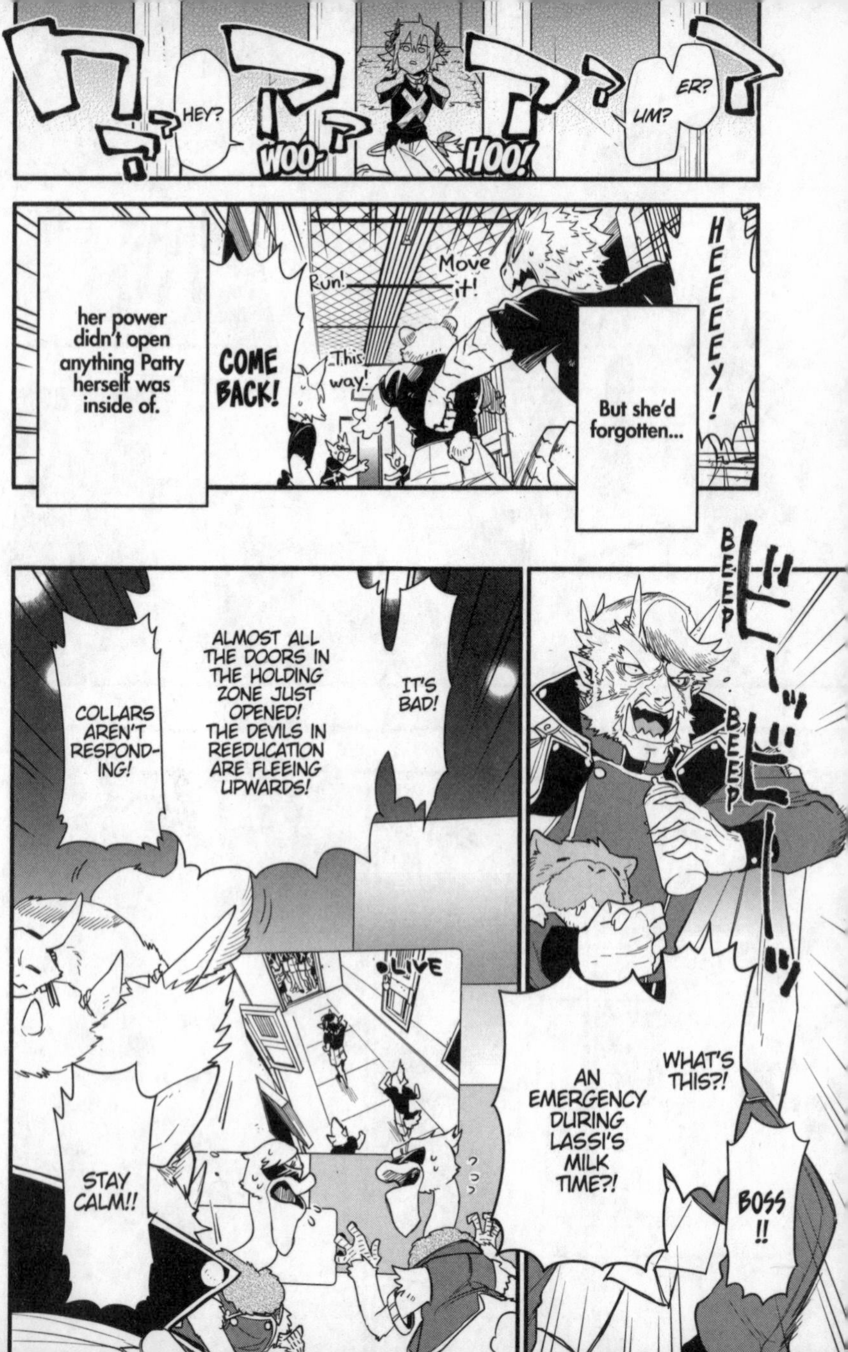
ER?
UM?
WOO-
HOO!
HEY?
HEEEEEY!
But she'd forgotten...
Move it!
Run!
This way!
COME BACK!
her power didn't open anything Patty herself was inside of.
BEEP
BEEP
BOSS!!
WHAT'S THIS?!
AN EMERGENCY DURING LASSI'S MILK TIME?!
IT'S BAD!
ALMOST ALL THE DOORS IN THE HOLDING ZONE JUST OPENED! THE DEVILS IN REEDUCATION ARE FLEEING UPWARDS!
COLLARS AREN'T RESPONDING!
LIVE
STAY CALM!!

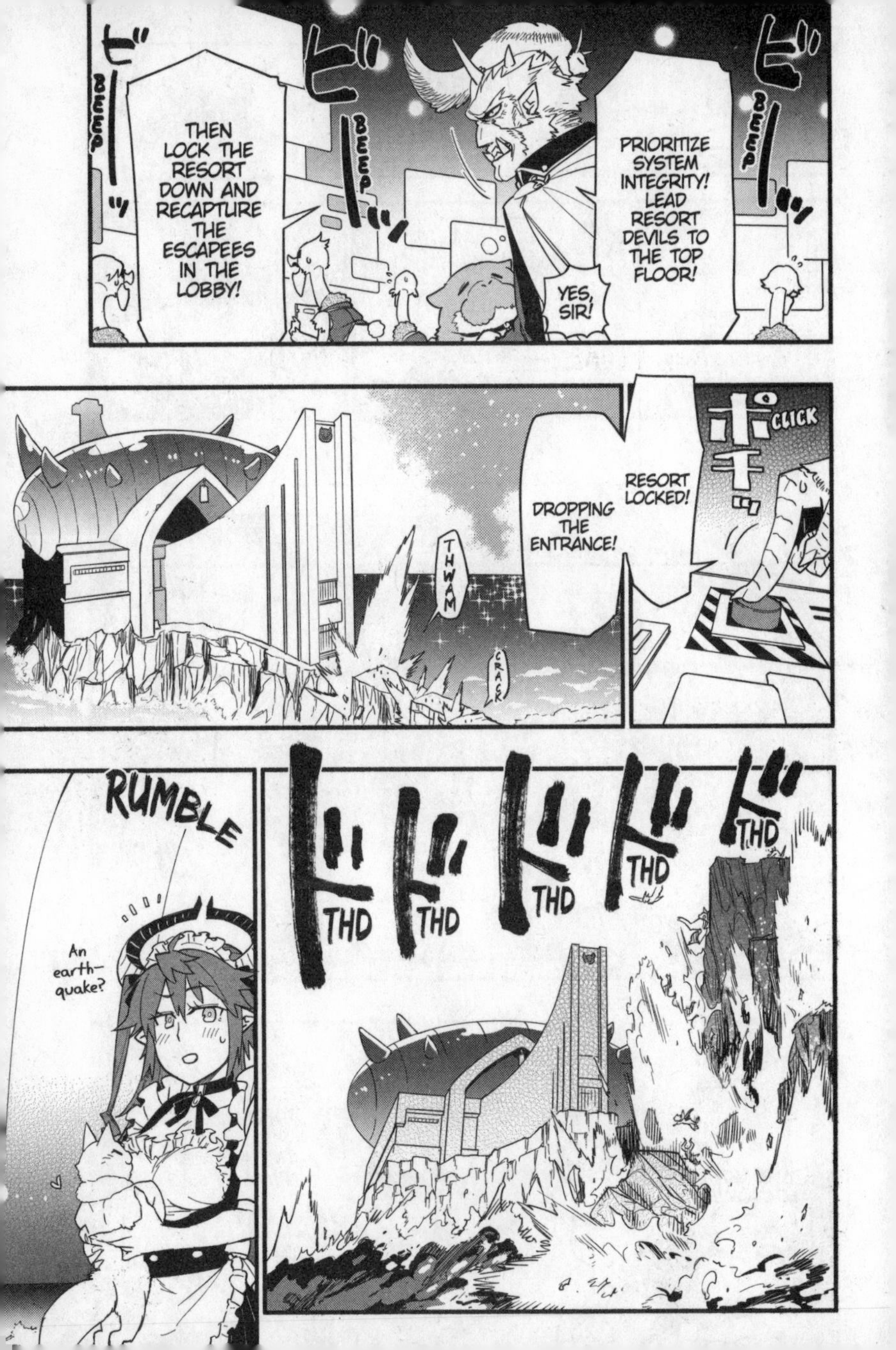
BEEP
PRIORITIZE SYSTEM INTEGRITY! LEAD RESORT DEVILS TO THE TOP FLOOR!
YES, SIR!
BEEP
THEN LOCK THE RESORT DOWN AND RECAPTURE THE ESCAPEES IN THE LOBBY!
BEEP
CLICK
RESORT LOCKED!
DROPPING THE ENTRANCE!
THWAM
CRACK
THD
THD
THD
THD
THD
THD
RUMBLE
An earth-quake?

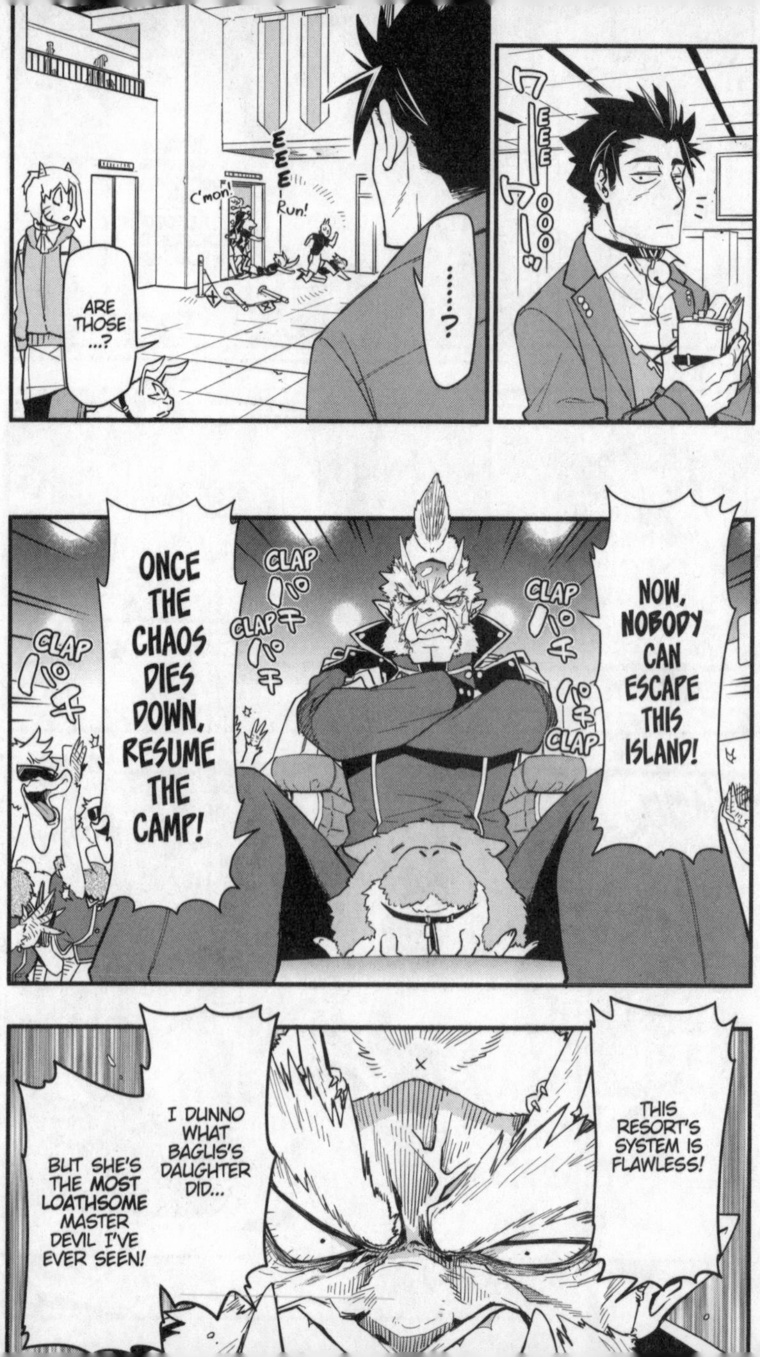

ワEEEーワーOOO!!
っ……
EEEE
C'mon!
Run!
ARE THOSE ...?
NOW, NOBODY CAN ESCAPE THIS ISLAND!
CLAP パチ
CLAP パチ
CLAP パチ
CLAP パチ
ONCE THE CHAOS DIES DOWN, RESUME THE CAMP!
THIS RESORT'S SYSTEM IS FLAWLESS!
I DUNNO WHAT BAGLIS'S DAUGHTER DID...
BUT SHE'S THE MOST LOATHSOME MASTER DEVIL I'VE EVER SEEN!

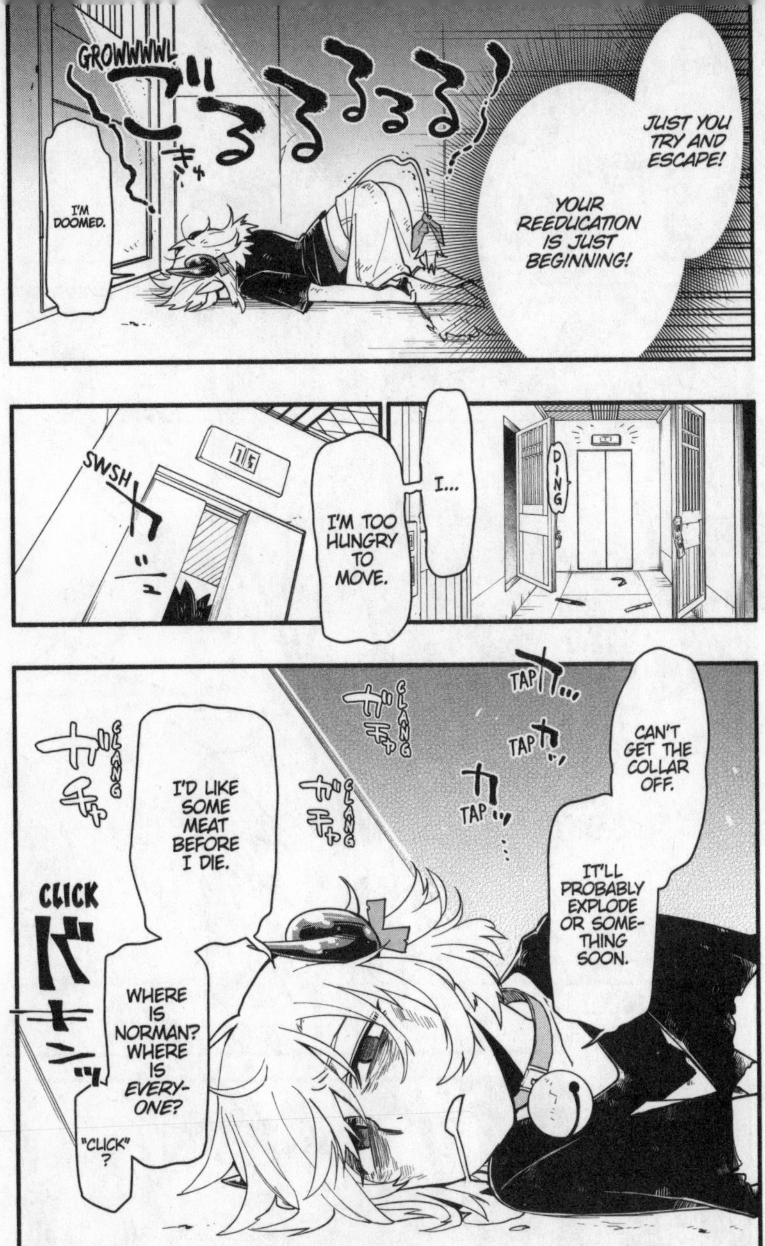

JUST YOU TRY AND ESCAPE!
YOUR REEDUCATION IS JUST BEGINNING!
GROWWWWL
I'M DOOMED.
DING
I...
I'M TOO HUNGRY TO MOVE.
SWSH
TAP
TAP
TAP
CAN'T GET THE COLLAR OFF.
IT'LL PROBABLY EXPLODE OR SOME-THING SOON.
CLANG
CLANG
I'D LIKE SOME MEAT BEFORE I DIE.
CLANG
CLICK
WHERE IS NORMAN? WHERE IS EVERY-ONE?
"CLICK"?

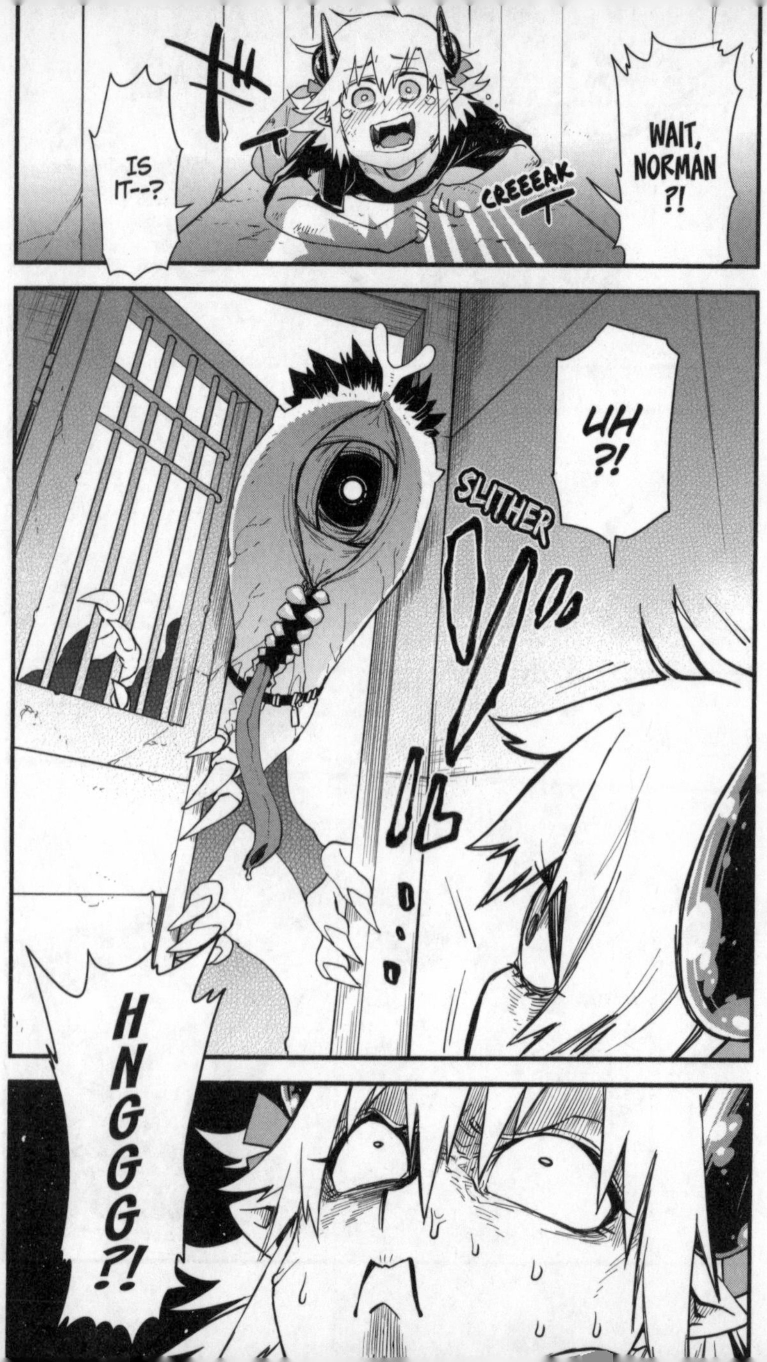
WAIT, NORMAN ?!
CREEEAK
IS IT--?
UH ?!
SLITHER
HNGGGG?!

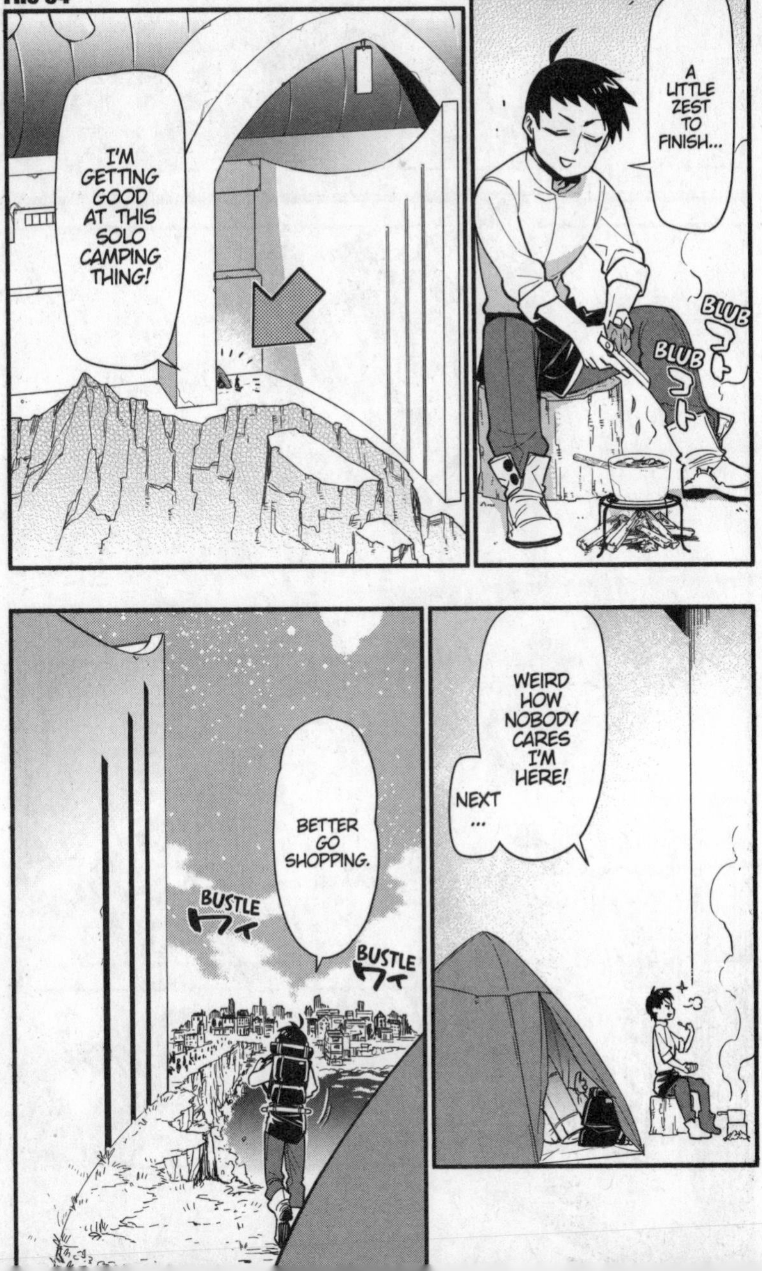
A LITTLE ZEST TO FINISH...
BLUB コト
BLUB コト
I'M GETTING GOOD AT THIS SOLO CAMPING THING!
WEIRD HOW NOBODY CARES I'M HERE!
NEXT ...
BETTER GO SHOPPING.
BUSTLE ワイ
BUSTLE ワイ

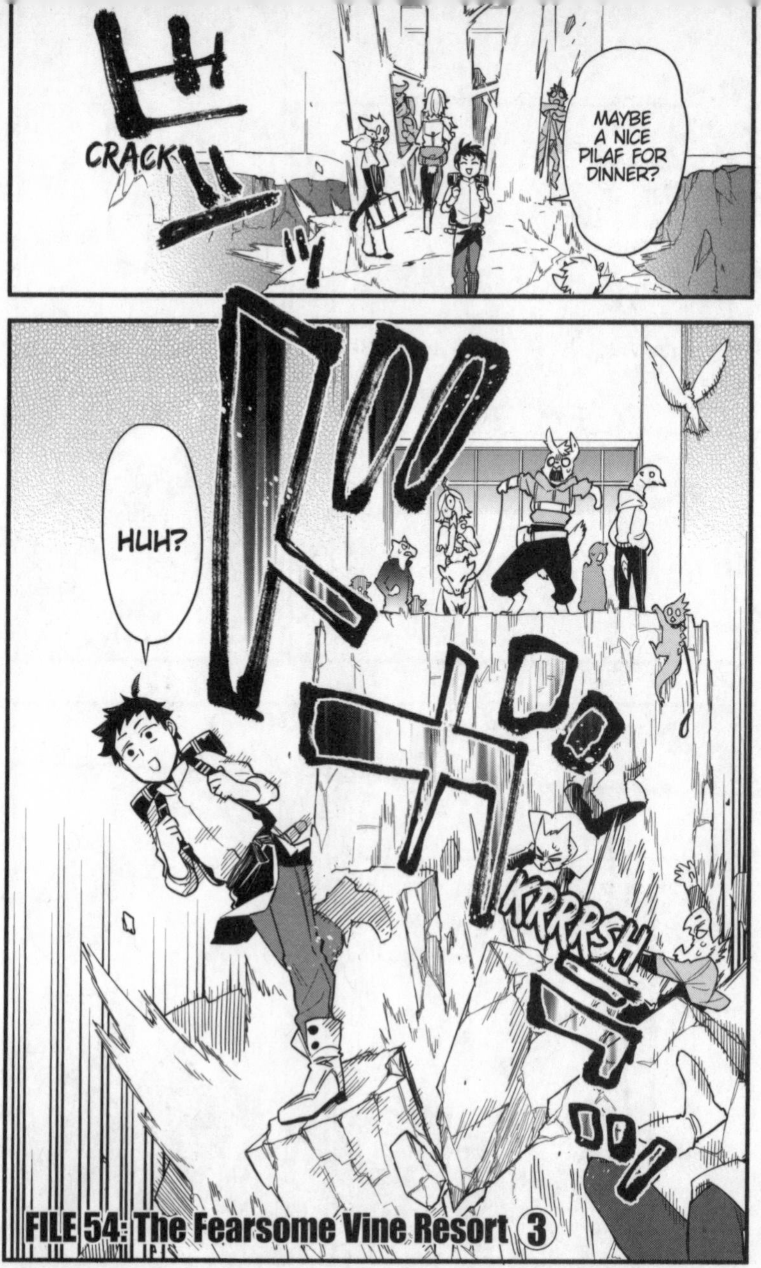
CRACK
MAYBE A NICE PILAF FOR DINNER?
HUH?
KRRRSH
FILE 54: The Fearsome Vine Resort 3

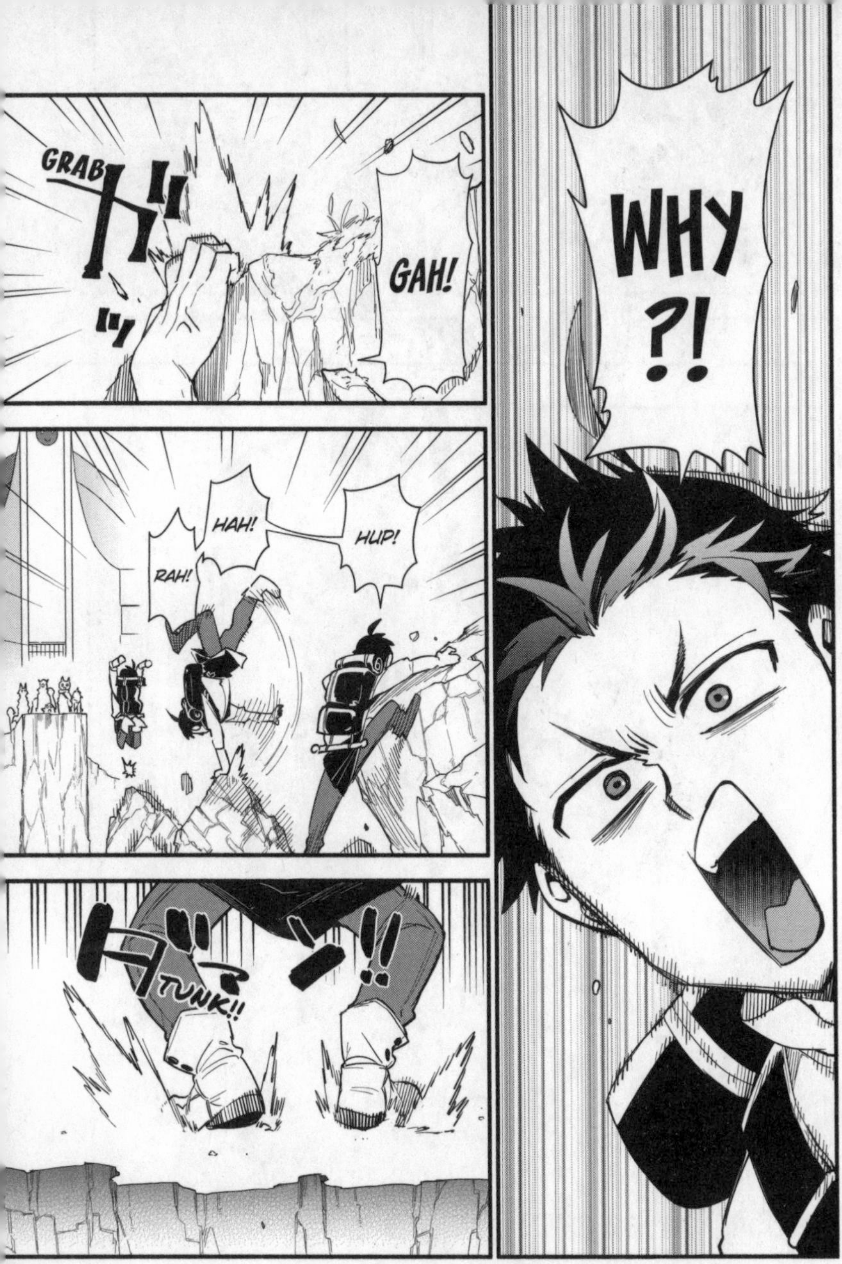
WHY ?!
GAH!
GRAB
HUP!
HAH!
RAH!
TUNK!!

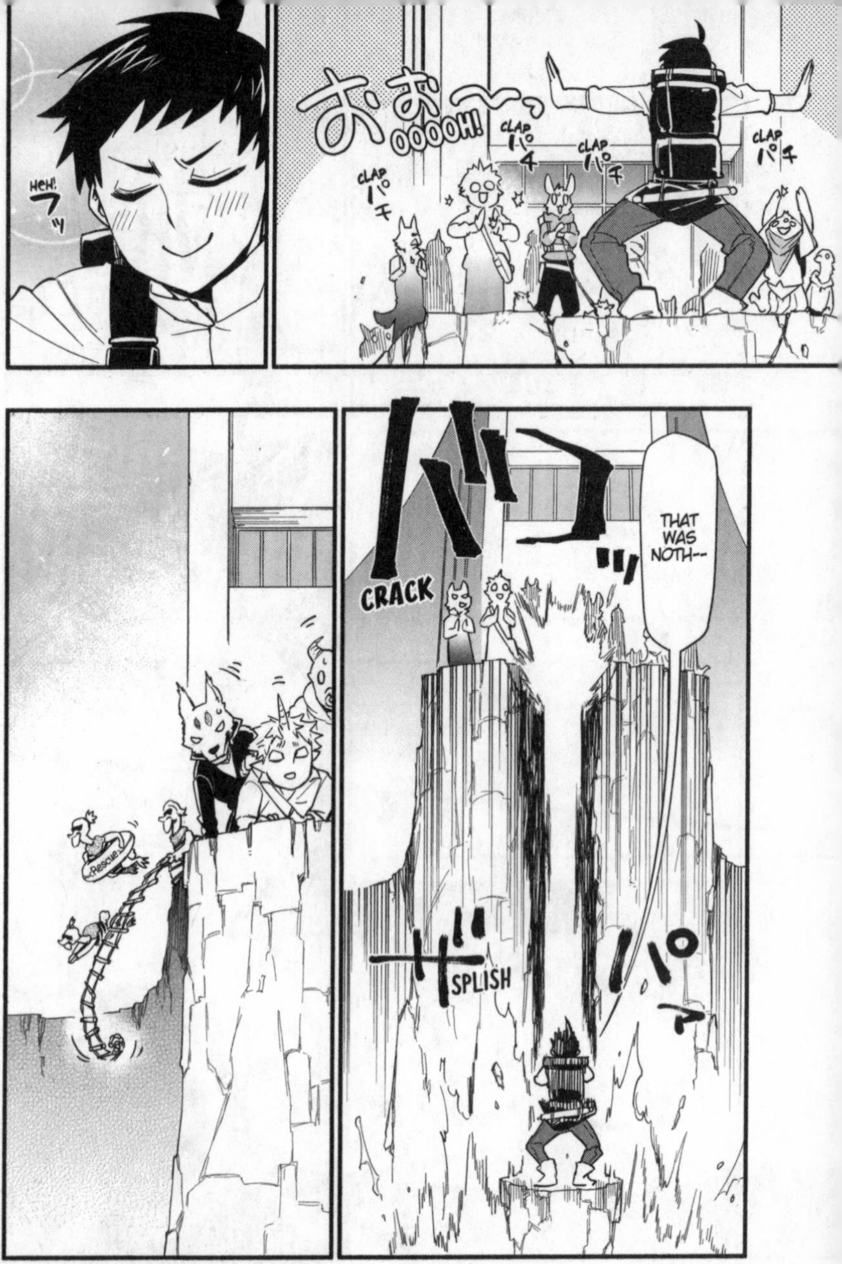

おお〜っ
OOOOH!
CLAP
パチ
CLAP
パチ
CLAP
パチ
CLAP
パチ
HEH!
フッ
THAT WAS NOTH--
バコッ
CRACK
ザ
SPLISH
Rescue

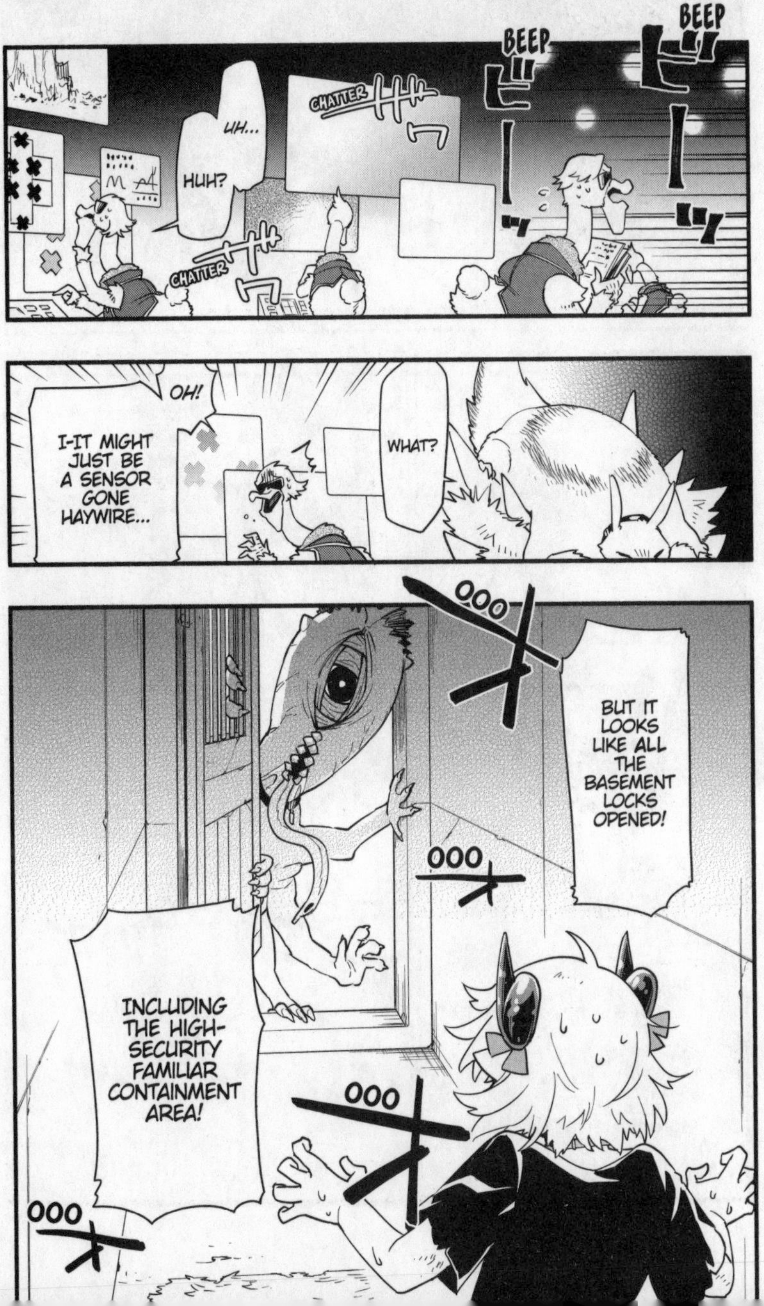
BEEP
BEEP
CHATTER
UH...
HUH?
CHATTER
WHAT?
OH!
I-IT MIGHT JUST BE A SENSOR GONE HAYWIRE...
OOO
BUT IT LOOKS LIKE ALL THE BASEMENT LOCKS OPENED!
OOO
INCLUDING THE HIGH-SECURITY FAMILIAR CONTAINMENT AREA!
OOO
OOO

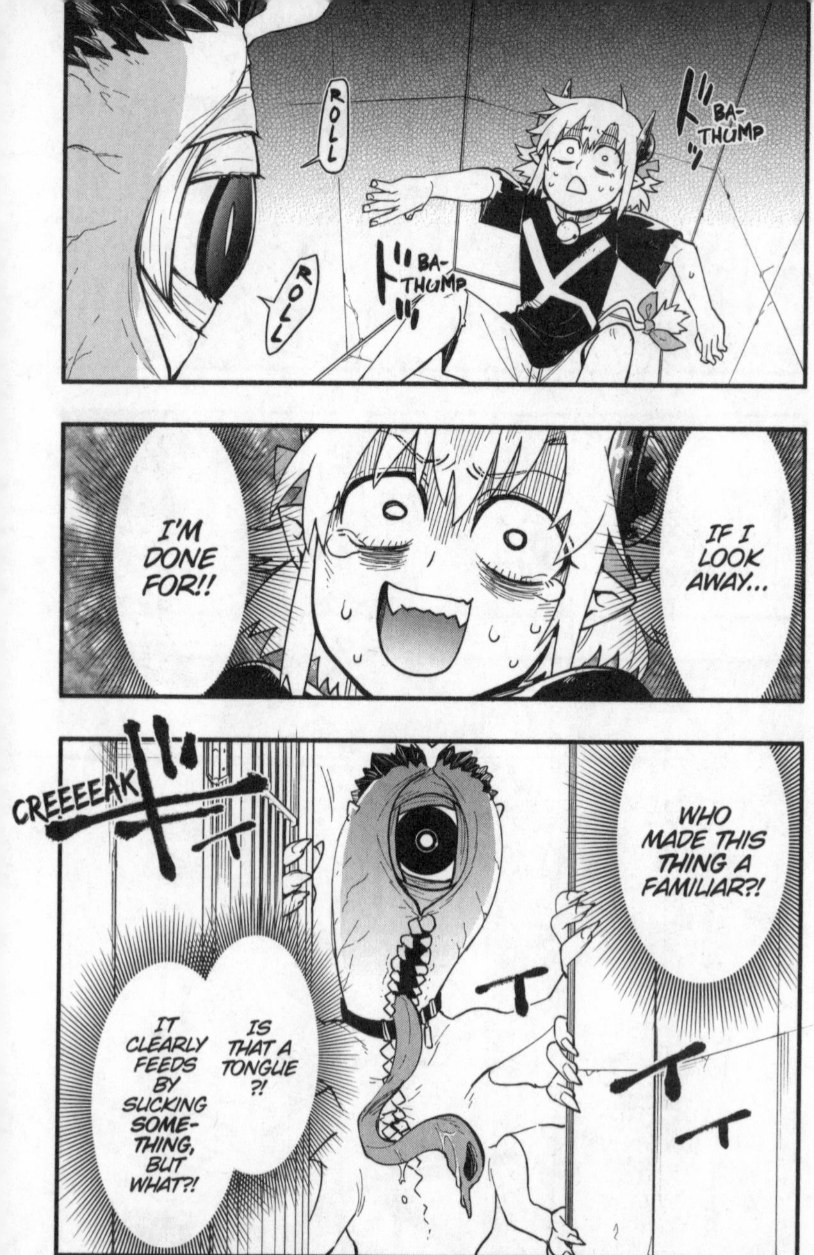
BA-THUMP
ROLL
ROLL
BA-THUMP
IF I LOOK AWAY...
I'M DONE FOR!!
WHO MADE THIS THING A FAMILIAR?!
CREEEEAK
IS THAT A TONGUE?!
IT CLEARLY FEEDS BY SUCKING SOMETHING, BUT WHAT?!

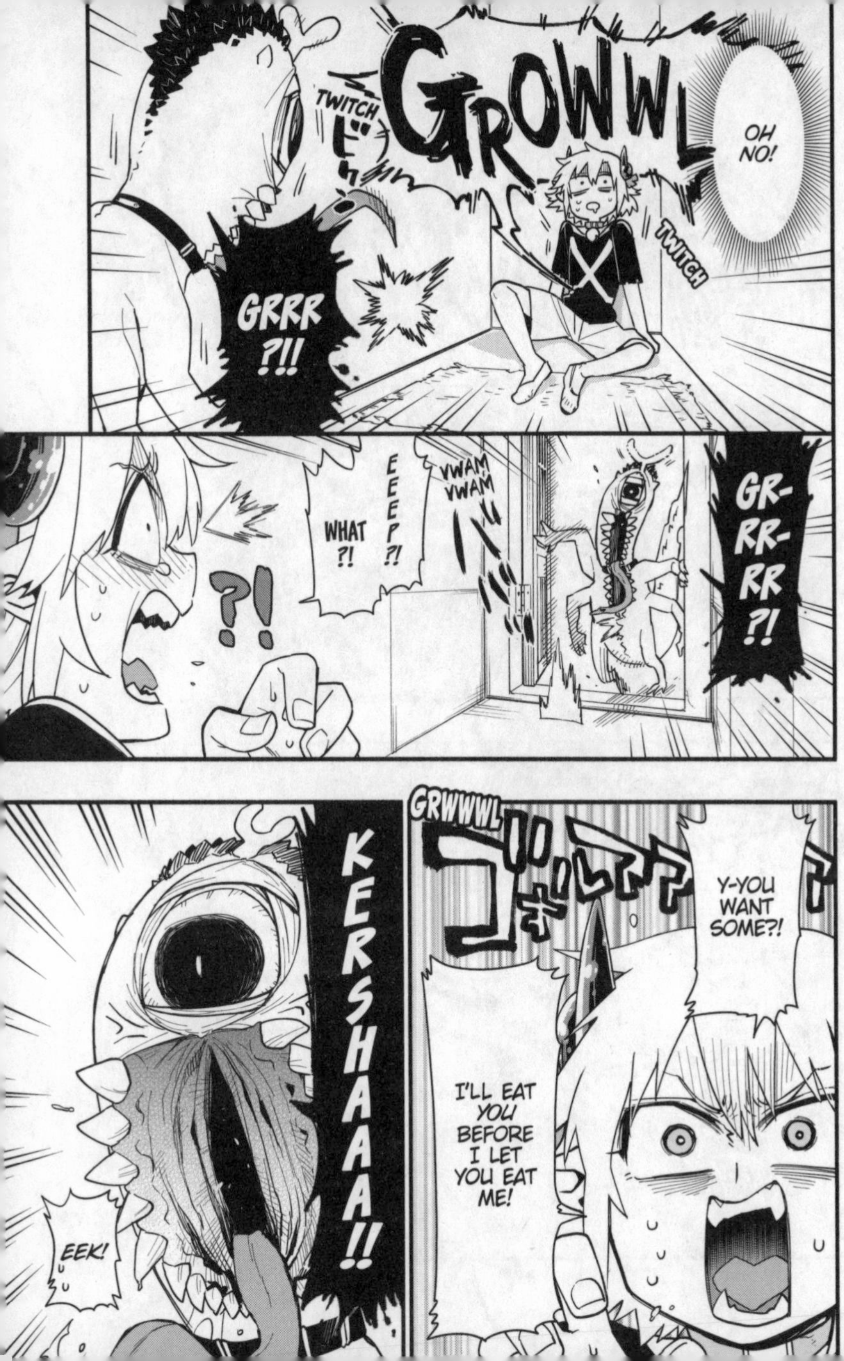
OH NO!
GROWWL
TWITCH
TWITCH
GRRR ?!!
GR-RR-RR ?!
VWAM VWAM
EEEEP ?!
WHAT ?!
GRWWL
Y-YOU WANT SOME?!
I'LL EAT YOU BEFORE I LET YOU EAT ME!
KERSHAAAA!!
EEK!

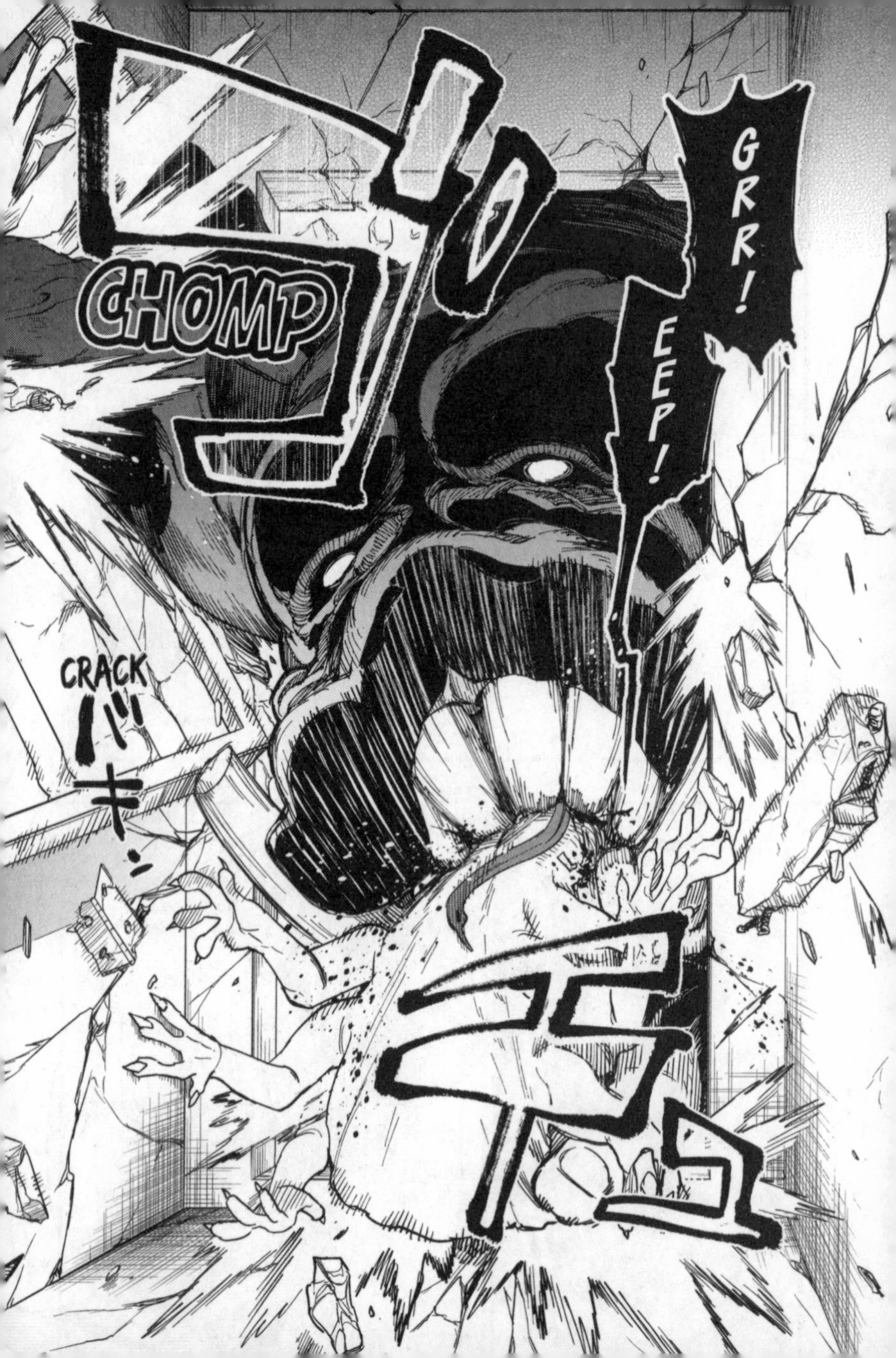
GRR!
EEP!
CHOMP
CRACK
バキッ

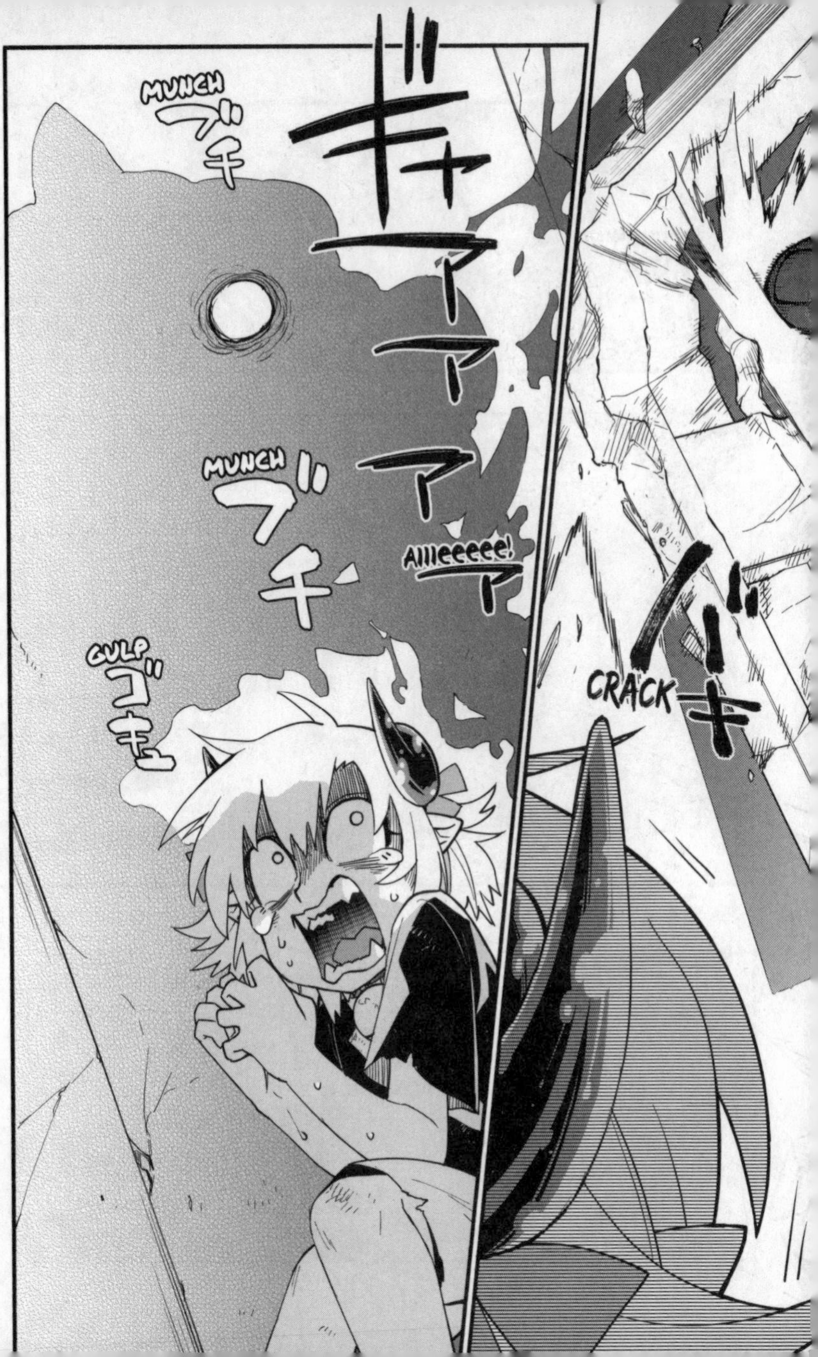
ギャアァアァ
Allleeeee!
MUNCH
ブチ
MUNCH
ブチ
GULP
ゴキュ
バキ
CRACK

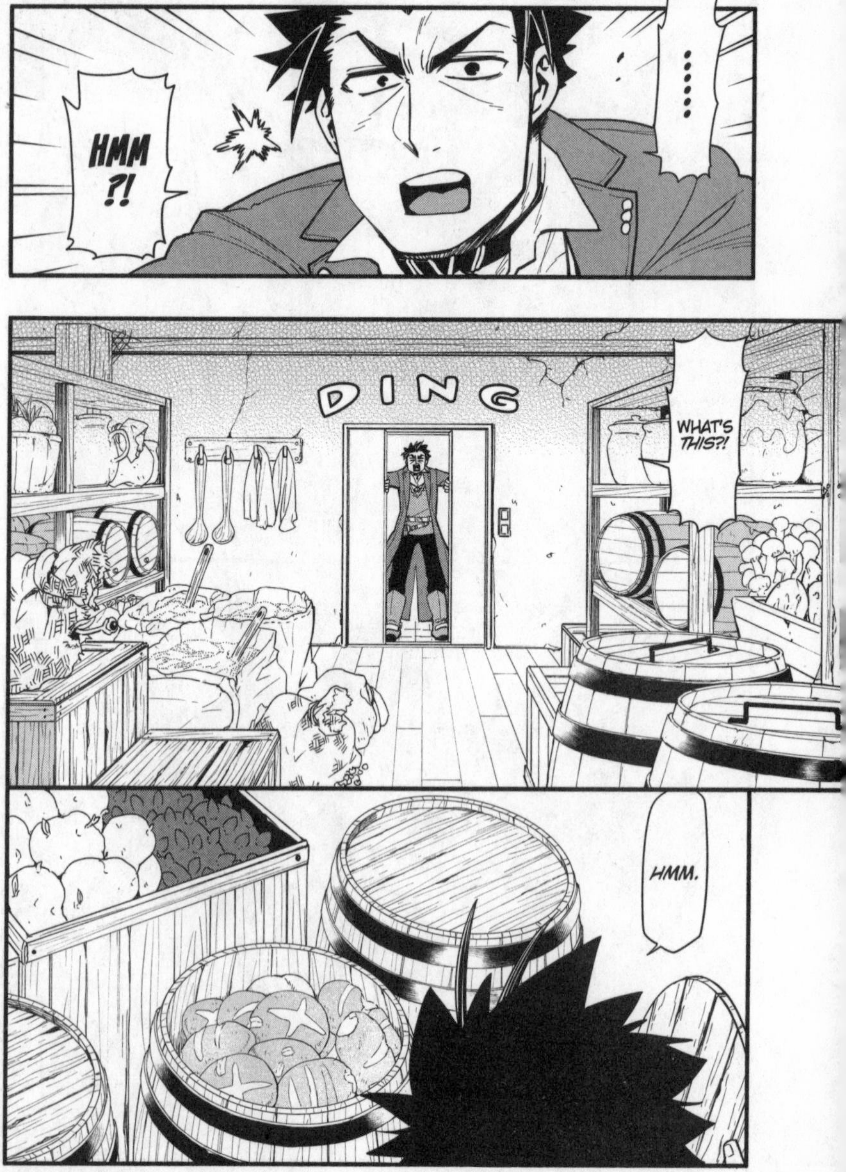
!
......
HMM ?!
DING
WHAT'S THIS?!
HMM.

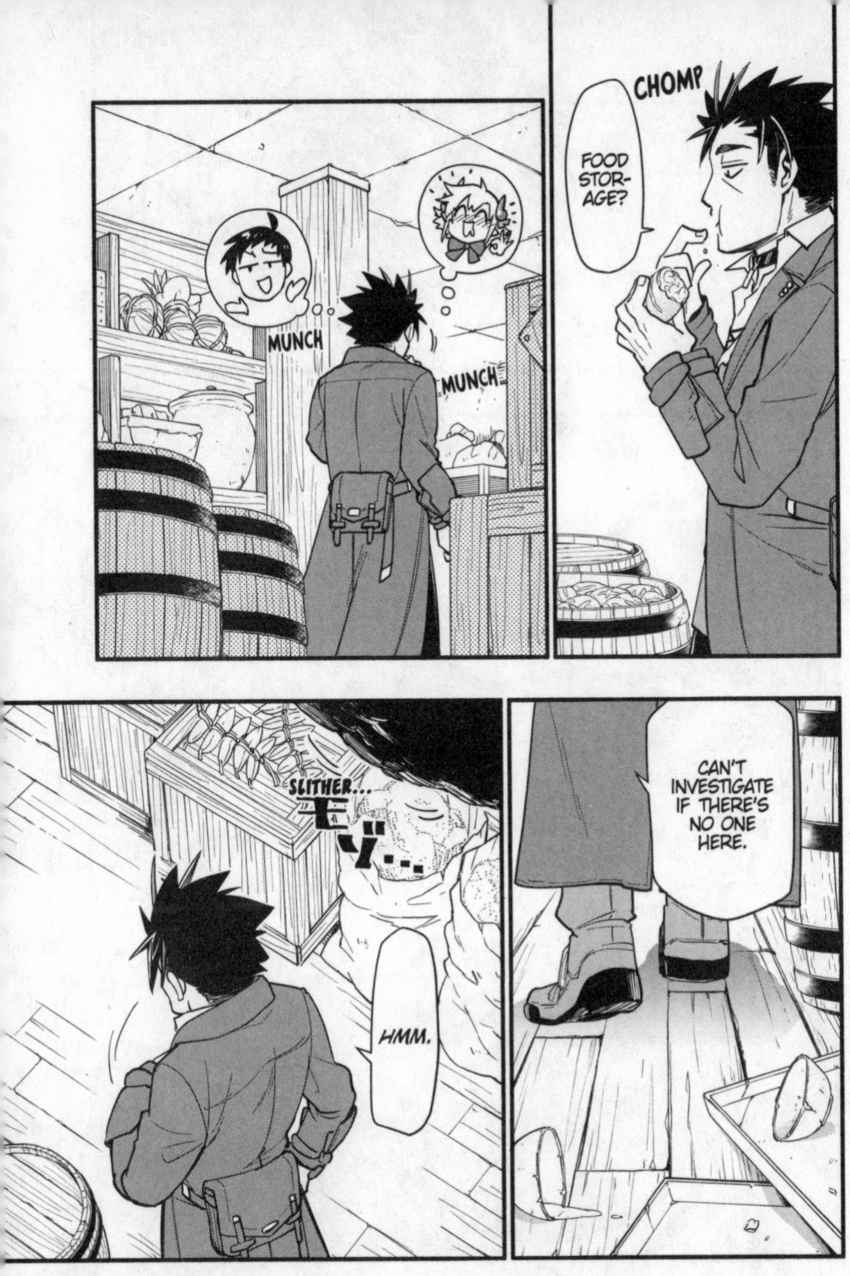
CHOMP
FOOD STOR-AGE?
MUNCH
MUNCH
CAN'T INVESTIGATE IF THERE'S NO ONE HERE.
SLITHER...
HMM.

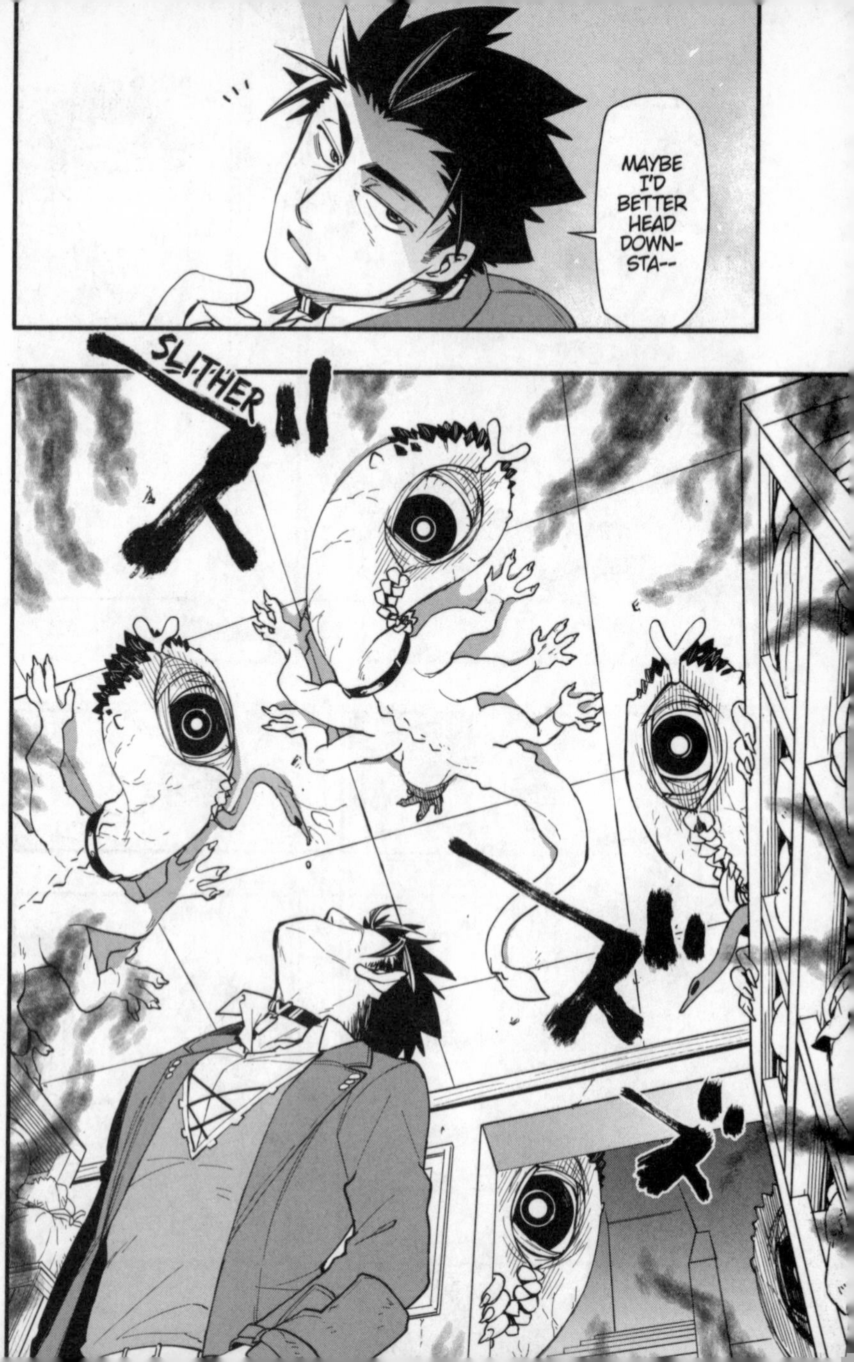
MAYBE I'D BETTER HEAD DOWN-STA--
SLITHER

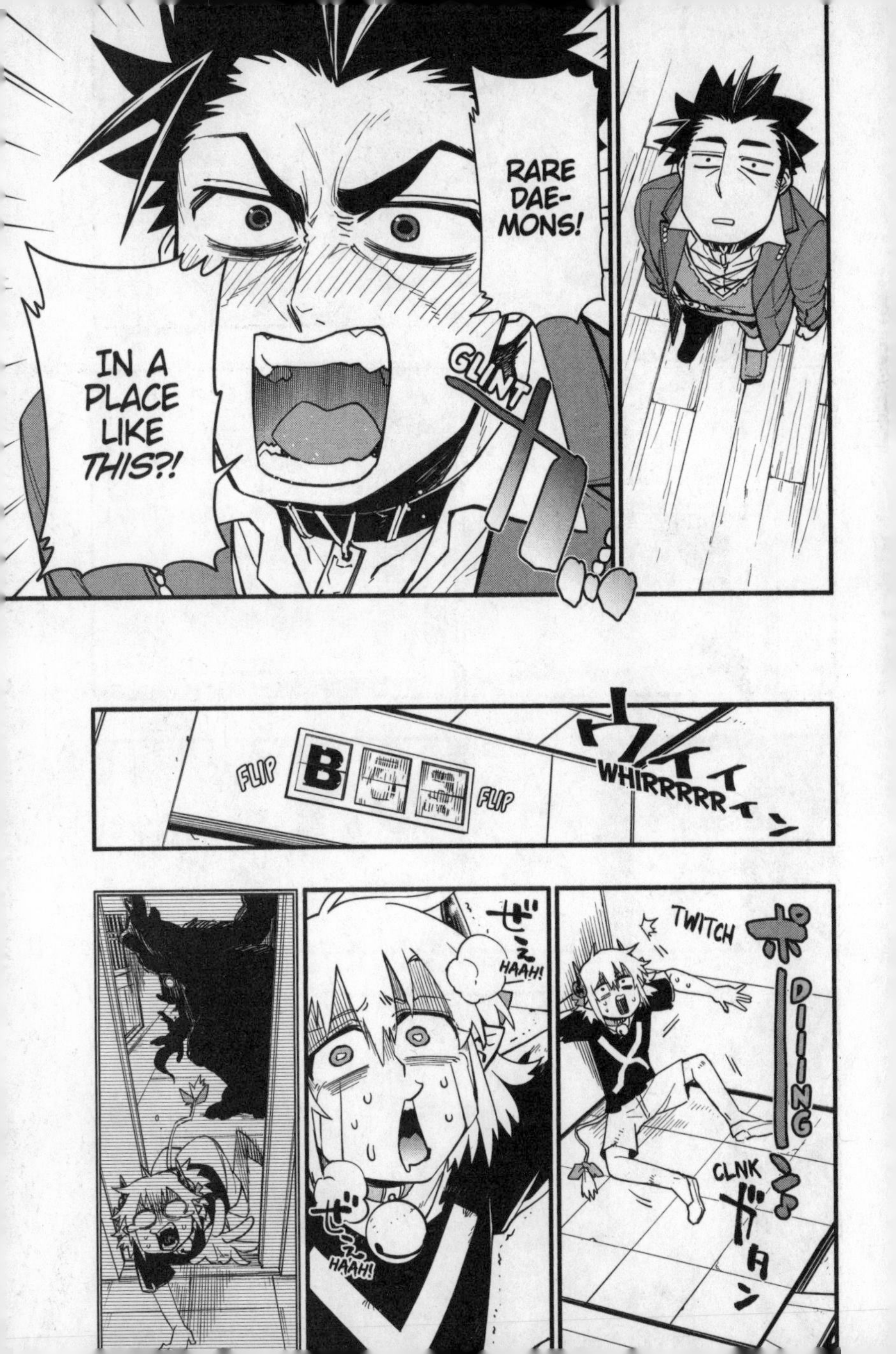
RARE DAE-MONS!
IN A PLACE LIKE THIS?!
GLINT
WHIRRRRRR
FLIP
B
FLIP
TWITCH
DIIIING
CLNK
HAAH!
HAAH!

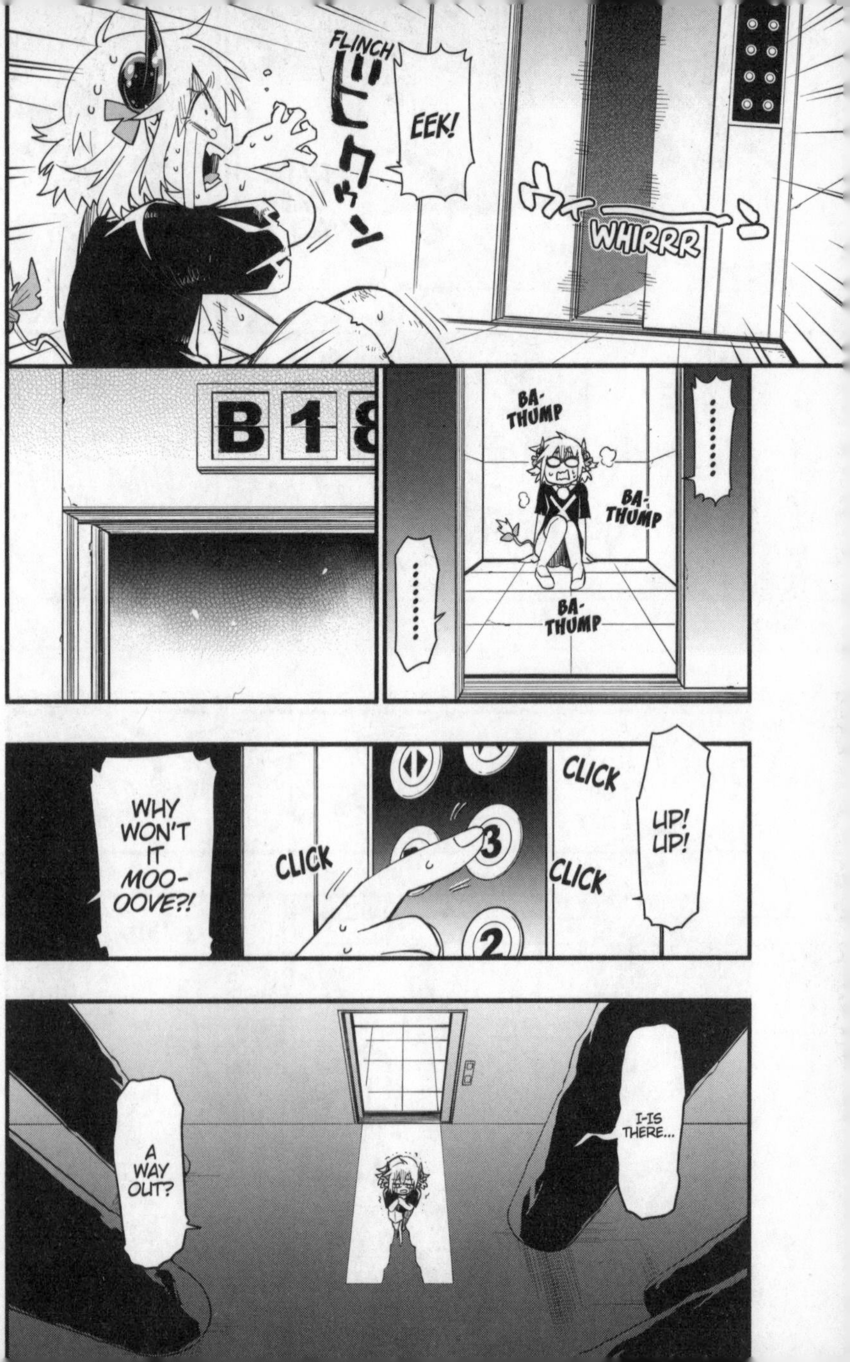
WHIRRR
EEK!
FLINCH
ビクゥン
......
BA-THUMP
BA-THUMP
BA-THUMP
......
B18
UP! UP!
CLICK
CLICK
CLICK
WHY WON'T IT MOOOOVE?!
I-IS THERE...
A WAY OUT?

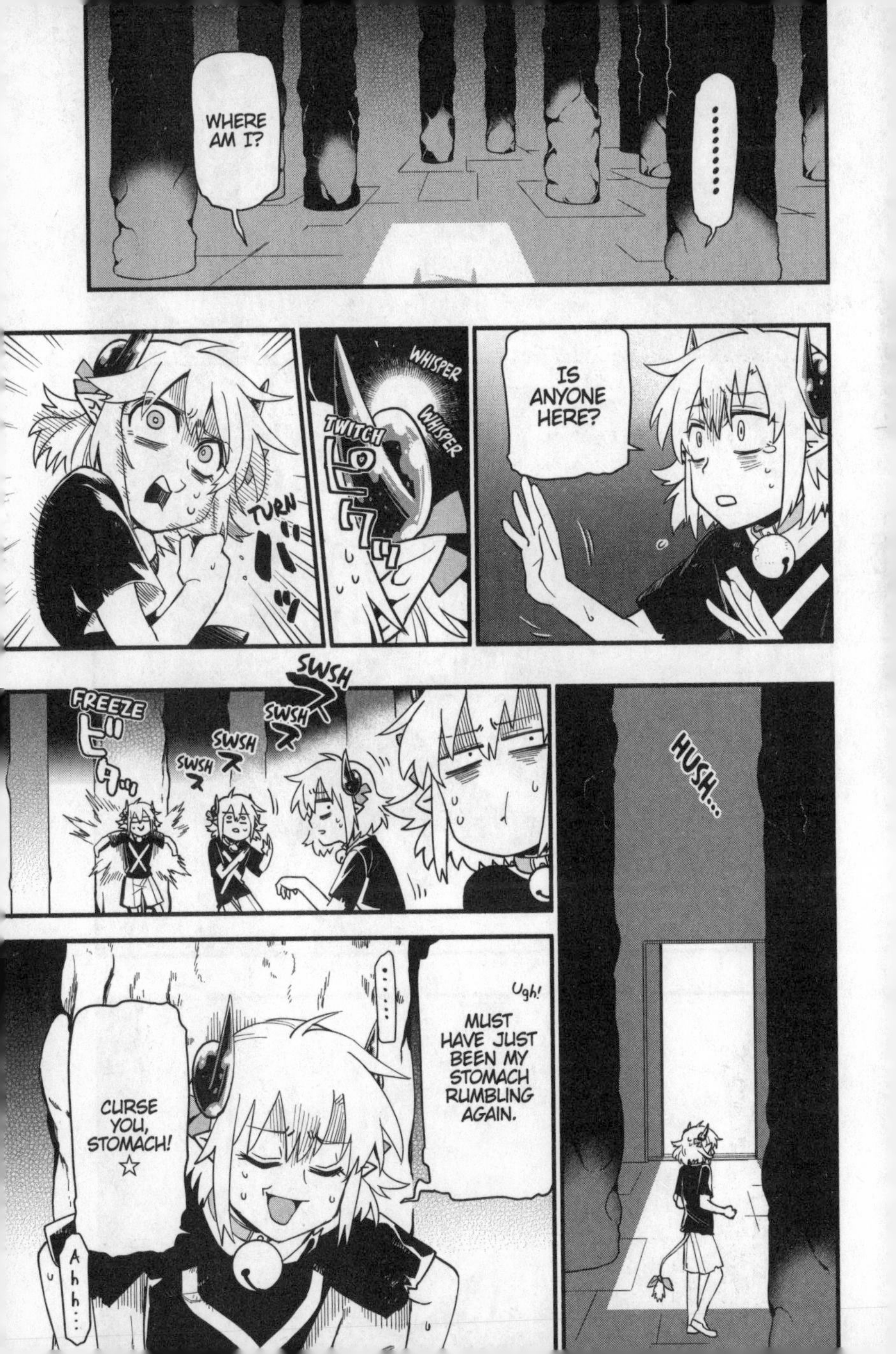
....
WHERE AM I?
IS ANYONE HERE?
WHISPER
WHISPER
TWITCH
TURN
HUSH...
SWSH
SWSH
SWSH
SWSH
FREEZE
Ugh!
MUST HAVE JUST BEEN MY STOMACH RUMBLING AGAIN.
......
CURSE YOU, STOMACH! ☆
Ahh...

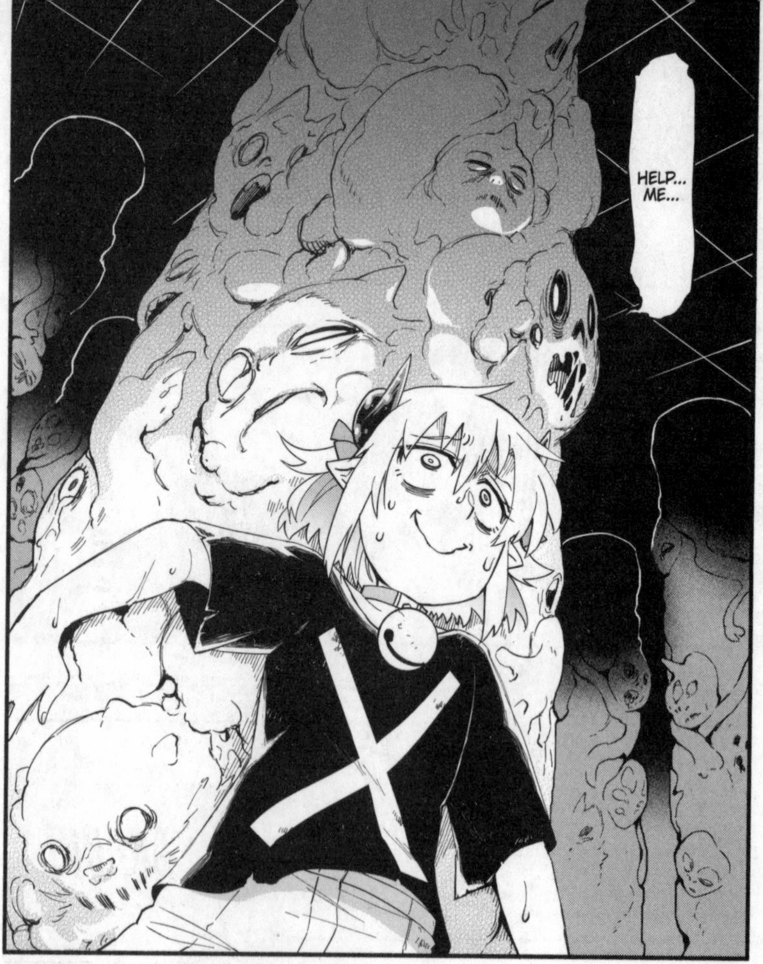
HELP... ME...
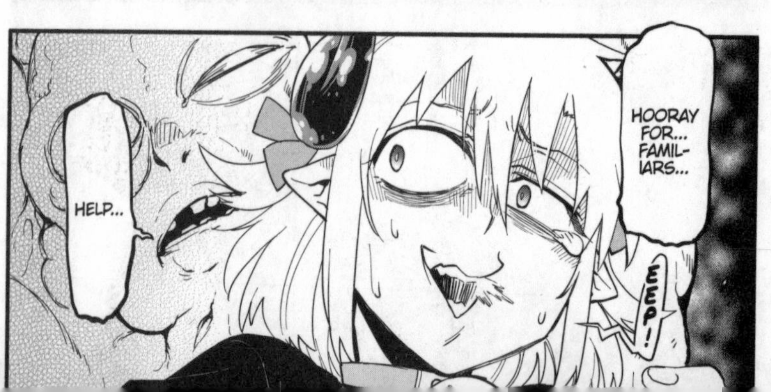
HOORAY FOR... FAMIL-IARS...
HELP...
EEEP!

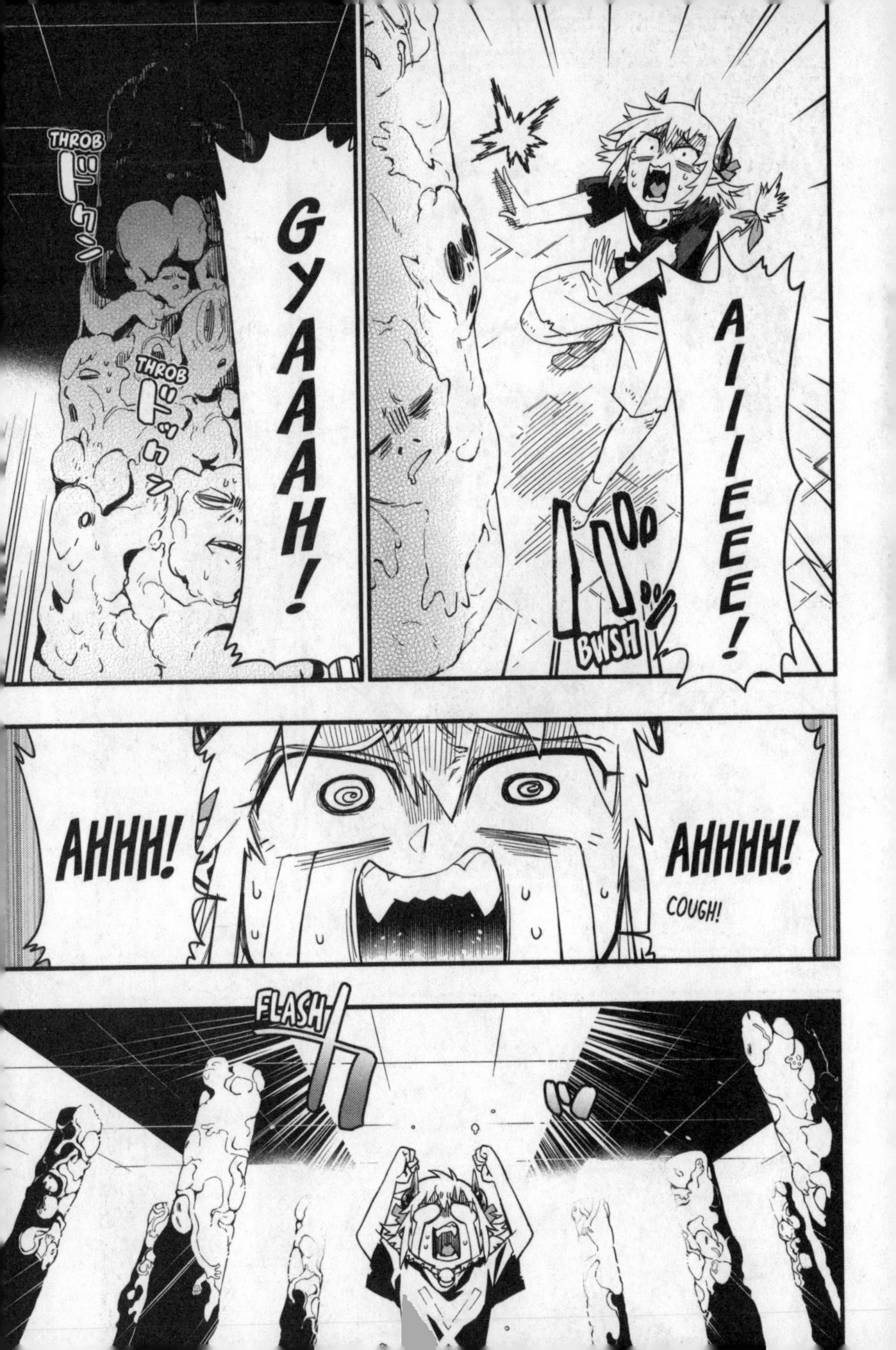
AIIIEEE!
BWSH
GYAAAH!
THROB
THROB
AHHHH!
COUGH!
AHHH!
FLASH

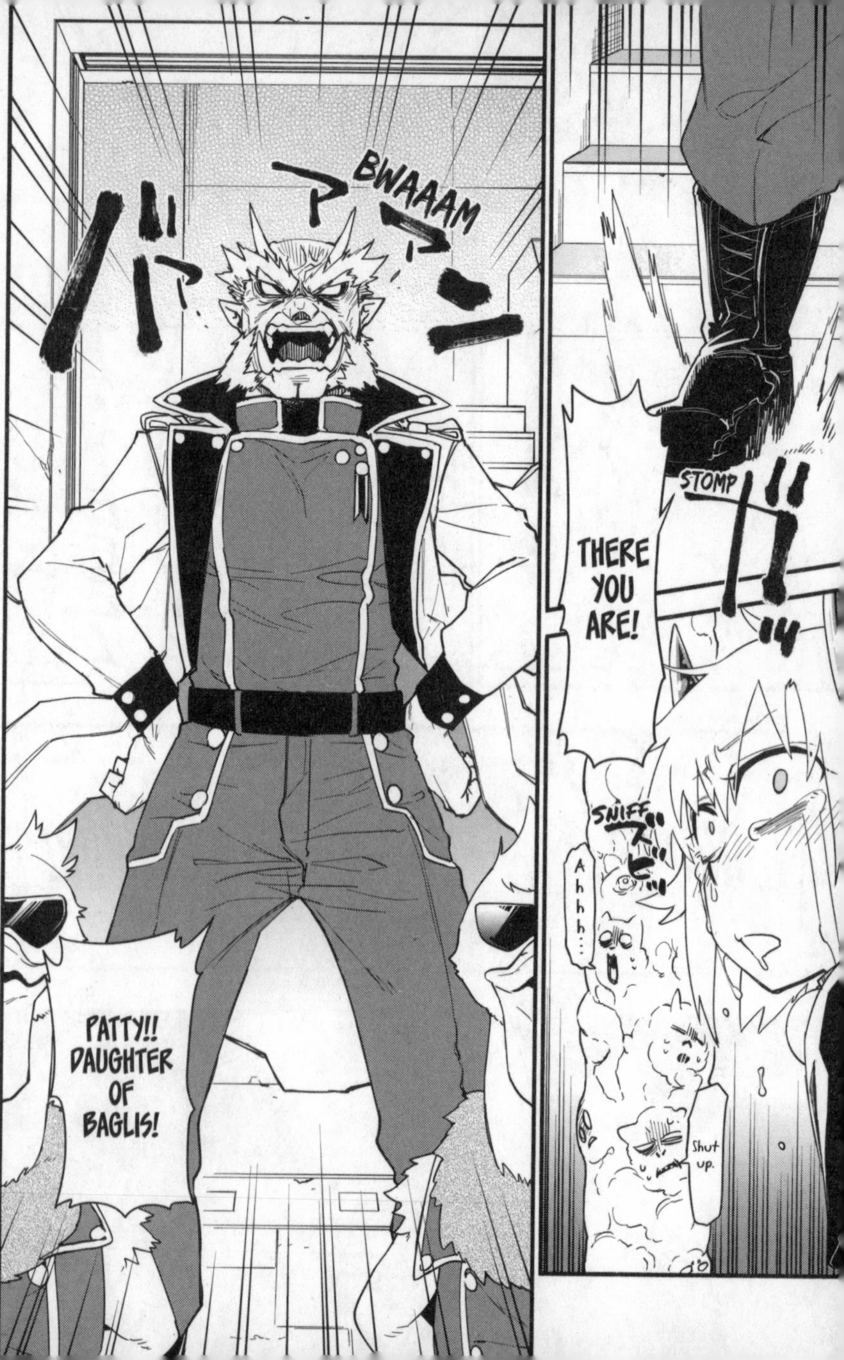
STOMP
THERE YOU ARE!
SNIFF...
Ahhh...
Shut up.
BWAAAM
PATTY!! DAUGHTER OF BAGLIS!

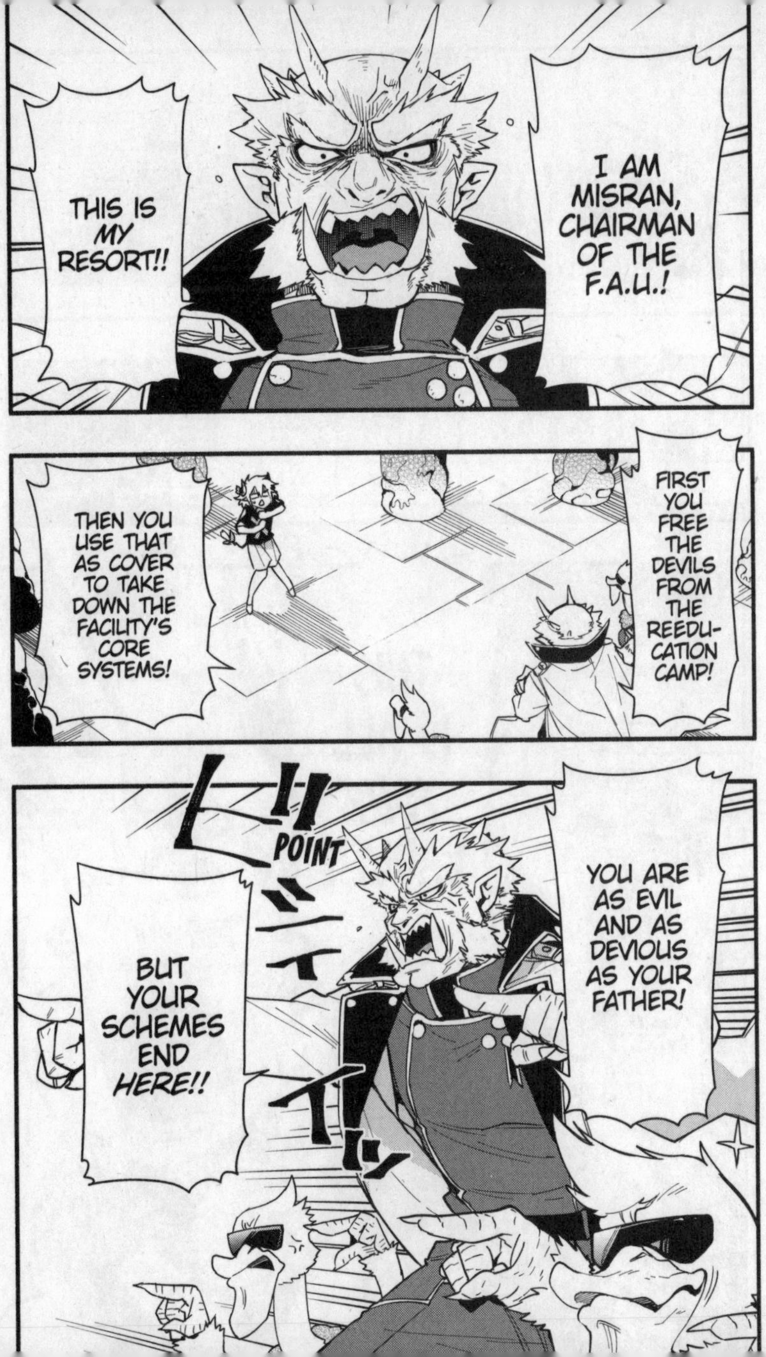
I AM MISRAN, CHAIRMAN OF THE F.A.U.!
THIS IS MY RESORT!!
FIRST YOU FREE THE DEVILS FROM THE REEDUCATION CAMP!
THEN YOU USE THAT AS COVER TO TAKE DOWN THE FACILITY'S CORE SYSTEMS!
YOU ARE AS EVIL AND AS DEVIOUS AS YOUR FATHER!
POINT
BUT YOUR SCHEMES END HERE!!

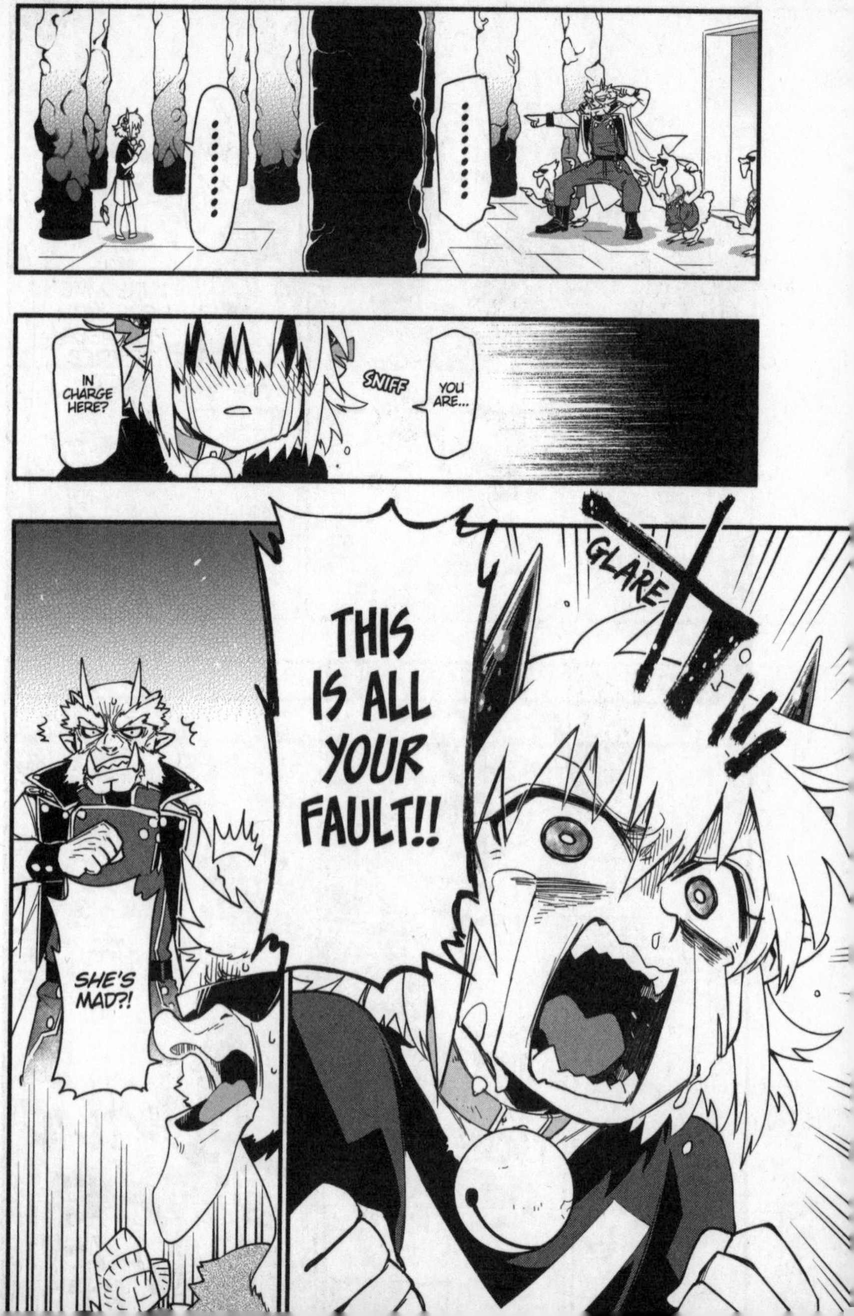
....
....
IN CHARGE HERE?
SNIFF
YOU ARE...
THIS IS ALL YOUR FAULT!!
GLARE
SHE'S MAD?!

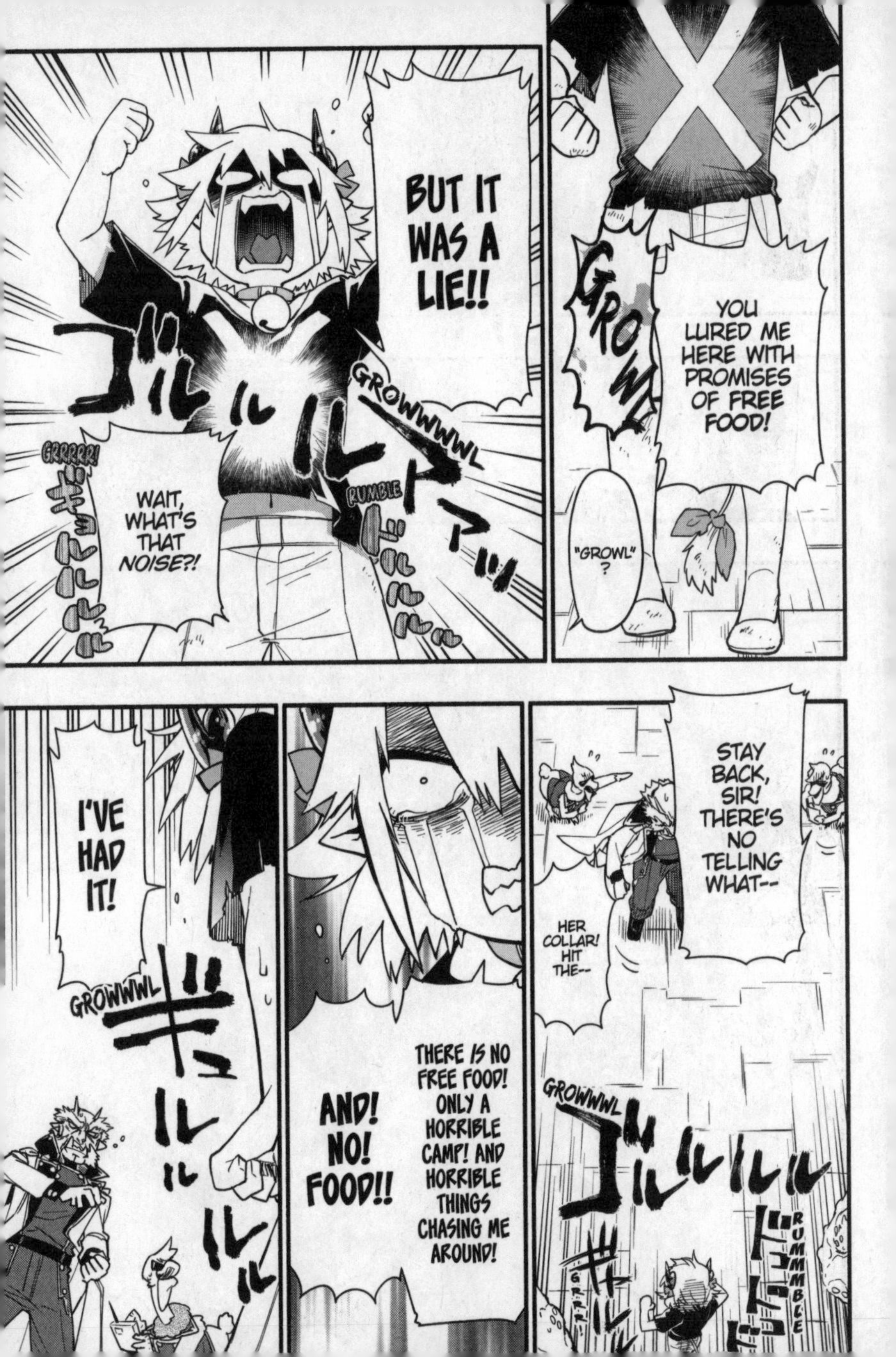

GROWL
YOU LURED ME HERE WITH PROMISES OF FREE FOOD!
"GROWL"?
BUT IT WAS A LIE!!
GROWWWWWL
RUMBLE
GRRRRR!
WAIT, WHAT'S THAT NOISE?!
STAY BACK, SIR! THERE'S NO TELLING WHAT--
HER COLLAR! HIT THE--
GROWWWL
RUMMMBLE
GRRR!
THERE IS NO FREE FOOD! ONLY A HORRIBLE CAMP! AND HORRIBLE THINGS CHASING ME AROUND!
AND! NO! FOOD!!
I'VE HAD IT!
GROWWWL

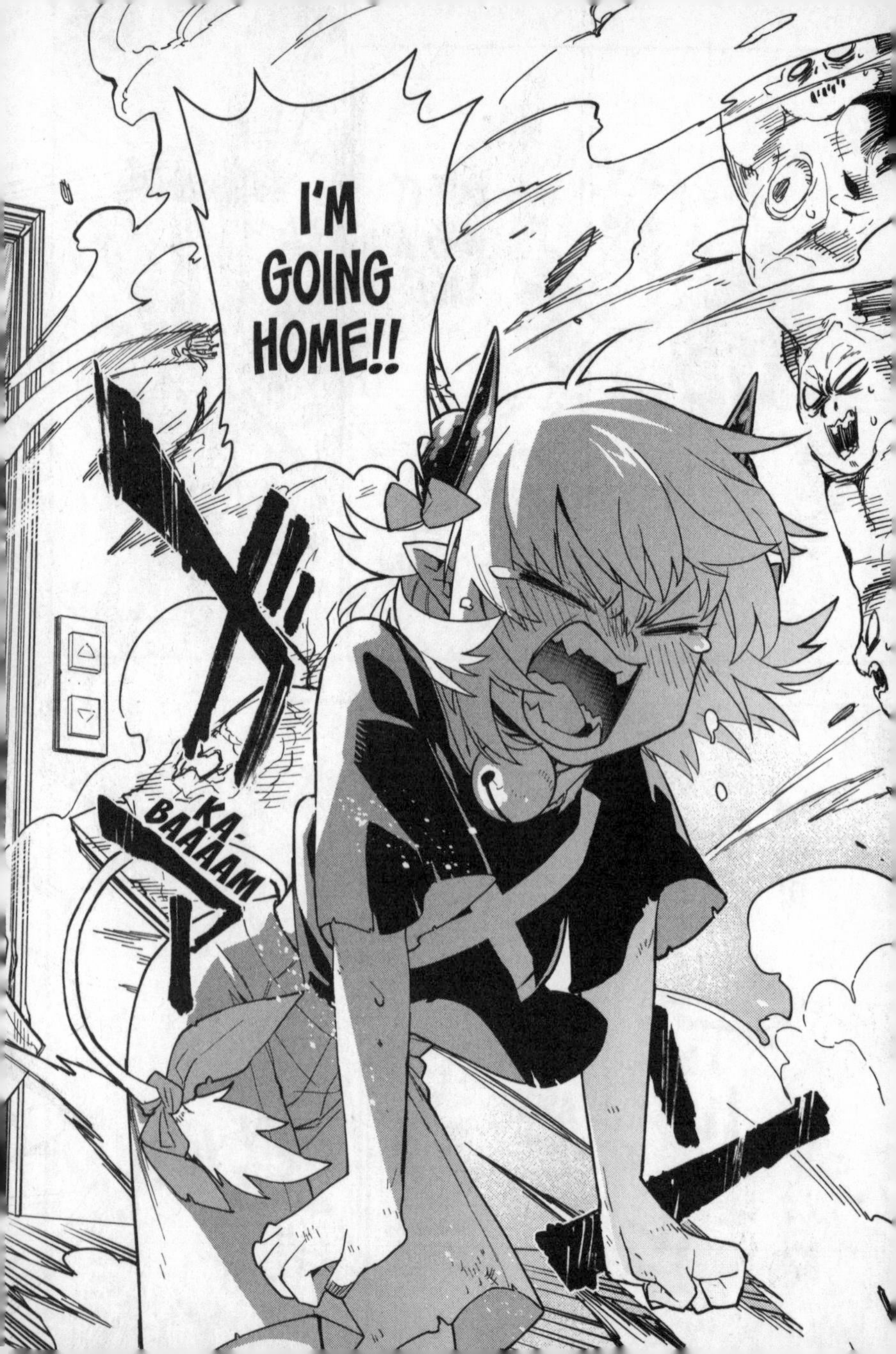
I'M GOING HOME!!
KA-BAAAAAM

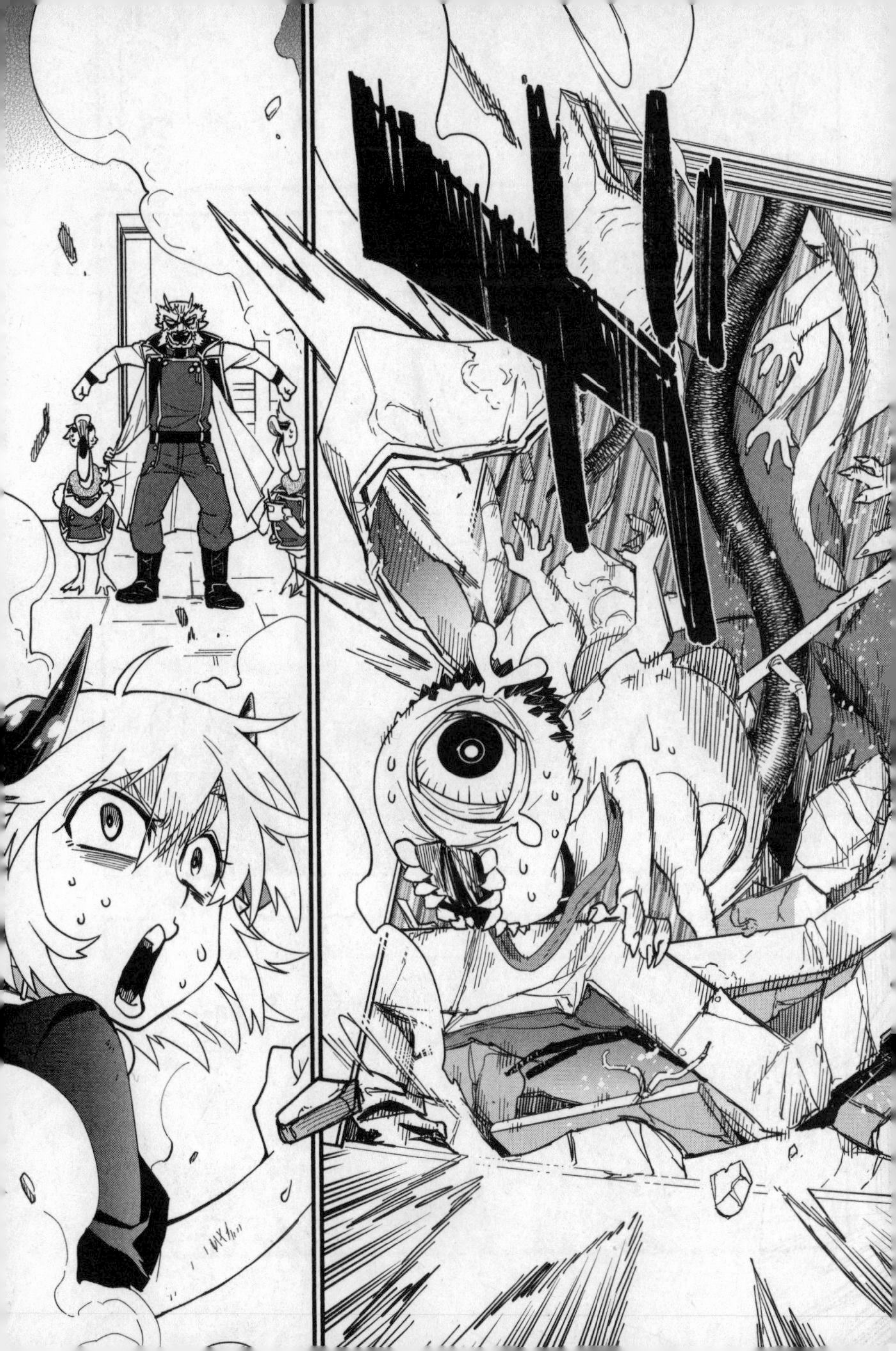

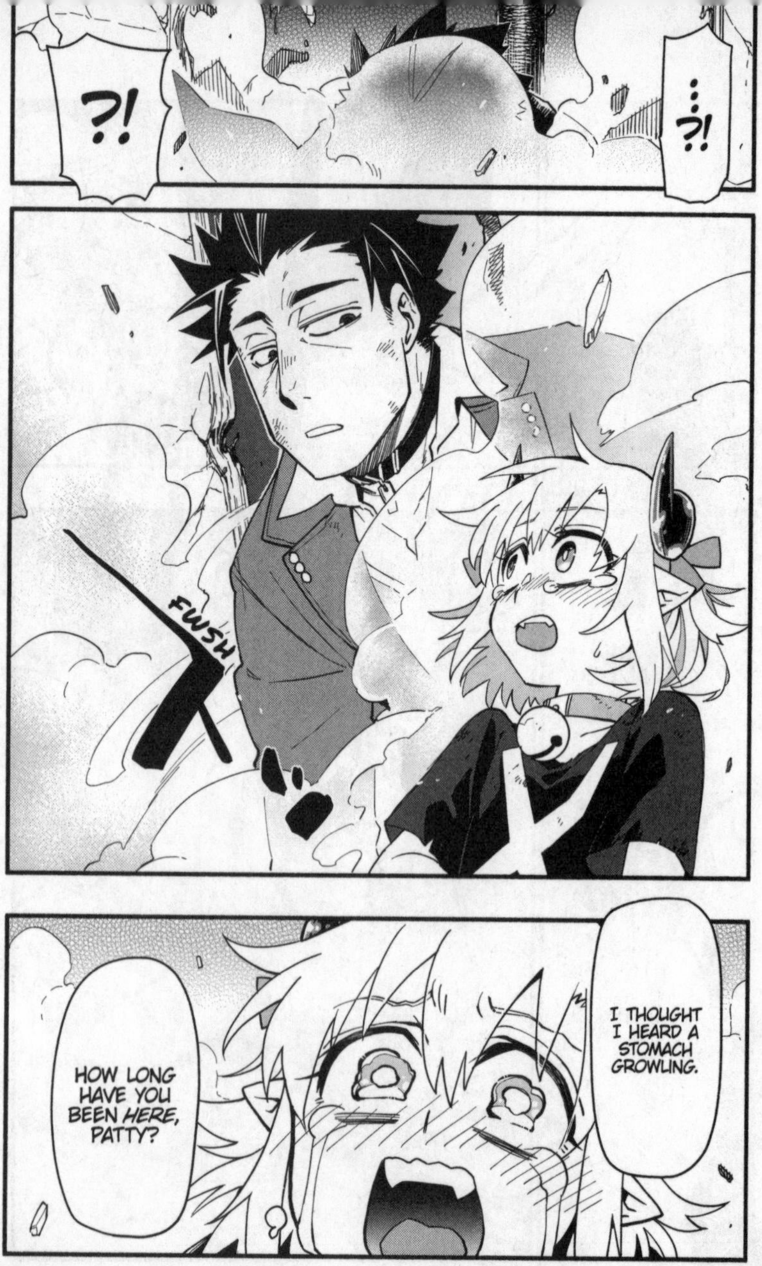
…?!
?!
FWSH
I THOUGHT I HEARD A STOMACH GROWLING.
HOW LONG HAVE YOU BEEN *HERE*, PATTY?

File 55

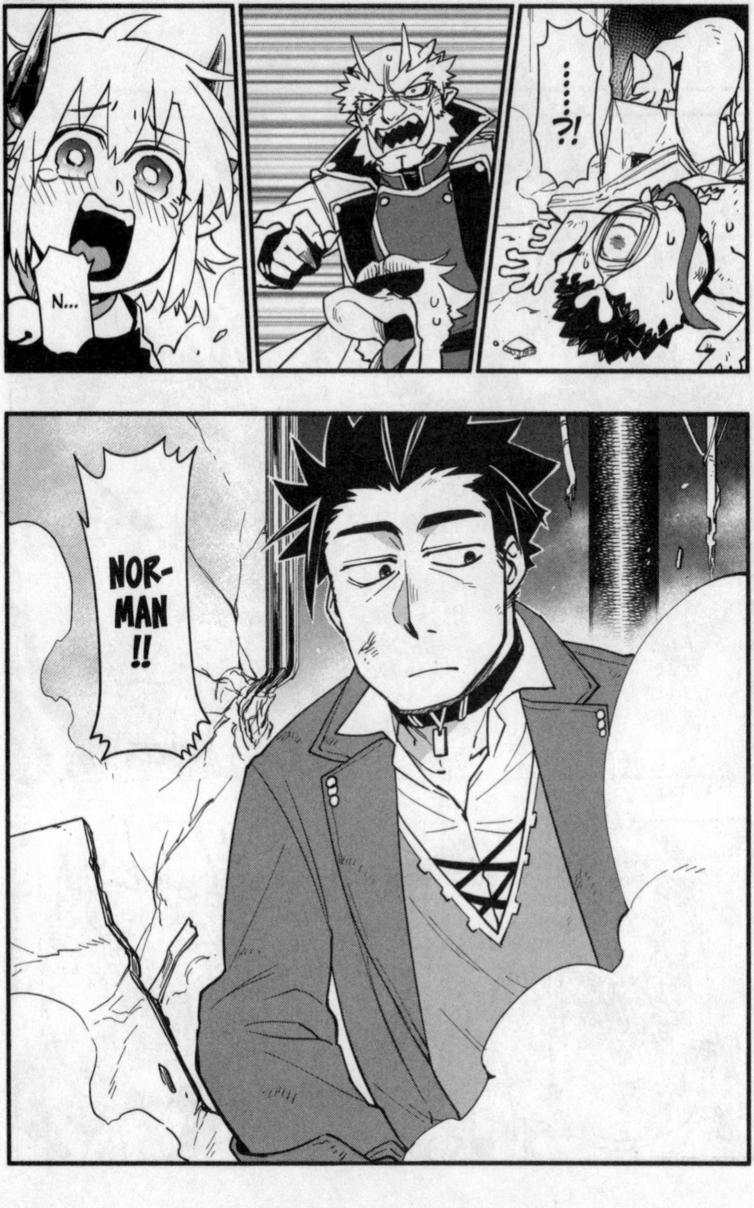
......?!
N...
NOR-MAN!!

FILE 55: The Fearsome Vine Resort ④

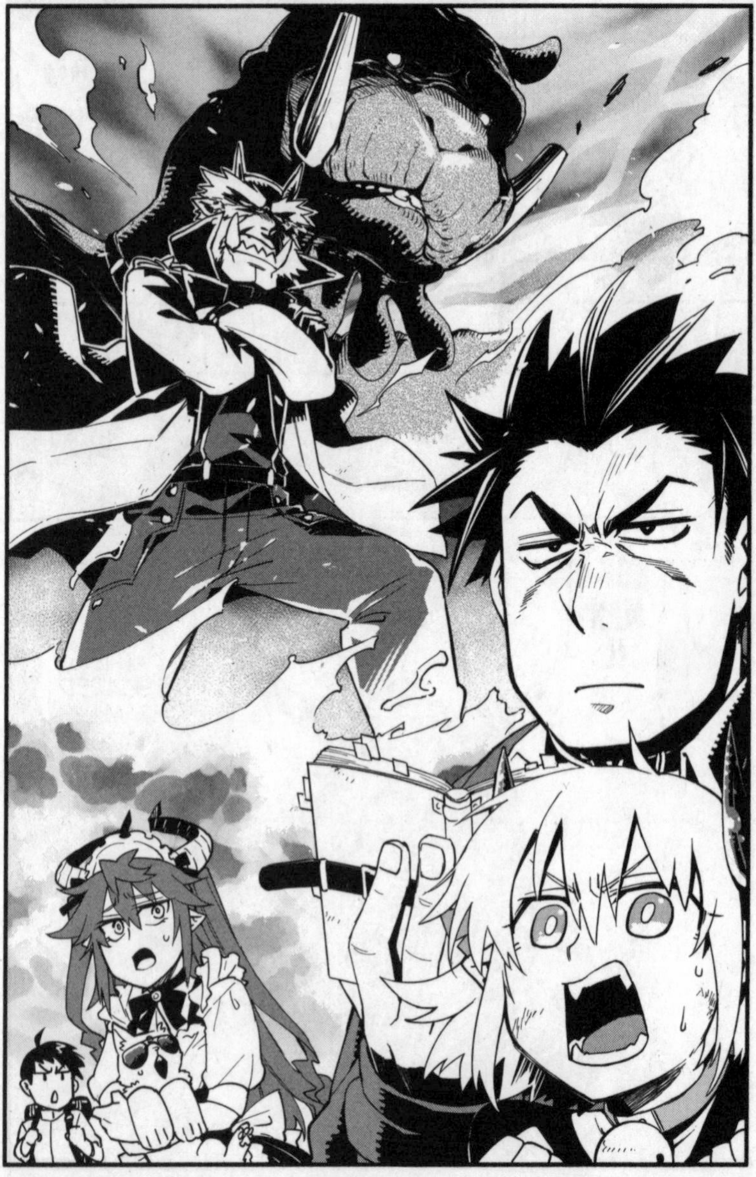

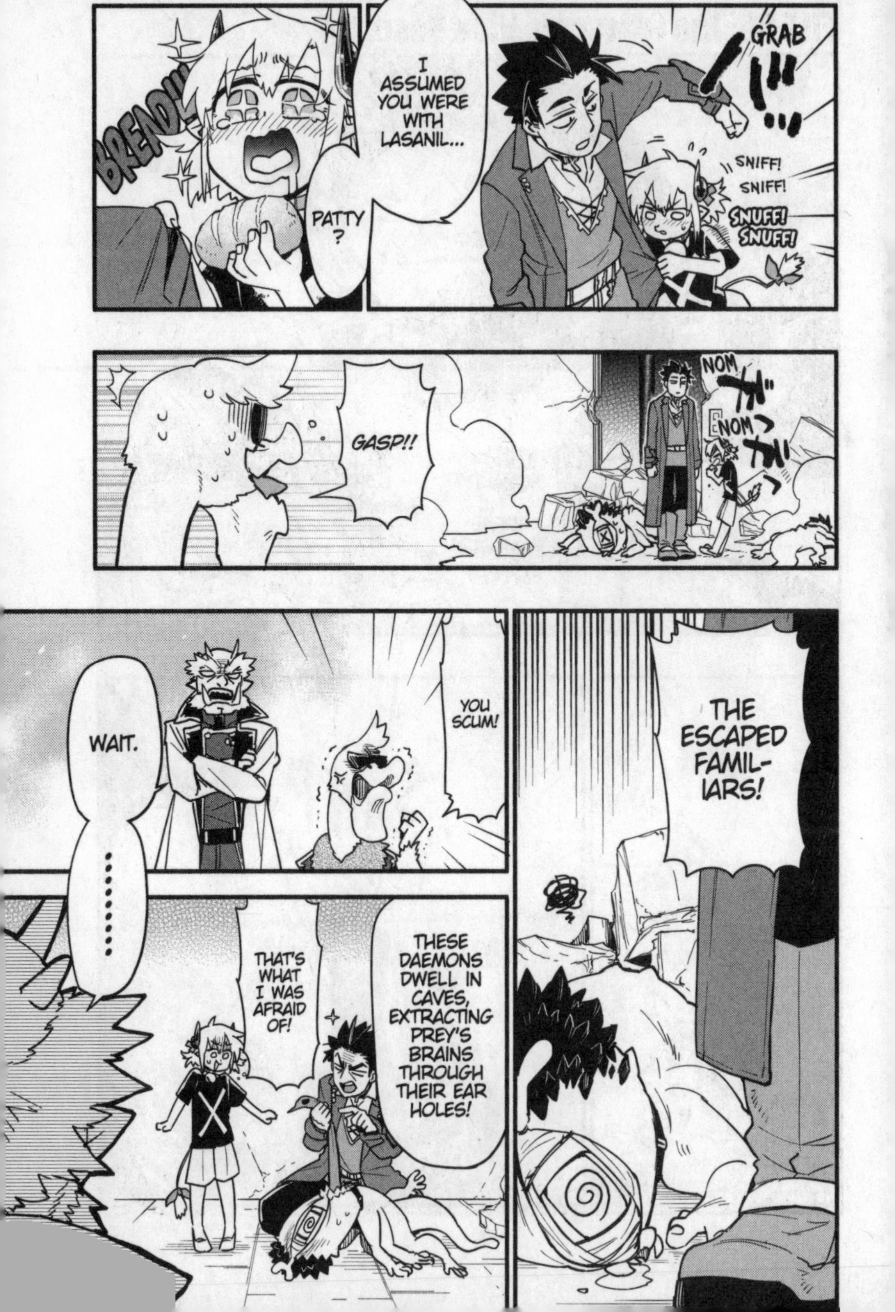
GRAB
SNIFF!
SNIFF!
SNUFF!
SNUFF!
I ASSUMED YOU WERE WITH LASANIL...
PATTY?
BREAD!!
NOM
NOM
GASP!!
THE ESCAPED FAMIL-IARS!
YOU SCUM!
WAIT.
......
THESE DAEMONS DWELL IN CAVES, EXTRACTING PREY'S BRAINS THROUGH THEIR EAR HOLES!
THAT'S WHAT I WAS AFRAID OF!

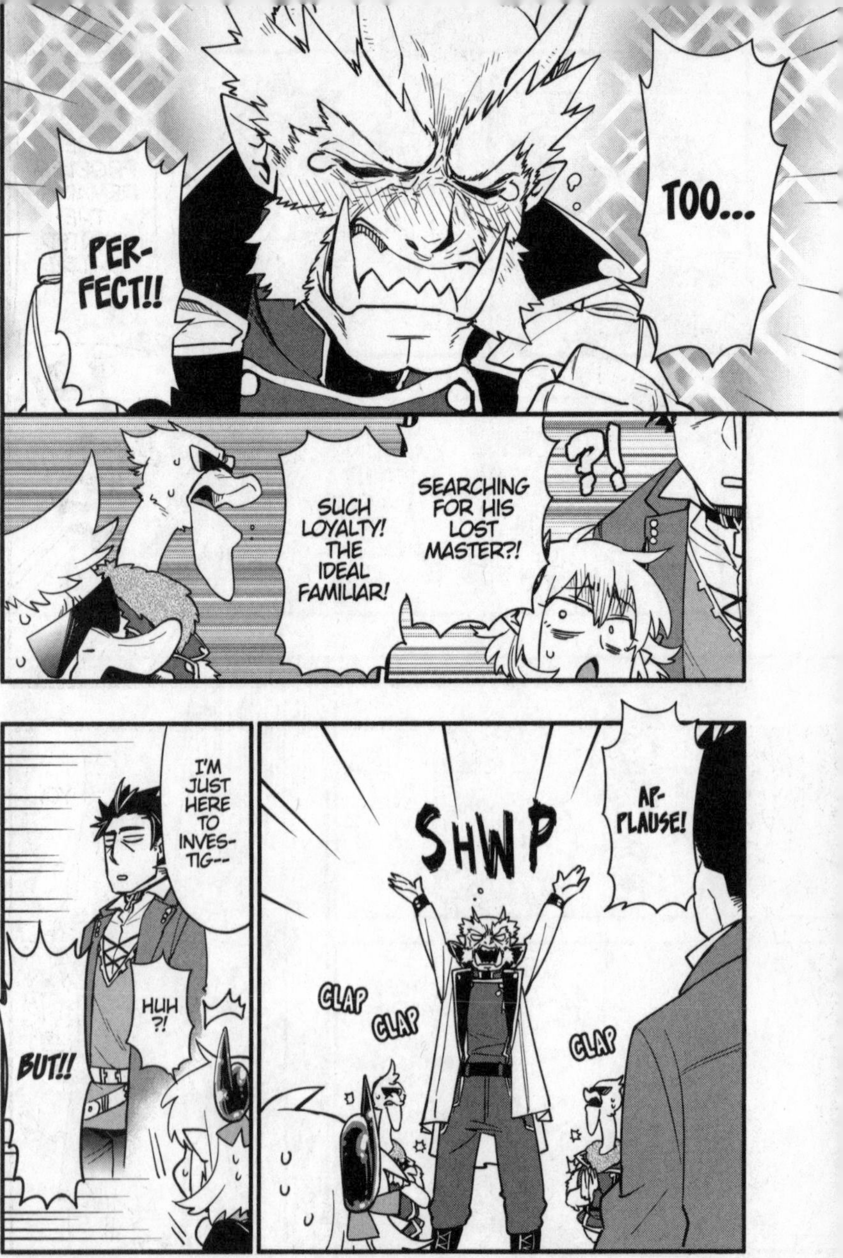
TOO...
PER-
FECT!!
SEARCHING FOR HIS LOST MASTER?!
SUCH LOYALTY! THE IDEAL FAMILIAR!
AP-
PLAUSE!
SHWP
CLAP
CLAP
CLAP
I'M JUST HERE TO INVES-
TIG--
HUH ?!
BUT!!

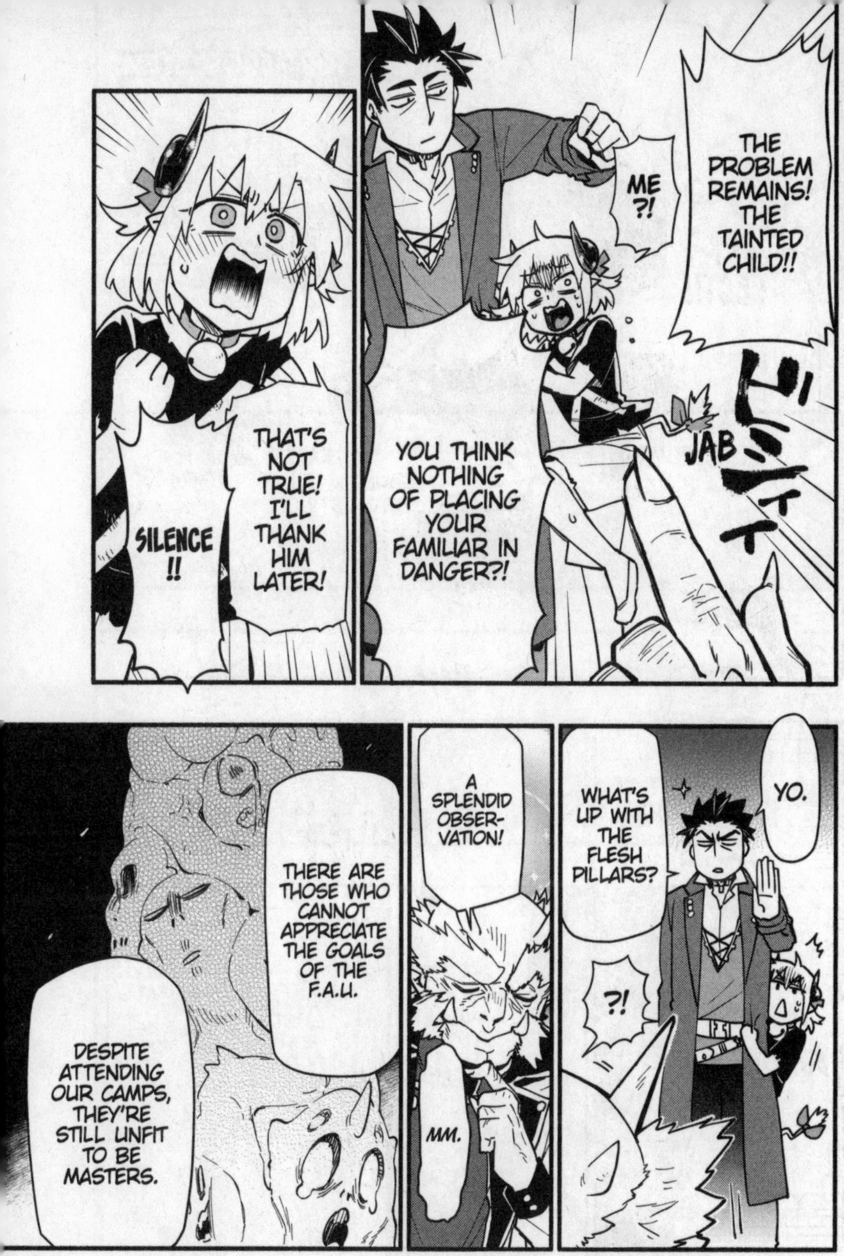
THE PROBLEM REMAINS! THE TAINTED CHILD!!
ME ?!
JAB
YOU THINK NOTHING OF PLACING YOUR FAMILIAR IN DANGER?!
THAT'S NOT TRUE! I'LL THANK HIM LATER!
SILENCE !!
YO.
WHAT'S UP WITH THE FLESH PILLARS?
?!
A SPLENDID OBSERVATION!
MM.
THERE ARE THOSE WHO CANNOT APPRECIATE THE GOALS OF THE F.A.U.
DESPITE ATTENDING OUR CAMPS, THEY'RE STILL UNFIT TO BE MASTERS.

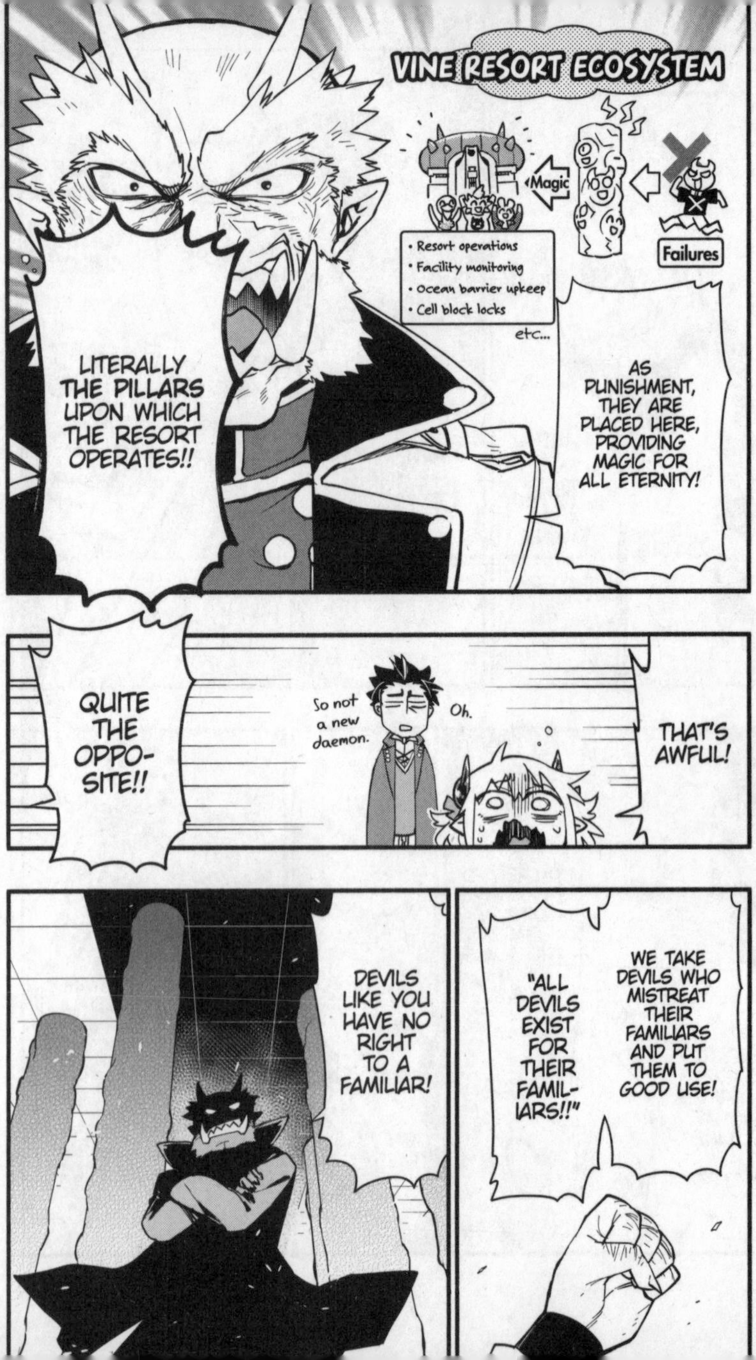
VINE RESORT ECOSYSTEM
Failures
Magic
• Resort operations
• Facility monitoring
• Ocean barrier upkeep
• Cell block locks
etc...
AS PUNISHMENT, THEY ARE PLACED HERE, PROVIDING MAGIC FOR ALL ETERNITY!
LITERALLY THE PILLARS UPON WHICH THE RESORT OPERATES!!
THAT'S AWFUL!
Oh.
So not a new daemon.
QUITE THE OPPO-SITE!!
WE TAKE DEVILS WHO MISTREAT THEIR FAMILIARS AND PUT THEM TO GOOD USE!
"ALL DEVILS EXIST FOR THEIR FAMIL-IARS!!"
DEVILS LIKE YOU HAVE NO RIGHT TO A FAMILIAR!

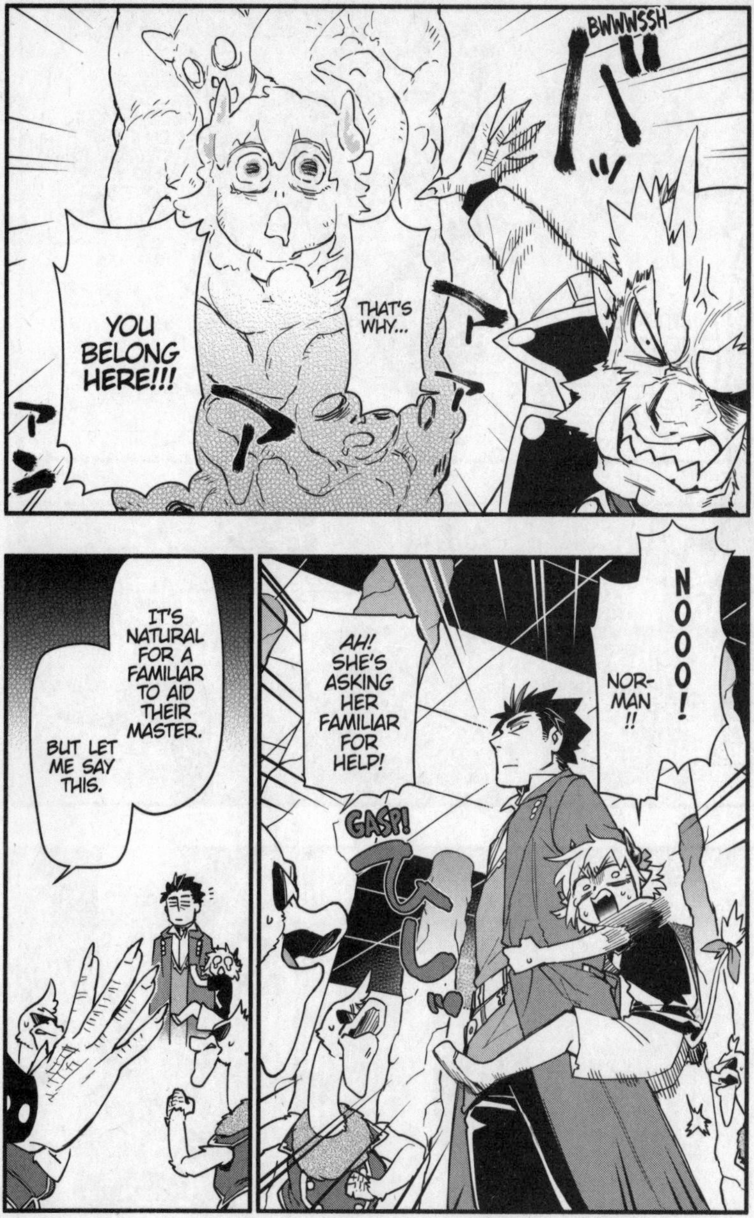
BWWWSSH
THAT'S WHY...
YOU BELONG HERE!!!
NOOOO!
NOR-MAN !!
AH! SHE'S ASKING HER FAMILIAR FOR HELP!
GASP!
IT'S NATURAL FOR A FAMILIAR TO AID THEIR MASTER.
BUT LET ME SAY THIS.

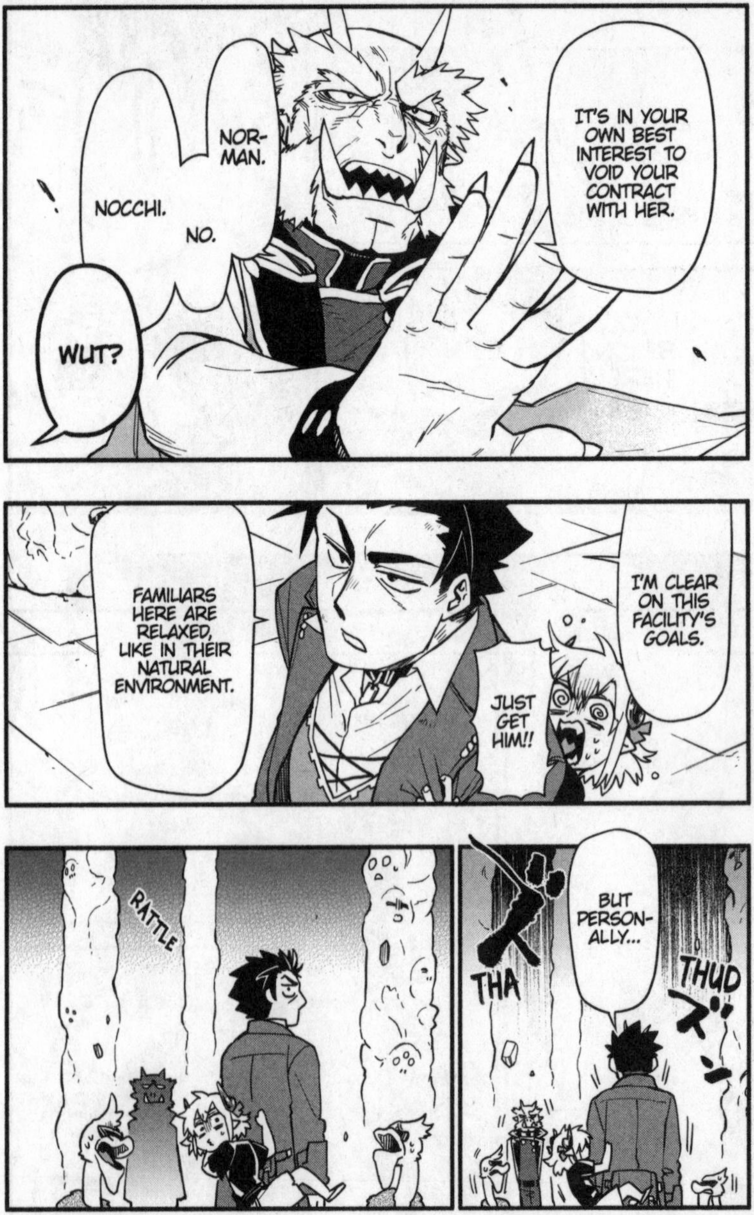
IT'S IN YOUR OWN BEST INTEREST TO VOID YOUR CONTRACT WITH HER.
NOR-MAN.
NOCCHI.
NO.
WUT?
I'M CLEAR ON THIS FACILITY'S GOALS.
JUST GET HIM!!
FAMILIARS HERE ARE RELAXED, LIKE IN THEIR NATURAL ENVIRONMENT.
BUT PERSON-ALLY...
THUD
THA
RATTLE

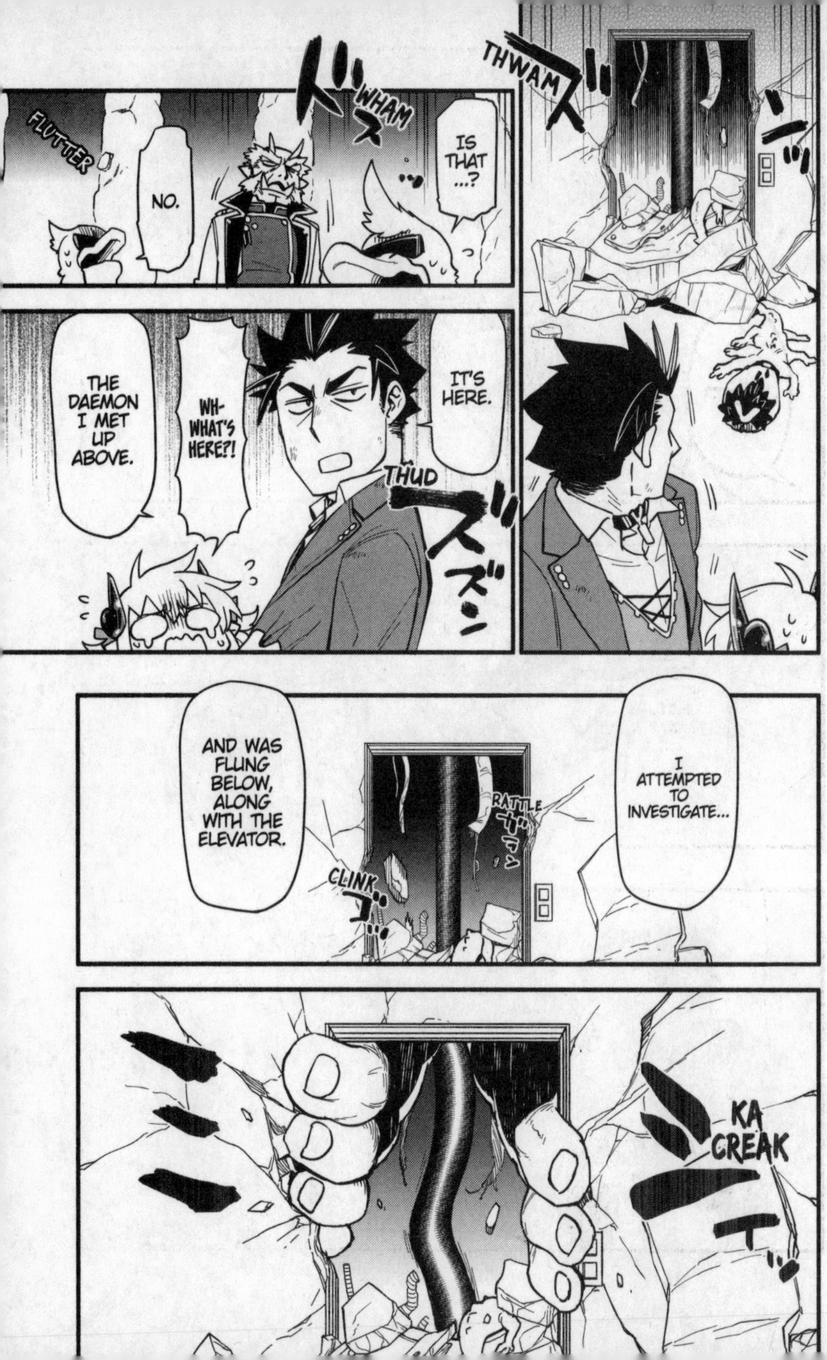
THWAM
WHAM
IS THAT ...?
NO.
FLUTTER
IT'S HERE.
THUD
WH-WHAT'S HERE?!
THE DAEMON I MET UP ABOVE.
I ATTEMPTED TO INVESTIGATE...
RATTLE
CLINK
AND WAS FLUNG BELOW, ALONG WITH THE ELEVATOR.
KA CREAK

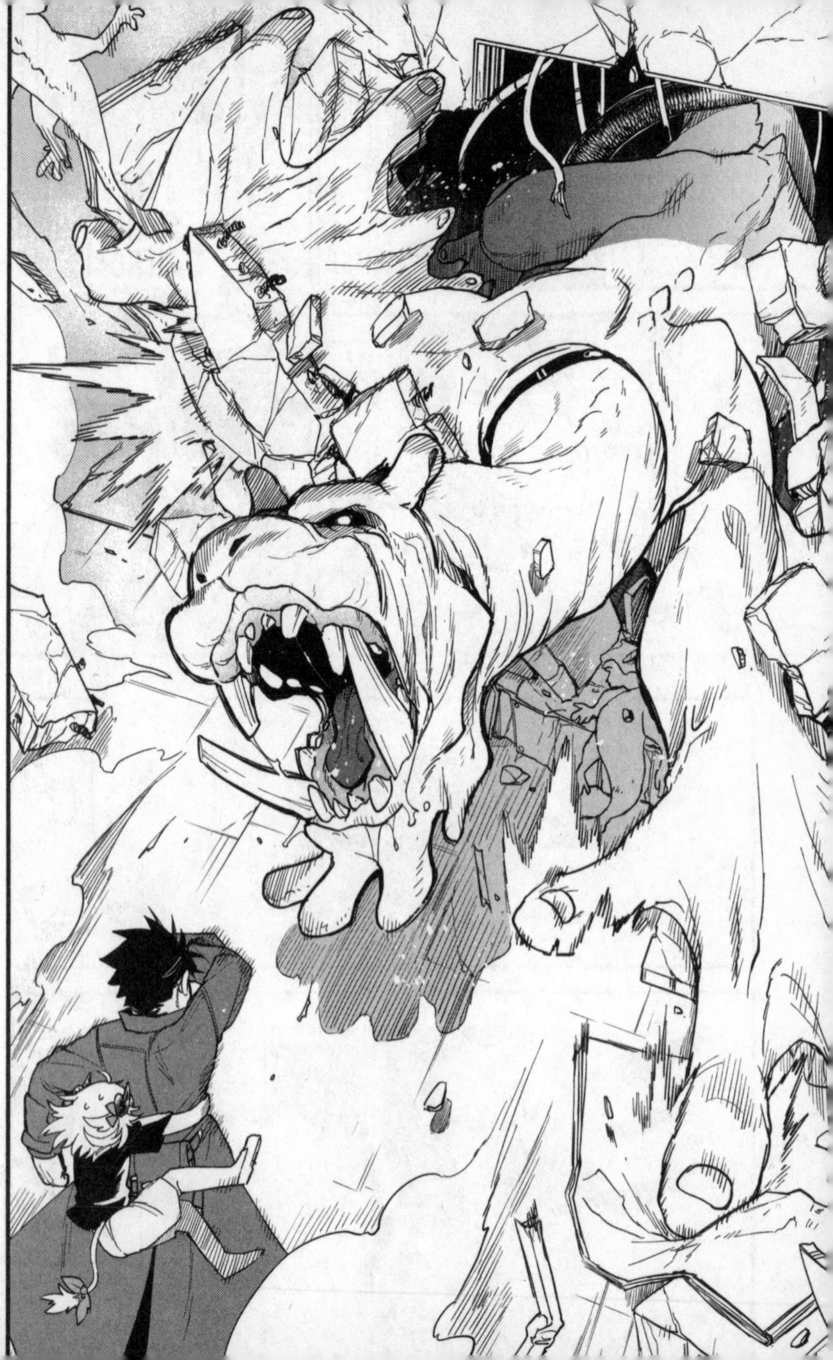

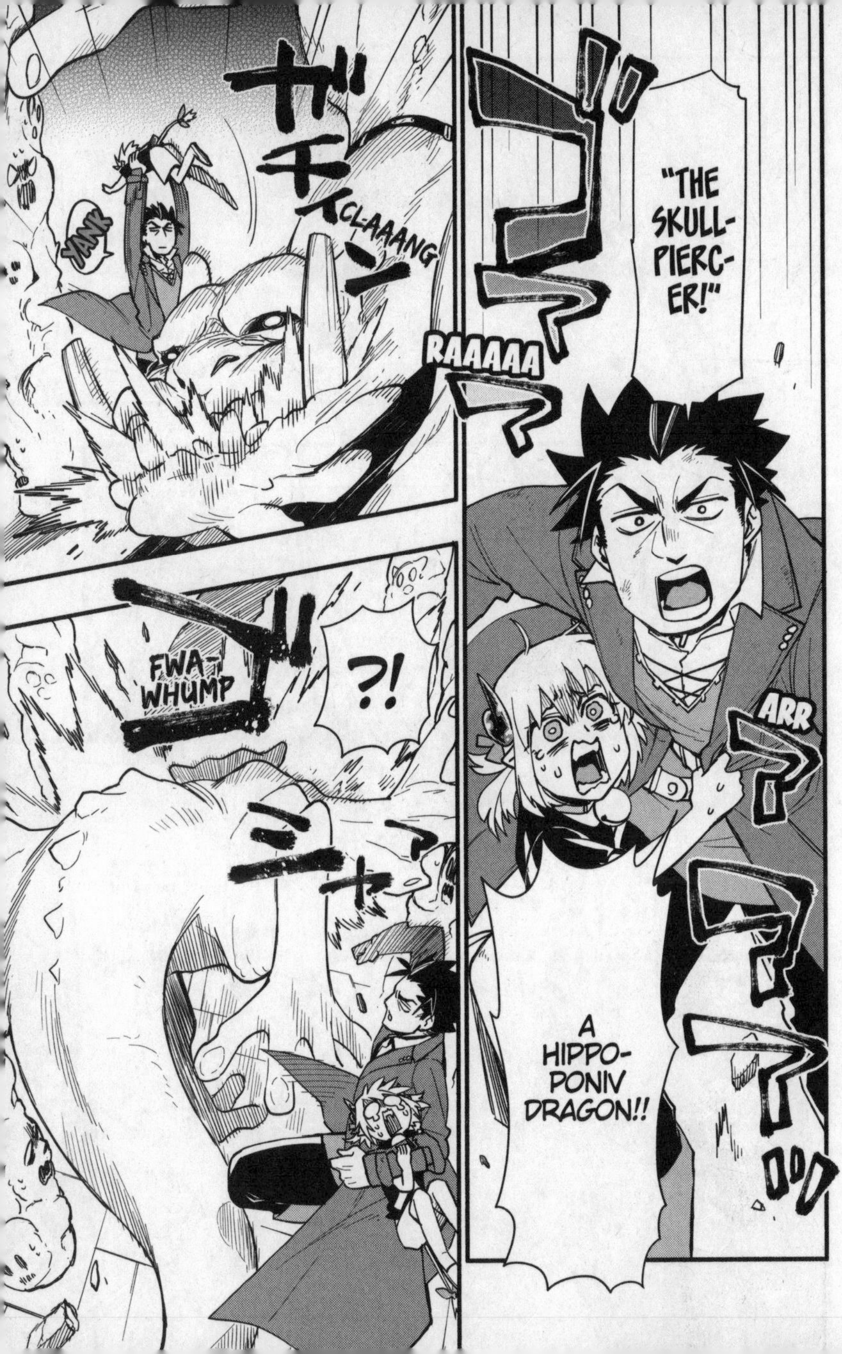
"THE SKULL-PIERCER!"
RAAAAA
ARR
A HIPPO-PONIV DRAGON!!
YANK
CL-AAANG
FWA-WHUMP
?!

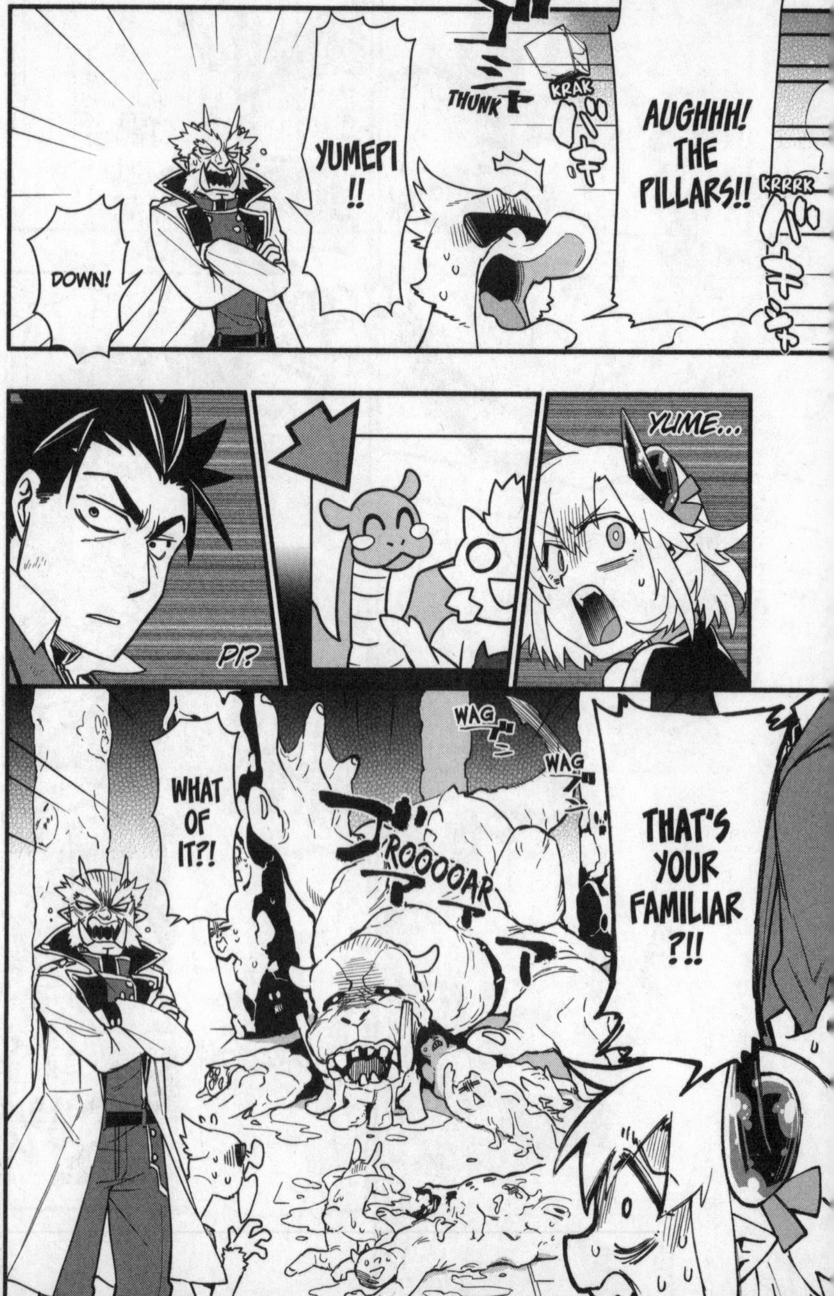
KRRRK
AUGHHH! THE PILLARS!!
KRAK
THUNK
YUMEPI !!
DOWN!
YUME...
PI?
THAT'S YOUR FAMILIAR ?!!
WAG
WAG
ROOOOAR
WHAT OF IT?!

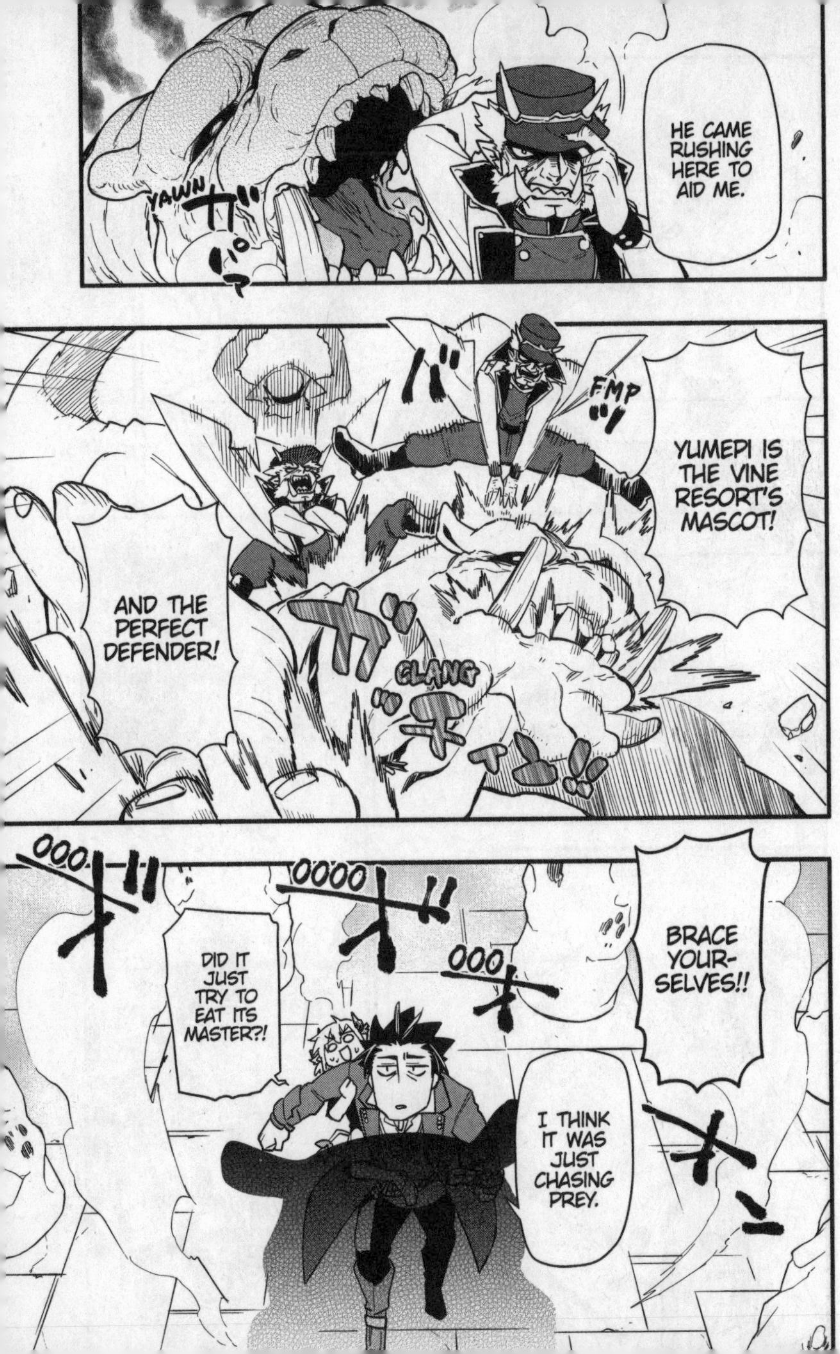
HE CAME RUSHING HERE TO AID ME.
YAWN
YUMEPI IS THE VINE RESORT'S MASCOT!
FMP
AND THE PERFECT DEFENDER!
CLANG
OOO
OOOO
OOO
BRACE YOURSELVES!!
DID IT JUST TRY TO EAT ITS MASTER?!
I THINK IT WAS JUST CHASING PREY.

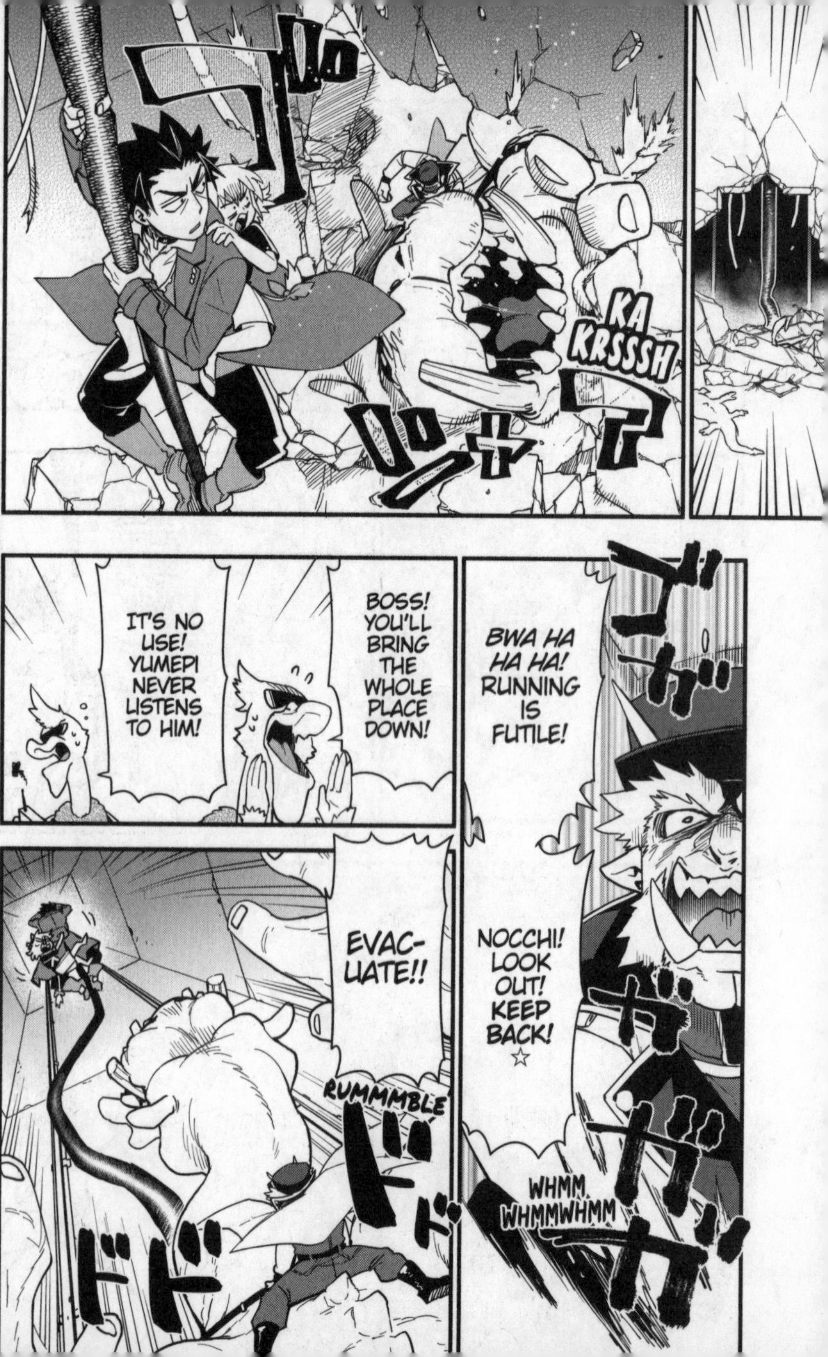
KA KRSSSH
BWA HA HA HA! RUNNING IS FUTILE!
BOSS! YOU'LL BRING THE WHOLE PLACE DOWN!
IT'S NO USE! YUMEPI NEVER LISTENS TO HIM!
NOCCHI! LOOK OUT! KEEP BACK! ☆
WHMM WHMMWHMM
EVACUATE!!
RUMMMBLE

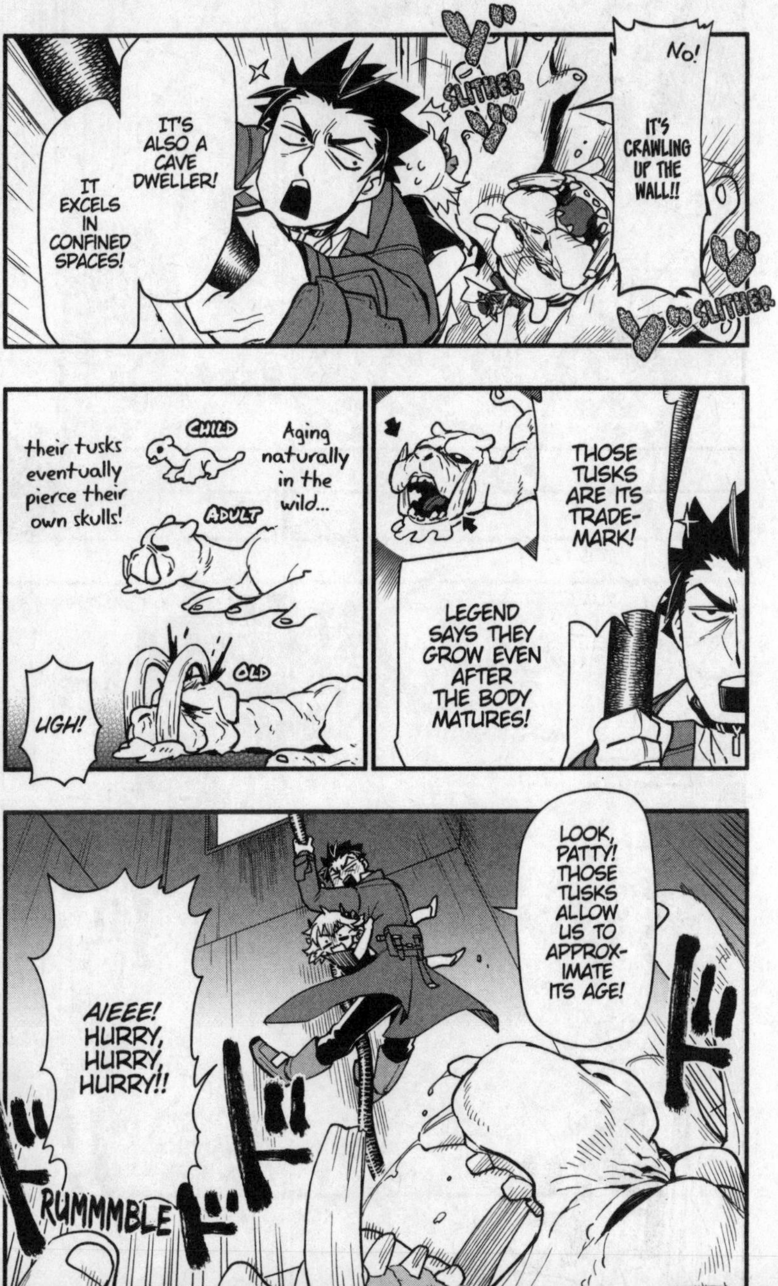

No!
IT'S CRAWLING UP THE WALL!!
SLITHER
SLITHER
IT'S ALSO A CAVE DWELLER!
IT EXCELS IN CONFINED SPACES!
THOSE TUSKS ARE ITS TRADE-MARK!
LEGEND SAYS THEY GROW EVEN AFTER THE BODY MATURES!
Aging naturally in the wild...
CHILD
ADULT
OLD
their tusks eventually pierce their own skulls!
UGH!
LOOK, PATTY! THOSE TUSKS ALLOW US TO APPROX-IMATE ITS AGE!
AIEEE! HURRY, HURRY, HURRY!!
RUMMMBLE

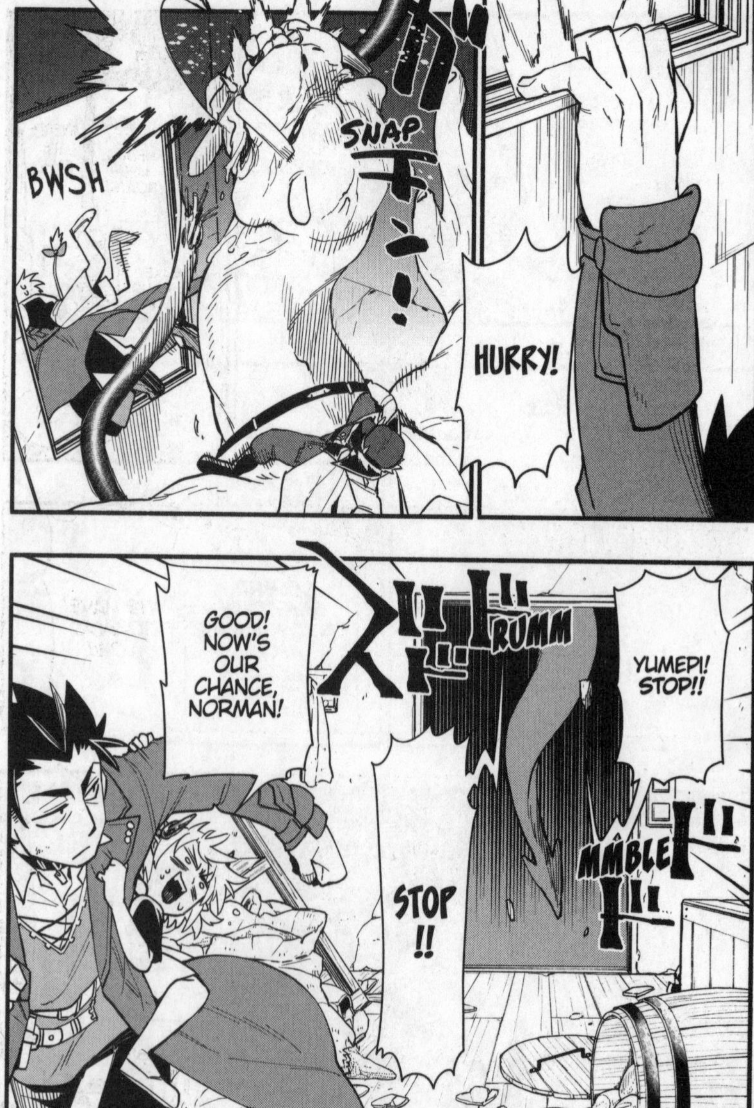
HURRY!
SNAP
BWSH
YUMEPI! STOP!!
RUMM
GOOD! NOW'S OUR CHANCE, NORMAN!
MMBLE
STOP !!

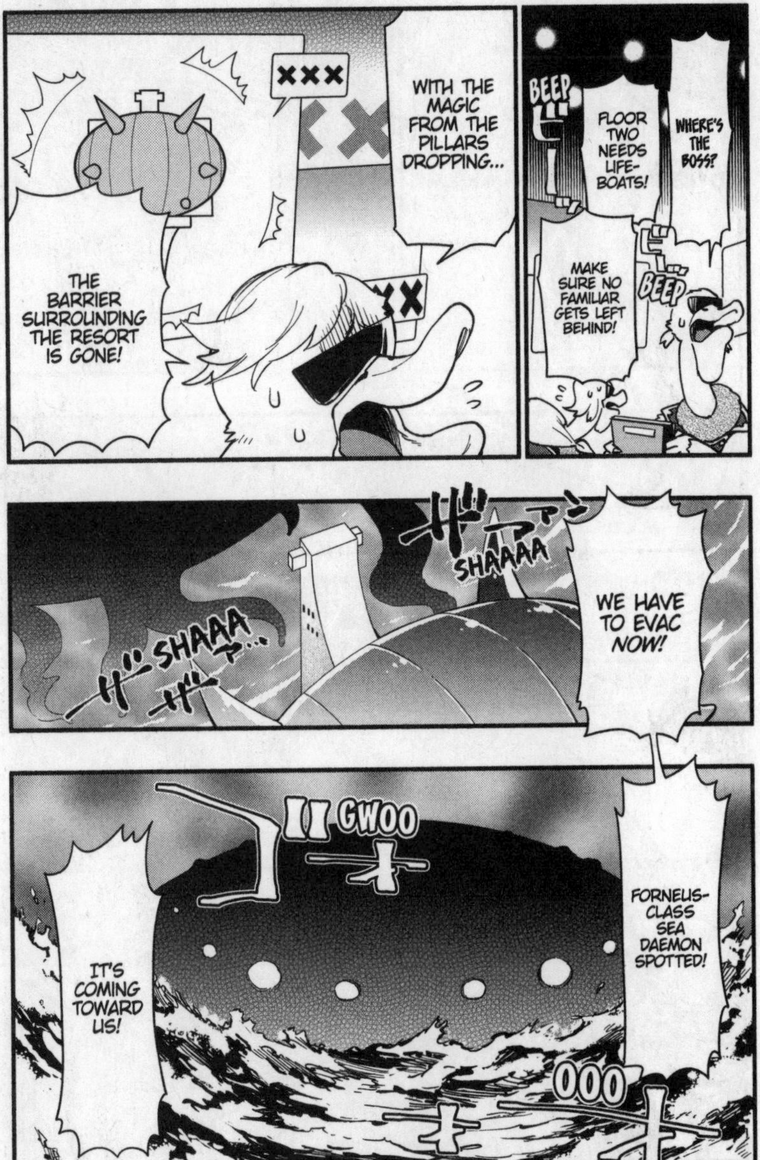
WHERE'S THE BOSS?
FLOOR TWO NEEDS LIFE-BOATS!
BEEP
MAKE SURE NO FAMILIAR GETS LEFT BEHIND!
BEEP
×××
WITH THE MAGIC FROM THE PILLARS DROPPING...
THE BARRIER SURROUNDING THE RESORT IS GONE!
SHAAAAA
WE HAVE TO EVAC NOW!
SHAAAA
FORNEUS-CLASS SEA DAEMON SPOTTED!
GWOO
OOO
IT'S COMING TOWARD US!

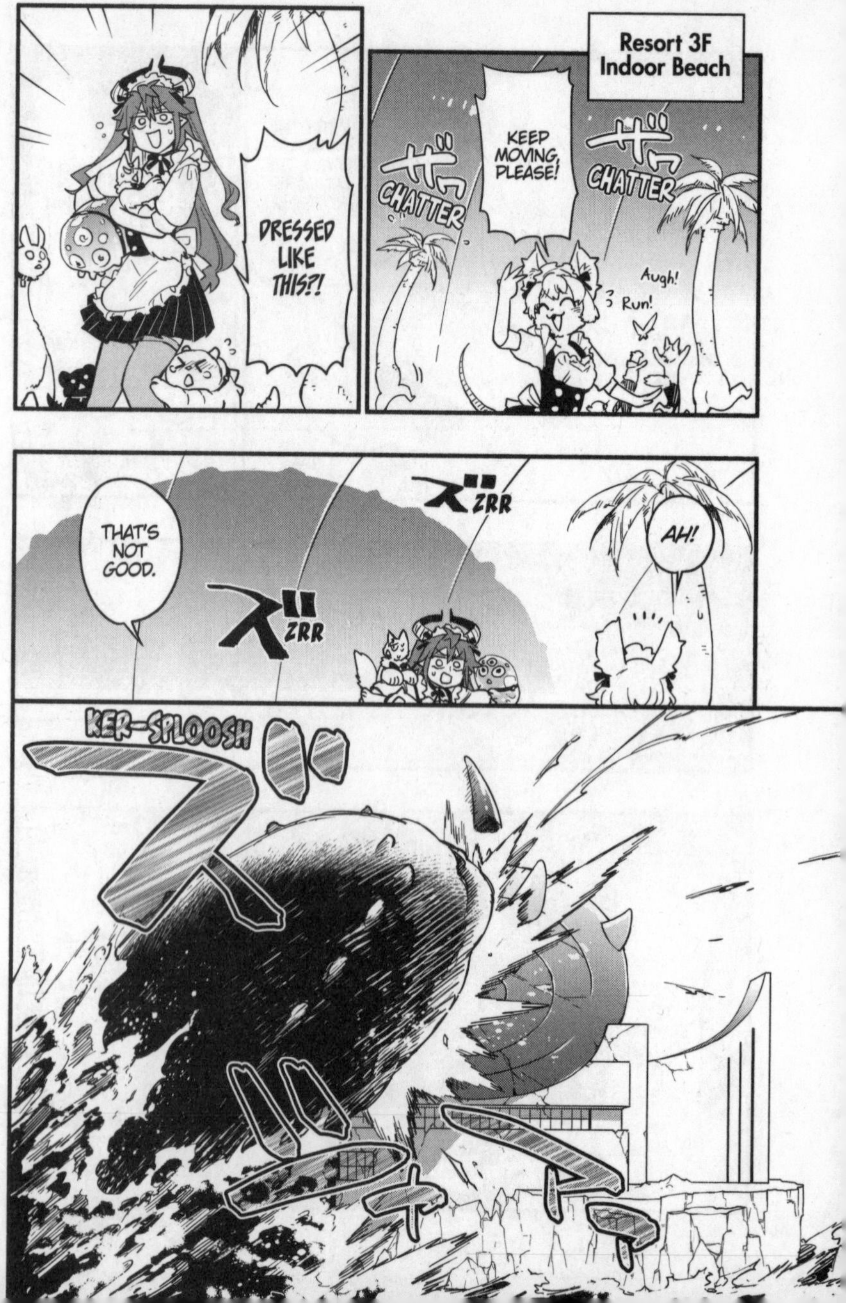

Resort 3F
Indoor Beach
KEEP MOVING, PLEASE!
CHATTER
CHATTER
Augh!
Run!
DRESSED LIKE THIS?!
ZRR
ZRR
THAT'S NOT GOOD.
AH!
KER-SPLOOSH

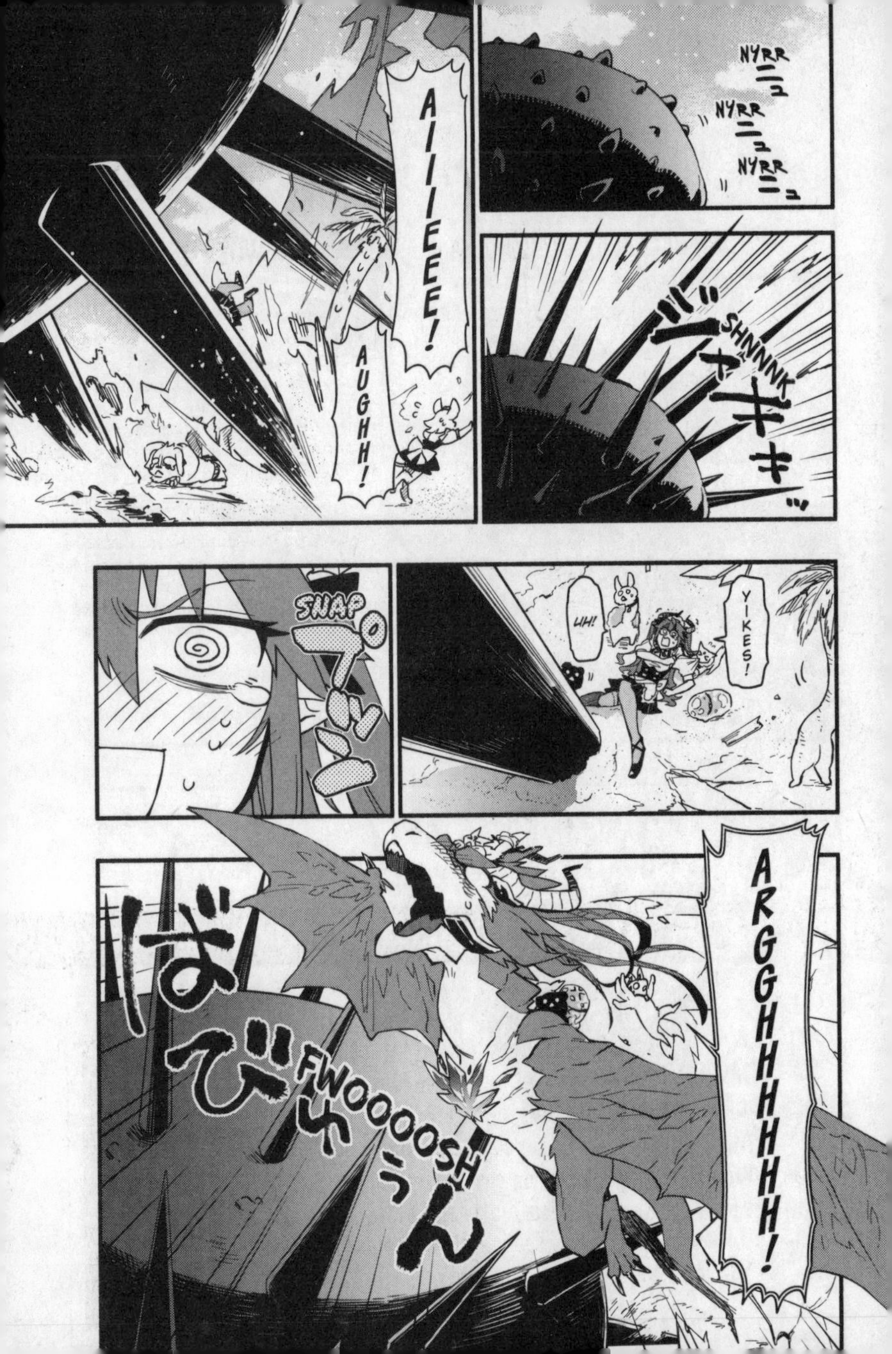

NYRR ニュ
NYRR ニュ
NYRR ニュ
SHNNNK
ジャキキッ
AIIIIEEEE!
AUGHH!
YIKES!
UH!
SNAP
プッツン
ARGGHHHHHHHH!
FWOOOOOSH
ばびゅうん

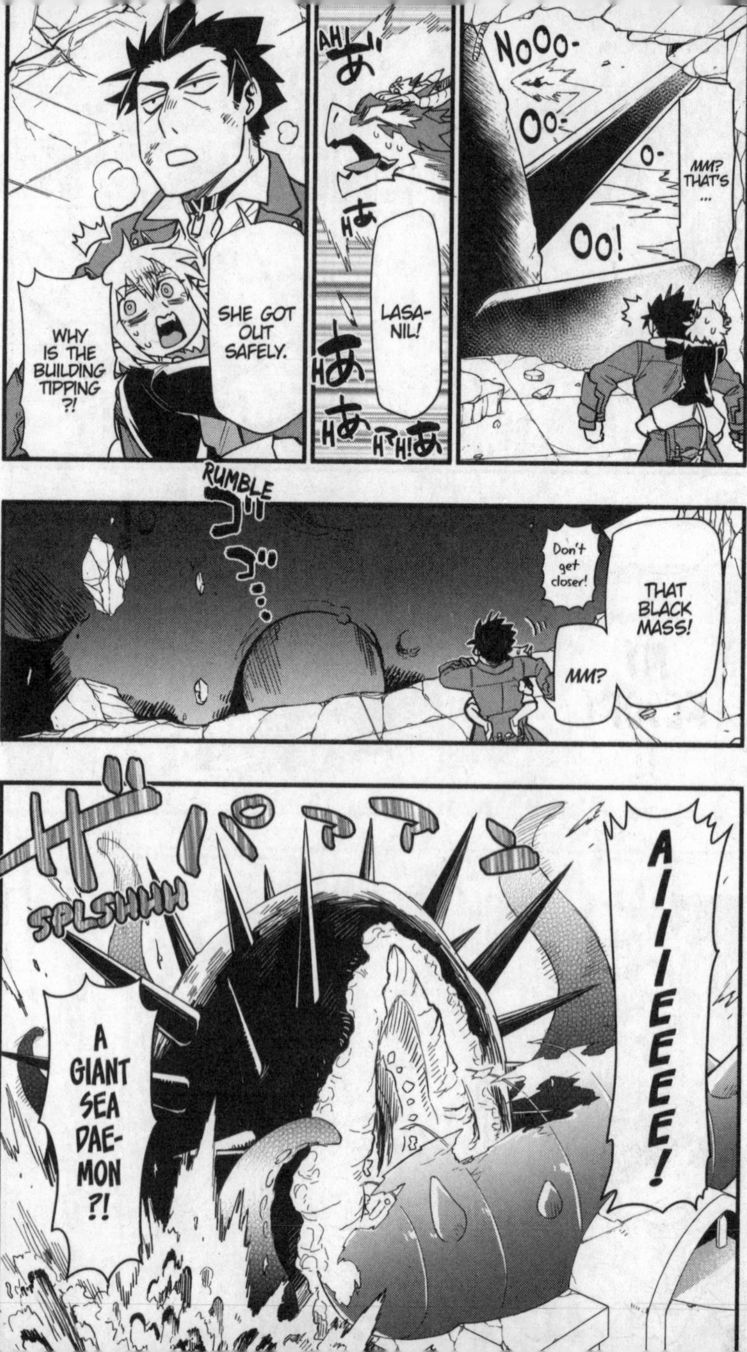
NOOO-OO-O-OO!
MM? THAT'S ...
AH あ
LASA-NIL!
H あ H あ H あ H あ H あ
SHE GOT OUT SAFELY.
WHY IS THE BUILDING TIPPING ?!
RUMBLE ゴゴ...
THAT BLACK MASS!
Don't get closer!
MM?
AIIIEEEEE!
ザパアアン
SPLSHHH
A GIANT SEA DAEMON ?!

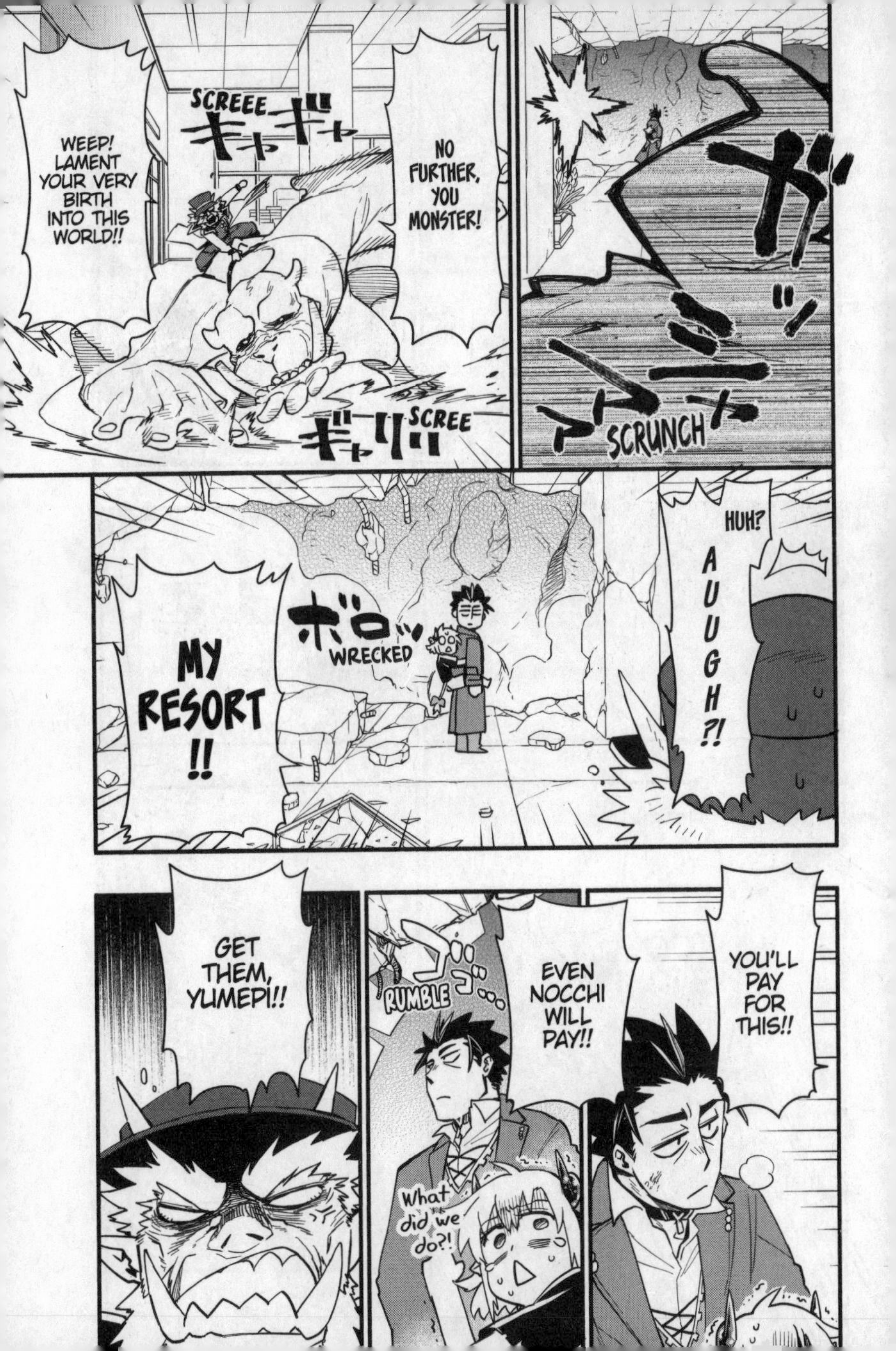
SCRUNCH
NO FURTHER, YOU MONSTER!
SCREEE
WEEP! LAMENT YOUR VERY BIRTH INTO THIS WORLD!!
SCREE
HUH?
AUUUGH?!
WRECKED
MY RESORT!!
YOU'LL PAY FOR THIS!!
EVEN NOCCHI WILL PAY!!
RUMBLE
What did we do?!
GET THEM, YUMEPI!!

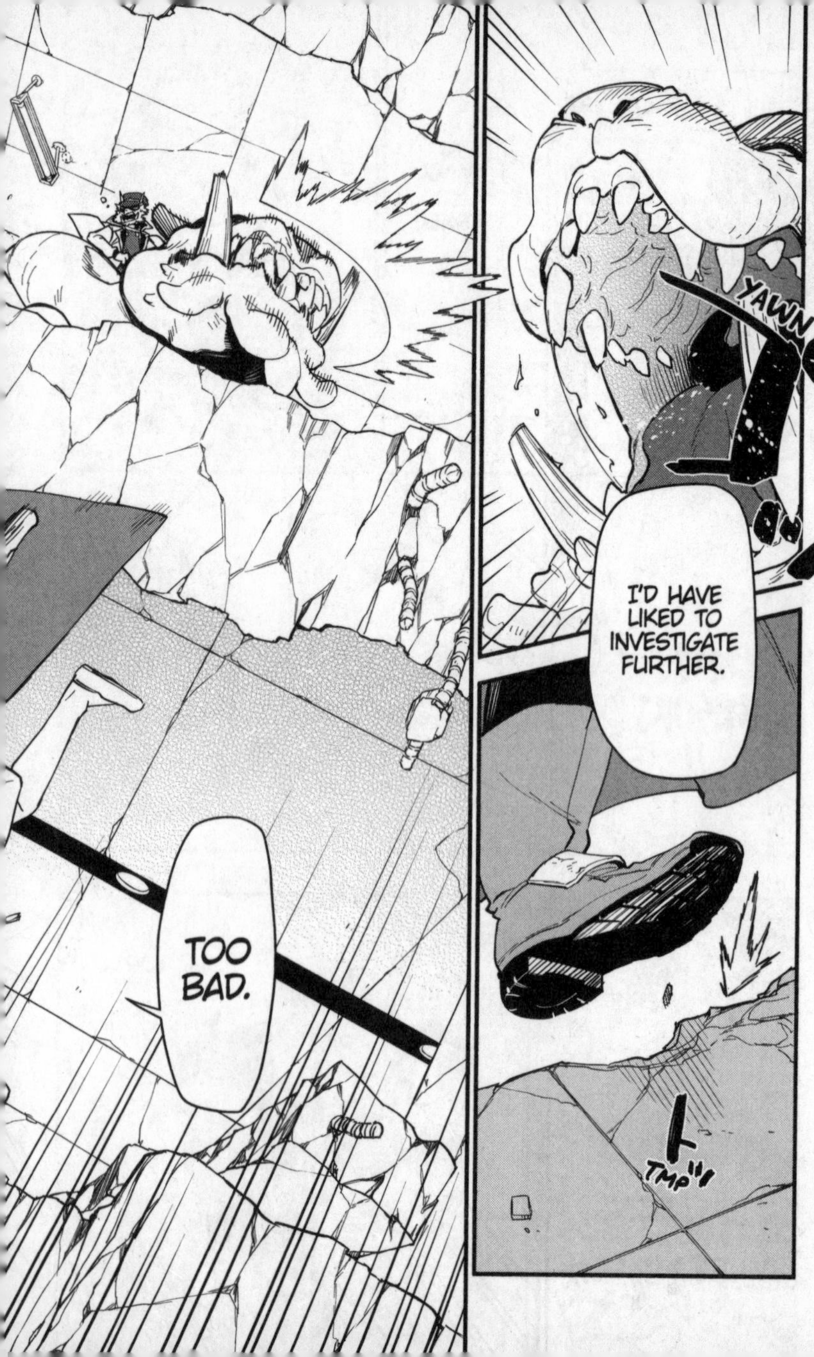
YAWN
I'D HAVE LIKED TO INVESTIGATE FURTHER.
TMP
TOO BAD.

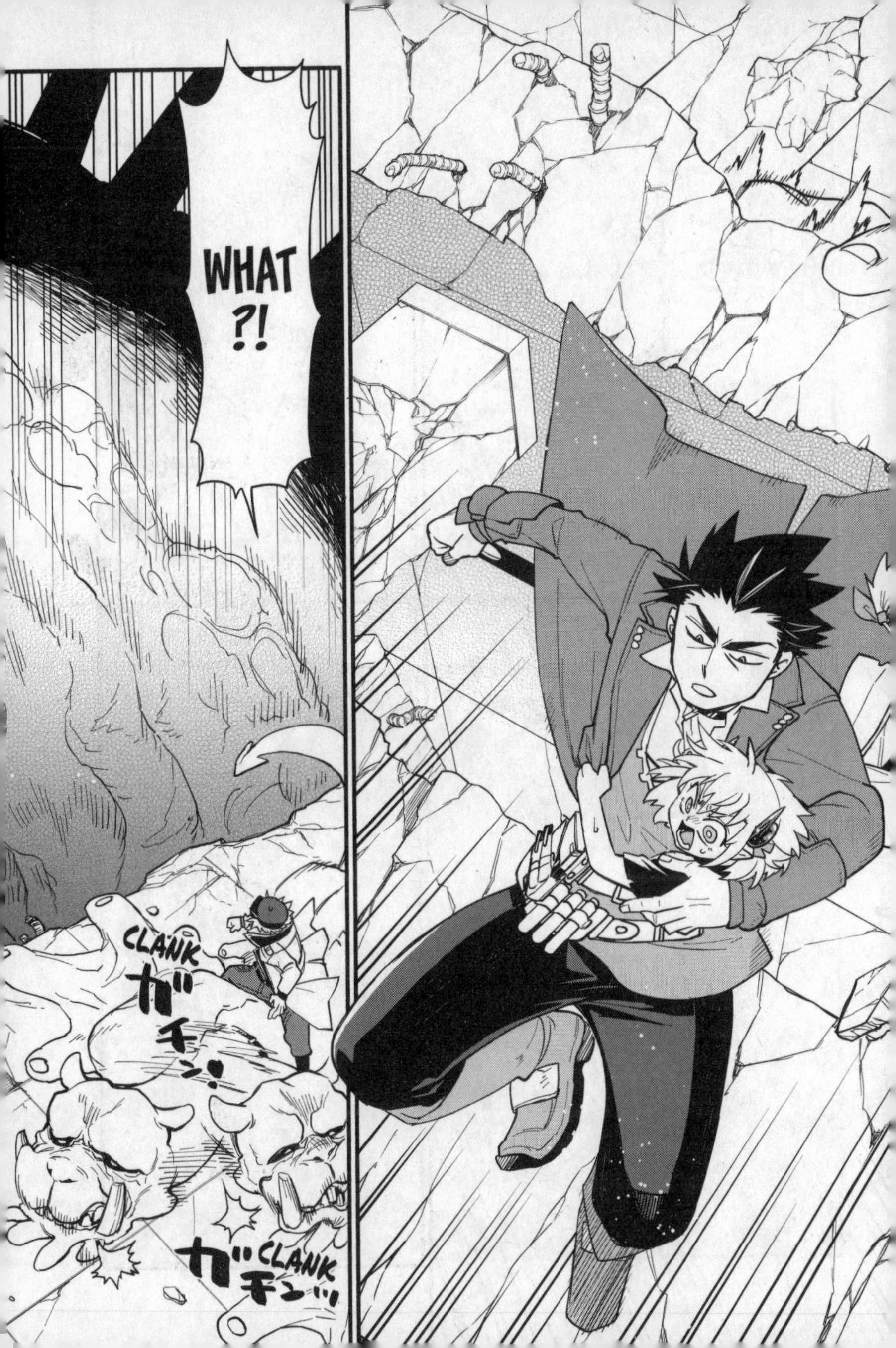
WHAT ?!
CLANK
ガチン!
ガチン…!!
CLANK

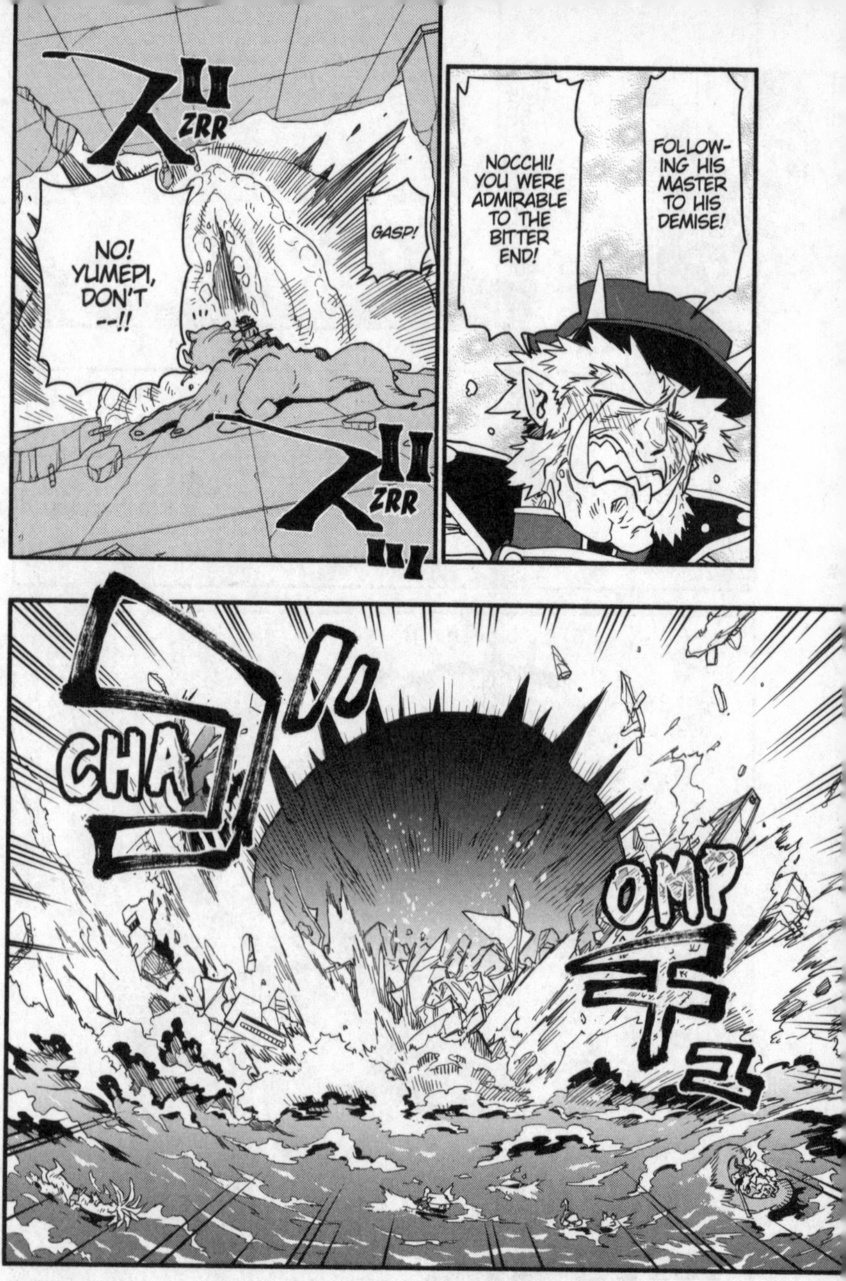
FOLLOW-
ING HIS
MASTER
TO HIS
DEMISE!
NOCCHI!
YOU WERE
ADMIRABLE
TO THE
BITTER
END!
GASP!
ZRR
NO!
YUMEPI,
DON'T
--!!
ZRR
CHA
OMP

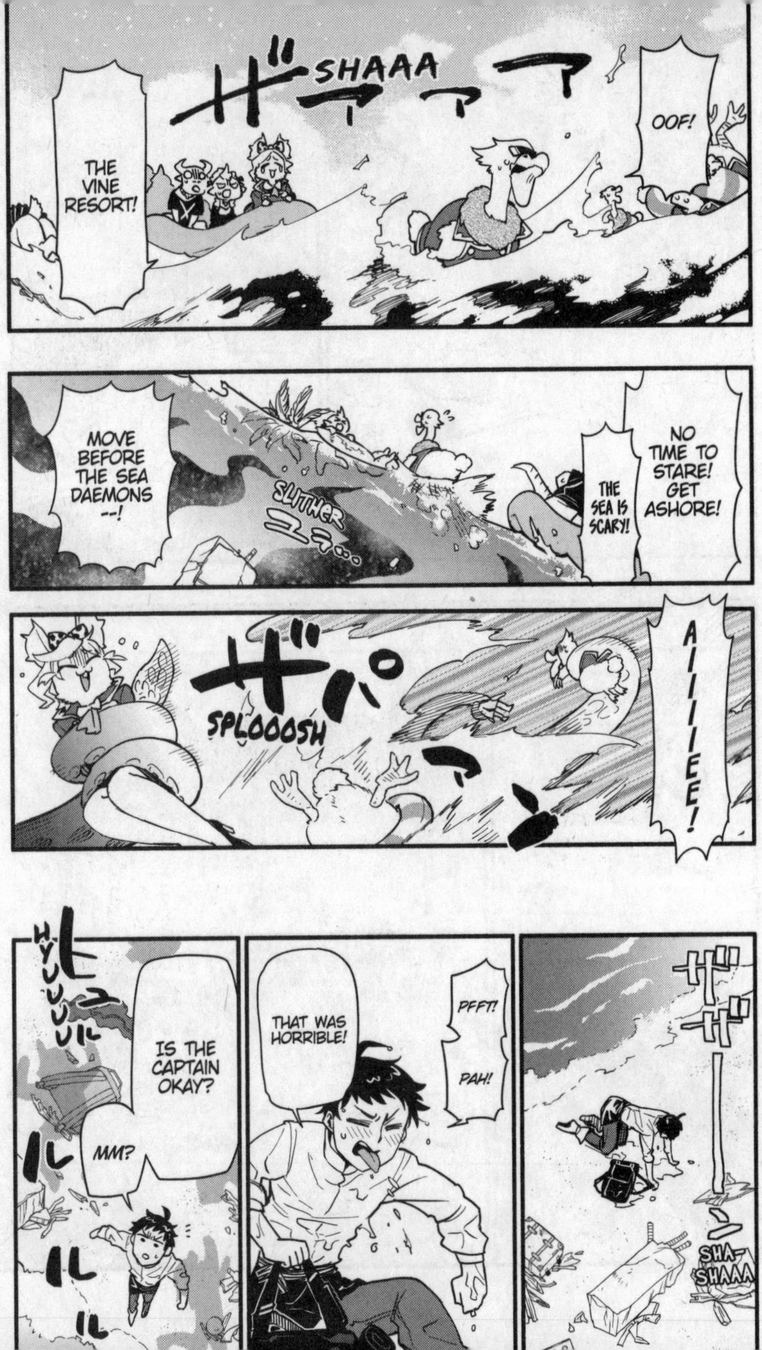
OOF!
SHAAA
THE VINE RESORT!
NO TIME TO STARE! GET ASHORE!
THE SEA IS SCARY!
SLITHER
MOVE BEFORE THE SEA DAEMONS --!
AIIIIIEE!
SPLOOOSH
SHA-SHAAA
PFFT!
PAH!
THAT WAS HORRIBLE!
HYUUUUL
IS THE CAPTAIN OKAY?
MM?

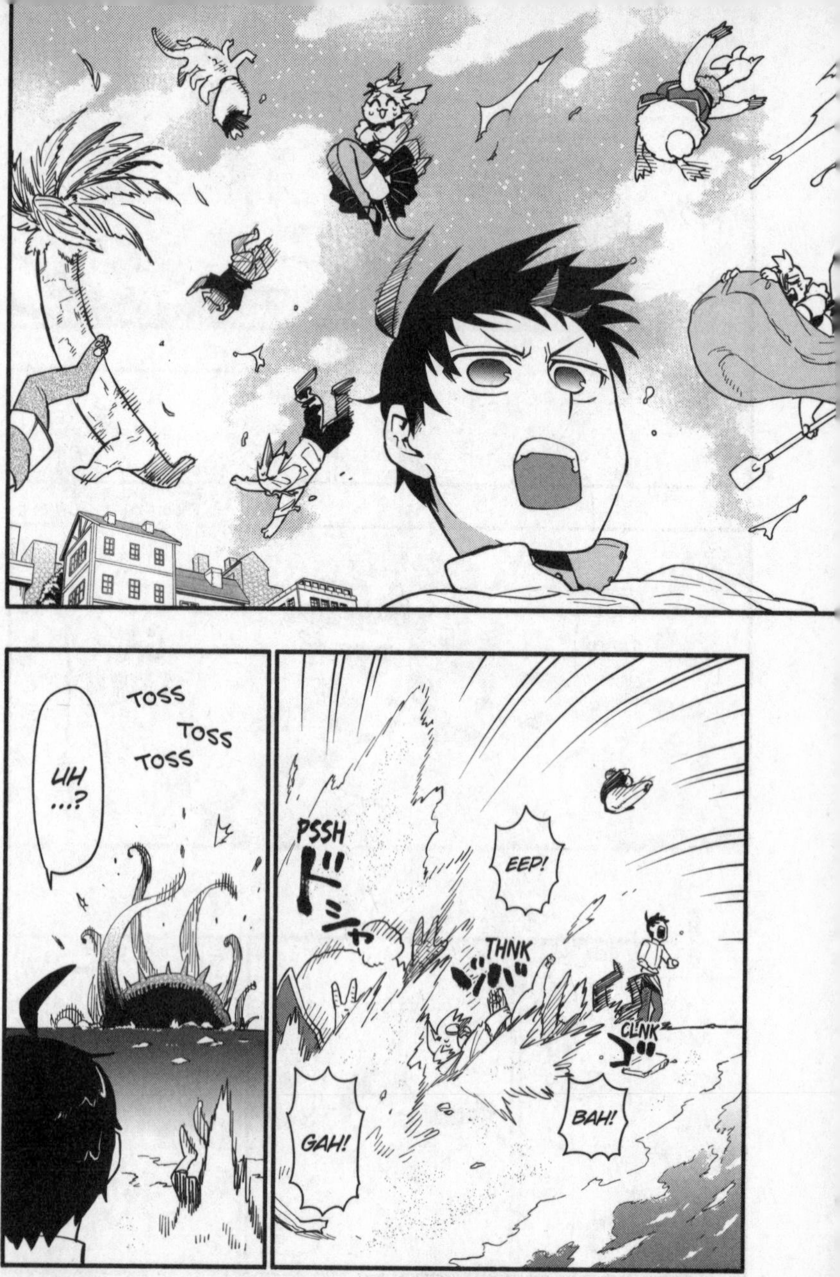
EEP!
PSSH
ドシャ
THNK
CLNK
BAH!
GAH!
TOSS
TOSS
TOSS
UH ...?

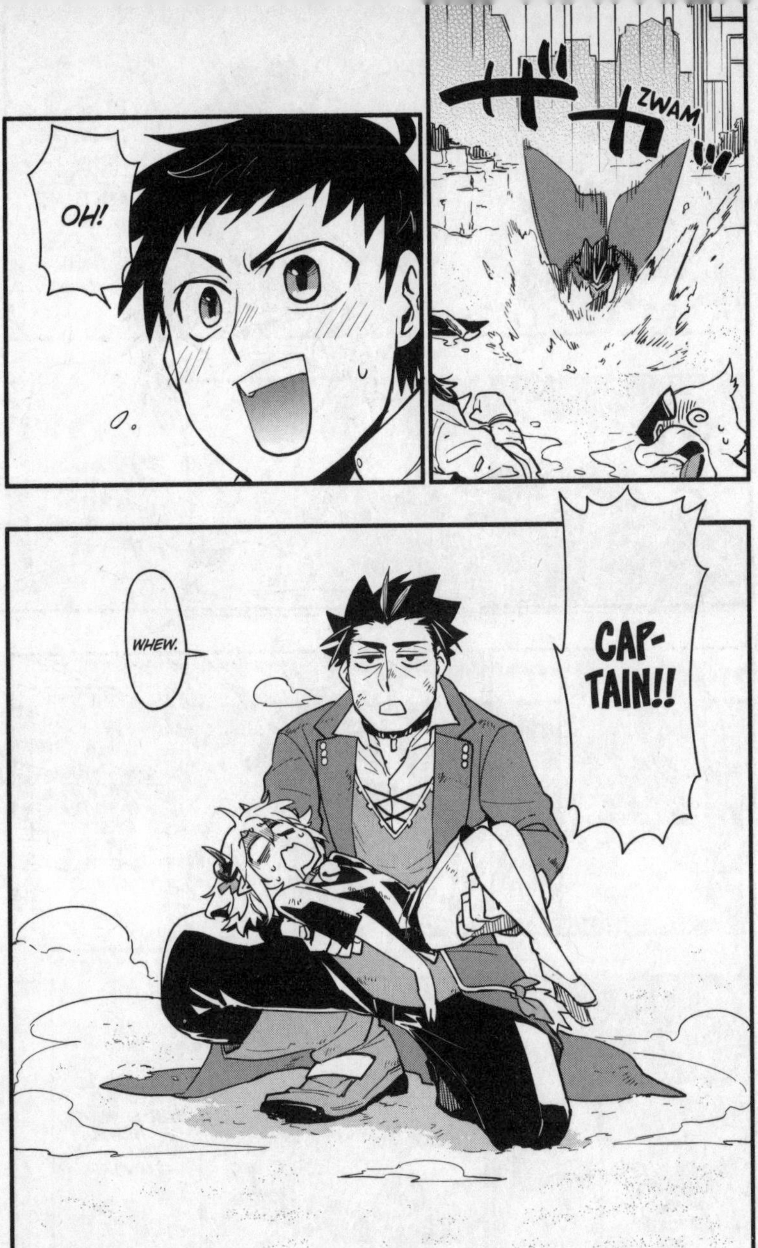
ZWAM
OH!
CAP-TAIN!!
WHEW.

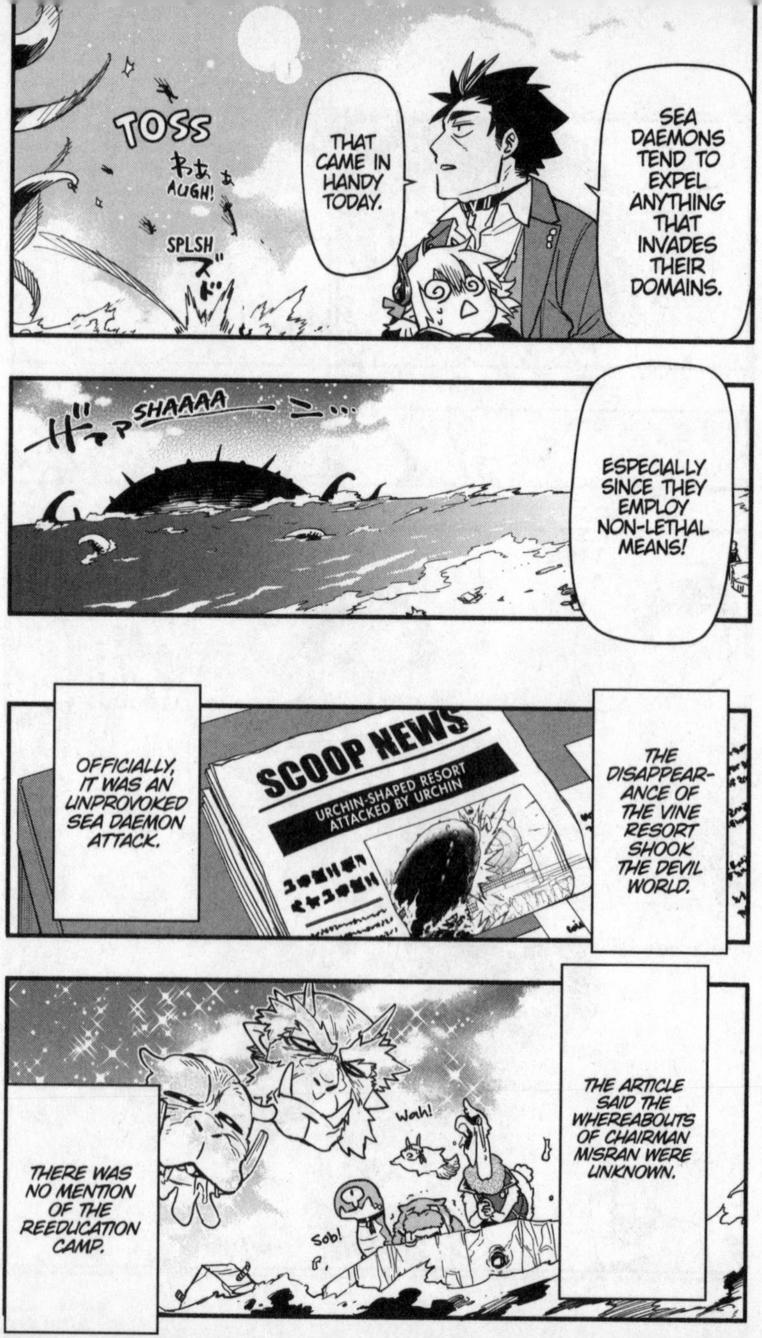
SEA DAEMONS TEND TO EXPEL ANYTHING THAT INVADES THEIR DOMAINS.
THAT CAME IN HANDY TODAY.
TOSS
AUGH!
SPLSH
ESPECIALLY SINCE THEY EMPLOY NON-LETHAL MEANS!
SHAAAA
THE DISAPPEARANCE OF THE VINE RESORT SHOOK THE DEVIL WORLD.
SCOOP NEWS
URCHIN-SHAPED RESORT ATTACKED BY URCHIN
OFFICIALLY, IT WAS AN UNPROVOKED SEA DAEMON ATTACK.
THE ARTICLE SAID THE WHEREABOUTS OF CHAIRMAN MISRAN WERE UNKNOWN.
Wah!
Sob!
THERE WAS NO MENTION OF THE REEDUCATION CAMP.

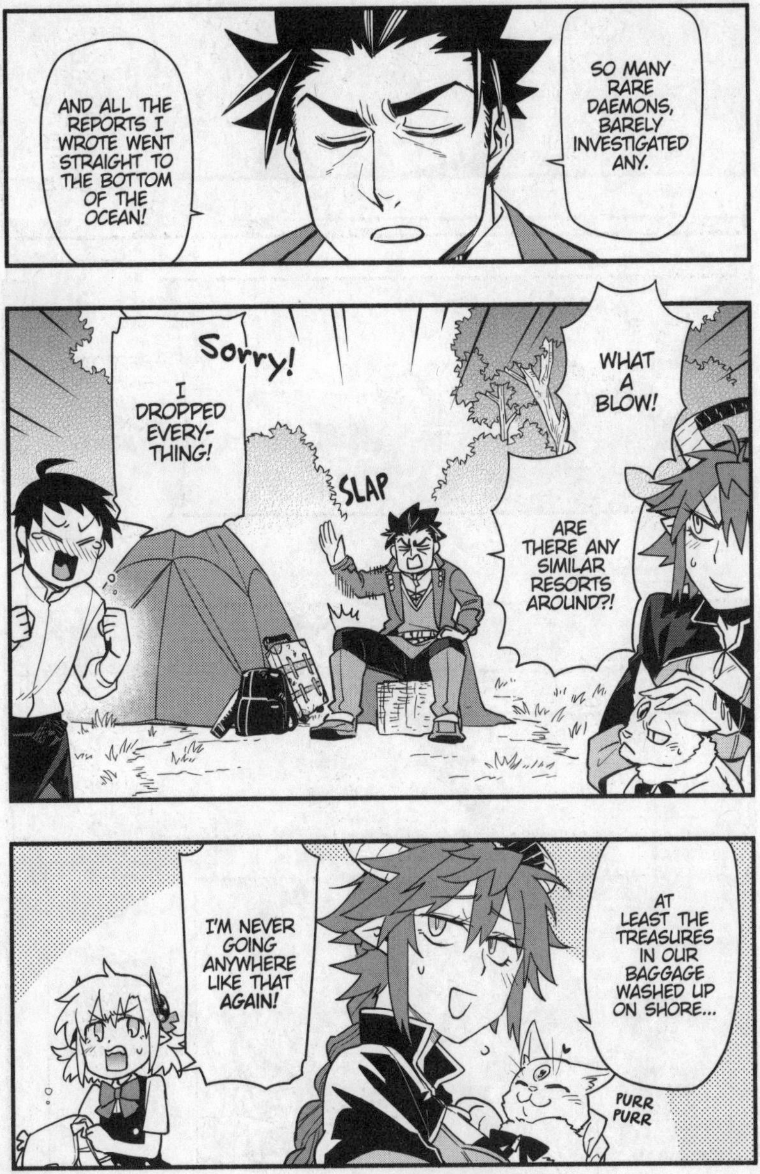
SO MANY RARE DAEMONS, BARELY INVESTIGATED ANY.
AND ALL THE REPORTS I WROTE WENT STRAIGHT TO THE BOTTOM OF THE OCEAN!
WHAT A BLOW!
SLAP
Sorry!
I DROPPED EVERY-THING!
ARE THERE ANY SIMILAR RESORTS AROUND?!
AT LEAST THE TREASURES IN OUR BAGGAGE WASHED UP ON SHORE...
I'M NEVER GOING ANYWHERE LIKE THAT AGAIN!
PURR PURR

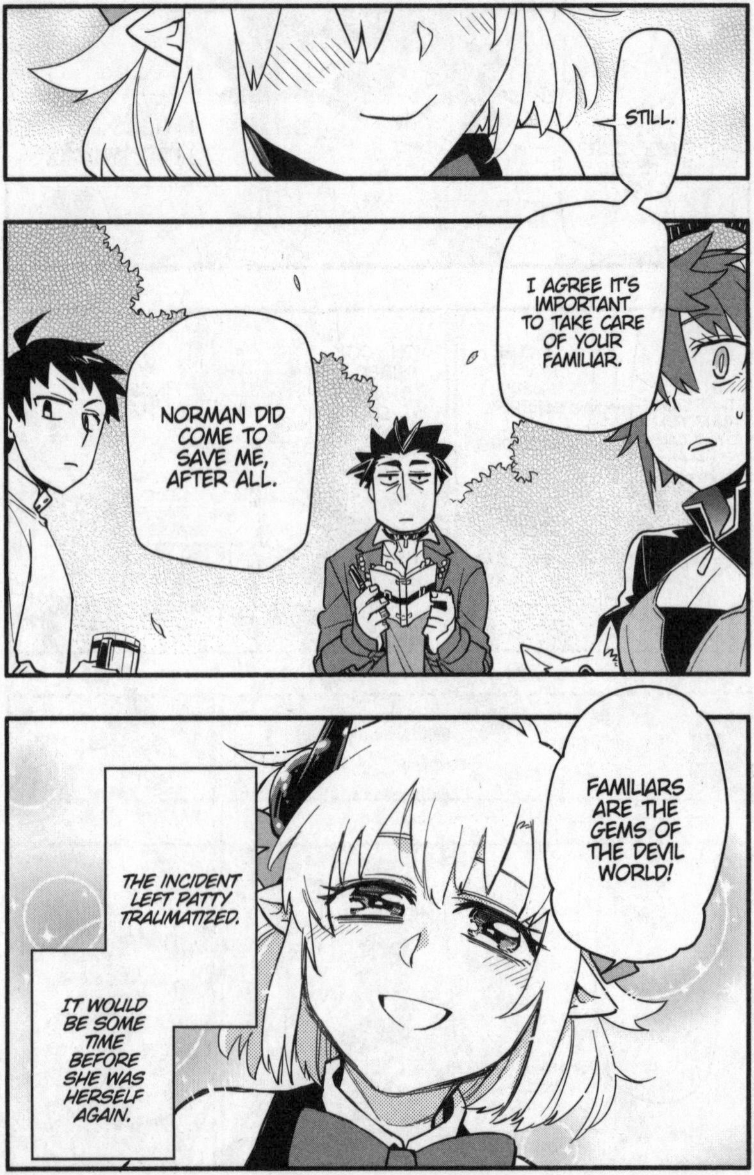
STILL.
I AGREE IT'S IMPORTANT TO TAKE CARE OF YOUR FAMILIAR.
NORMAN DID COME TO SAVE ME, AFTER ALL.
FAMILIARS ARE THE GEMS OF THE DEVIL WORLD!
THE INCIDENT LEFT PATTY TRAUMATIZED.
IT WOULD BE SOME TIME BEFORE SHE WAS HERSELF AGAIN.

File 56

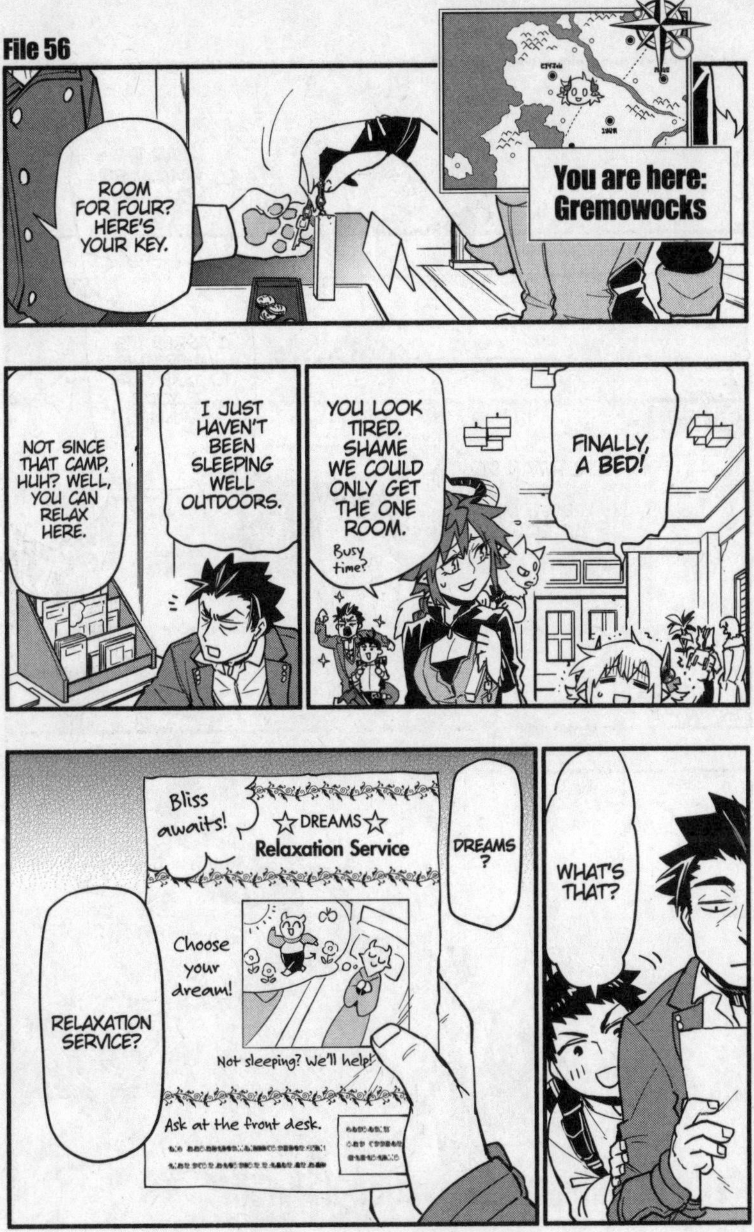

You are here: Gremowocks
ROOM FOR FOUR? HERE'S YOUR KEY.
FINALLY, A BED!
YOU LOOK TIRED. SHAME WE COULD ONLY GET THE ONE ROOM.
Busy time?
I JUST HAVEN'T BEEN SLEEPING WELL OUTDOORS.
NOT SINCE THAT CAMP, HUH? WELL, YOU CAN RELAX HERE.
WHAT'S THAT?
DREAMS?
RELAXATION SERVICE?
Bliss awaits!
☆DREAMS☆
Relaxation Service
Choose your dream!
Not sleeping? We'll help!
Ask at the front desk.

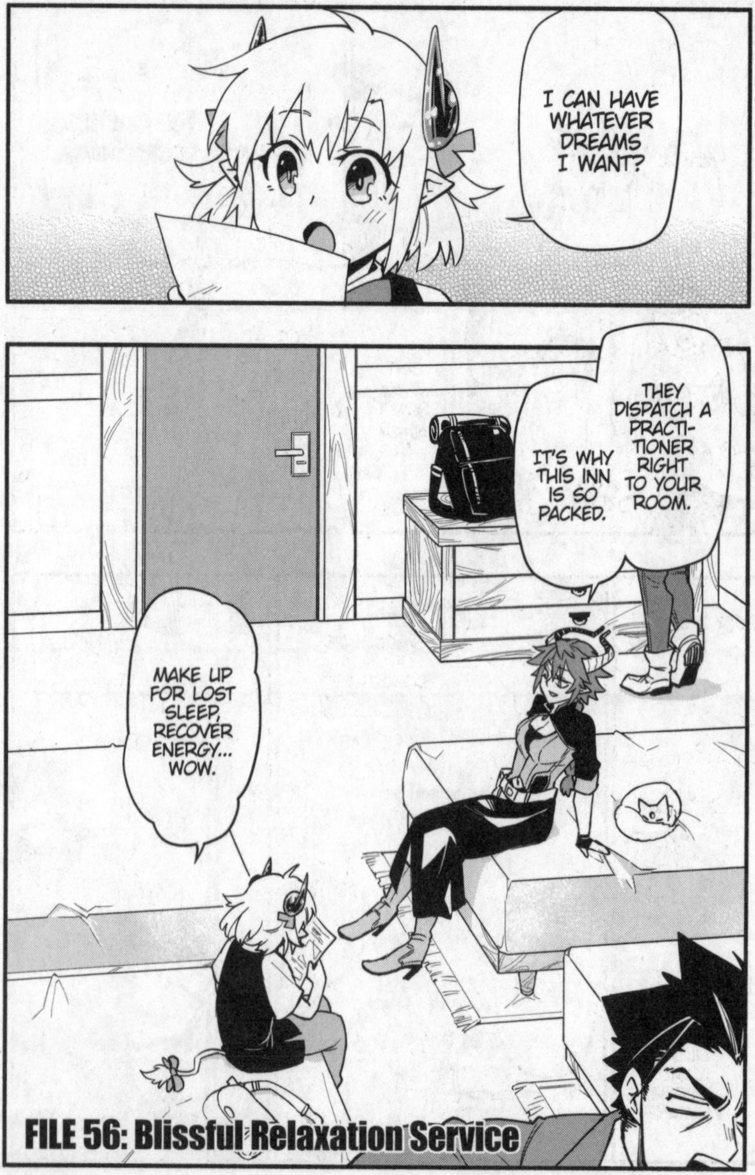
I CAN HAVE WHATEVER DREAMS I WANT?
THEY DISPATCH A PRACTI-TIONER RIGHT TO YOUR ROOM.
IT'S WHY THIS INN IS SO PACKED.
MAKE UP FOR LOST SLEEP, RECOVER ENERGY... WOW.
FILE 56: Blissful Relaxation Service

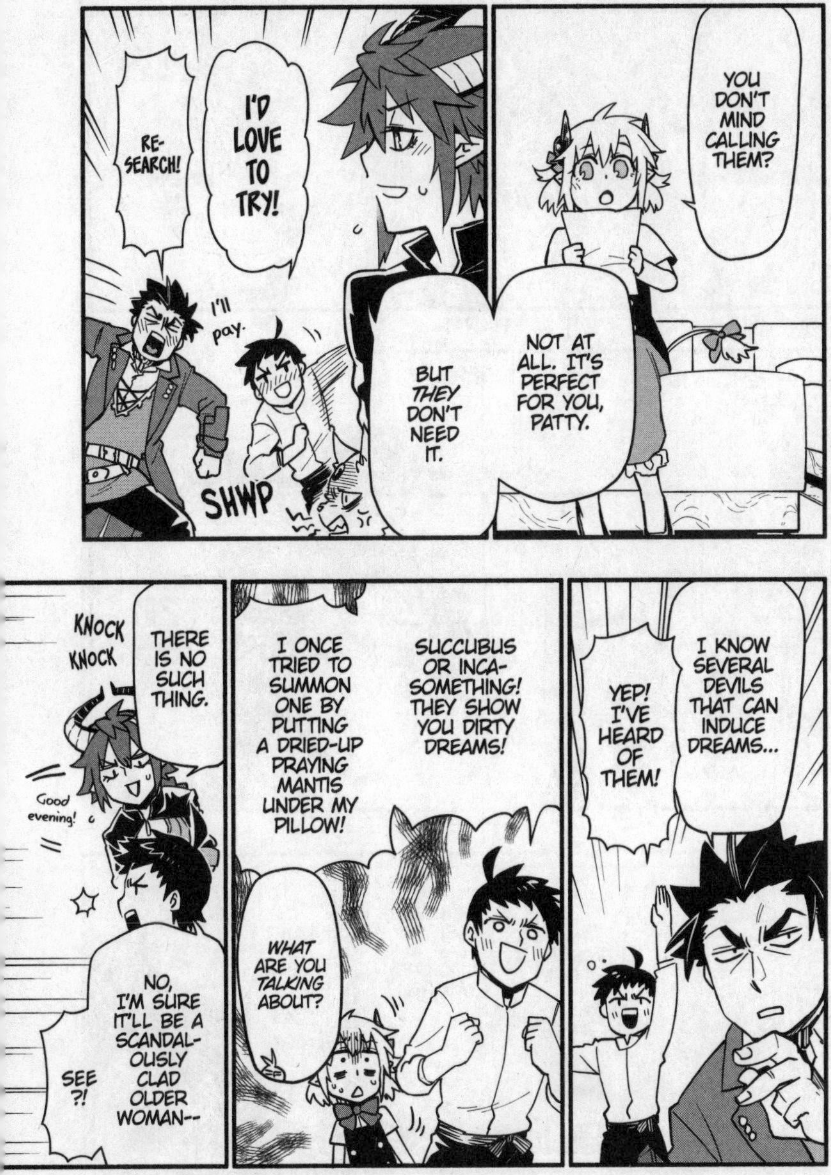
YOU DON'T MIND CALLING THEM?
NOT AT ALL. IT'S PERFECT FOR YOU, PATTY.
BUT *THEY* DON'T NEED IT.
I'D LOVE TO TRY!
RE-SEARCH!
I'll pay.
SHWP
I KNOW SEVERAL DEVILS THAT CAN INDUCE DREAMS...
YEP! I'VE HEARD OF THEM!
SUCCUBUS OR INCA-SOMETHING! THEY SHOW YOU DIRTY DREAMS!
I ONCE TRIED TO SUMMON ONE BY PUTTING A DRIED-UP PRAYING MANTIS UNDER MY PILLOW!
WHAT ARE YOU *TALKING* ABOUT?
THERE IS NO SUCH THING.
NO, I'M SURE IT'LL BE A SCANDAL-OUSLY CLAD OLDER WOMAN--
SEE?!
KNOCK KNOCK
Good evening!

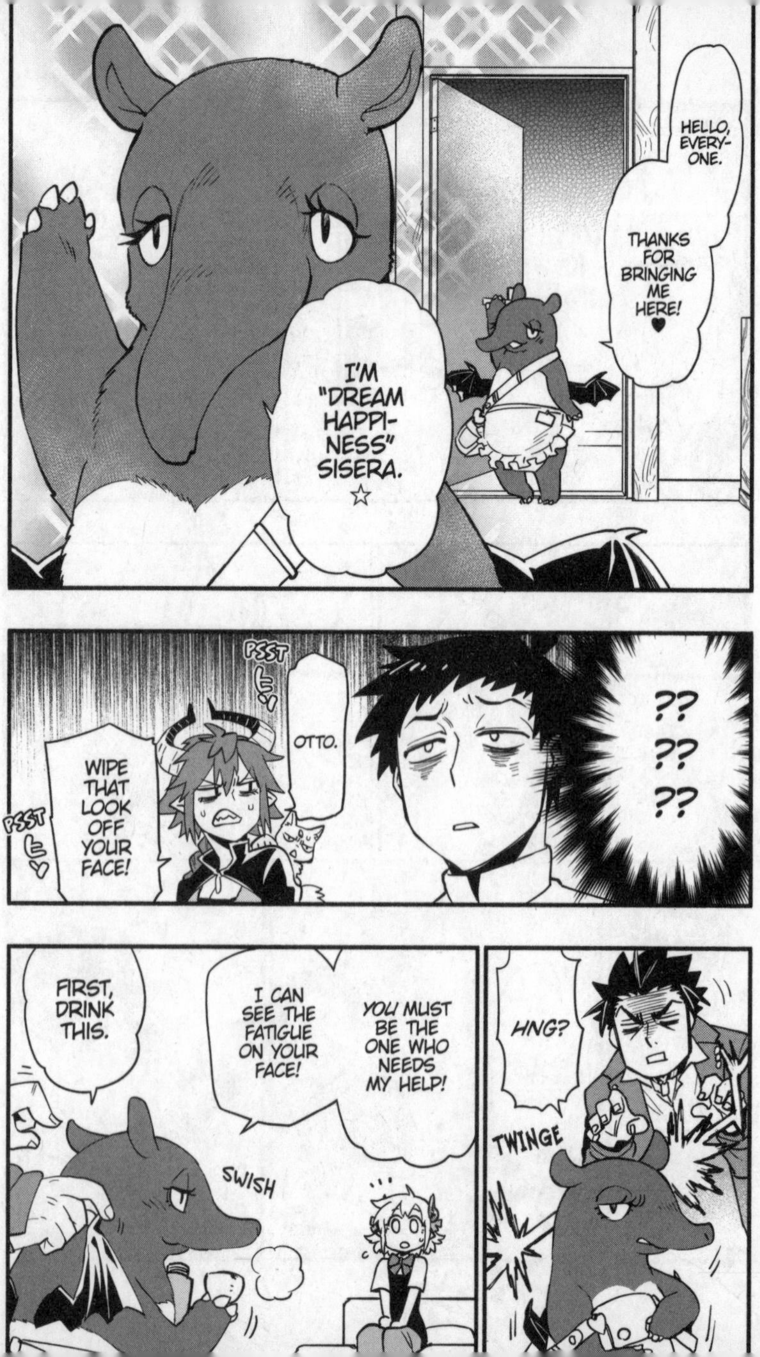
HELLO, EVERYONE.
THANKS FOR BRINGING ME HERE! ♥
I'M "DREAM HAPPINESS" SISERA. ☆
?? ?? ??
PSSST
OTTO.
WIPE THAT LOOK OFF YOUR FACE!
PSSST
HNG?
TWINGE
YOU MUST BE THE ONE WHO NEEDS MY HELP!
I CAN SEE THE FATIGUE ON YOUR FACE!
FIRST, DRINK THIS.
SWISH

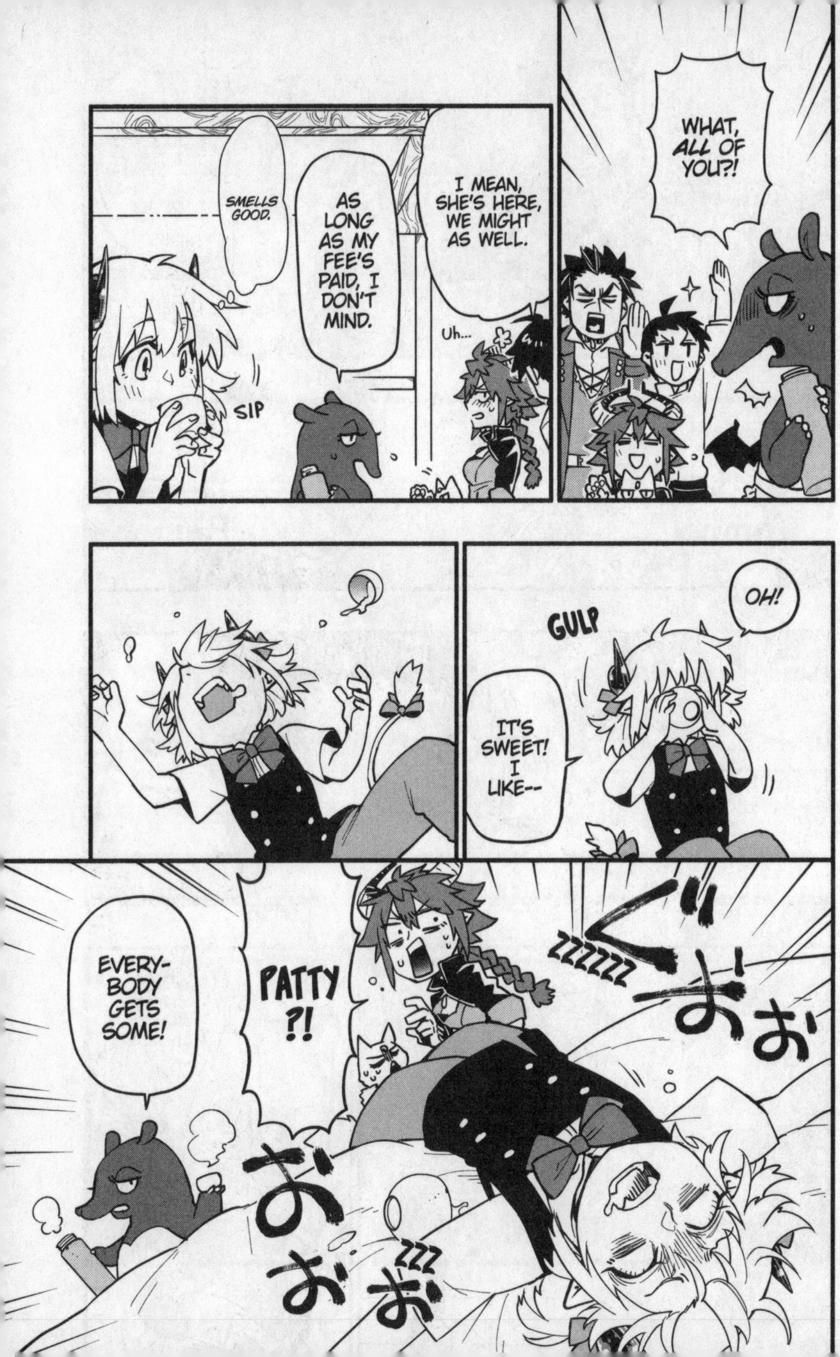

WHAT, ALL OF YOU?!
I MEAN, SHE'S HERE, WE MIGHT AS WELL.
Uh...
AS LONG AS MY FEE'S PAID, I DON'T MIND.
SMELLS GOOD.
SIP
OH!
GULP
IT'S SWEET! I LIKE--
ZZZZZZ
PATTY?!
EVERY-BODY GETS SOME!
おお
おお
おお
ZZZ

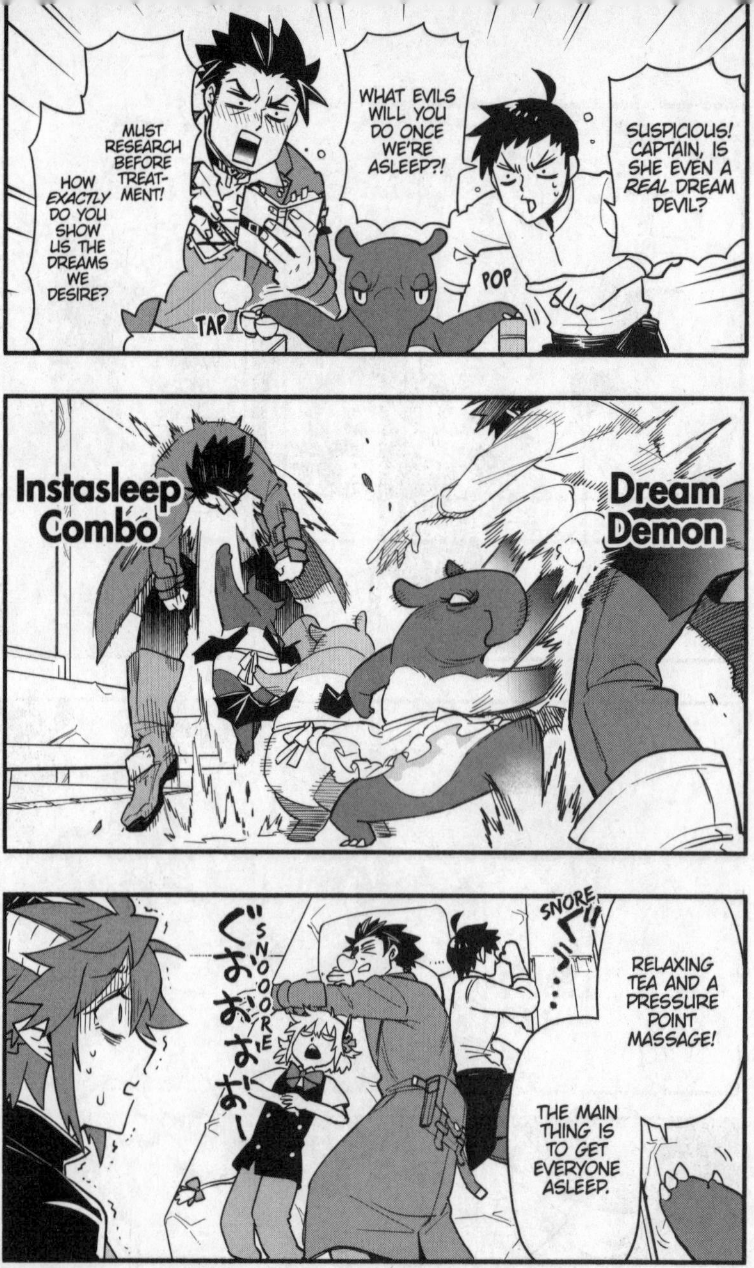
SUSPICIOUS! CAPTAIN, IS SHE EVEN A *REAL* DREAM DEVIL?
WHAT EVILS WILL YOU DO ONCE WE'RE ASLEEP?!
MUST RESEARCH BEFORE TREATMENT!
HOW *EXACTLY* DO YOU SHOW US THE DREAMS WE DESIRE?
POP
TAP
Dream Demon
Instasleep Combo
RELAXING TEA AND A PRESSURE POINT MASSAGE!
THE MAIN THING IS TO GET EVERYONE ASLEEP.
SNORE
ぐ〜…
SNOOOORE
ぐおおおおー

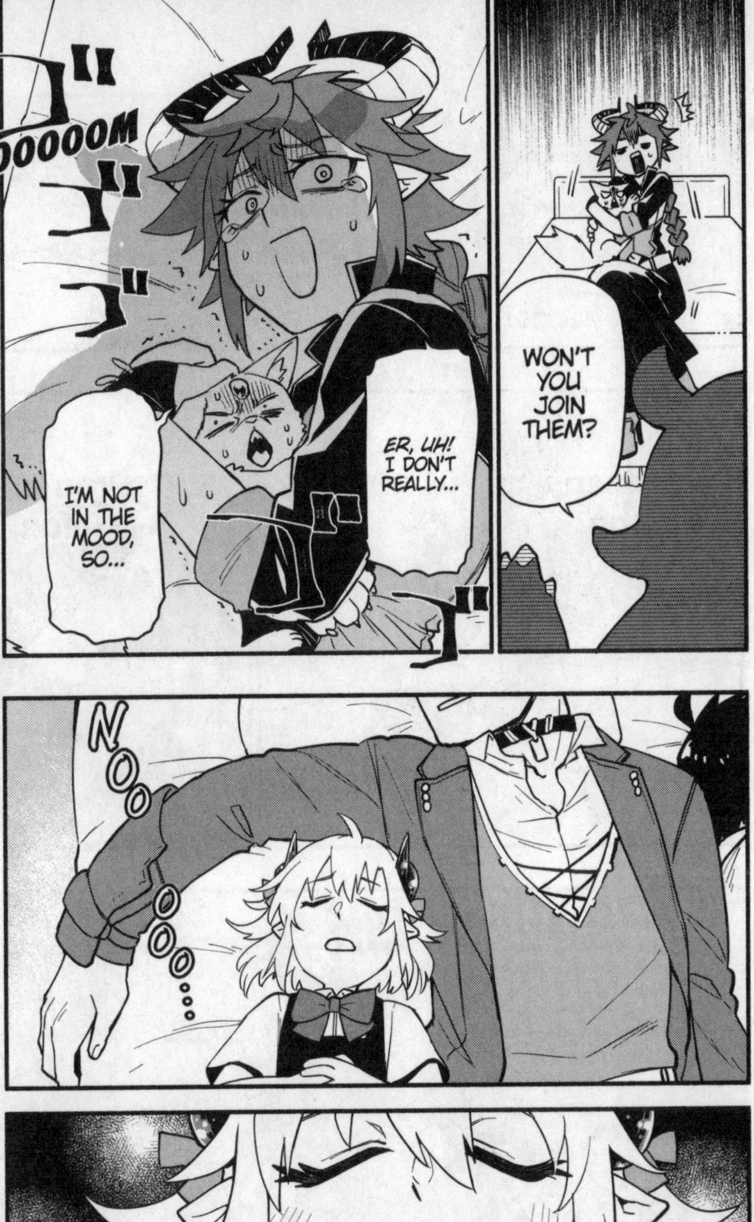

WON'T YOU JOIN THEM?
ER, UH! I DON'T REALLY...
I'M NOT IN THE MOOD, SO...
LOOOOOM
NOOOOOO...

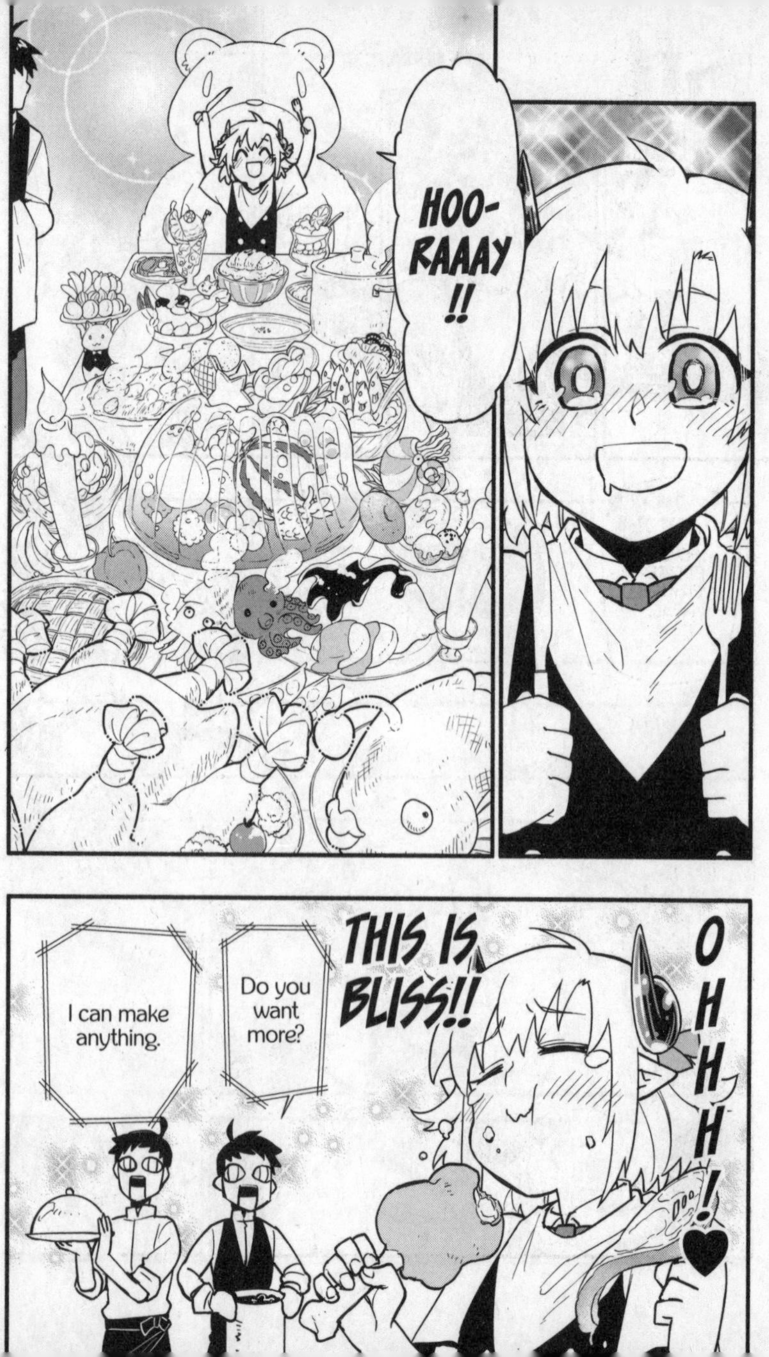
HOO-RAAAY!!
THIS IS BLISS!!
OHHHH!
Do you want more?
I can make anything.

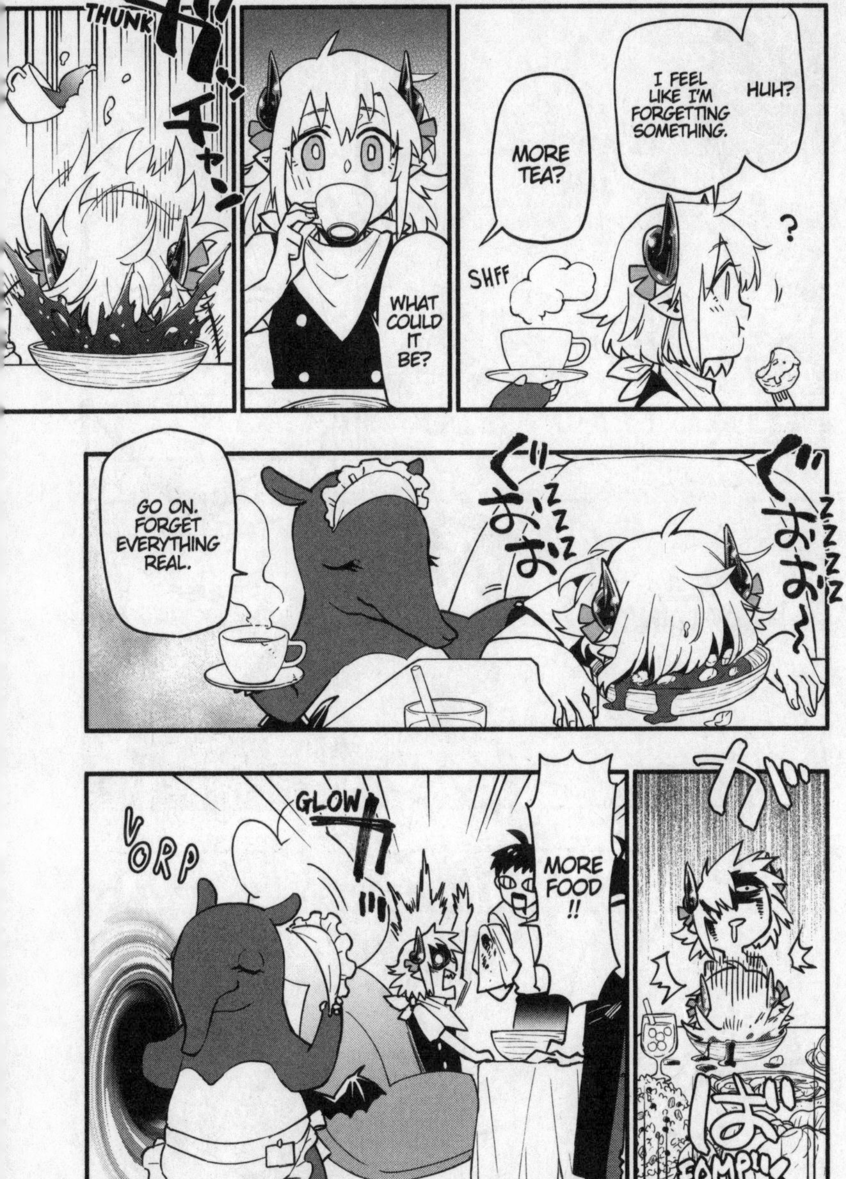

HUH?
I FEEL LIKE I'M FORGETTING SOMETHING.
?
MORE TEA?
SHFF
WHAT COULD IT BE?
THUNK
ガチャン
ぐおおZZZ
ぐおおZZZ~
GO ON. FORGET EVERYTHING REAL.
ガバ
MORE FOOD!!
GLOW
VORP
ぼ
FOMP!!

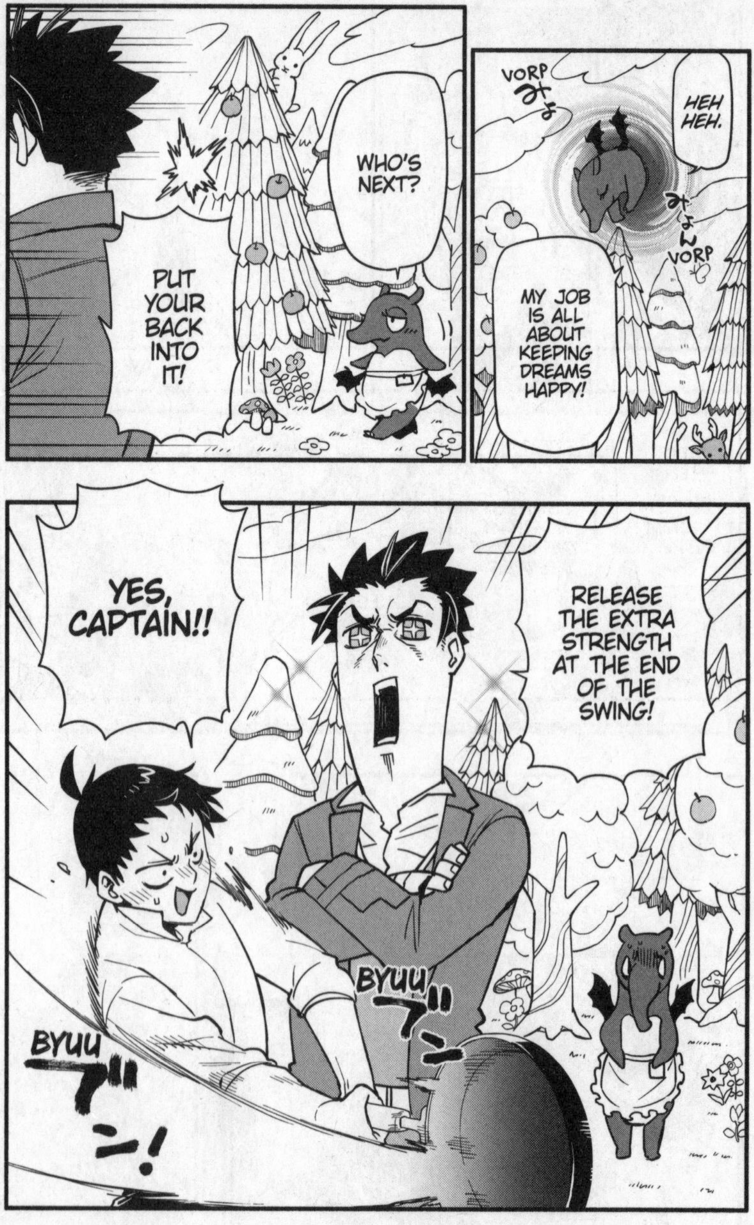
VORP みょ
HEH HEH.
みょん VORP
MY JOB IS ALL ABOUT KEEPING DREAMS HAPPY!
WHO'S NEXT?
PUT YOUR BACK INTO IT!
RELEASE THE EXTRA STRENGTH AT THE END OF THE SWING!
YES, CAPTAIN!!
BYUU ブー
BYUU ブーン!

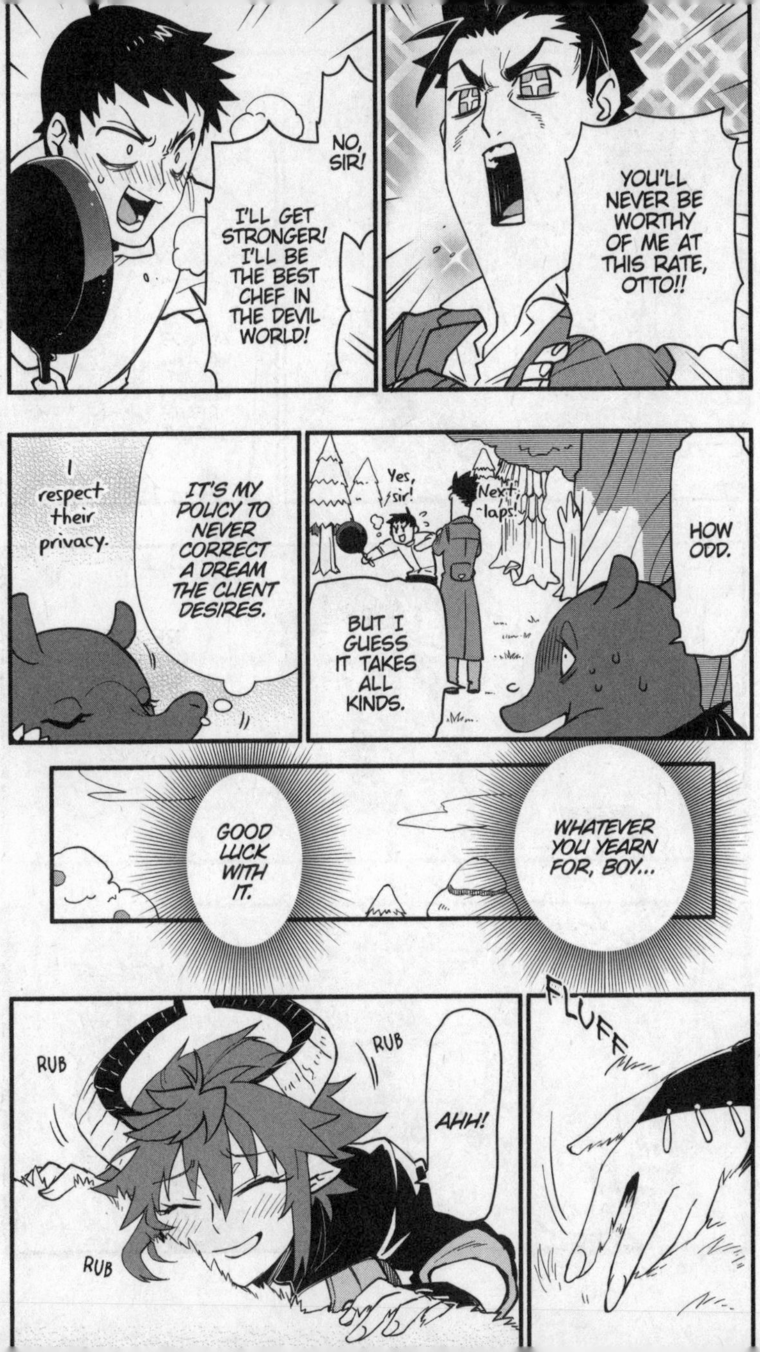
YOU'LL NEVER BE WORTHY OF ME AT THIS RATE, OTTO!!
NO, SIR!
I'LL GET STRONGER! I'LL BE THE BEST CHEF IN THE DEVIL WORLD!
HOW ODD.
Next laps!
Yes, sir!
BUT I GUESS IT TAKES ALL KINDS.
IT'S MY POLICY TO NEVER CORRECT A DREAM THE CLIENT DESIRES.
I respect their privacy.
WHATEVER YOU YEARN FOR, BOY...
GOOD LUCK WITH IT.
FLUFF
AHH!
RUB
RUB
RUB

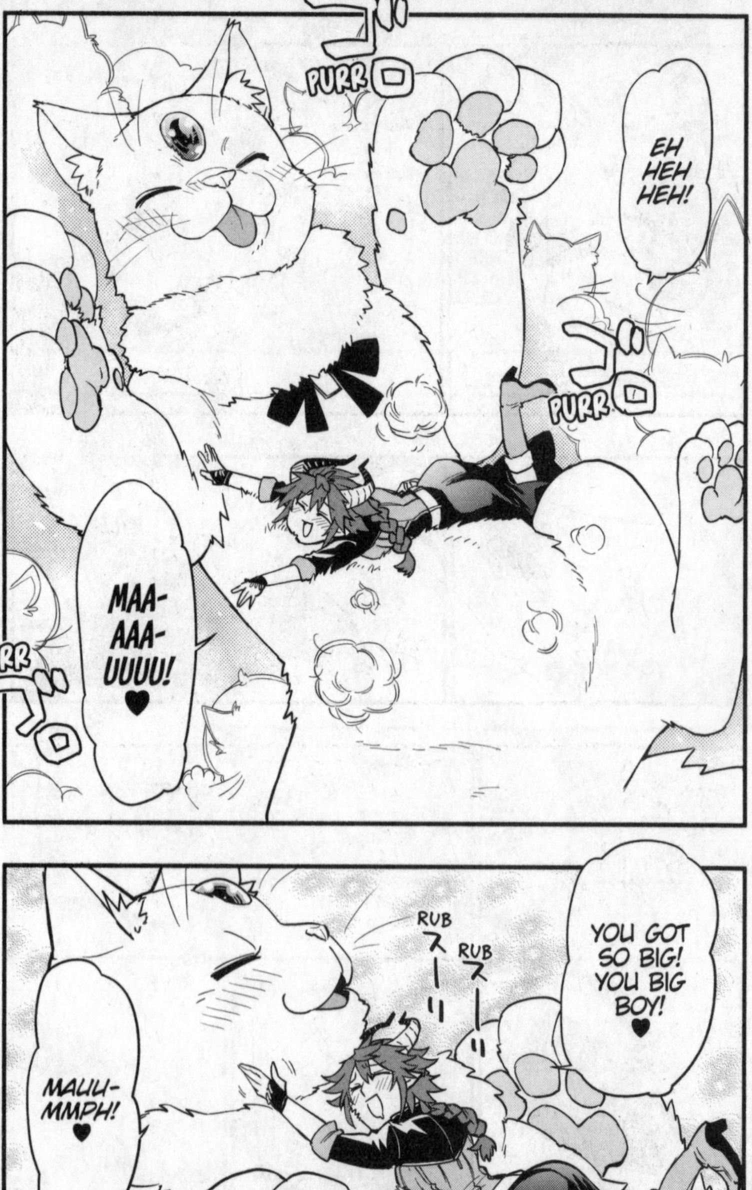
PURR ゴロ
EH HEH HEH!
PURR ゴロ
MAA-AAA-UUUU! ♥
PURR ゴロ
YOU GOT SO BIG! YOU BIG BOY! ♥
RUB スーッ
RUB スーッ
MAUU-MMPH! ♥

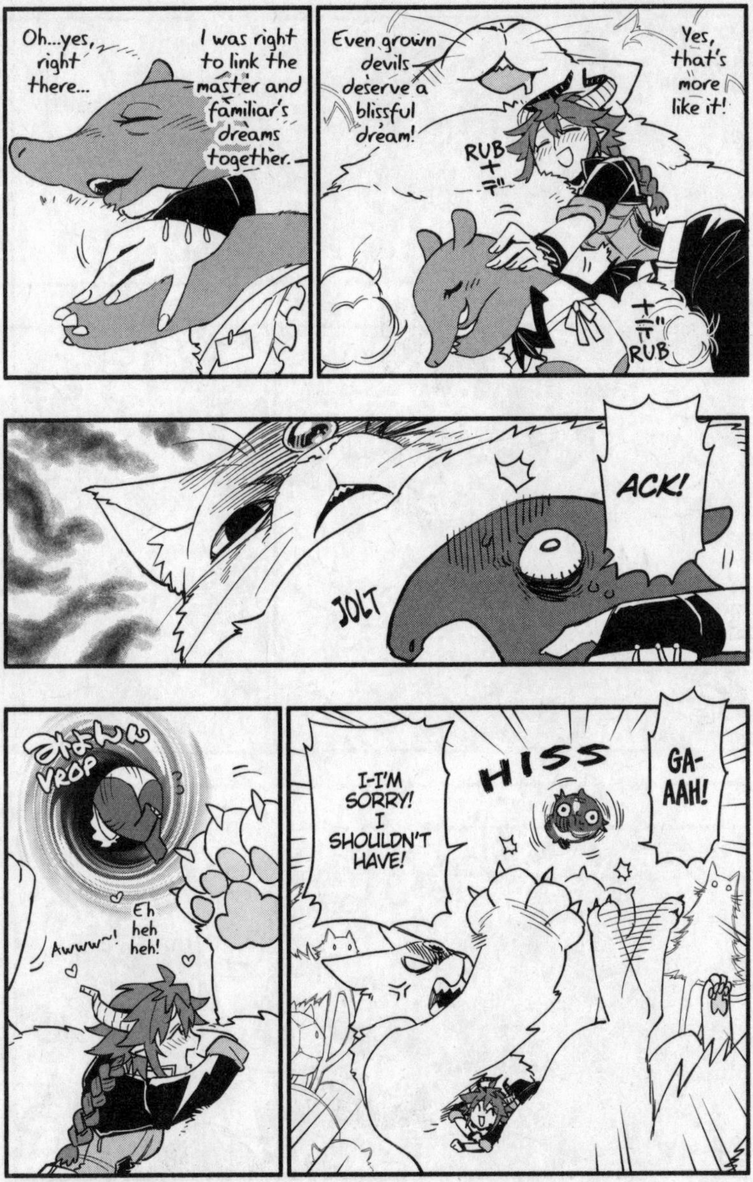
Oh...yes, right there...
I was right to link the master and familiar's dreams together.
Even grown devils deserve a blissful dream!
Yes, that's more like it!
RUB
RUB
ACK!
JOLT
みよんん
VROP
Eh heh heh!
Awww~!
GA-AAH!
HISS
I-I'M SORRY! I SHOULDN'T HAVE!

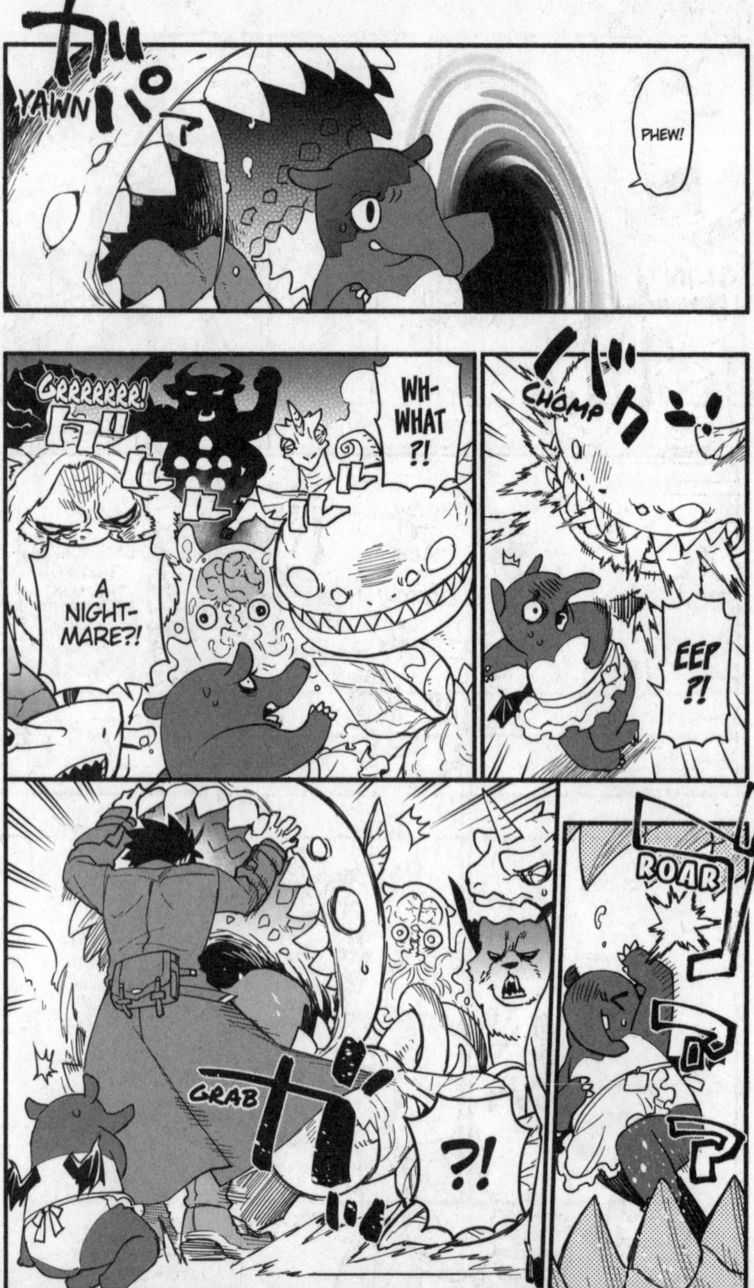
YAWN
PHEW!
CHOMP
EEP?!
GRRRRRRR!
WH-WHAT?!
A NIGHT-MARE?!
ROAR
GRAB
?!

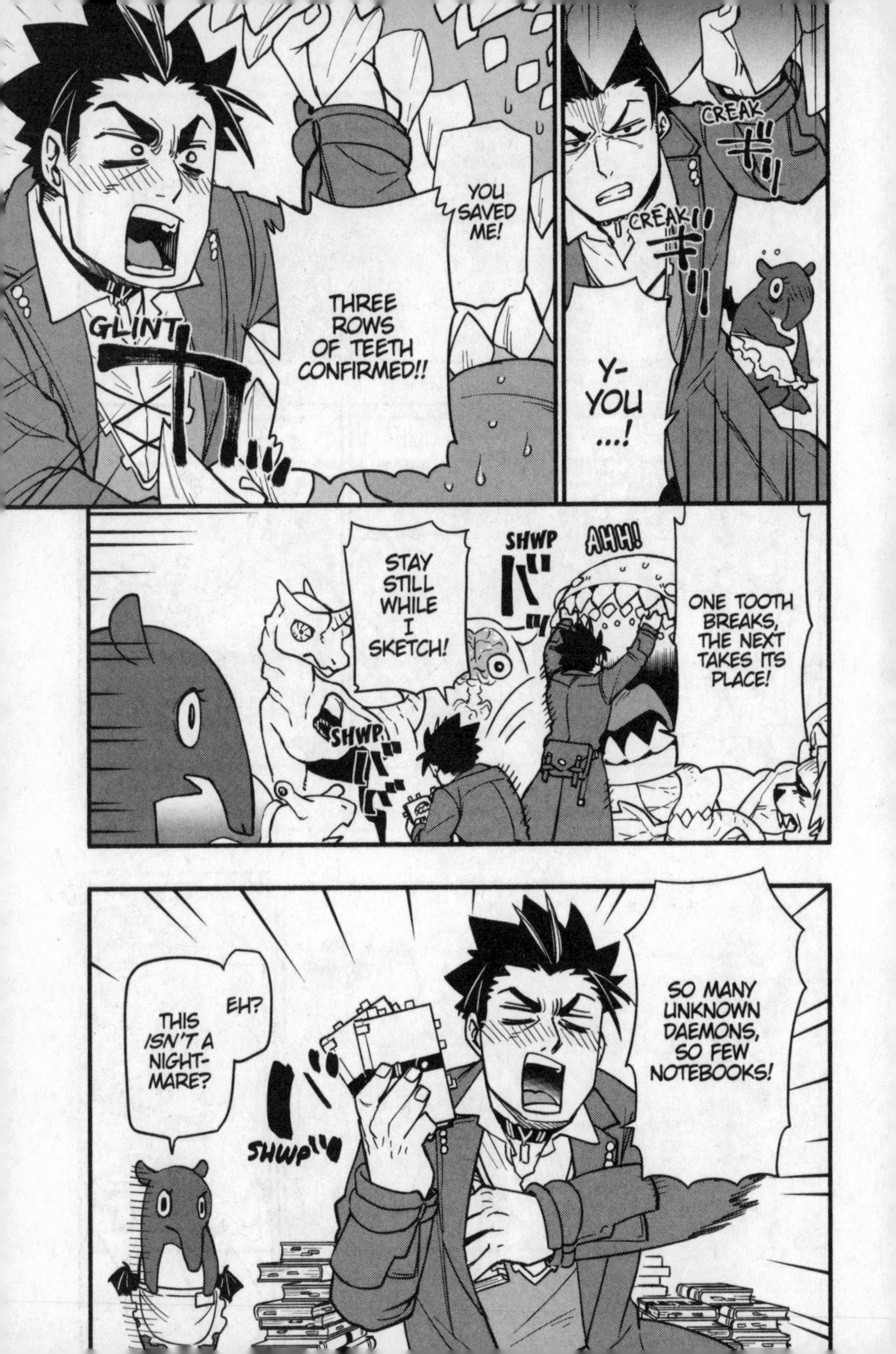
CREAK
CREAK
Y-YOU ...!
YOU SAVED ME!
THREE ROWS OF TEETH CONFIRMED!!
GLINT
ONE TOOTH BREAKS, THE NEXT TAKES ITS PLACE!
AHH!
SHWP
STAY STILL WHILE I SKETCH!
SHWP
SO MANY UNKNOWN DAEMONS, SO FEW NOTEBOOKS!
SHWP
EH?
THIS ISN'T A NIGHT-MARE?

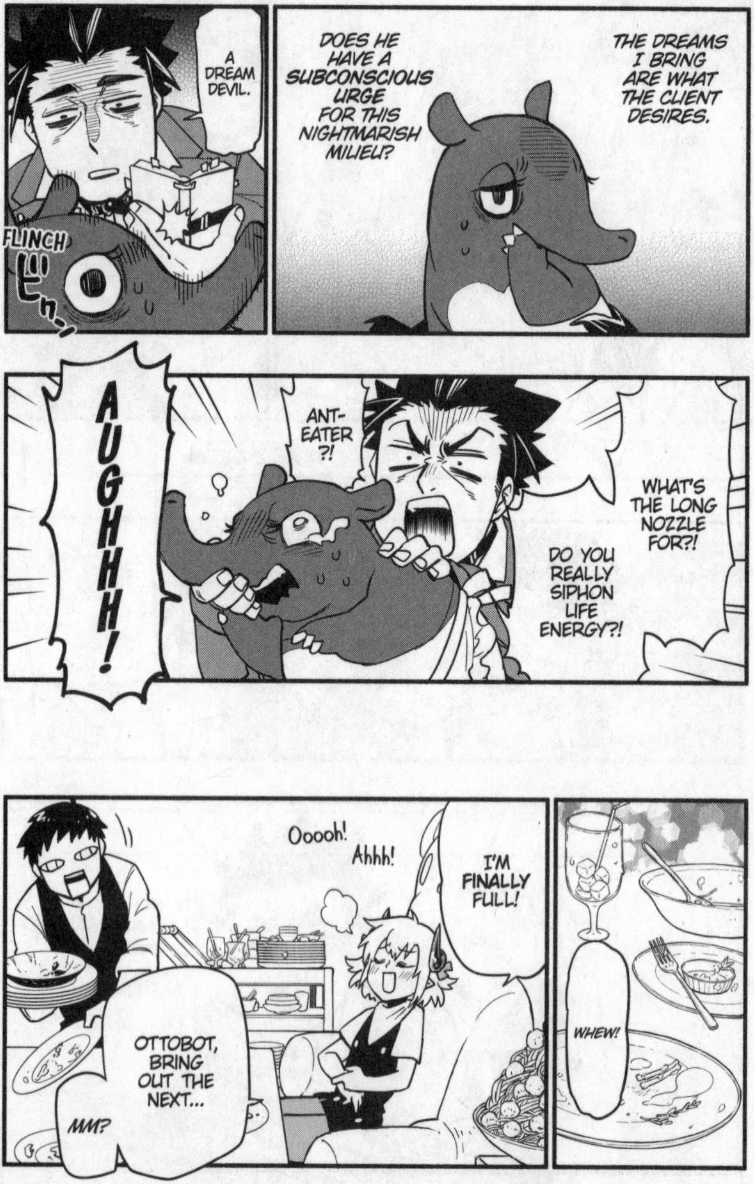
THE DREAMS I BRING ARE WHAT THE CLIENT DESIRES.
DOES HE HAVE A SUBCONSCIOUS URGE FOR THIS NIGHTMARISH MILIEU?
A DREAM DEVIL.
FLINCH
WHAT'S THE LONG NOZZLE FOR?!
DO YOU REALLY SIPHON LIFE ENERGY?!
ANT-EATER?!
AUGHHHH!
WHEW!
I'M FINALLY FULL!
Ooooh!
Ahhh!
OTTOBOT, BRING OUT THE NEXT...
MM?

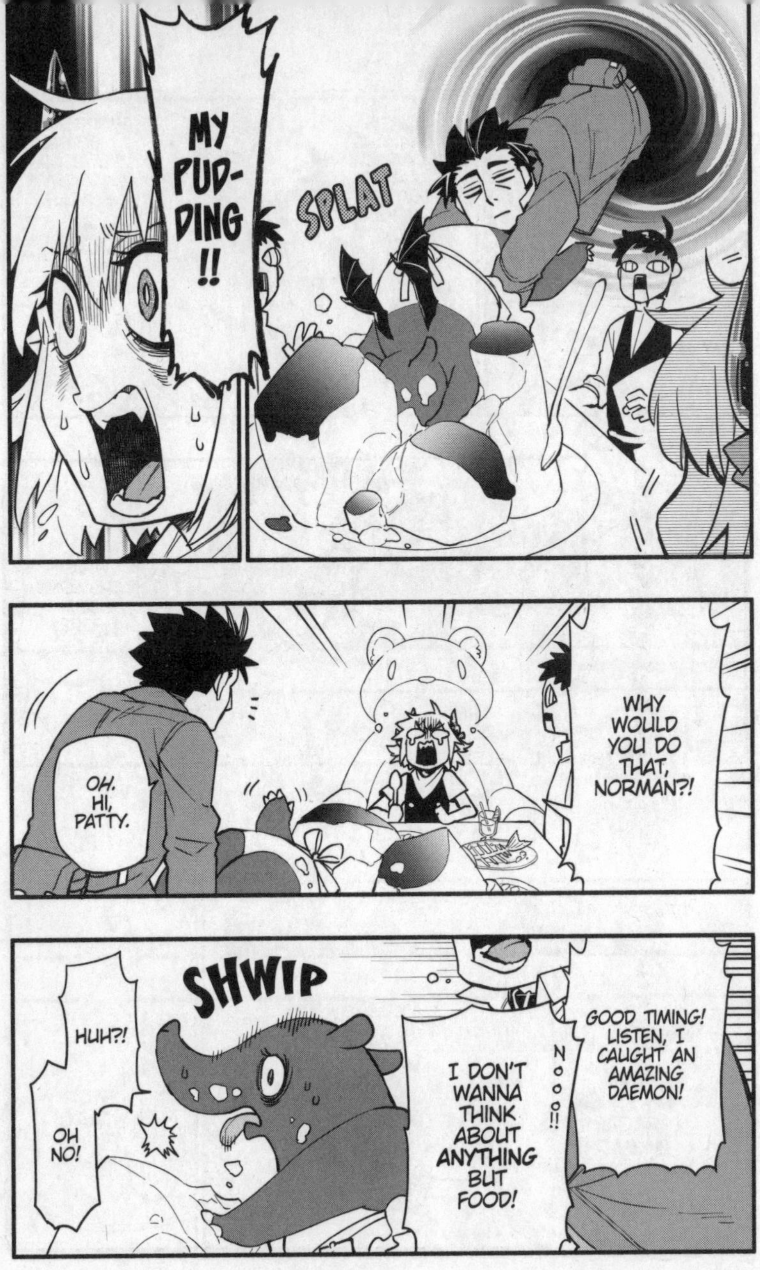
SPLAT
MY PUDDING!!
WHY WOULD YOU DO THAT, NORMAN?!
OH. HI, PATTY.
GOOD TIMING! LISTEN, I CAUGHT AN AMAZING DAEMON!
NOOOO!!
I DON'T WANNA THINK ABOUT ANYTHING BUT FOOD!
SHWIP
HUH?!
OH NO!

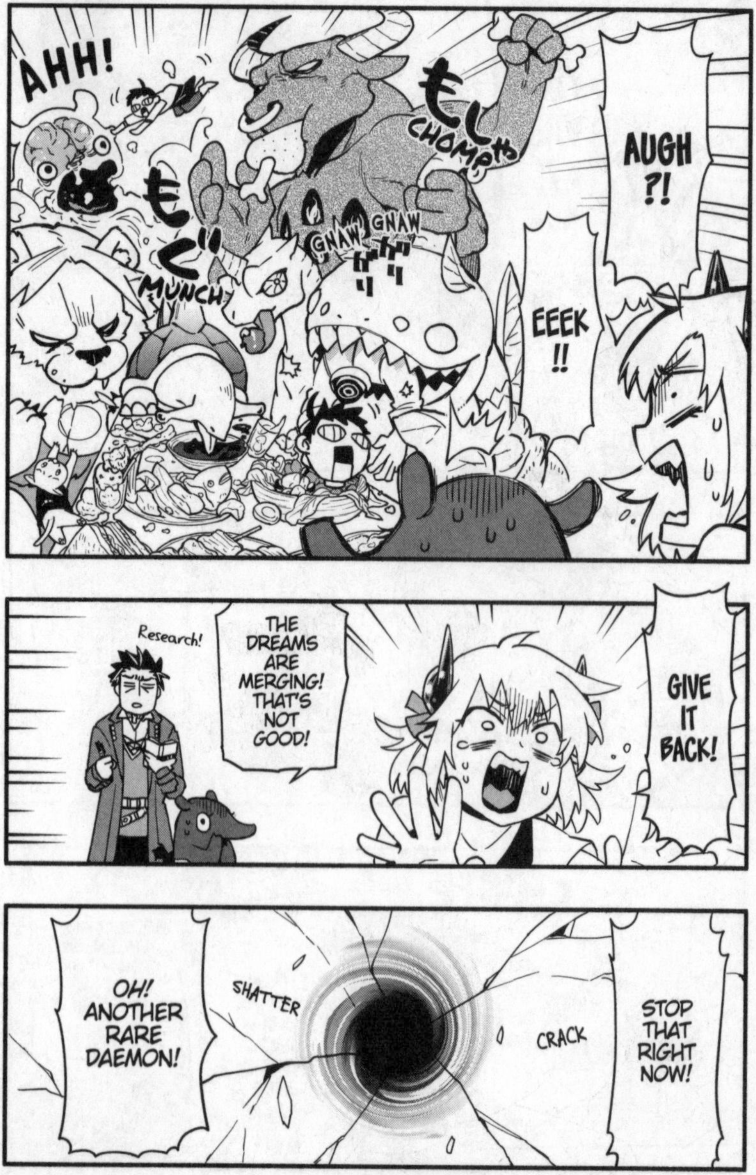
AUGH?!
EEEK!!
CHOMP
GNAW GNAW
MUNCH
AHH!
GIVE IT BACK!
THE DREAMS ARE MERGING! THAT'S NOT GOOD!
Research!
STOP THAT RIGHT NOW!
CRACK
SHATTER
OH! ANOTHER RARE DAEMON!

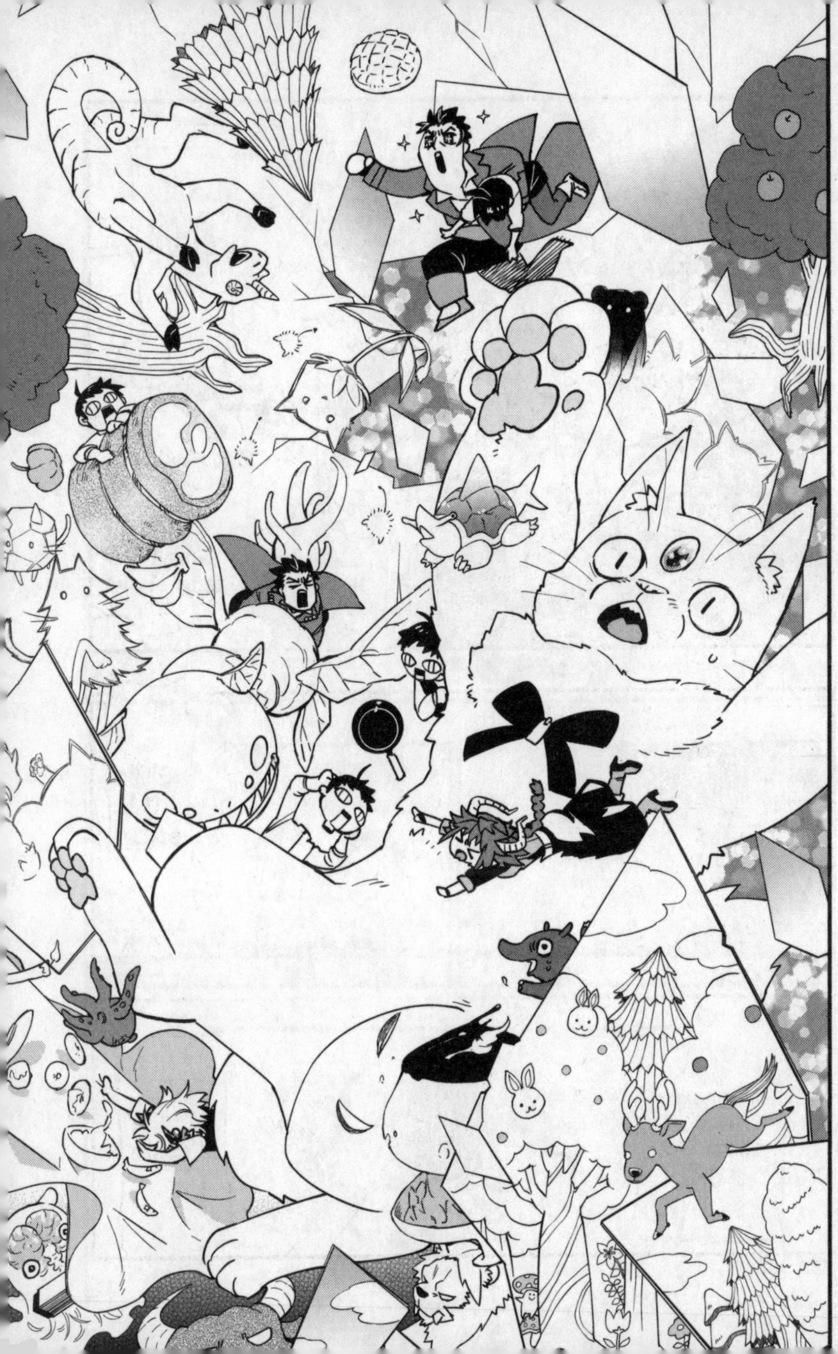

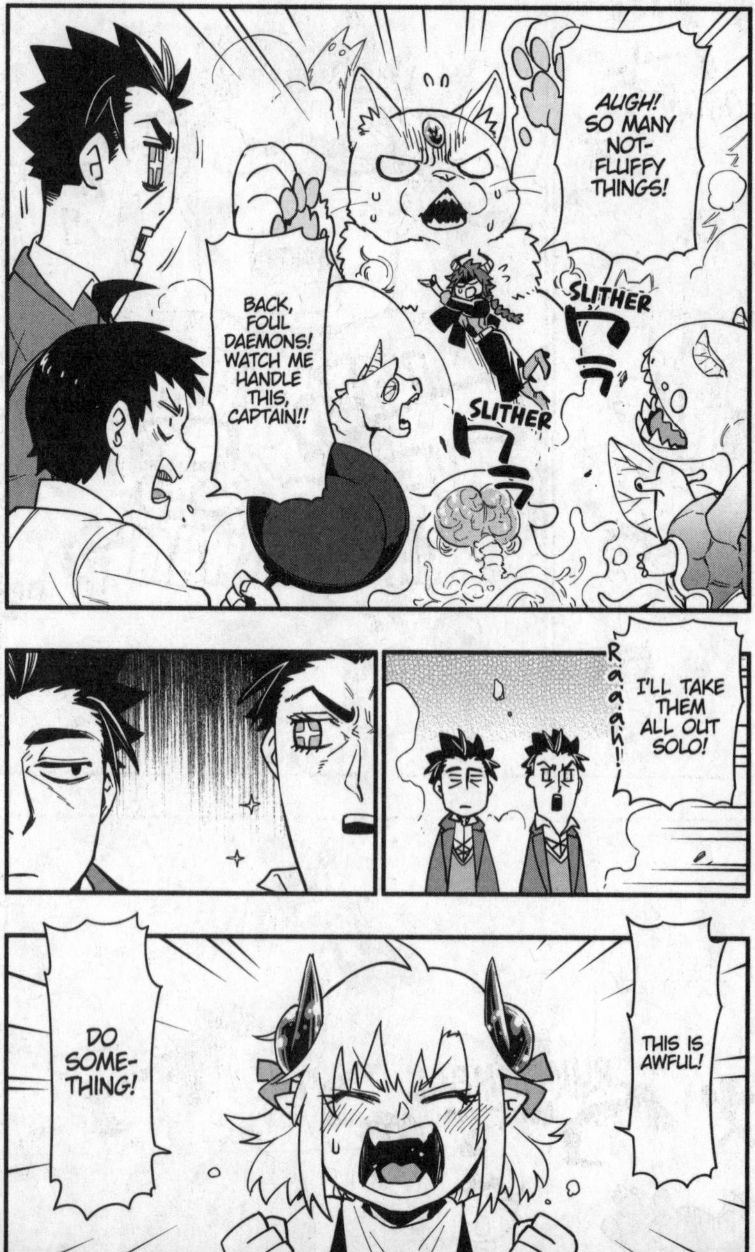
AUGH! SO MANY NOT-FLUFFY THINGS!
BACK, FOUL DAEMONS! WATCH ME HANDLE THIS, CAPTAIN!!
SLITHER
SLITHER
I'LL TAKE THEM ALL OUT SOLO!
Raaah!!
THIS IS AWFUL!
DO SOME-THING!

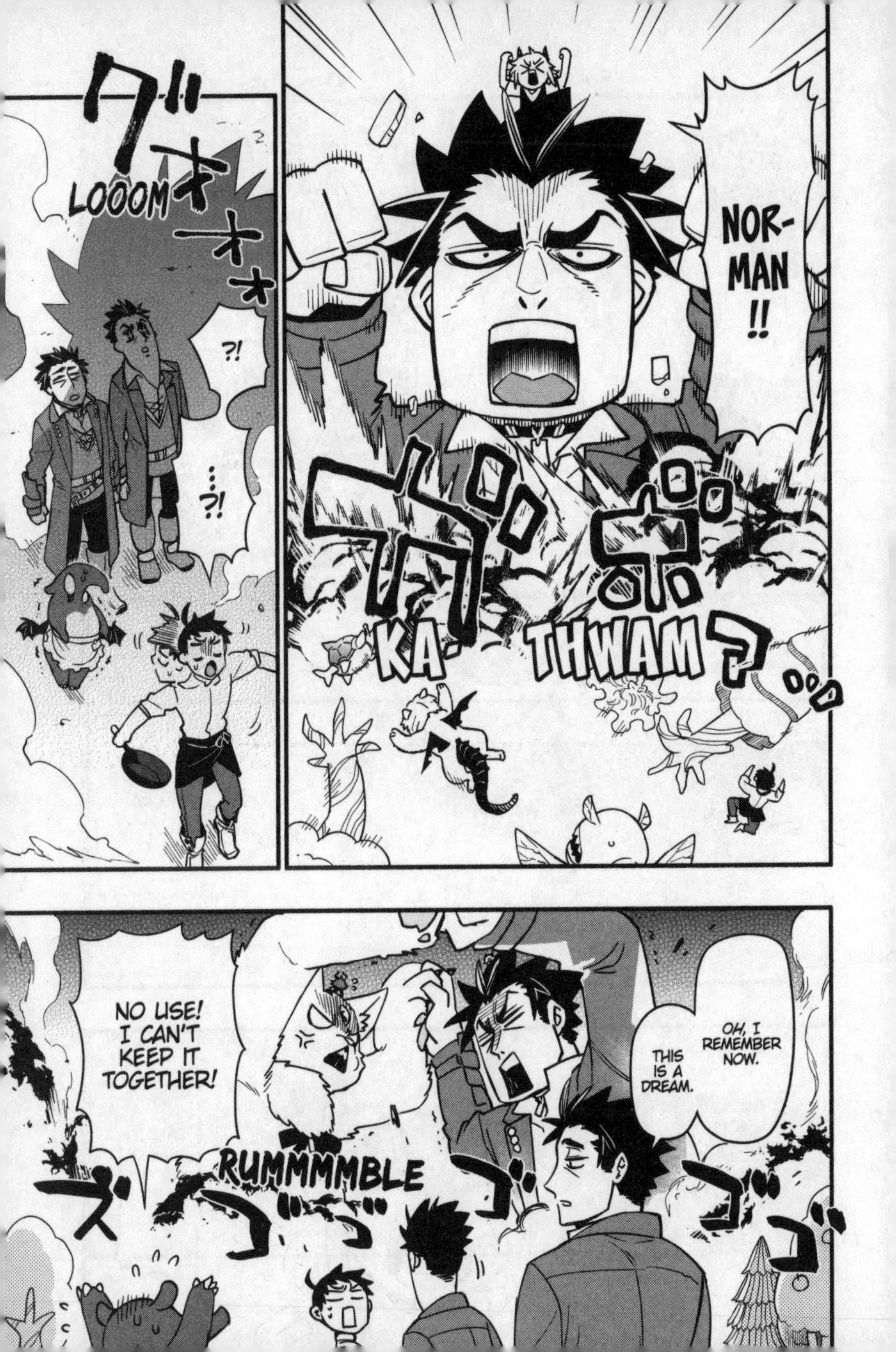
NOR-MAN!!
KA-THWAM
LOOOM
?!
...?!
OH, I REMEMBER NOW.
THIS IS A DREAM.
NO USE! I CAN'T KEEP IT TOGETHER!
RUMMMMBLE

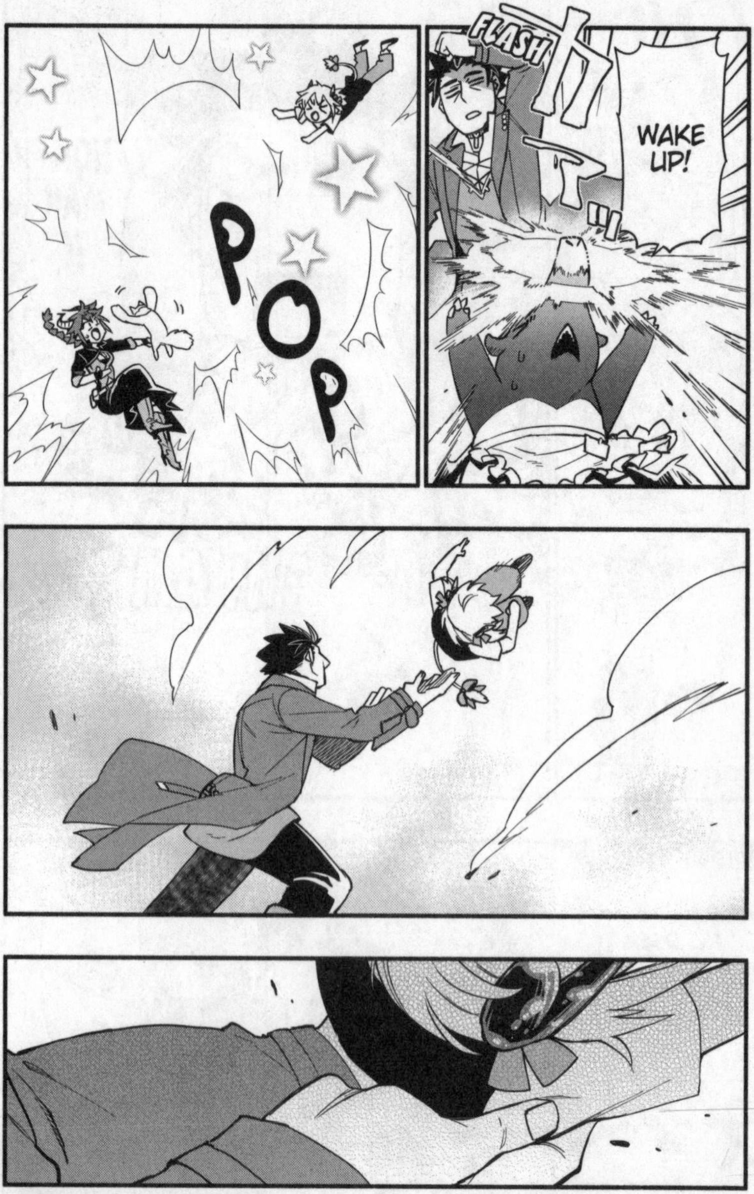
FLASH
WAKE UP!
POP

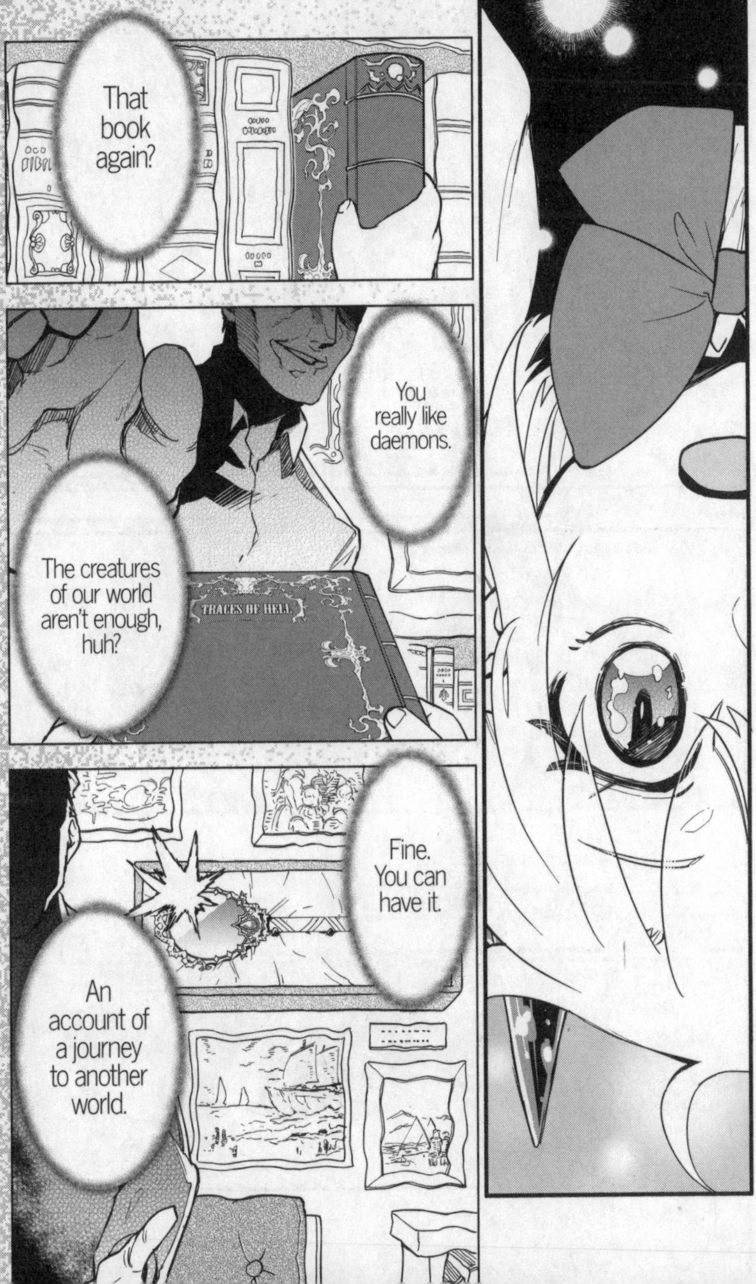
That book again?
You really like daemons.
The creatures of our world aren't enough, huh?
TRACES OF HELL
Fine. You can have it.
An account of a journey to another world.

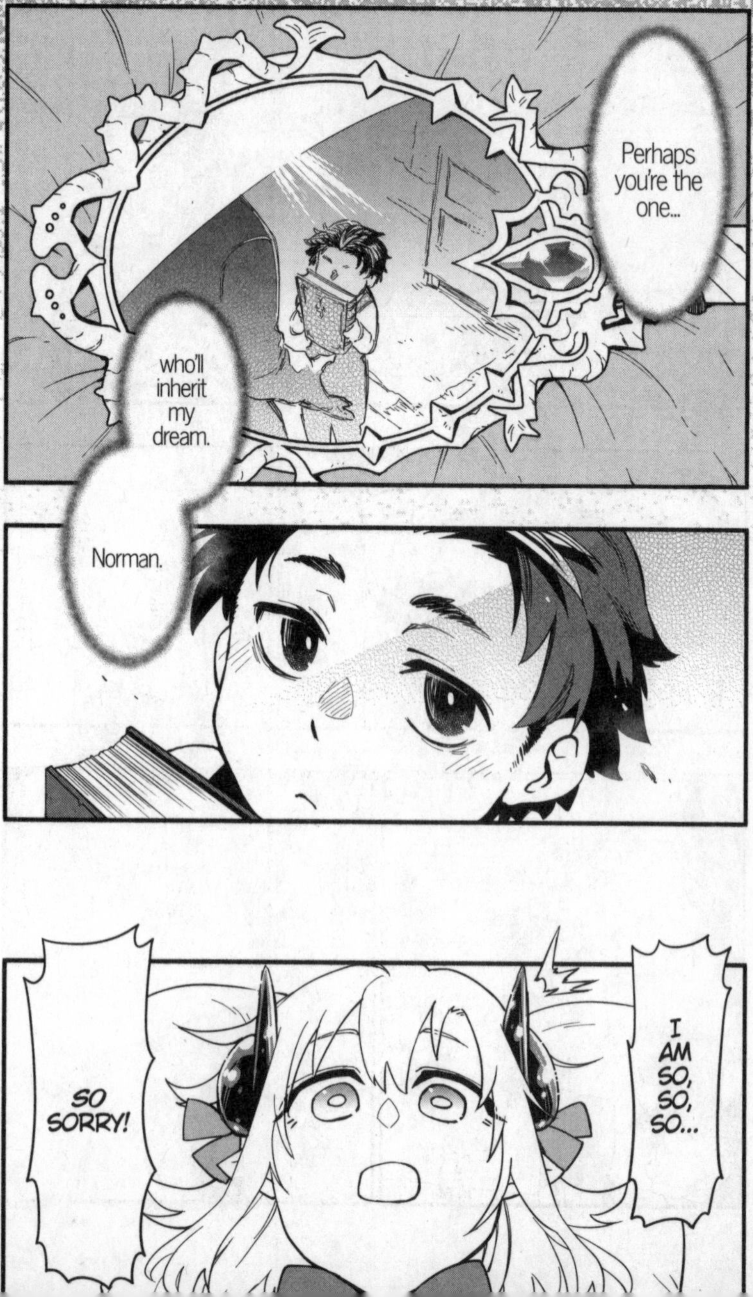
Perhaps you're the one...
who'll inherit my dream.
Norman.
I AM SO, SO, SO...
SO SORRY!

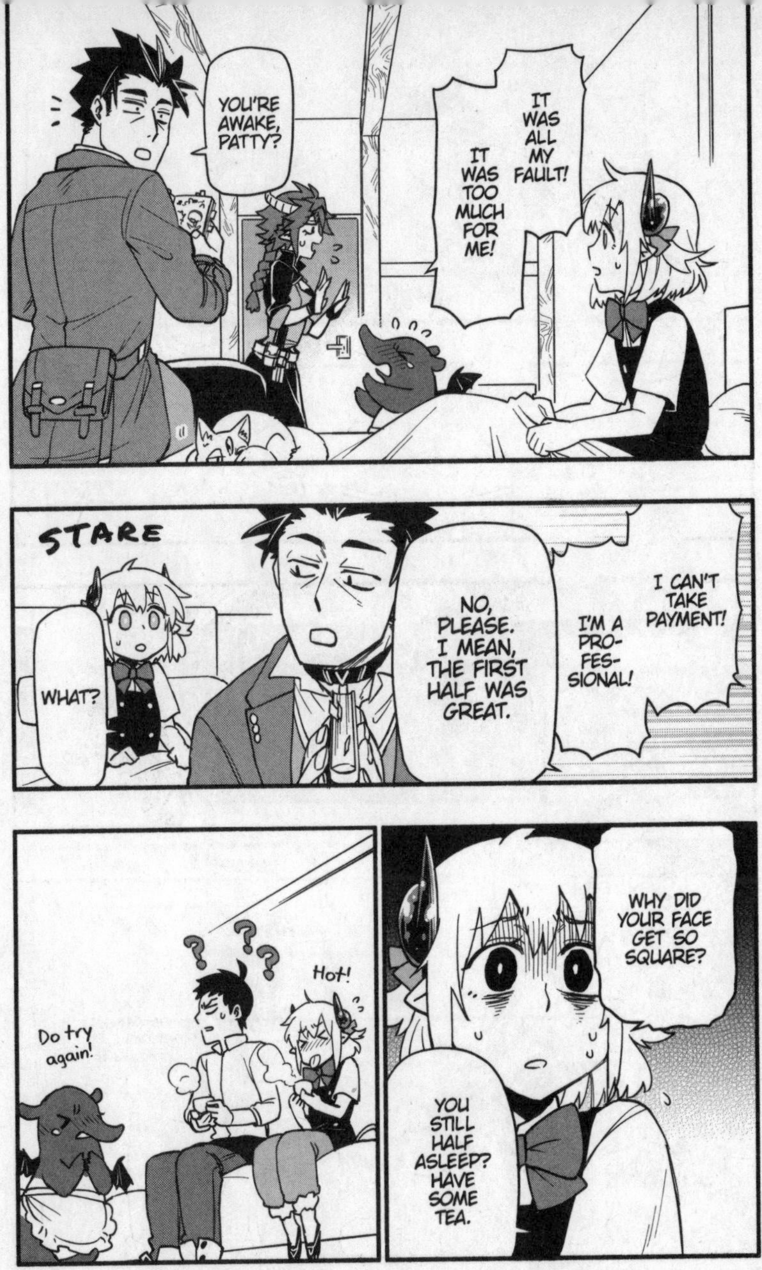
IT WAS ALL MY FAULT!
IT WAS TOO MUCH FOR ME!
YOU'RE AWAKE, PATTY?
I CAN'T TAKE PAYMENT!
I'M A PRO-FES-SIONAL!
NO, PLEASE. I MEAN, THE FIRST HALF WAS GREAT.
STARE
WHAT?
WHY DID YOUR FACE GET SO SQUARE?
YOU STILL HALF ASLEEP? HAVE SOME TEA.
Hot!
Do try again!

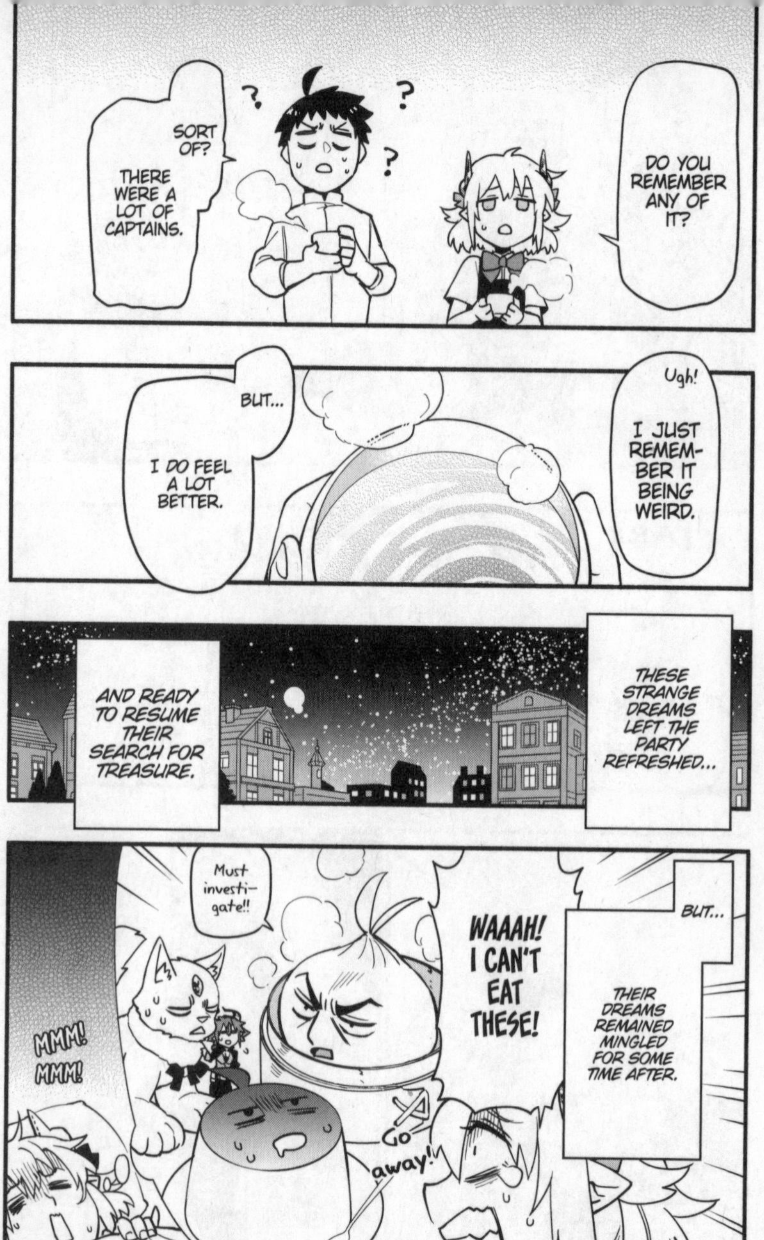
DO YOU REMEMBER ANY OF IT?
SORT OF?
THERE WERE A LOT OF CAPTAINS.
Ugh!
I JUST REMEMBER IT BEING WEIRD.
BUT...
I DO FEEL A LOT BETTER.
THESE STRANGE DREAMS LEFT THE PARTY REFRESHED...
AND READY TO RESUME THEIR SEARCH FOR TREASURE.
BUT...
THEIR DREAMS REMAINED MINGLED FOR SOME TIME AFTER.
WAAAH! I CAN'T EAT THESE!
Must investigate!!
Go away!
MMM! MMM!

To be continued!

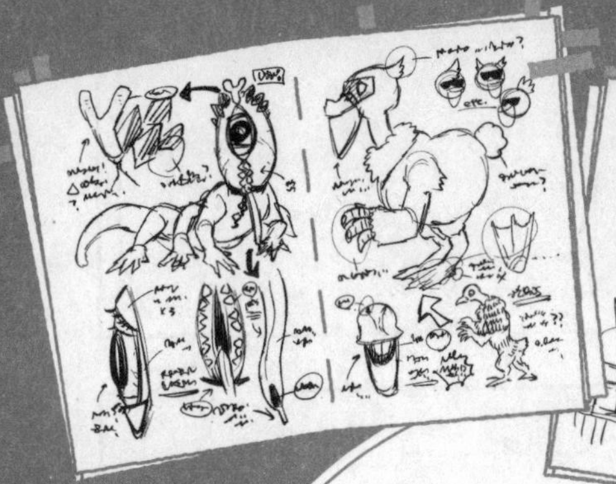
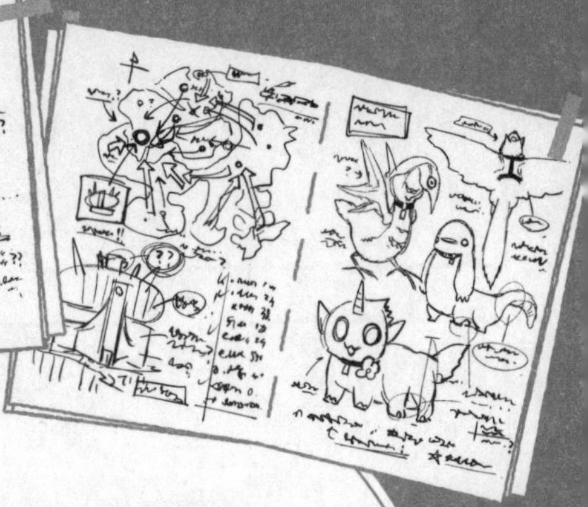

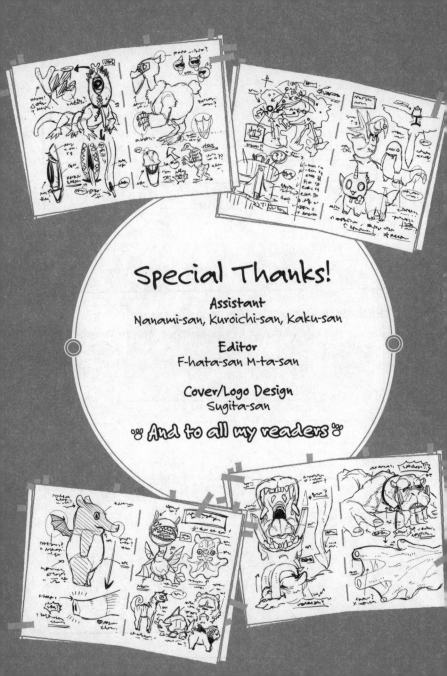

Special Thanks!

Assistant
Nanami-san, Kuroichi-san, Kaku-san

Editor
F-hata-san M-ta-san

Cover/Logo Design
Sugita-san

And to all my readers

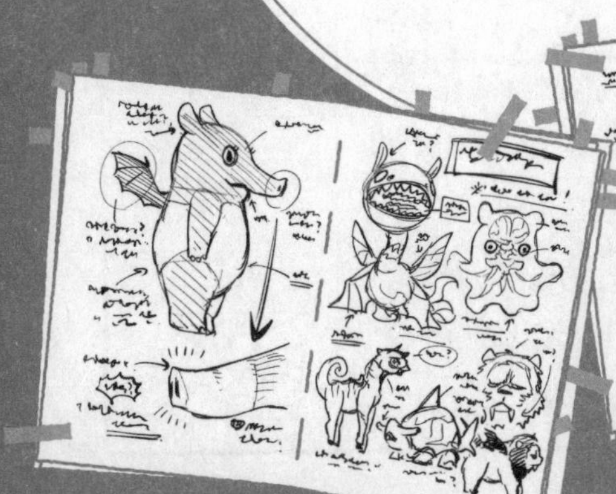
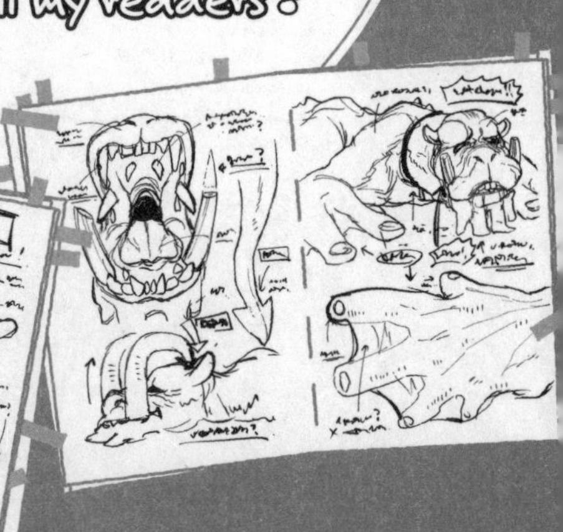

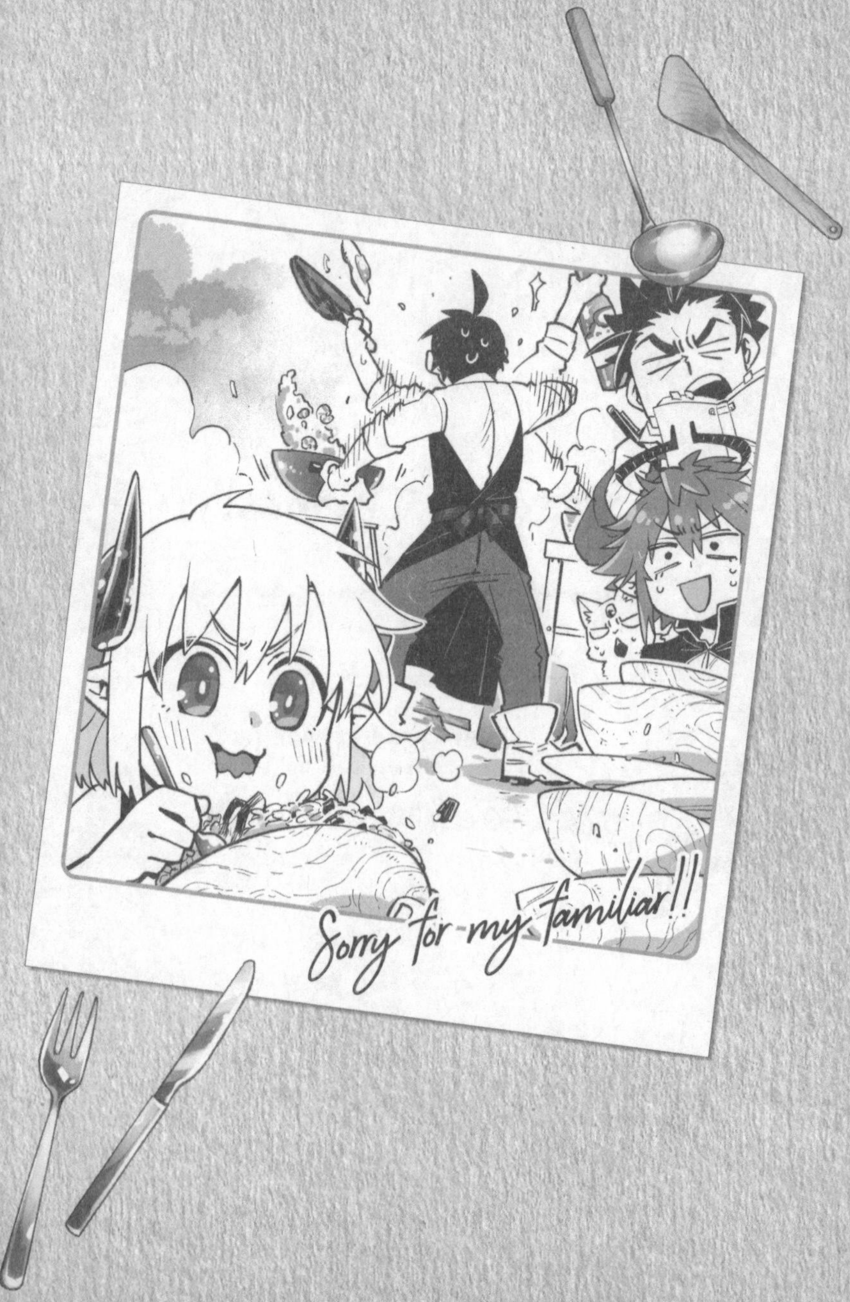
Sorry for my familiar!!

Sorry for my familiar

Sorry For My Familiar

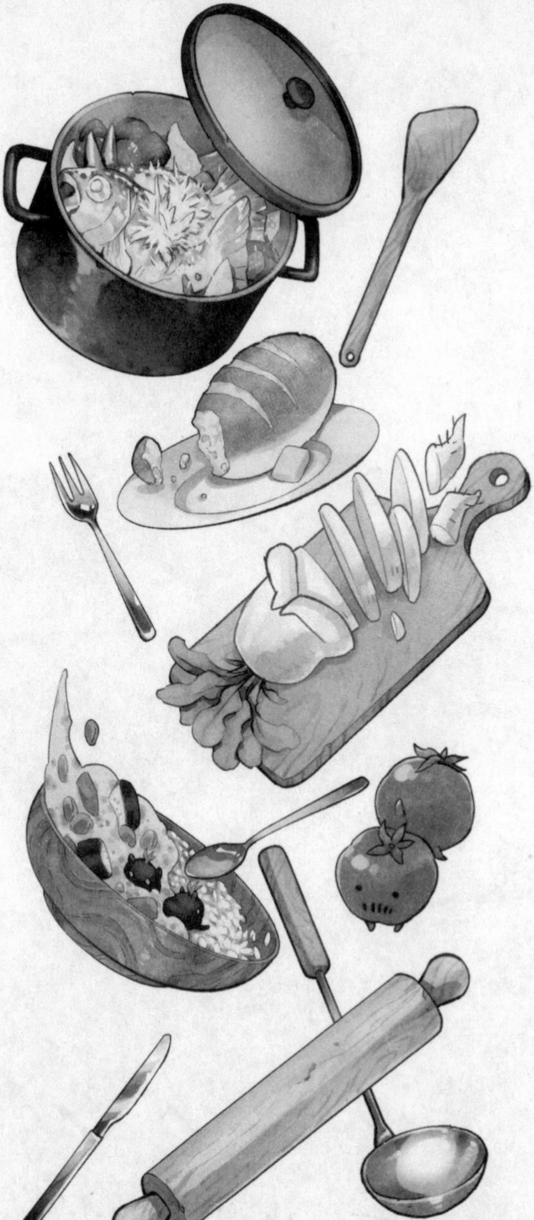

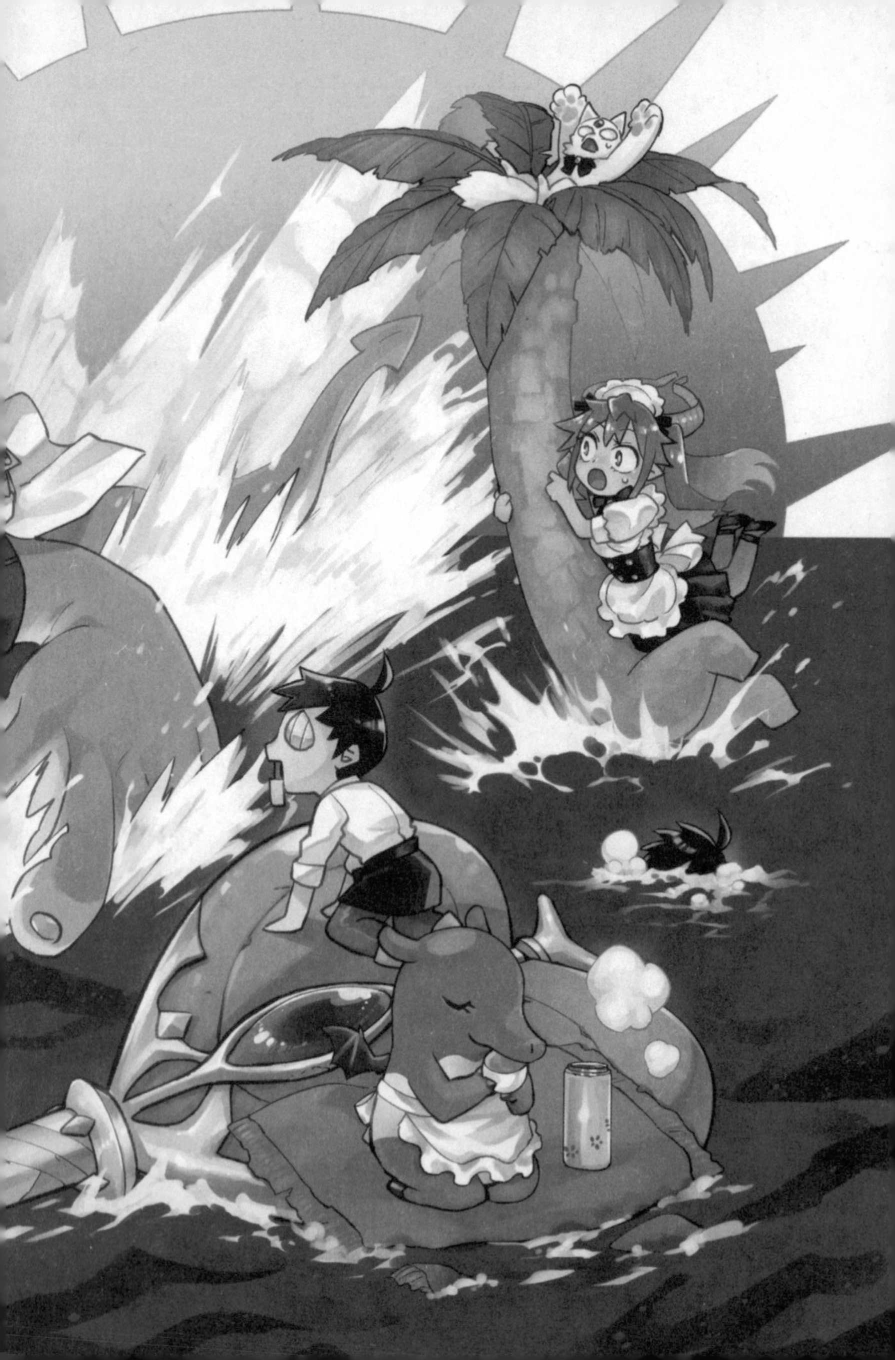

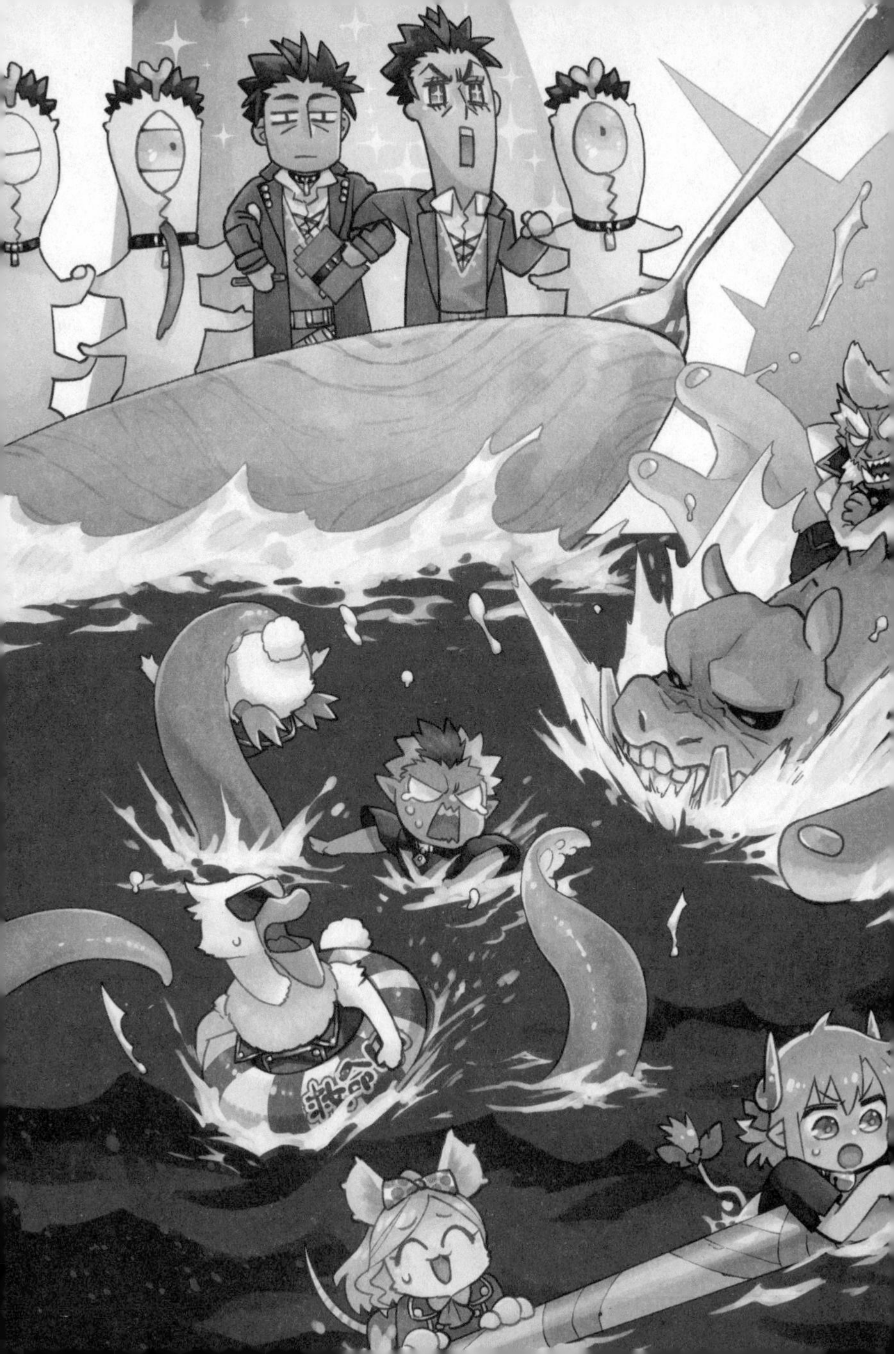
救命

Sorry For My Familiar